THE
SILENT
CHILD

About the Author

James Kelly is the author of the Nighthawk crime series for Alison and Busby, and the Philip Dryden series for Penguin. He was born in 1957 and is the son of a Scotland Yard detective. He went to university in Sheffield, later training as a journalist and worked on the *Bedfordshire Times*, *Yorkshire Evening Press* and the *Financial Times*. His first book, *The Water Clock*, was shortlisted for the John Creasey Award and he has since won a CWA Dagger in the Library and the New Angle Prize for Literature. He lives in Ely, Cambridgeshire.

THE
SILENT
CHILD

J.G. KELLY

HODDER

First published in Great Britain in 2022 by Hodder & Stoughton
An Hachette UK company

This paperback edition published in 2023

2

A CIP catalogue record for this title is available from the British Library

Paperback ISBN 978 1 529 35782 0

Typeset in Plantin by Manipal Technologies Limited

Printed and bound in Great Britain by Clays Ltd, Elcograf S.p.A.

Hodder & Stoughton policy is to use papers that are natural, renewable
and recyclable products and made from wood grown in sustainable forests.
The logging and manufacturing processes are expected to conform to the
environmental regulations of the country of origin.

Hodder & Stoughton Ltd
Carmelite House
50 Victoria Embankment
London EC4Y 0DZ

www.hodder.co.uk

For Mike and Justyna,
for the invitation

AUTHOR'S NOTE

History is made by real people, and it's important not to ap-propriate their lives in the interests of fiction. *The Silent Child* sits squarely in two historical frameworks – Berlin in 1961 and Poland in 1944 – but the characters are fictional, as are the landscapes through which they move, and the story they tell. The camp at Borek – for example – did not exist. The chateau at Łabędzie lives only in my mind. Even Swan House, on its lonely Fen, cannot be found on any real map. In the in-terest of drama and clarity I have simplified a complex world, torn apart by the Second World War, and then the Cold War. I hope the truth that remains reveals the mind of Hanna Stern, *the silent child*, a fictional character who is real to me.

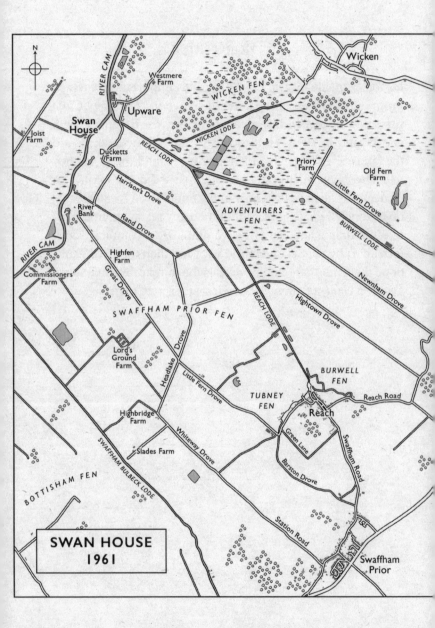

SWAN HOUSE
1961

BOREK 1944

A. Railway Station   C. Watchtower   E. Die Himmelstrasse
B. The Lazarette   D. Water Tower   F. SS Compound

PROLOGUE

Hanna sat alone on the back seat of the polished black car, her battered suitcase on her lap, the world outside only dimly seen through the misted windows. The engine, cooling, made an odd ticking sound, but otherwise there was silence, until she heard crows calling. She cleared a porthole in the condensation with her glove. The landscape was entirely flat, but upside down: the sky grey and sooty, while the snow-covered fields seemed to pulse with a gentle current of inner light. Her breath kept obscuring the scene, so that she had repeatedly to wipe the glass clear, each time noting another visual detail: a lone willow, a string of telegraph poles running to the horizon, a stretch of water-filled ditch, the surface glazed with ice as if by cataracts.

Setting the case carefully down she slid across the leather seat and cleared a circle in the window on the opposite side of the car. Mr Hasard, the driver, was smoking by a mailbox mounted on a metal post. When they'd come to a halt after the journey north from London, he'd wound down his window and sounded the horn, and Hanna had counted out the triple echo. He'd done it again before switching off the engine and getting out, his shoes making a brittle crunch in the snow.

'They'll be here soon,' he'd said, although who 'they' were had not been clear. Hanna was inured to these moments, when the adult world seemed to require only that she sat quietly and waited politely for the future to unfold.

She watched Mr Hasard throw the cigarette away with an impatient gesture, stamping his feet, looking towards a house in the distance that stood half a mile away, at the end of a rutted track.

Hanna read the sign that hung from an iron arm on the mailbox:

SWAN HOUSE
MAZUREK

Mr Hasard came back to the car, threw open the door, and pressed down on the horn, the cigarette hanging from his mouth.

'We'll have you warm and safe soon,' he said, checking his watch.

When he'd come to the chateau in Poland to fetch her – the car was black again, but smaller, battered and dusty – he'd taken her hand and said he was 'Mr Hasard-with-one-S', and that he was her *provisional guardian*. His duty was to collect Hanna and take her to Paris where 'further decisions' would be made about her future.

They had driven for three days, skirting towns where it was possible, but where they couldn't, edging through streets full of rubble, past sullen crowds gathered around bonfires against the cold. The fires carried ash up into the sky, and Hanna watched the rising smoke, craning her neck to see the clouds, while everyone else seemed hypnotised by the flames.

When Hanna wasn't asleep on the back seat she sat next to Mr Hasard, who asked her gentle questions she couldn't answer. There was something wrong with Hanna's memory. The last year, which she'd spent in the caretaker's cottage on the estate, was vivid: from the swans on the frozen lake at Christmas to the rabbits running from the last stook of hay at harvest time. But back beyond these images there was nothing. The first six years of her life were lost, and when she was urged to see into that darkness she had to look away, although she never cried.

They reached Paris, a pale city, where all the buildings had been arranged in squares, and around parks, or along wooded streets, and all the fountains were dry, and full of snow. The apartment was on rue Delambre and had so many mirrors, and tall windows, Hanna felt constantly unsure if she was looking at the real world of rooftops and drifting smoke, or its reflection. The rooms were bare, but the plaster was ornate, and depicted swans, just like the ceilings at the chateau. Mr Hasard came each day and explained that he was waiting for what he always called 'instructions'. A tutor visited in the afternoons to teach Hanna English and French, but she still thought in German, although some of the few words she said out loud, and unbidden, were Yiddish – words she was urged to forget.

A woman called Suzanne looked after her and cooked her meals, and was always there, beside her bed, when she woke up pooled in sweat, rigid with nightmares she couldn't remember. In the dusty park by the apartment, Suzanne told her that the doctor, who had examined her twice in the yellow day room, thought she'd had a great shock, which had upset her so much that the past was lost, but that it might be found, if they were patient and kind. Hanna asked for a sketch-book and pencils, and Mr Hasard admired her work, although it revealed nothing of the past.

Finally, after three months, instructions did arrive in Paris, and now here she was, after a journey of trains and boats, somewhere north of a city called Cambridge, in England, on what Mr Hasard called a 'fen' – a frozen landscape of fields and poplars, which reminded her of Poland, as if her journey had described a great but pointless circle.

She heard brittle footsteps on ice, and then voices close to the car, and through the porthole that she'd cleared she saw that two elderly people had arrived and were shaking hands with Mr Hasard. The three adults, dimly seen as a single shadow, came to the side of the car. The door opened, and Hanna had to jump down, clutching her case.

Mr Hasard performed a slight bow towards an old man. 'Hanna, this is Count Mazurek.'

'Welcome to Swan House, Hanna,' said the old man, in what Hanna recognised as English, which he spoke very slowly.

'You can call me Uncle Marcin. This is my wife.' It wasn't an old man's voice, Hanna thought, and she saw that his hair – which was swept back off a broad face, was only streaked with grey. He had a peasant's great hands – like those of the estate workers back in Poland – and broad shoulders, and a round head that hung forward, as if its weight was too much.

He took her hand gently in what Hanna felt was a sign of welcome.

But his wife, who was bird-like and still, stood back watching them both.

'She remembers nothing?' said the count to Mr Hasard.

'No. As I said in my letter, she can recall nothing before the estate at Łabędzie,' he said, slipping on a pair of driving gloves. He opened the boot of the car, retrieved a large flat brown paper parcel, and gave it to the woman, who clutched it to her chest.

'But she *can* speak?' asked the count, looking at Hanna, and then Mr Hasard, a smile widening.

'Oh yes. When spoken to.'

They all looked at Hanna, who looked at them back.

Mr Hasard touched the rim of his hat. 'I must get the ferry, and the roads are bad. The car has to be back by nightfall.'

A minute later, after a conversation Hanna did not understand involving 'expenses' and an 'invoice', Mr Hasard shook her hand and then they all stood back and watched the shiny black car drive away, until it seemed to tip over the distant horizon.

Marcin took Hanna's suitcase, and they set out on the rough, icy track to the house. He told Hanna that they too had once lived in the great chateau at Łabędzie and that his wife was a *countess*, but Hanna could call her Aunt Lydia. They had fled Poland when the Germans invaded in the first days of the war so that the count could continue the battle in the sky. Their grown-up daughter Natasza had been left behind, trapped in a city called Warsaw, where she had bravely helped hide Jewish children like Hanna away from the Nazis who wanted to kill them. Finally, she'd escaped with Hanna to the family estate, and hidden her safely away again. But Natasza had been killed helping others reach freedom.

All this, the most important words Hanna had ever heard, came from the mouths of these two strangers out on this wide fen, under a tin-lid sky, on a still-born day, already close to dusk. Hanna felt she should mark the moment, so she stopped walking and turned to face the countess. 'I'm sorry I don't remember,' she said.

'In time,' said Aunt Lydia, smiling with her lips, but not her eyes, which never seemed to meet Hanna's.

The house had a brick façade – flat and foursquare, with blank windows – and a central door with two pillars that held up a little roof, which tilted giddily to the left. It looked like the house was falling over very slowly. Smoke dribbled from a chimney in a black lazy line.

The front door swung open to reveal a bare hallway, with worn wallpaper, and floorboards. The house smelt of cabbage and polish. In a kitchen with a stone floor Aunt Lydia gave her a glass of milk and boiled her an egg, which Hanna ate with bread and butter in front of a coal fire. Lydia also gave her a cup of black tea that tasted of herbs, which Hanna sipped, staring into the flames. She felt that if she kept very still, and silent, and remained well-behaved, things she wanted to happen would keep happening; she'd be left alone in a room of her own, and then she could open her suitcase and take out her sketch-book and pencils.

Lydia announced that Hanna was tired and should go to bed.

'It's gone bedtime for little girls,' she said, but Hanna felt this remark wasn't for her at all, but someone in the past.

They climbed up uneven wooden steps to the second floor, and then to an attic, which comprised several rooms off a wide corridor. Lydia showed her into one, at the front of the house, with a sloping ceiling and a single window. Marcin pulled back a heavy curtain to show Hanna that snowflakes were touching the glass.

The bed was big enough for two grown-ups and was made of iron, and Lydia had to help Hanna turn back a wedge of blankets so that she could slip beneath. Her suitcase was set on a wooden chest while Marcin fetched a glass and a jug of water. Finally, the old man stood at the door, his hand on the light switch, smiling shyly before letting the darkness flood out from the corners of the room to press against Hanna's eyes.

She heard them say goodnight.

Sleepless an hour later, she burrowed her way from underneath the covers, drew back the curtains, and looked out over the strange flat country, disguised by snow, but now under the light of a familiar moon, by which she opened her sketch-book and drew the first line, describing the pale horizon.

Chapter 1

Long Fen, January 1961

Hanna remembered the shoebox at the last moment, as she climbed the stairs in the gathering dark, ferrying a canvas away from the rising flood. The banks had broken the night before, the great river spewing out across the fields, so that at first light they'd watched the waters spreading over Long Fen; an infinite grey sea flecked with white horses, running to the same horizon over which Mr Hasard's car had tipped fifteen years earlier.

Any memory of what went before was still lost, a silent history, but the precious shoebox contained all of her memories since: photographs, letters, keepsakes, postcards and diaries. Tonight, of all nights, she needed the shoebox beside her, so that she could set out the past, and decide on the future. A decision had to be made, the biggest decision of her remembered life. But the shoebox was in the old fruit store, surrounded by the flood.

She hauled the painting up the stairs to what Lydia had always called the 'schoolroom' – where Hanna had faced her various tutors over the years. She blew out the candle on the table, and went to the window, opening it with difficulty against the gale. A moon appeared briefly between shredded clouds. A tree – an oak from the north – sailed past in the mid-distance, half submerged. The line of poplars along Siberia Belt flexed, and she heard the sound of snapping branches, and waves breaking around the house. If she was quick, and sure-footed, she could get to the fruit store before the water rose too far. She ran back to the stairs and sat down to pull on Marcin's old waders. The count's winter coat hung on the newel post, and so she shrugged it on as well, feeling the damp weight of it, and catching a memory of the old man in the hint of pipe smoke in the collar.

She stepped from the stairs into a foot of floodwater, which had been flowing through the house since early afternoon, so that they'd had to drag away the sandbags across the front door to let it drain out to the fen. The flood reeked of greens and leeks, and black earth, and now, tonight, there was the unmistakable tang of the sea. It seemed to boil with eddies and currents, its surface encrusted with silver bubbles.

She took the first step across the hallway and set her hand flat against the far wall.

'This is madness, Hanna.'

Aunt Lydia stood on the stairs wrapped in a housecoat and carrying a candle in a pewter bowl. She'd gone to the warmth of her room an hour ago to sleep, because the power had failed, and she couldn't read for long by candlelight.

'You can't go out, child. Not now.' Lydia's world encompassed the house and little more, a fearful, timid outlook against which Hanna had fought with increasing success over the years. She took another brave step towards the open door that framed the night, pausing to push her hair back from her face, readjusting a clip, and buttoning up the old coat.

'I have to save the Lambretta,' she said, lying easily. 'There's just time. They've opened the sluices to the sea. If saltwater reaches the engine it will never start again. I need to get it up on blocks.'

She edged further along the hallway, her hand flat against the wall, which was marked by the coloured lines she'd drawn as a child with a crayon in her trailing hand, marking the passing years as surely as a doorframe marked with feet and inches. Lydia had been outraged by this outburst of artistic expression, but Marcin had been forgiving, a breaking of ranks that defined their taut, triangular, relationship.

Hanna saw two rats in the flood, sleek and dark like slugs.

'They won't bother us,' shouted Hanna. Lydia had never overcome a lifetime's fear of vermin.

Halfway out of the front door, Hanna met the wind, a gale that guttered as if trapped in a great sail. Close by, a chimney pot smashed, and then a pane of glass. Once away from the bright pinpoint of the candle flame, her eyes switched to night vision, and she could see that the storm had ripped the clouds away. The black water was studded with torn branches and flotsam, broken fence posts, a flooded dinghy, thorn and bramble, all sweeping past. The illusion that *she* was being swept north, leaving Long Fen behind, made her dizzy.

The water was two foot deep in front of the house, and her torch beam failed to penetrate to the path beneath. Once clear of the building, the air was full of spray and foam whipped off the surface of the river that ran between its high banks behind the house. Within seconds her hair was wet, water running down her face. She stumbled once but reached a low wall that sheltered the cottage garden. The old store, a shed set on brick foundations, stood among the count's apple trees. She had to lean her weight on the door to push against the flood inside. The lemon yellow Lambretta, with its CND sticker, a source of perpetual tension with Lydia in Hanna's teenage years, stood high and dry on the workbench where she'd left it that morning.

Since the count's death the shed had been neglected, making it the perfect hiding place from Lydia's tireless regime of order and the random forays of the cleaner who came from the village each Friday. Hanna stood on her toes to reach the shelf and retrieve the shoebox, which she slipped into the poacher's pocket of the old coat. Back outside, she found herself wading now against the current, and was quickly out of breath. The spray in the air was as dense as rain, the old waxed coat streaming. The floodwater was higher, rising, and she had to stop to rest and still her heartbeat, which is when she heard a single bell in a sudden silence between gusts of wind. She turned north, towards the little chapel at River Bank, and wondered if a hand had pulled a rope, or if the storm had rung its own warning.

The unseen path was slippery and she nearly fell taking her next step, scrambling at the last moment to find a foot-hold. The mud, the darkness, the thundering current, made her think that it was quite possible her life could end here, if she wanted it to. She could make the decision right now, and simply let herself be swept away. It was a moment rehearsed many times in the last two weeks. The shoebox would be lost too, with all its memories, which seemed fitting.

She stood, swaying in the current. Out in the night she heard the terrified lowing of a cow and, staring into the moonlit distance, saw the beast itself, wall-eyed with terror, struggling to keep its great head above water. It reached a narrow bank that ran over the fen, marking the line of the dyke. Hanna saw it rise up, first on its knees, and then on shaking legs, until it stood facing into the gale, stunned and lost, before it settled, folding itself down into a foetal ball, as if for comfort.

The fatal moment passed, and so Hanna set out back along the path to the house.

When she reached the door, she saw Lydia sitting halfway up the stairs. Her brittle hands were knotted together, and she realised with a shock that her aunt was frightened for Hanna's safety, not of the storm.

'Aunt. There was no need.'

'We should have given up and gone when we had the chance. It's my fault,' Lydia said stiffly. Two men from the vil-lage had come in a boat to take them away, but Lydia had said the old house had served them well and they'd seen out the floods in '47 and this was no worse. The people of the Black Fens took inundation in their stride.

'If they come back in the boat tomorrow, we should go,' said her aunt.

Hanna went to the phone, which was fixed to the wall, and picked up the receiver, but the line was still dead. The water was running through the house strongly now, pulsing, as if propelled by a great heart, slopping up against the walls and doors.

'Let's see what dawn brings,' said Hanna, taking the last few steps to the stairs, her feet shuffling on the muddy boards. 'The boatmen said it would peak at midnight. The worst may be past soon.'

Hanna watched Lydia's pale heels as she climbed the stairs to the attic. Her studio bedroom was on the ground floor, with long south-facing windows, but she'd had to abandon it to the flood. In the old schoolroom the paraffin heater was ticking, the metal warming, but it had hardly taken the chill off the air, so she set a fire in the grate, and then put the shoebox on the camp-bed. Taking off the rest of her clothes, she hung them on chairs, wrapped a towel around her hair, and draped a blanket over her shoulders. Then, with an eye on the door, she opened the shoebox and set out the contents. Some were found objects: beach pebbles from Norfolk, a piece of plaster from a church in Padua with the fragment of fresco attached, and the bowl of a clay pipe she'd dug up in the vegetable garden, helping Marcin plant broad beans. And finally, the diaries that she was so keen to keep from her aunt's eyes. She'd made daily entries since her twenty-first birthday, confiding difficult emotions, often about Lydia, who had never disguised the fact that as Hanna grew up, she had become a poor substitute for the lost Natasza.

Beneath the diaries was a wad of photographs and she picked out the oldest and pinned it to the corkboard on the wall.

A studio shot, it showed her face, artfully lit. It had been taken in Cambridge the weekend after her arrival. The purpose of that strange outing had been disguised as a shopping trip for much-needed shoes: the sturdy brown leather pair that had once filled the coveted box. The real mission was to get an official picture of Hanna to forward to an organisation in Germany that helped parents track down children lost in the war. She had no name – no *surname* – and nobody knew anything more about her, not even Mr Hasard-with-one-S. The portrait photograph was striking: the round broad face, the large brown eyes, the curving arched eyebrows, and the peculiar intensity of the blank face, which seemed lost and dignified in the same moment. But no one had recognised her, and so from being 'hidden' she was translated to 'lost'. Other photos followed: her again, standing glumly at the playground gate to the school at Upware; the inevitable Lambretta, with her student flatmate Vanessa hanging on, with the Brighton Pavilion in the background; and then finally a rare sighting of Hanna's smile, clutching her degree certificate from art college on the steps off Long Acre, the shadowy outline of a London backstreet running into the distance.

She pinned them all up and then picked up the bundle of postcards. Most were from Peter. She slipped off the elastic band and spread them out. The latest was a black-and-white shot of the National Gallery, which marked the last time they'd met. It had been a week before Christmas and they'd gone to the gallery to avoid continuing the row that had begun the night before in Peter's bedsit in Earl's Court.

It was early morning and the pigeons in Trafalgar Square were untroubled by tourists.

The gallery was deserted too, except for the sullen attendants who sat on chairs staring at everything but the art. She'd wandered with her sketch-book for an hour and then caught up with him where she knew she would, in front of a wide landscape of the American West, with towering clouds casting a shadow over the Great Plains, a herd of bison in the distance, a broken tree to the foreground, under which a family sat by their chuck-wagon.

The author's name was on a gold-leaf plaque: Albert Bierstadt 1881: *Beyond the Sierra Nevada*.

'Homesick?' she'd asked, taking his arm.

Peter, six foot one inches tall, looked down at her. 'Sure. This guy's a kraut – well he was before his parents set sail for the Land of the Free. I like the light – not fashionable now. They said he was a *luminist*. They're never going to say that about me.'

Peter's work was jet-black and jagged, full of angry architectural shapes in violent motion.

'The boat sails next week, Han, and my offer still stands. The *Empress of Britain*, from Southampton. As I said, I have to get back and a loft's come up. Five days at sea, then New York. Double cabin – you can still come. It ain't first class – but there's a porthole. I checked.'

Hanna sighed. 'It wouldn't work, Pete. It's not my home; it's yours. Besides, you're famous.'

It was a familiar argument, which they'd circled like birds of prey, even though the carcass was down to the bones.

He shook his head, narrowing his eyes as if he could see something in the dusty distance of Bierstadt's painting. 'One show on the East Side and a piece down-page in the *New York Times* doesn't make me the next-big-thing.'

Hanna shrugged. 'Well, you *look* famous. I look like a twenty-three-year-old art student. Over there I'd be the great man's girlfriend. And what am I going to paint? It's your landscape, not mine. Wherever I'm going, I have to start on Long Fen.

'I need to paint, Pete. I need to paint better.'

Hanna's abstract canvases were full of intense colour, and geometrical form, and some even sold, but to her they were devoid of emotional content, as if she'd reached out for an idea, and felt nothing at her fingertips.

'I've told you how to paint better, Han. Paint what you feel.'

'I've tried,' she said, and shook her head, staring into Bierstadt's endless sky. 'But sometimes I don't know who I am.'

Hanna took a step back, as if trying to reassess Bierstadt's landscape. 'And as I've said, Lydia's frail. The doctor says another stroke's possible. I know she's independent, but I feel a duty, to stay close, at least for now. I do owe her, Pete.'

Peter shook his head. 'The old girl'll make a hundred, you'll see. That type always does. Eats like a bird.'

He'd visited Swan House in the summer but left his paints in his suitcase under the bed, spending his time swimming in the river or sitting in front of the house on a swing-chair drinking whiskey. He thought the house gloomy, and suggested that skylights in the attic was the only solution. Oddly, he'd liked the Fens, explaining to Hanna that the grid-like mathematical landscape reminded him of a great chequerboard. At dusk they'd played draughts on the stoop. Lydia had been a shadowy presence, coldly polite, a figure glimpsed in the corner of his eye.

'She hates me,' he said. 'I'm a drunk. Sorry, an old drunk, who paints his nightmares.'

'You were in the war. She understands. She has her own nightmares. And you're not old: you're thirty-eight.'

Peter had been called up in the last year of the war and spent six weeks in a shell-hole in a snowy forest in Belgium. Then they'd discovered his grandparents were German and he could speak like a native, so they assigned him to *special duties*. He hardly ever talked about those months, but Hanna had been woken by the muffled screams at night. The war brought them together, because he couldn't forget what he'd seen, and she couldn't remember.

They'd sensed the bond the day they met. She'd spent a term at Padua at the art school, staying with Lydia's sister in Venice. She'd lingered in the city, waiting for Lydia's annual visit. August had been sweltering and so she'd taken the boat to the Lido, and they'd sat alone, fifty yards apart, looking out to sea, then chosen the same moment to swim. Back on dry land he'd offered her a cigarette with a dripping hand and she'd liked his face; handsome still, but the features settled, buckling slightly under the force of gravity, the blue eyes still holding a thousand-yard stare. The art-school boys had never had a past to share.

They'd ended up back at his studio in a side street in the Arsenale, and in the weeks that followed, they spent every moment together when Hanna could shake off the attentions of her chaperone, Lydia's sister. At five o'clock they'd take a shower, using the tin can he'd rigged up in the yard, and walk out into the city and find another bar or café beside the jade-green water of a sluggish canal. They'd talk about art, because he understood why she was driven to paint, that it was a way to try and connect with the world she'd lost when she was six years old. And for the first time in someone's company, she felt that she could just *be*: she could share his studio, work in the same space, and he would ask no questions, or demand anything of her but her presence. The rest of her life often felt like a summons to be someone else, a series of appointments to meet the expectations of others.

The light seemed to fade from Bierstadt's landscape. Peter wanted a cigarette, so they'd made for the exit.

Outside, a few people were strolling in the anaemic sunshine, and the great Christmas tree looked out of season. They found an empty bench where the wind blew spray from the fountains in a thin mist, so the wooden seat was damp.

Peter's face had hardened, the cigarette between thin lips, and she knew there would be one last effort to get her to follow him to New York.

'I know I shouldn't have mentioned kids,' he said, using a Zippo lighter, which left a whiff of fuel on the air. 'It's mortality kicking in. It's not important.'

But it was. He'd come home after the war to small-town America – Artesia, Nebraska – and married a local girl. Working in a real estate office, he painted at night in the garage in an effort to exorcise his demons. Ten years later he went to work one day and didn't come back home – hitchhiking fifty miles, then getting the Greyhound to New York. He'd left a son behind, five years old, who he hadn't seen since. He said he often wondered what the boy was doing – not in a general sense, but in the sense of *right now*.

She took the pack of Lucky Strike out of his overcoat pocket and lit one.

The wind blew a shower of droplets on her face.

'Maybe I'll have children one day – maybe, but not now. I've got to learn to paint first – that's what you always say. I'm sorry.' There was another reason that she left unsaid: how could she think about a new family if she hadn't found the one she'd lost?

Peter picked a shred of tobacco off his lower lip. 'I've been thinking. I might go back to Artesia and see if they'll let me see the boy. He'll be ten – eleven.'

'If it's what you want, go. I hope it's enough,' said Hanna.

Before he could say anything more, she'd stood up. 'Ring, when you can. Or write.'

She'd walked away and when she got to the corner of the Strand she looked back, and he was still sitting on the bench, watching her through the drifting spray. Turning away, she wondered if she'd see him again.

His card had arrived two weeks later with a New York postmark. On the back he'd written: *You took my Lucky Strike. Happy Christmas.*

She now pinned the card on the wall next to the photographs; her past laid out, in time to make a decision about the future.

The fire was radiating heat, and she felt feverish, so she let the blanket fall from her shoulders, and stood naked in front of the long cold mirror she'd once used to check her school uniform. She let her hair fall free, taking out the clip.

If she'd been one of the art-school models, shivering in the studio, she'd have said she was tall and well-made, with long limbs leading to slender hands and narrow feet. Her face was indeed broad: Marcin had suggested there was a hint here of the steppes and the Mongol hordes, but she always thought the wide-eyed look was a mirror to the horizon that encircled her life. Her hair, which she always wore pinned back, was long and brown and pulsed with light, even here, in a shadowy room on a stormy night on an island in the flooded Fens.

From the mantelpiece over the fire she retrieved her diary and a *Gitane* from its stylish packet – an art-school affectation she couldn't drop. She lit the cigarette from the flame in the heater and let the smoke drift from her nose, so that the image in the mirror showed a naked woman with the protoplasm of a ghost over her left shoulder.

This image and the sense it conjured up – that while she was indeed alone, she was in some way *accompanied* – brought the decision she needed to make frighteningly close. She thought about a dingy bedsit in Earl's Court, then turned sideways and examined her high, small, breasts – which seemed different to her touch already – then her flat narrow waist, her slender neck. (Never as slender as Natasza's of course; only the daughter murdered by the Nazis was truly swan-like.

J. G. Kelly

The painting that proved the point hung now in Lydia's attic room, having arrived in Mr Hasard's car, wrapped up in brown paper.)

Placing a hand on her stomach, she knew that while her eyes told one story her body told another, although for now it told her alone. But the weeks and months would pass quickly, and her body would betray her.

Chapter 2

Three days later they heard the sound of an outboard motor an hour short of dusk, and when Hanna ran to the window in the schoolroom she saw the white gash of the wake across Long Fen, a widening V that perfectly mirrored the geese in the sky above, rising from the flooded washes. It took her a minute – sitting on the stairs – to struggle back into the waders, which gave Lydia time to reach the landing above. The water level had risen to the third step that first night, but had dropped each day since, so that the hallway was now a muddy path. The flood had left a silt-red tidemark on the plaster, between Hanna's crayon lines.

Lydia was agitated, her hand turning on the newel post.

'It's Bowyer, the ferryman from the village,' she said. 'Can you ask him about the telephone, Hanna. The lines are still strung between the poles, but the line's dead – what *is* their problem? What will they be thinking in Cannaregio?'

Given the annual *acqua alta*, Hanna doubted her aunt's sister would be in the least worried about flooding in the Fens, if the news had made it to the Veneto at all.

'I'll ask about the line, Aunt,' she said, standing unsteadily in the waders.

Hanna threw open the front door, the sandbags piled neatly now to one side.

Long Fen was still a wide sea, a deep marine blue today, thanks to the evening sky above. The north wind had flattened the water, but strange ripples still signalled the currents below, streaming back north, the pumps raising the water slowly up into the high river, the breach in the banks repaired. A beach had formed about fifty yards from the front door of Swan House, their 'island' expanding as the water retreated.

Lydia was right – she had keen eyes – for old man Bowyer was at the helm.

He let the boat idle until it grounded lightly, leapt over the side, and stood in two foot of water. 'Do you want to go?' he said. 'There's food and heat at The Five Miles.'

The village inn at Upware had a slipway and a dock, and rooms for travellers on the river. The bar was used by that half of the community that didn't attend the Methodist Chapel.

'You've done well to stick it out,' he said, lighting a cigarette and looking up at the old house. 'Most of the others have cut and run.'

'Long Fen's got the worst of it,' he added. 'The banks are fine upriver. Bad luck really.'

'We're happy to stay,' said Hanna. 'The power's back, and we've a larder full of cans; we've always got a larder full of cans.'

'There's post,' said Bowyer, rummaging in a bag. 'And Bryant's sent these …'

Carefully he handed Hanna four pints of milk, and a loaf of bread, as well as some letters, a postcard, and finally a telegram.

'Hope it's not bad tidings,' he said. Telegrams in the Black Fens were still items of wonder.

Hanna ripped it open. It was from Peter.

Hope you're OK. I have NEWS. SENSATIONAL NEWS. Phone usual time if you can. Px

'No – all's well,' said Hanna. There had been regular calls from Peter since Christmas, the tone cool and practical. But the telegram seemed to radiate breakneck optimism and immediate action, both of which made her feel uneasy.

'The telephone's down, that's the only thing,' she said.

'There's a problem at Waterbeach,' said Bowyer. 'The flood took a whole load of poles down. They reckon tomorrow they'll get the line back up. Maybe the day after. They've sent soldiers from Newmarket, which won't make anything easier – they don't know up from down. Are you sure you don't want to come with us? Your aunt?'

'She's fine. We're fine,' said Hanna, stepping back, but allowing a hand to creep over her stomach.

'Your decision. Just that the shipping forecast for the North Sea is snow,' he said, climbing back in the boat.

She took a few steps forward in the waders. 'Can you take a note for me to post – for Haysom & Haysom. I've put on stamps.'

Hanna worked for an architect in Cambridge producing technical drawings and artist's impressions of new buildings. Marcin had left her an allowance in his will – to Lydia's obvious disapproval – but the job provided her with the daily reality of independence, a wage, and a life beyond Swan House. Even when her art sold, the prices were modest. Leaving Long Fen each morning, the Lambretta whining, always lifted her spirits. Hanna's hasty letter simply outlined the situation, which would come as no surprise given the flood, and explained that she had to stay to look after her aunt, which was partly true.

'If I can, I'll swing back tomorrow,' said Bowyer, touching the rim of his hat, which struck Hanna as a faintly feudal gesture.

She watched the boat dwindle, the engine's whine prompting water birds to take flight in a flock that faded to a fingerprint in the eastern sky.

'I heard,' said Lydia, when Hanna retreated to the kitchen. 'Snow. Thank goodness for the woodpile.'

Her aunt took two letters, no doubt recognising the handwriting. Lydia lived at the centre of a web of Mazureks – the count's aristocratic family – and of her own – the Wotyas, who

were even more lofty in social terms but even more impover-
ished in real terms. Letters arrived in spidery *fin de siècle* style
with almost every post.

The card depicted a Flemish masterpiece that Hanna recognised, showing the animals being loaded into Noah's Ark.
She flipped it over:

Han. Hope it doesn't come to this. Tried to call. V

Vanessa, her old friend from art school, worked in London,
designing fabrics. Hanna visited often, but the thought of being able to talk to her now, of hearing her steady, matter-of-
fact voice, made her wish the soldiers from Newmarket had
set out earlier.

The third letter was for Hanna, with Polish stamps, post-
marked WARSAW, the address neatly typed. She took it upstairs to the schoolroom, which was still her billet, because the
studio was damp and muddy. She lit a cigarette, enjoying the
distinctive edge to the smell of the tobacco, placing a finger
on the letter, hoping for news, delaying the possibility of disappointment.

For most of her childhood she had been forced to make do
with the brief – even curt – version of her early life given on
the day she arrived: that she was a Jewish child hidden away
in Warsaw by Natasza Mazurek for nearly four years after the
German invasion, and finally delivered safely to Łabędzie as
the Red Army forged its victorious path towards Berlin. The
only addition to the picture had come from the count, unbidden, one night after he'd taken his usual glass of whiskey
in his office. It had been Natasza's birthday, and Lydia had
gone to attend mass in Cambridge. The count made an annual donation to church funds on the anniversary; a gesture
that appeared to free him from the need to actually attend.
Lighting the fire, he offered, without warning, the thought

that Natasza had at least died without pain. Having secured Hanna a hiding place on the estate, she had been returning by horse and cart from the railhead at Kraśnik – where she had delivered two Jews fleeing west – when a German fighter had strafed a column of refugees on the road. She'd been found, in the ditch, her swan-like neck broken, and taken back to the estate to be buried in the family plot.

'I hope she lies in peace,' the count had said, and then quietly cried, so that Hanna had felt moved to hold his hand. In all the years of her childhood, these were the only tears, other than her own, that she saw fall in Swan House.

But despite Marcin's enquiries, on her own childhood, and the fate of her family, the passing years had shed no light.

It had been Peter who made her question the assertion that the past was lost for ever.

Europe had been in ruins when the count had sent out his letters. That first summer in Venice, Peter said they could try again – together; they didn't know very much it was true, but they knew where to start. The Mazureks were a great family, part of high society. Did Natasza really disappear in Warsaw, hiding Hanna away? Did nobody ask questions about little Hanna when she turned up at the estate in Poland in 1945? Why had she accepted this version of the past? Peter asked. She'd hated him then because she knew the answer – that it was her fear of what she might find that held her back: a list of names, a camp in the East, the gas chamber demolished. A tragedy from which she was excluded. They'd died together; she lived alone.

Peter had taken her to the ghetto in Venice, to the old synagogue, where a few Jews, transported east, had survived the camps and returned to the neighbourhood. They put her in contact with the United Jewish Appeal, and there were groups in Warsaw too, trying to match the 'hidden' with the 'lost'. They told a very different story to the one Peter and Hanna had imagined: the truth was that the Jewish children had been hidden *in plain sight*. Those who didn't look Jewish were simply slotted into Aryan families. Forgery was a backstreet industry. They weren't really hidden at all, they were *disguised*. Hanna had sent many letters, but there had been no word of Natasza or young Hanna.

But there was always hope, and it often came with the post. She was about to open the envelope when she heard the distinct sound of crockery breaking. Lydia had recovered well from her last stroke, but Hanna had been warned to be vigilant, so she went quickly out to the landing.

'Aunt. Can I help?' she asked, throwing her voice into the stairwell.

She heard the old woman's footsteps.

'What is it?' asked Lydia.

'I heard something,' said Hanna. 'The wind's probably blown something over in the kitchen.'

They both stood unseen, listening to the wind buffet the old house.

'It will be one of the cats,' said Lydia. The count had introduced 'mousers', which had multiplied.

Lydia's footsteps retreated, and Hanna was about to go back into the schoolroom, when she heard a second sound, an indeterminate sliding, but with some heft, as if something was falling in slow motion.

But this sound definitely didn't come from the kitchen. She was quite certain it came from the door at the end of the hallway, which Marcin had christened the Imperial Red Door, because it reminded him of the grand interior of the chateau at Łabędzie – although the scale was reduced. It was covered in crimson leather pinned to the wood with gold studs; Marcin had bought it at an auction in Ely, because he said it set the tone for the work that had to be undertaken within. This was the count's office, where he went each evening, until his death just two years ago, in the bitter winter of 1958. From here, letters winged out to the capitals of Europe on behalf of the Polish government-in-exile, and others too, seeking any trace of Hanna, and her lost family.

In her bare feet she crept to the threshold and listened, holding her breath. The door was locked and had been since Marcin's death. A man in an impeccable grey suit had attended the funeral service in Cambridge and introduced himself to Lydia as a representative of the Foreign Office. He'd asked polite but persistent questions about the count's papers, and suggested that they should be left untouched, and secure, pending a possible visit from officials. Given the situation in Poland – still firmly under Soviet control – the count's correspondence could be highly sensitive. But since then, there had been no further word, except a brief telephone call apologising for the delay. It seemed that the machinations of emigrés in the wartime years had slipped down the order of priorities in London. Lydia, nevertheless, had ruled the room off limits, and there were no exceptions, as she had the key. But her aunt's determination to keep her out had always made Hanna suspect that the countess had other motives for leaving the past untouched.

Swan House had been Hanna's home for more than fifteen years; most of the happy times she could remember took place behind the Imperial Red Door. Even in that first summer, she'd been allowed to play in the evenings on the floor while the count worked. There was a threadbare rug, and a great desk in dark wood carved with bears and wolves, and a small fire that the count kept glowing with coke and bog oak from the fen. Hanna sketched and coloured, while the count wrote letters. Lydia came and went with tea for Marcin, but her domain was the kitchen, or her bedroom with its writing desk. Her aunt and uncle seemed to revolve around each other without ever touching. Lydia's life was centred elsewhere, either in Cambridge where she organised volunteers to work among the poor, or in her annual visits to her own family in Venice. She inhabited Swan House, but never seemed to live there.

In those early years the count left each morning for the air base – just over the eastern horizon, ferried in a staff car by his own driver. But by dusk he'd be home, cosseted in his office, and Hanna, stretched out on the old rug by the desk, was allowed to do her homework beside the fire if she remained silent. After tea, the count would tell her stories, about the old estate, about the Mazureks, and even fairy tales from the Polish woods. On her tenth birthday she was granted the honour of her own chair, and the freedom to curl her legs up away from the draught that blew under the door. Art school took her to London, but when she thought of home she thought of the count's office, and when she *came home* she craved the particular silence that descended when they both read their books – broken only by the crump of the fire settling, or Lydia's slippered feet ascending to her room.

Now, down on her knees, a hand to the leather door, Hanna thought she heard the scratch of a pen on paper, but knew this was a sad illusion, and so went back to the schoolroom. It would be mice of course, or worse, rats, seeking high ground above the suffocating waters, safe from the cats.

She knelt before the schoolroom grate, lit a *Gitane*, and tore open the letter.

It was typewritten and short – a single page – which was never a good sign.

It was stamped: NO RECORD.

She was good at this now: allowing the disappointment to somehow settle at a distance, while she engaged her conscious mind in reading the Polish text, an intellectual effort that kept the reality of failure just beyond her grasp.

Despite this, her eyes had clouded, and she struggled to read on.

She was aware of being overcome by an emotion, but, as so often, powerless to identify its precise origin. What had she hoped for? A name, an old photograph, a fleeting likeness?

The writer, secretary to a society devoted to reuniting Jewish families, said she was sorry but there was no trace of such a girl as Hanna. The Mazurek 'house' was in fact a smart apartment, in a block now demolished, and as far as she could discover, it had been blown up during the great uprising at the end of the war. One former neighbour – from the same street – said she didn't recall anyone in the flat during the occupation, but then all the grand buildings were boarded up, so Hanna might have been inside. Natasza was remembered, certainly – 'fun-loving' was the description, part of Warsaw society, and a fixture at aristocratic parties and balls. Perhaps Natasza had stayed with friends, or family, in a different part of the city?

It was another dead-end.

Hanna folded the letter, considered writing a polite reply immediately, and then burst into tears. Head up, refusing to slump, she acknowledged the sense in which she often came close to the lost past, and the people who lived there, but never close enough to be touched.

In all the futures she could now imagine, she was alone. She wept silently, knowing that Lydia had an ear for slight sounds, and the house was quiet. She didn't weep often, indeed it was rare, but it continued, until her breathing became disrupted, and she put on the radio to cover the noise. There was a play, with rough northern voices arguing over money. On the hour there were six pips, and before the news she switched it off, because she'd finally stopped crying.

Her tears gave way to the sudden vertigo of despair. To fend it off she stood quickly and went to the far end of the room where her latest work was on the easel: a canvas in oils, two foot by four. This had been a reflex for as far back as she could remember, even to the day Mr Hasard had brought her to Long Fen. When she couldn't face the present, she tried to capture something of the past on paper – a detail, a line, an emotion. This latest work – *Green, Silver, Red* – consisted of three panels of colour, in the order from the left indicated by the title. For twenty minutes she worked with a manic intensity, her face a few inches from the surface of the canvas, two brushes held in her right hand, a wrist movement switching from one to the other, while her left hand held the palette knife, ready to create a three-dimensional surface in the red panel, the ridges and troughs caught by the flickering light of the fire.

Spent, she stepped back, and turned away to the window where she kept a bottle of the Wotyas' family Soave – of which there was always a crate in the kitchen, sent from Venice. It was white and dry and as cold as the ice that obscured the glass. She took a sip, sat on the high stool, and looked back at *Green, Silver, Red*. In the act of painting, the mixing of the colours, the application of the brushstrokes, she'd felt alive. Now, when she tried to make a connection with this abstract image, it felt cold and dead, a message without coherent content. She got up abruptly and went to look in the fire, because all she saw on the canvas was what she always saw: her art was like a window, which held her own reflection, and obscured what was beyond.

And it was in the hollow silence of this moment that she heard the noise again, out in the icy corridor.

She shut the door behind her to harbour the heat. The corridor was freezing. At one end stood a window, bare to the night, so that she could see snowflakes kissing the glass, just as she had on that first night years ago. But these were not large feathery flakes, but small icy flecks, which hissed as they touched the glass. At the other end of the corridor was Marcin's red door. Hanna walked to it and stood a few inches from the wood, turning her head and resting her ear against the leather.

She knew it was mice, or rats, but she so wanted it to be something else. She heard then the turning of something impossibly fragile, like the page of an old book.

'Uncle?' she said, knowing there would never be an answer.

And then she heard the phone ring.

Chapter 3

'Swan House,' said Hanna, the two words leaving a veneer of condensation on the black Bakelite mouthpiece of the phone, because the hallway was freezing, the night frost having slipped in under doors and through the old sash windows.

'Oh, hello you. I've been trying for days.'

Hanna felt the sudden intimacy of the much-loved voice, which seemed to collapse the distance between them.

''Nessa. Thank God. You're the first one to get through.'

Hanna sat on the seat she'd dragged out of the kitchen – on Lydia's instructions – so that she could diligently try the line for twenty minutes at a time.

She pressed the cold plastic phone to her ear and heard the distinct whisper of a cigarette, which brought with it the whole picture: Vanessa at the drawing board by the north-facing window, on the tall stylish stool.

'Are you all right, Han? You sound odd.'

'I got another letter from Poland – another dead-end. I burst into tears.'

'It's allowed,' said Vanessa, who had the gift of making Hanna feel like a normal human being, with everyday problems, and occasional joys. A telephone call from Vanessa had become one of the treasures of life. For a moment they smoked in silent intimacy.

They'd become friends that first term at art school. Vanessa had offered Hanna a room in Gladstone Mansions so that she could escape a bedsit in Tufnell Park. They'd travelled together: India one summer, Greece the next. Vanessa was a fixed point in Hanna's life; in the drifting minutes before sleep, she always speculated on exactly where 'Nessa was, what she was doing, and who else was there.

'It's deathly dull here,' Vanessa added. 'London's in a grey mood.'

'What, no suitors?' asked Hanna, feeling better. The taut tensions of the last few days seemed to dissolve, and she heard herself laughing.

'I fought one off. Double-barrelled, again. Another of father's ideas I suspect.'

Vanessa's parents lived in Hong Kong, exporting art from China and Japan.

'He wanted to take me to the Criterion,' she added, with a note of weary boredom.

'What did you say?'

'That I had work to do. Which I have; I can't seem to say no. Liberty's want ideas for spring.'

In the background there was the unmistakable clatter of the metal gates on the lift outside her friend's door. Vanessa lived in the family flat in a mansion block in Knightsbridge. The doorman always called Vanessa 'Miss Gore-Smythe' and touched the rim of his bowler hat to her. He'd struggled with Miss Mazurek, but after a brief consultation was persuaded to use Miss Hanna.

'Hold on,' said Vanessa. 'That might be for me.'

There was a muffled conversation and then Vanessa was back: 'Samples,' she said. 'The deadline's tight but I wanted to see how the colours showed up on the material.'

'And?'

'I think we're in business,' she said.

Hanna lit another cigarette, creating a layer of mist that hung in the damp hallway. There was a soft, enveloping silence in the house, and she wondered if the snow was settling already.

'There was a picture on the news of the flood,' said Vanessa. 'They said north of Cambridge was worst – but a near miss everywhere else.' The flat had a television set. Vanessa craved independence, especially financial, but she enjoyed the trappings of the modern world.

'What's it like?' she asked.

'Desperate,' said Hanna. 'But the water level's dropping fast. Now they've forecast snow. We'll be cut off again I expect.'

Vanessa picked up on the note of despair.

'It's just you and the *countess* then,' she said. Vanessa had stayed at Swan House for Christmas one year, not willing to face the boat or the plane out east. She'd found it unsettling that Lydia could appear in a room without the usual precondition of coming through the door.

'Lydia's not the problem. I was fine, then the letter arrived. It was stamped 'no record' just like all the rest. Sometimes I wonder if I exist at all.'

'Bad day, then?' said Vanessa.

Hanna laughed, the relief like a drug, making her suddenly optimistic. 'Did the suitor try again?' she asked.

'No. He gave up. Pathetic really. I got the strong impression that the word "work" was alien to him.'

There was a silence and Vanessa decided they'd done with small talk.

'Did you see the article in the *Observer*?' she asked.

'Of course.'

Hanna had been instructed by Peter to buy five copies and post them to New York. They'd done a picture special on the Cedar Tree Tavern, E. 8th Street – unofficial headquarters of the latest wave of the abstract impressionists. All the big names had been there, including Peter Portland Cassidy, partly obscured by a cloud of cigarette smoke, but nonetheless the Kerouacian character he wanted to appear: craggy, handsome, if a bit puffy round the eyes.

'They said *Voices!* was going on tour – all twenty canvases. Do you know where?' Vanessa asked. 'They didn't say.'

'The world's his apparently: Paris, Milan, London.'

'So you're still speaking?' Hanna had given her friend a vivid cameo of their last meeting in London.

'Yes. By phone every Sunday. It's a ritual. Well, it was until the line came down. And there's a telegram today.' She paused. 'He wants me to call New York. There's good news.'

'What did he say last time?'

'Nothing's changed. I should come and live in New York, and then he'd buy a house back out West. It's all planned, you see.'

She took her time, drawing on the cigarette, then watching the smoke rise in the cold air.

'Problem is he's big time. I'm small time. I like here, he likes there. And I think we can agree I don't want a family. He keeps talking about going back to see his son, but I think that's a smokescreen.'

'Will you ring this week?'

'Yes.'

'And you won't tell him, Han? You're really sure?' Vanessa's relationships were distinguished by emotional directness. She was the only person in the world who knew about the pregnancy.

'No. Never. This is my life – and besides, it's too cruel. I can't tell him that I have what he wants most in the world, and then just take it away. And he thinks he's a man of action, so he'd come back – no doubt he can afford to fly now. He'd try to persuade me, and he might succeed. And that's not what I want.

'Anyway. I've decided, I decided last night. I got out some of the old photos – you know, like the one you took on Long Acre after we got our degrees. I thought about the past, and what I hoped was the future.

'So, will you help?'

Saying the words out loud seemed to move something inside her.

'There's an agency,' said Vanessa briskly. 'One of the counter girls at Liberty's told us the details in the staff room over a slice of Battenberg – entirely unprompted, which was a bit shocking. Anyway, they pay the confinement costs; the hospital is in Park Royal, which is out of the way I suppose, if a tiny bit grotty. But you have to sign it away Han – there's no second thoughts. You'll see it once – so I guess you'll know if it's a boy or a girl – and then they'll take it away.'

Adoption had been one of the options they'd discussed. There were others, even if the law still threatened prison for *child destruction*.

'That wasn't what I meant,' said Hanna.

'Oh God, Han. Not St Pelagia's?'

The Catholic Church ran a home for fallen mothers, from a Gothic pile on the edge of Cambridge, and found homes for the children. It was the option that involved telling Lydia.

'No. Not that. I just don't think I can do it,' Nessa – have a child I can't love.' She looked up the stairs, suddenly terrified Lydia would be at the top step.

Which left one option.

'Fine,' said Vanessa. 'That's *fine*, Han.'

'I've got Marcin's money. I thought London …'

'I'll ask,' said Vanessa. 'I know the ropes. It's Harley Street, or just off. It's perfectly respectable from the outside so there's nothing lost if I get spotted. I'll get some dates and then we'll just make a plan. Leave it to me, Han.'

Hanna was aware that she was making the telephone receiver hot, although the air was getting colder in the hallway, and she could see her breath.

'Will it hurt?' The question made her feel vulnerable, as if she'd caved in on herself.

She was shivering, despite the coat, and a second cigarette.

'No. I just felt sick and that passed. Frankly the relief was enough. I thought: *I can take London now*. It's freedom, Han. If you don't want to be a mother, now – or ever – that's perfectly all right. It's 1960, not 1860.'

They smoked together for a few silent moments, the illusion that they were together, in the same room, complete.

'You know you could just stay here,' said Vanessa, always business-like. 'Father's gone to Shanghai to look at warehouse space, and Mother's redecorating the house in Victoria Peak. I won't see them 'til late summer. Come and stay, Han. Maybe London's what you need.'

They made plans and set dates. Hanna said Lydia would be fine – the flood seemed to have given her a new lease of life – but she'd arrange for the district nurse to call on her rounds.

'Anyway, I'd better go,' said Vanessa. 'Ring at the weekend. My deadline's Friday. So Saturday is cocktail hour.'

Hanna pictured her then, the glass rim at her lips, the cigarette elegantly poised.

'Thanks,' Hanna said. 'If I couldn't talk to you, I don't know what I'd do,' she added, and put the phone down.

Chapter 4

Overnight, the fen froze, and so Swan House was no longer an island. Hanna laid salt along the drove road to the mailbox so that at noon the taxi could pick Lydia up as usual, the back seat crowded with a family from Wicken, a mother and two children, both altar boys. Their destination was the Catholic church on the corner of Parker's Piece in Cambridge: a cathedral in all but name. Marcin, whose veneration for the Church was less heartfelt than Lydia's, had once told Hanna where the money had come from to erect this edifice: a Victorian businessman had inherited a Portuguese factory making glass, and patented the design of the eyes set in children's dolls, which moved from side to side – a glimpse into an unknown childhood that had always terrified Hanna. Whenever she thought of the church she thought of those lifeless, erratic, eyes.

Her aunt would be gone until late evening, because after sung mass there would be lunch, and then Benediction, and even a glass of wine with the priests, especially if the bishop was their guest. Marcin's will had left a bequest for the diocese, and so his widow was always an honoured visitor. Sunday afternoons were therefore Hanna's favourite time, because she had the house to herself. Today, this sense of isolation was almost magical, with Swan House set in its icy landscape, like a miniature version of itself, in a paperweight. This state of wonder helped offset her anxieties about the future. She'd put aside her disappointment with the letter from Warsaw, but her conversation with 'Nessa had set in motion a series of events that she now felt powerless to stop, all of which led to the clinic off Harley Street, and a day soon to be noted in red ink in her diary.

The day was crystalline with light, and so after lunch she shrugged on Marcin's old coat, and threw open the front door of Swan House. For an hour she cleared the flotsam of the storm, dragging broken branches and straw away from the back of the house, and building a bonfire. The white smoke, untroubled by the slightest breeze, rose up into the still-blue sky, but an icy mist was already creeping out of the frozen ditches, which made Hanna think of the Lambretta, in the old fruit store. A foot of snow lay on the path, and every reed and blade of grass was a shard of ice. The air, so cold and metallic, caught at the back of her throat. She found the shed clogged with silt, the scooter still safely high and dry, so she rolled it back down the plank and up on to its stand, and then wrapped it in some old sheets and blankets Marcin had used as covers when painting in the house. From a hook she took down a small paraffin heater and lit the wick against the inevitable hard frost.

Overcome with a sudden urge for adventure, she retrieved the Lambretta's keys from a drawer in the count's workbench. Astride the scooter she turned the ignition, prompting a cloud of noxious gas and an ear-splitting whine. She enjoyed a minute of imaginary speed, then cut the engine, the silence settling again. Reluctant to dismount, she lit a cigarette, threw her head back, and blew out the smoke. Above her, hanging from a rusty nail, was a bunch of keys she'd never noticed before. She reached up and took them down, recognising a spare for the front door among several others. The image of the Imperial Red Door came to mind: it would be typical of the count to keep a complete set of spares safely at hand. With Lydia out she had the perfect opportunity to test her theory. She put the keys in her pocket, grabbed a small can of oil with a nozzle like an oyster-catcher's bill, and patted the scooter goodbye.

Outside, the mist had thickened to a fog, so that she couldn't see the house, and the sun was just a pale disc, the heat gone. The hallway was shadowy now, dusk close, so she turned the light on, went to the kitchen and found some stale bread, a piece of cheese rind, and a biscuit, and climbed the stairs. Dropping down on her knees, she listened at the keyhole of the count's old office. In the night she'd heard it twice, a skittering, and once the distinct thud of something falling to the bare boards of the floor. She knew it was mice, but half asleep, she'd imagined the count, a ghostly scribe, still working away sending letters out, trying to find Hanna's family.

Ear to the door she caught again the lightweight rustle, and imagined the delicate mouse running along the skirting board, nosing curiously among the documents on the great desk. The noise, the fragile scuffle, was very close for a second. It felt as if she was listening to something inside her own head.

'Are you hungry?' she asked. The thought of the creature starving to death troubled her. Hunger had always made her anxious. Her own eating habits had unnerved Lydia and Marcin, who treated every meal as a kind of ceremony, played out to old established rules. She found the plates of meat and vegetables unappetising, preferring to graze on pockets full of raisins or nuts, sweets and biscuits, apples and cakes.

Her voice seemed to still the movement within, so she stood up and began to try the keys. It took her a few minutes to test the set, and none of them worked. She put a drop of oil in the keyhole and tried each again, giving it time, reminding herself that if Lydia's rule that the office should be locked had been assiduously followed, the mechanism had not been turned in more than two years.

Finally it gave, with such a loud iron clunk that she was thankful for her aunt's absence.

It was now four o'clock, and virtually dark. The fog – glimpsed through the long window at the far end of the corridor – had thickened to a phlegm-like veil. She'd brought a candle in case the electrics were shot, and so she lit that, and opening the door crossed the threshold. Immediately, the flame guttered, and she felt the cold air, laced with damp, blowing in from the solid frozen river. It brushed her cheek, flooding out through the open door into the house beyond.

The flame reflected off the black panes of glass in the two windows, and she saw that one was smashed, while the other bore an image she recognised, because they were common in the Fens, often incorporating the delicate tracery of a wing, each feather etched in white. In that instant of impact, how did the bird impart its own image to the glass? It always made her think of a votive picture that hung in Lydia's room of the Turin Shroud. She'd thought then, as a child, confronted with a miracle, that perhaps the moment of reincarnation had somehow blazed out of Christ's skin into the fabric. But the passing years had brought another thought: that it was the moment of death that left its mark: an exhalation perhaps, a gasp, a final breath.

She went to the marked window and saw, by the candle's light, the dead bird on the outer sill, frozen stiff. She imagined two birds rising from the river, seeing perhaps the sky reflected, and flying together into the shocking reality of glass. But where was the bird that had broken the other window? Was that the noise she'd been hearing? There were several feathers on the desk, and a book and a broken cup on the floor.

A standard lamp was to hand, so she reached up to the switch. The result was such a shock that she stumbled against the desk, her legs giving at the knees. In the sudden light, there was a monstrous shadow on the walls: her mind raced for a moment with fabulous possibilities – a clawed dragon, a great hawk, her ghostly uncle. The apparition screamed, terribly, and the beating of its wings seemed to touch her ears. On her knees looking up she saw a crow sitting on the metal frame in-

side the lampshade. Its shadows, magnified, had terrified the
bird itself. The base, Hanna saw, was sticky with droppings.
The small black eyes scanned the room, the head tilted this
way and that, so that Hanna was reminded of Victorian dolls.

She opened both the windows and tilted the lamp to
set it free, but the bird simply hung on with its claws and
screeched, so she gave up, closed the windows, and surveyed
the room. It was much smaller than she recalled, with the
great desk taking up the space in the middle, behind a captain's chair, all set on a threadbare rug depicting yet another
hunting scene. One wall was a bookcase, the other covered
entirely in pigeon-holes. There was a pull-down lamp attached to the ceiling and held by a counterweight, so that
she could bring it right over the blotter, where it produced a
brilliant circle of light.

Hanna sat at the chair and examined the desktop, running a finger over the studded leather. Was this how the
count had left it – precisely in this way? There was a fine
fountain pen, in black and gold, with the cap left off. Hanna tried it on the blotter, and it made a scratching sound.
The ink-well was solid. There was an ashtray with the end
of a cigar. She picked it up and held it to her nose, but there
was hardly any aroma.

Standing up, she examined the bookcase. The volumes were
broadly categorised by subject, but the languages – mostly
German, Polish and French – were mixed. There was a section
on law, estate management, and the collectivisation of farms
in the Eastern Bloc – as well as a five-volume copy of the
constitution of the Polish Republic of 1952. The section on
the Second World War included more in English on the RAF,
the Battle of Britain, the Polish Free Air Force, and various
technical books on aircraft, navigation and pilot training. The
top shelf was set aside entirely for books in Polish and what
Hanna took to be Lithuanian or Lettish, on the history of the

Polish aristocracy, including a lavish volume that illustrated the coats of arms and heraldry of the various noble families, which fell open at Mazurek, and the inevitable swans.

The crow fidgeted on its unseen perch, unsettled by human company. When Hanna went to cradle it, ferry it perhaps to the broken window, the bird flew to the corner and came to rest on what looked like a low table covered with a dusty velvet cloth. Its clumsy landing dislodged the material so that it slid to the ground to reveal a stout metal safe box. Hanna knelt beside it on the bare floor, prompting the crow to return to the lampshade. She tried the handle, but it was locked fast.

The classification system for the pigeon-holes was not difficult to decipher. Marcin had a logical mind, which drew him to machines, and certainties. He'd made ten rows, with twelve compartments, each with a small brass bracket that could take a stiff cardboard label. The system ran from top left to bottom right in the series A–Z. Each label was afforded a sub-division, such as S – Swan House (deeds). Not every letter was given the same number of pigeon-holes; for example, L had nearly half an entire row, and most of these were marked for the Mazurek family seat at Łabędzie. This intrigued Hanna, because it was part of her story – the sleepy sunlit estate where she'd spent the first year of her remembered life. So she took down the first parcel of documents and set them on the desk. The broken window meant the air temperature was several degrees below freezing, so she fetched the paraffin heater from the schoolroom and used some masking tape to put a square of cardboard up at the window, closing off the view from the back of the house, which was dank and shadowy, the grassy bank rising steeply up to the river.

The crow, trapped, shuffled on its wire perch.

She went back to the files, surprised by the amount of correspondence related to the old estate in Poland, because Marcin had always lamented that the house and grounds, and the treasures within, were irretrievably lost. In the schoolroom, or at bedtime, he had patiently outlined to Hanna the brutal realities of post-war Polish politics: that in the wake of victory, Stalin had forced the Allies to break their promise to install a democratic government. Instead, the government-in-exile – which Marcin served – was set aside, and a communist, pro-Soviet regime had been installed in Warsaw. Private property was outlawed while the collectivisation of the land destroyed the old aristocratic families.

Nonetheless, the files under L revealed that Marcin had patiently sought compensation for the loss. Different pigeon-holes were set aside for correspondence with the new cooperative farm, and a state-run orphanage that had been installed in the house. Various departments of the British state had been urged to support the case – notably the Ministry of Defence and the Foreign & Commonwealth Office, but with no apparent success. There was a file of old photographs of the house, with its grand porch and turrets, as well as one of a ballroom with chandeliers. Separate efforts had been made to purchase specific items from the house: paintings, ceramics, furniture, tapestries – and a collection of clocks. But Hanna knew the truth: that the only item ever salvaged was the portrait of Natasza, delivered by Mr Hasard.

Downstairs, in the hallway, the clock chimed eight.

She'd been reading for hours and her eyes were tired and strained. Lydia would be back soon and expect food. She'd keep the keys and return to the documents when she could. Putting back the last of the files under L, her eye was caught by the single pigeon-hole directly above marked H – Hanna.

Unable to resist, she took down the file, which was full of documents: school certificates from Upware, an old passport, an illustrated parchment that recorded her First Communion. There were also various letters of appointment for the tutors who'd made their way to Swan House to teach her

Polish, German and French. (Lydia had been scandalised by the British suspicion of foreign languages.) Of all these, Polish had proved the problem for Hanna, and there was no certificate here, despite the hours spent in the schoolroom conjugating verbs. Finally, there was a sheaf of her childish drawings, which she'd often slipped inside birthday and Christmas cards: a delicate outline of Swan House, a sinuous sketch of the count asleep in his favourite armchair.

The next pigeon-hole along was marked H, too – but she had to squint to see the sub-division: H – Stern inquiry. She picked it out, aware her heart had missed a beat, opened the file, and what she read made her feel many things, but first of all was a sense of betrayal, that the two people who had become her guardians, and had given her a home, had withheld from her a precious gift: her family name.

Chapter 5

The soup was root vegetable, the turnips and carrots glistening in a thin liquor. As Hanna stirred the pot she heard Lydia's car arriving at the distant mailbox. The prospect of confrontation, which was now inevitable, made her place a hand over her heart. But for a few minutes the routine would remain unchanged, as ritualistic as the mass. Her aunt would go first into Hanna's studio, a small incursion mutually agreed after Lydia's last bout of illness. Here she would sit – where she had once knelt – before the shrine Marcin had constructed to the lost Natasza. This consisted of a photograph in a silver frame, and a candle, set on a wooden ledge below a simple cross, another testament to the count's skills at carpentry. Silent prayers would fill a few minutes, punctuated only by the rhythmic click of rosary beads. Then Lydia would come to the kitchen door, smile, and appear to struggle with some inner turmoil. The soup would be inspected, a short sharp sniff, and then a smile.

'I'm tired,' said Lydia. 'The sermon was tedious and long. I thought that combination was reserved for the Protestants. At least the mass was in Latin, although the bishop tells me that won't last, and then it will be English, of all things.'

Hanna hadn't said a word. She wondered if Lydia had sensed the change, the way in which the antagonism between them wasn't a relic any more, an empty ritual; that it was something alive, and dangerous. Hanna added salt and pepper to the soup.

'The house is icy. I've set the fire in your room.' Hanna's hands shook very slightly, but she was amazed to hear her own voice, still calm, measured, even distant.

'Thank you. The soup smells good,' said Lydia. 'And I am cold. The taxi driver said there were skaters on the river.'

Hanna silently stirred the soup.

'I'll go up,' said Lydia. She always ate her evening meal in the attic at her table, and took a glass of sweet wine, while Hanna sat in her aunt's armchair by the fire. This had been their routine since Marcin's death.

While the soup warmed, Hanna wandered the ground floor of the house, a yellow crayon in her hand, adding a new vivid line to the others on the whitewashed walls, above the ugly stain of the flood. But this addition did not follow the sensuous curves of its predecessors; it was jagged, uneven. It was only during this simple act of rebellion, crayon in hand, that she analysed how she felt. Of itself, anger was a rare emotion; she'd often been angry about *things*, but rarely angry *with* anyone, except herself. She hung on to this idea, as if it were a source of power, for she felt desperately insecure as well: Lydia and Marcin had given her the life she had, so the concept of an overt challenge threatened everything.

She put the hot soup on a tray with some bread.

At the top of the last flight of steps, she paused as she always did. 'Aunt?'

If there had been a door, she would have knocked. She never passed this point without permission. She had considered breaking that rule today, but decided it would be a petty victory when a larger one was within reach.

'Yes, Hanna,' said her aunt, the vigour always surprising.

Lydia's room was small, so the air was warm and mildly scented with the old woman's soap. The three bars of an electric fire glowed. The lamp on the desk, an elegant porcelain piece that used to sit in the front room, threw light over letters and a half-open book of poetry. Hanna always suspected that such elaborate arrangements of chiaroscuro were timed for her arrival, to indicate that Lydia's life was busy and rich despite illness and old age.

The room was dominated by the portrait of Natasza. In the half-light at the gable-end, Hanna could just see the white of the perfect skin.

'Hanna, thank you. Sit, talk. The bishop asked me to mention his blessing – Father Joseph as well, although he looked dreadful. There are rumours. But we shouldn't gossip.'

Lydia's world was a small one, so she was able to keep a constant watch on everyone, although she tried to disguise her pleasure in scandal. Father Joseph, who smelt not unpleasantly of whiskey, had taught Hanna the catechism for her Confirmation. He had two nicotine-brown fingers, and a sideways smile, and had even suggested she might one day investigate her lost religion, which made her wonder about his own faith.

'He drinks, you mean,' said Hanna, determined that they were going to have a forthright conversation, devoid of the usual evasions.

Lydia blinked, perhaps sensing the brittle atmosphere, and then carefully resumed her task of breaking the roll set beside the soup, before beginning to ferry small spoonfuls of the broth to her mouth.

'Will you phone Peter now the line is back?' she asked, and Hanna knew that in her own subtle way her aunt had picked up the taut emotional atmosphere, and was spoiling for a fight, although such draining exchanges had never yet reached boiling point.

'I'll try later. I think he's been away – Bowyer brought a telegram. There's been a lot of interest from galleries …'

'What is his secret?' asked Lydia; a pointed observation of Hanna's inability to make money. Marcin had kept his own counsel, but Lydia had hoped Hanna's education might lead to teaching, or even the law. 'And Vanessa too. I suppose that's just hard work and application; I don't doubt Liberty's pays handsomely for those gorgeous prints.'

She set down the spoon and edged the soup bowl away. 'This is delicious, but hot. I'll let it cool.'

Hanna pulled up a chair and then went to the decanter by the window and poured out two glasses of the sweet white wine from Venice.

Her aunt's eyes lingered on the second glass, which constituted an affront to the daily routine. They never drank together.

Hanna retrieved a sheet of paper from the pocket in her painter's overalls and placed it on the table.

'What's this?' asked Lydia.

'Did you know my real name was Hanna Stern?' Hanna said, draining the glass of wine and returning it to the table with a sharp crack. The sense of power she felt, the sense of *self*, was intoxicating and for the first time in her life she understood the strange thrill of holding power over another human being.

'N-no …' stammered Lydia. But she stared at Hanna, the whites of her eyes catching the light, until she had to look away, making an elaborate ritual of dabbing the napkin at her lips. Hanna sensed this was the truth, but that it was offered now as a distraction from other, nameless, lies.

Hanna placed a finger on the single sheet of paper, which appeared to be an official document, typed in a German Gothic font.

'I found this in the count's office. It was in a file marked H – Stern Inquiry. That's my name – my *family* name.' Hanna recognised that she was being cruel but was unable to temper the urge to persist.

Lydia shook her head: 'You are Hanna Mazurek to me,' she said, her chin coming up. 'That door is locked, child,' she said, trying to hit back. 'Are you a common thief?'

'The count kept spare keys in the apple store, Aunt. Not a complete set – there's a safe too, but that has retained its secrets. Do you have the key?'

Lydia shook her head, her lips pressed tight.

'Did you know this was my name?' asked Hanna again, sensing that repeating a lie would be beyond her aunt's powers. The force of the question seemed to drive Lydia back into her cushioned seat.

'I did not,' said Lydia, calmer now. 'The estate manager at Łabędzie did not know your family name. Mr Hasard did not know. *I* did not know your name.'

Lydia's hands clutched each other. Hanna thought of the old woman's heart, labouring in the narrow chest, squeezing tired blood around her thin body.

'We did all we could for you,' said her aunt; five words that opened up the past like a book. 'We took you in to our family. We gave you a name. You had no name but Hanna, child. That was all I knew. That is all I knew until this moment ...'

She noted the use of I, and realised that the old woman had swiftly acknowledged that she too had been led astray by lies. (The count was buried at River Bank and Hanna knew Lydia would go there tomorrow, to talk to the stone.)

'So the count knew and kept the truth from us both,' said Hanna. 'I am nearly twenty-three years old and today, in a forbidden room, and on a forbidden page, I found that name for the first time. Why did he do this to me?'

Externalising the question made it almost unbearable. An echo of the count's gentle kindness had sustained her each day since his death. Had she mistaken love for something else?

Lydia's eyes flooded, and her fingers shook as she pressed a tissue to her mouth.

Hanna took a deep breath, aware that she might break down. Efficient communication was required here, not self-pity. She picked up the sheet of paper. It had the quality of a photograph, with a slightly gloss finish. Blackness crowded around the white page, and the letters, in the fussy German script, were slightly blurred.

'There are several of these in the file, as if the photographer was trying to get the most legible copy. Some prints are clearer than others. Whoever sent them to the count included a typed note. It says the form shown in the picture was a record taken for the Gauleiter of Poland, based on information from the Judenrat – that's a Jewish council, I think. The document is a list of all those boarding Transport 573 at the Radegast railway station in the city of Lodz – about a hundred miles south of Warsaw – on 1 July 1944; all those, that is, with a surname beginning with S.'

Lydia reached out for the wine glass, but then changed her mind.

'There was a carbon copy of the letter to the photographer, which makes it clear the count was *looking* for a family called Stern. So perhaps he didn't know that first day when Mr Hasard brought me here. But he found out.'

Hanna glanced at the list again, quickly finding the four listed Sterns: 'This family – the Sterns – appears on the list. He's marked the names you see, with a blood-red tick. Read them, Aunt.'

Lydia's glasses, on a chain around her neck, had to be positioned first. Then she licked her thin lips: 'Leopold, Irena, Judith and Hanna.' Her voice broke on the last word.

Hanna's eyes had filled with tears, but it was a sign of the power she felt, a derivative of her anger, that she could hold them back, could stop them falling. She retrieved the paper, but the names were blurred now, and swimming. She was intoxicated by the idea that her family was alive when these words were typed, and that *she had been with them*: that she hadn't been left behind, and certainly not hidden.

For the first time she thought about the order of the names: Leopold, Irena – father and mother? Judith an older sister, perhaps? They'd all been on the train together. And before that there had been a home, and grandparents, and parties, and outings, and picnics, and birthdays and holydays, and a polished wooden synagogue. And there'd been nights of sickness when she'd been held against her mother's skin.

She thought of the life that she had lost and let the tears fall, brushing them aside, before setting the page down again.

'There is more. Do you see, Aunt? Beside each name is stamped the same words.' She read aloud:

VERARBEITET:
BOREK, JULY 8th 1944

'Processed,' said Hanna. 'I looked it up. Uncle always said the Germans had a genius for euphemism.

'It's all official – the list was made in Lodz and counter-signed, and then verified by what is called here 'the officer responsible for the census' – another euphemism. Julius Sandberger, a lieutenant. Look, his name is at the bottom, just here. I think this means we arrived at the camp and that we were sent to the gas chamber.'

'Borek?' asked her aunt, as if they'd wandered into a casual geography lesson.

'A camp in Poland, a hundred and fifty miles south-east of Lodz. I looked it up in Uncle's books – the history books. It was like Treblinka and Majdanek, Sobibor, like Chełmno. A death camp. The camps from which nobody returned.'

She took a breath. 'But I returned. I wasn't processed, I wasn't killed, I'm here, talking to you. How did that happen?'

'I don't know,' said Lydia, and this too was clearly the truth.

It occurred to Hanna that the old woman had also been betrayed.

She retreated to the shadows at the end of the room and came back with the portrait of Natasza, setting it up on her chair, upright, still catching the light.

'If I was taken to the death camp at Borek from the ghetto in Lodz, I wasn't being hidden away in Warsaw. So where was Natasza, Aunt? What is the truth about her?'

Lydia studied the painted face before them, looking at the picture, looking *into* the picture, and Hanna was moved to see she too was bewildered, frightened even, but most of all heart-broken.

Chapter 6

Hanna always rang on the dot of eleven, five o'clock Eastern
Standard Time on a Sunday, a time that suited them both: she
was usually finished for the day in the studio, and Peter was
taking a break, sitting on the stairs by the phone, with a can of
beer in his New York loft. Such calls had become a tradition
the first winter they were apart, in that way that small ceremo-
nies can define a relationship. And his first question was part
of the ritual too: 'what are you working on?' To which she had
an answer, because her hands were sticky with paint, a new
canvas drying on the easel.

The earlier confrontation with Lydia had drained them
both: her aunt had asked to be left alone, while Hanna had
gone to the old schoolroom, her mind still full of that shared
journey east from the Radegast station, with Leopold, Irena
and Judith. The lost details haunted her: did the boxcar lurch
from side to side? Did the whistle sound? Could they see the
landscape passing? The precise images were still locked away,
but when she came down from the attic, she'd felt inspired to
paint, to try and reach back into that lost world. She applied
the familiar three colour panels to a canvas, but then she set
it flat on the floor, mixing the oils with turpentine to thin the
paint, letting her hands hang free, painting with a slow-motion, dreaming action, then adding charcoal lines. She tried
not to think, but to let her body decide. And what, finally, did
she see? *Green, Silver, Red* again, the second iteration of what
she felt certain would be a series, but now *inhabited*, popu-
lated by insubstantial forms, the lines an echo of something
she'd once felt.

She took up the charcoal and added a signature to the canvas:

Hanna Stern

The simple physical act of inscribing the letters of her surname for the first time made her heartbeat rise.

The clock chimed the hour. She clattered down the stairs into the cold hallway and rang the exchange at Cambridge to ask for the line she'd booked to Albany, for a New York City number. The line crackled, and the hiss rose to become a note. The operator told her they'd had to patch four lines together to make the connection. Another conversation was going on in the background, waxing and waning in a giddy cycle.

A final click and there was Peter.

'Han? What you working on? You OK? Above water?'

It was only now, hearing his voice, with its furred edge of nicotine, that she realised the danger of the call: that she might say what she'd promised herself she'd never say.

'Han?'

She heard voices in the background, familiar but suddenly hushed.

'A party?' she asked.

'Maybe. Sure – we're celebrating, I've taken the plunge, Han. I'm off to Berlin next week. Everyone's come round to say goodbye.'

'*Berlin?*'

She heard him laugh, and, more faintly, a scuffling. She imagined friends pushing past in the narrow stairwell, heading for the loft loaded down with bottles.

'That's it,' said Peter. 'Berlin. There's a studio on the Ku'Damm – and a venue close to the Neue Galerie is going to hang *Voices!* And there's dollars, Han – like a salary – for three months. The State Department's picking up the tab.'

His voice was light, even joyful, rising above the damage caused by bourbon and cigarettes. 'I've sold my soul. The US wants to push Western Art – show the Soviets that we're the future, they're the past. I can't argue with that. Paris would have been great, but why should I have to be poor for ever?'

She heard a glass touch a bottle.

'Pete. Something's happened.'

'Can you hear me?' he said. 'Coz I can't hear you. This is crazy. Look. I'll try you; it saves money, and I bet the line's better. Stay by the phone.'

The line went dead, so she put the receiver down and stood for a moment, thinking that the party must be reaching full swing soon and that he'd get distracted. It was too cold to stay in the hall, so she went back to the schoolroom.

Green, Silver, Red II lay in the shadows, wet patches of paint still catching the light flickering from the fire.

She heard the phone then – a single ring, half finished – so she went out into the corridor and waited. But the silence was mid-winter deep. Maybe the operator was struggling to make the connection. Then she heard the flutter from behind the Imperial Red Door: despite her best efforts she'd failed to entice the crow to the open window, but she'd left it food. It remained trapped, despite the clear prospect of freedom.

She went back to the schoolroom, took down her shoebox from the shelf, lit a cigarette and spread out Peter's postcards, until she spotted the one she wanted. In sepia, an old shot of a chateau, marked on the back in type as Hotel Palaise, Mondorf-les-Bains, Luxembourg. He'd found the postcard clearing out his old papers and sent it to her with a few lines. She knew a lot already because of the nightmares. He had the gift of tongues – German, because of his grandparents, and then French at Lafayette, so he'd been seconded into intelligence.

This is the place, Han. Camp Ashcan. Once upon a time, before the war, it was a fairy-tale castle for rich Americans. This is where they made me listen to the tapes. I hear they knocked it down. Maybe I'll sleep better. Px

Sometimes he'd tell her more to try and clear his head for sleep. The prisoners, all high-level German officers, were led in through a gate in an electrified fence. Their sins would fall eventually under two headings: *crimes against humanity*, and *genocide*. At night, Klieg lights, flown in from Hollywood, lit the perimeter in a searing impersonation of daylight. The captives were held in the old cellars. Taped interviews were conducted by senior intelligence staff in the suites on the first floor.

On the first day he was issued with a tape-recorder – a state-of-the-art German Magnetophon, commandeered from the Gestapo headquarters in Paris – and taken to a booth, one of nearly fifty constructed of chipboard and sacking. There were two grades of tape: alpha and beta. Alpha tapes were made at Ashcan during interviews. Beta tapes arrived by motorcycle messenger and contained recorded testimony from suspects and witnesses. Peter's daily ten-hour shifts involved making verbatim accounts of the Alpha tapes, or creating brief abstracts of the Beta. All the transcripts were sent by motorcycle messenger to the Palace of Justice at Nuremberg, for use in the trials to come.

The extraordinary quality of the stories that he heard was that they had no visual component, only an auditory one. His mind was therefore required to provide the images, a feat of creative imagination to which he was appallingly well suited. He was entirely defenceless against the words that fell, unbidden, into the silent, soundproof, booth. An interview subject, an SS officer perhaps, serving in the advance guard of the assault on Russia, might suddenly switch from a colourless exposition on the destruction of a field of corn to a vivid cameo of a roadside execution, the visceral jolt of the bullet going home, the folding marionette's legs. A Jew, doomed to the long march west, might talk for several minutes about the minutiae of the roadside diet: spring bulbs under the snow, a rotten turnip, a frozen crab apple, and then simply append a vision glimpsed at a crossroads – three Polish partisans, their bare bloodied feet swinging an inch above the vivid yellow snow. Relentlessly, each day, Peter's memory recorded these images, until his head was full of the hellish visions of others.

Hanna pinned the card up on the wall.

The phone rang, so she ran down the stairs and grabbed at the receiver, so that it fell, turning on its twisted cord.

'Pete,' she said, breathless.

'Sorry. They couldn't get a line. This is good for me?'

'Me too.'

'You said something happened?'

She told him what she'd found beyond the Imperial Red Door.

Peter needed no framework, no context. He knew her remembered life as well as she did. In her pocket she had the single sheet of photographic paper, so she read out the names, not caring for once if Lydia could hear from the attic above.

'I'm Hanna Stern,' she said, finally.

She heard him light a new cigarette. 'Hallo, Hanna Stern.'

'There's an archive in Berlin, in the US sector. It's called the Berlin Document Centre – the BDC. It's the best place to find out what happened at the camp. Myda – the woman from the synagogue in Venice – mentioned it way back, but said they'd need the family name, or an address, somewhere to start.

'Well, now we have it. There's a chance, a real chance. We can find out for sure what happened to them, and what happened to me, Pete. How I survived.'

Saying this out loud made her believe in the possibility of success; that she might know who she was, who she'd been at the start of her life.

'Sure,' said Peter. 'They've got all the Nuremberg evidence, and the rest.'

'I know it's a lot to ask …' Hanna began.

'Depends what you're asking, Han,' he said, and she could picture his smile.

'Now we know the camp, and their names, there'll be statements, witnesses.'

'Tapes,' he said.

Hanna had begun to shiver, icy air seeping under the front door, creating a thin mist.

'Someone knew, Pete. Why I'm here and my family aren't. I can write again to the others with the surname: the Red Cross, the United Jewish Appeal. But the BDC's different, you have to apply, you've got to be there. Would you look for me, Pete? Make a start.'

She could hear music blare and fade, and a siren on the streets of New York.

'Sure. I'll do it, Han. I'll do that for you.'

She would have touched him then, pushing her fingers into his hair, if he'd been in the hallway.

'The State Department might help – right?' she asked.

'Yeah. They might. Carlson at the Cedar Tree says the CIA's in on this Berlin project too. There's a front organisation that's paying my tab: the Congress for Cultural Freedom. Sounds pretty creepy but what the hell.'

She heard someone calling his name, a sudden swelling of jazz and voices.

'But if I do this, how about you do something in return for me?'

'Of course,' she said, a hand on her stomach. The lie that lay between them, the unspoken truth, made her feel afraid of what he might ask.

'Like you said, I'll make a start. But if I find anything, I'll send you a return ticket. Will you do that for me, Han? Come to Berlin?'

Chapter 7

Long Fen had lost its echo: the brittle landscape of ice lay quilted under an inch of snow, so that as Hanna paused on the doorstep she was able to examine the quality of the silence, which seemed to press against her ears. Transatlantic calls always left her dizzy, her brain overheated, and tired of words, tired even of thought itself. The idea of stepping out into this silent world was bewitching. The dull percussion of closing the front door was lost instantly, swallowed up, followed by each separate footstep, creaking as it compressed the snow, circling the house, climbing the steep slope that ran up to the river, and the towpath. From the top she could see the white fens spread out like a sheet of paper beneath a sickle moon.

A breeze blew, along the frozen river, creating strange weaving patterns of snowflakes on ice. Hanna imagined the water below, glacier-like, inching its way towards the distant sea. Which set her walking north as well, along the great slow uncurling bend, until the village of Upware revealed itself, a hamlet clustered by a slipway and a ferry, and the old inn. The moonlight picked out several listless smoke trails rising from chimney pots. There was even a light at a cottage window, beside the old wooden wharf.

A cluster of poplars hid the school. She'd walked each morning, and then hailed the ferry over the water. The memory of her first day, breathing in the damp reek of the other children, from the hats and scarves, made her heart freeze with self-pity. Her classmates were alien to her: sudden and uncanny, each with a past and a childhood remembered, and parents, and grandparents, and a familiar path to a familiar front door.

She had wondered then what it was like to be a child. The girls were conspiratorial, the boys randomly cruel. The games they played defied logic. But they knew who she was, they understood *her*. She was the Jew-girl who hardly spoke and lived with the Polacks on Long Fen and was so clever she was attended by tutors at home. The girl with the still face and the watchful eyes. They were proud of legends of webbed feet and the fact that there were only six surnames on the school register; five before Mazurek had been added.

The classroom had been claustrophobic, but when the bell rang, her isolation was transferred to the playground, where it seemed to deepen and solidify, because the rest ran wild, but together, the chaotic motion somehow following a plan she could not follow. On windy days – which were almost every other day in the Black Fen – she'd let the breeze buffet her ears, standing by the fence, watching the boys career, and the girls scream and join hands in a trailing line that never opened up for her: all those hands tightly held but never offered.

Hanna heard a noise behind her, a broom-like swishing, and turned to see a light in the distance to the south, cherry-red and warm, moving with a swaying rhythm along the river. So Lydia was right, the Fen skaters had taken their chance for sport. She watched, bewitched, until the leading man came close, holding a guttering torch high in one hand, behind him a phalanx of Fenmen in pursuit, arms swinging, hurtling past. And perhaps she hadn't been alone in keeping watch, because ahead now she saw more lights of welcome on the slipway at Upware. One or two of the men called out, and she thought she heard her name, although she recognised no one as they swept past.

The moment broke the spell of the night, and so she turned back for home.

From the high bank the view was studded with lights; the distant villages of Landbeach and Waterbeach, the runway beacons at Mildenhall and even Feltwell, and the orange blush above unseen Cambridge. To the far west the horizontal glow of a train slid silently across the darkness, heading for Lynn. After a few minutes, as the long curve of the river unwound again, she saw ahead the attic light at Swan House at the very moment it blinked out. She imagined Lydia, her lips moving perhaps with the last prayer of the day, staring at Natasza's pale painted face by moonlight, wondering like Hanna if *her* story would ever be told. Then the line of poplars came into view, dark shards against a star-scape, shielding the house, until she reached the wooden steps down the bank.

She'd closed the front door carefully behind her, but now it stood open, the porch light shining on a parallelogram of golden snow.

Night-walking had not been part of Lydia's decline, but Hanna found her aunt's boot-prints heading out towards the fen. Leaving the door open seemed like an act of dereliction, and it made Hanna call out for her aunt; there was no echo and no answer. She followed the tracks to a belt of trees, beyond which was a small lake, no more than a flooded pit, from which the clay for the riverbanks had been dredged. As a child she'd swum in the river every day, even in winter, enchanted by the sense of *otherness* she felt freely floating in the water. But she'd always been wary of the old pit's depthless stillness.

Lydia's tracks led through a gap in barbed wire, a thicket of thorn, to the edge of the water. The flat oval surface of the lake caught the moonlight. Her aunt was shuffling her way towards the centre, leaving a twin trail in the newly fallen snow.

'Lydia,' said Hanna: the whisper must have sped across the surface of the ice, because her aunt turned. She was thirty yards away but Hanna thought she detected a smile. The old woman raised a single heel and brought it down with a sharp crack.

Hanna's ears registered the blow, the shifting pressures of ice and air. She wondered if their confrontation had unhinged the old woman's mind.

'It's safe, child,' said Lydia. She sounded lucid, calm, in control.

Hanna slid her feet forward as if she wore snowshoes. The air above the ice was refrigerated, shockingly cold. By the time she'd reached her aunt she could see that the old woman was shivering. The ice at the centre of the lake had been blown clear of snow and was glass-like and clear. A spider's web of harmless cracks radiated from her aunt's left shoe.

'We should go back,' said Hanna.

'This is rather wonderful,' said Lydia. 'I was considering the past and couldn't sleep. At Łabędzie the lake froze every winter and we would skate. The swans never stayed; they sat stupidly in the ridged fields. It gives you a different perspective. Look ...'

She pointed back at the house through a gap in the trees. The portico, lit, framed the blackness beyond the open door, and made it look like an entrance to the night itself.

'I've never been happy here,' said Lydia, and the moonlight caught tears in her eyes.

'I've only just admitted that to myself after twenty years. Well – hardly that. I knew of course. But it was under the surface ...'

She tapped her shoe lightly on the ice.

Hanna thought this was a deft confession, and wondered if her aunt had contrived it, and what she would say to the priest at her next confession.

'Marcin lied to us both,' she said, her jaw beginning to shiver.

'We must go back,' said Hanna.

Lydia's hand emerged from a sleeve, and Hanna took it, feeling the heat of her blood, and the pulse.

'In Paris,' said Lydia, taking the first steps of return. 'In Paris, when the radio reported the German attack on Poland,

I had no news of Marcin, no news of Natasza. There was talk
of an assault on France. I took the night train to Venice. There
was a great ...'

She swirled a single finger. 'Debate, perhaps. A family
council. We were lucky after all: wealth, connections, property.' She shook her head. 'So lucky. I took the train to Dieppe.
My family had a house in London. Six weeks later Marcin
joined me. I was told a story.'

A note of mockery had crept into her voice.

'Marcin said that Natasza had left Łabędzie a week before
the attack, intent on seeing friends in Warsaw. The estate was
a bore. The harvest dusty. Tensions were high in the city, there
was feverish political activity, furious debate, the swirl of café
society. She sought the city's excitements, its pleasures, as I
once did. Everyone thought there would be ample time for
her to return to Łabędzie if the Germans attacked. Marcin
was in the high command of the air force. If the battle was
lost, they would fly together to France – or to England.

'But when news came to Łabędzie of the German advance,
the tanks were twenty miles away. Marcin admitted that while
we had all heard the word *blitzkrieg*, the reality was far more
brutal than anyone had imagined.

'So Marcin drove east, to a small country airfield and took
to the sky. It is a desperate, but heroic story.'

She looked away, shaking her head.

The ice was smoking, the cold threads weaving between
them.

'The story is untrue, I always knew it wasn't true,' said Lydia.

She folded both her hands around Hanna's. 'The flat
in Warsaw did not belong to Marcin's family. It belonged
to my sister, and her children, but it had become ours by
use, as it were. In August – before the attack – it was sold.
Marcin had advised against this; he had a high view of
his financial acumen, and he found it convenient when he

visited the Academy, or the government offices. But never-theless, my sister ignored him, and sold it, as was her right.

'We decided not to bother Marcin with the news. But I did tell Natasza.'

Hanna shrugged. 'Perhaps Natasza went to stay with friends and did not wish to worry her father or break unwel-come news.'

Lydia closed her eyes. 'Marcin said he telephoned to see that she had arrived safely. The maid answered the call. The maid we had dismissed three months previously. The maid who did not exist. He spoke to Natasza in the flat that did not exist and reported that she said he was to make a point of telling me that she sent her dearest love.'

Lydia looked back at the house. 'Why the lie? If I'd had the courage, child …'

With a shock, Hanna realised Lydia wanted to be forgiven.

'I could have confronted Marcin. But I told myself the sub-terfuge may have been innocent – a white lie to cover a minor indiscretion.'

She shook her head, and smiled sadly, perhaps at her own self-deceit.

'But lies are corrosive, Hanna. The loss of our daughter could not bring us together. It is astonishing that a marriage can be destroyed by something that remains unspoken. And now we know there were other lies. He withheld from you the story of your family – *your* story. And you're right, where did Natasza go in the war? How did you both come to Łabędzie at the end?

'I think Marcin worked tirelessly to find the truth about your family, Hanna, so that he could hide it away. He had to control the past, to obscure the truth. But in the end the lies have led us back to you, and Natasza.'

They'd reached firm ground and the silhouette of the house stood up against the stars.

'I was afraid of the truth, and that it might lie beyond the Imperial Red Door. The Foreign Office wrote last year to say they have no interest in the count's papers. It was locked because I wanted it locked.'

Lydia gave Hanna a key. 'He always said the safe held government papers – confidential papers – of little note. Perhaps this is the last lie.'

Chapter 8

Hanna looked out of the attic window while Lydia undressed behind her screen and slipped into bed. More snow was falling, but this time in large flakes, obscuring the view. She fetched an extra blanket from the cupboard and kissed her aunt on the cheek before turning off the bedside light, stepping away, wondering if the old woman was already asleep, because her whistling cat-like breath was so even and untroubled. It struck her that she was putting the old woman to bed, as she had been put to bed, a circle she found unexpectedly comforting.

Unlocking Marcin's office a minute later, she thought she heard a footstep above, and stood listening, but it must have been the frost making the old house creak. Before she turned on the standard lamp, she looked inside the shade, and saw the crow, sitting watchfully. She'd put seed on the floorboards, and a dish of water was frozen, because she'd left the broken window open, offering escape. The crow's black eyes examined her, before the beak returned to the ritual ruffling of feathers.

Hanna knelt by the safe and turned the key. The lock was slightly rusted and so she took the oil can she'd left on the old desk and inserted the long bird-like bill into the mechanism, pressing the trigger until a teardrop of oil welled up and fell, before seeping away.

Then she sat, wrapped up in the count's old coat, rhythmically trying the lock. She'd been out in the night air for an hour before finding Lydia and she was still shivering, an involuntary rhythmic judder that shook her shoulders, although her hands stayed steady. It took ten minutes for the key to turn a half-circle; then finally the lid sprang open a half-inch, giving out a sigh as the stale air escaped.

Inside she found a bankbook, the account holder listed as *Rząd Rzeczypospolitej Polskiej na uchodźstwie* – The Polish Government-in-Exile.

There was also a British passport, dated 1946, with a picture inside of the count in a flying jacket.

And there was a single large envelope. The handwriting on the front was workmanlike, with a slightly brittle jagged stroke, and gave the address of Swan House, with the addition of United Kingdom.

The addressee was Hanna Stern.

She sat at the count's desk and looked steadily at the name as if it might simply float free of the paper.

The letter had been opened. The postmark was BERLIN SOVIET SECTOR, dated 6 December 1957 – a year before Marcin's death. Inside was a single sheet of paper.

Hanna.
I promised your father. So here it is. He is alive, but I can tell you no more. Not even where to start. I can ask no more questions. Forgive me.

There was no signature.

Hanna sat in the silence of the old house, listening to the clock tick, her hands set down on the plain deal table, which felt oddly insubstantial, as if it might tip and veer beneath her touch.

The single word *alive* seemed to pulse. Her father felt suddenly close, and she looked up, expecting to see him perhaps, emerging from the corner shadows. The idea that anyone from her family had actually survived Borek – as she had – made her feel alive too. She had to stand, the chair falling back to the floor with a crash, and she gripped the edge of the desk as if she might faint.

She heard the inevitable footsteps above and her aunt's voice: 'Hanna?'

Out on the landing she craned her neck to see the old woman in the shadows above.

'It's nothing. Go back to bed. I'll tell you everything tomorrow.'

Back at the count's desk she set the chair on its legs again and forced herself to sit down, before tipping up the envelope.

A small wooden carving fell out. It was quite light, made of a cheap wood, but well-fashioned in the shape of the knight on a chessboard. Hanna thought immediately of the German: *der Springer*. She pressed the wooden carving against her cheek. It must be a gift from her father. *I promised your father. So here it is*. A toy at last; maybe for the child she had been.

The room felt suddenly crowded: her father, the writer of the letter who was forbidden to say more, and others perhaps still lost in the dark – her mother, her sister. She held the single sheet of paper to her lips, closed her eyes, and tried to imagine the writing hand that had put the words to paper. She felt herself drawn back into a past she had never remembered, and thrown forwards too, along what felt, even then, like a path.

She stood up, startling the crow, which rustled its wings one last time and left its perch, swooping lazily across the room in a sinuous dip, to fly free through the open window into the freezing night.

Chapter 9

The Greater Government, July 1944

They went on, because their lives had become a journey, and nothing else. They'd been in the boxcars for three days and two nights since departing the Radegast railway station in the city of Lodz aboard Transport 573. By the time the train left, each boxcar had a number chalked on the outside indicating the tally of occupants: they'd seen the numbers when the train took a long slow bend that first evening. The nominated leader in boxcar 14, Dr Leopold Stern, had counted nineteen women, twenty-three men, and eight children in his truck. The roll-call included Stern's wife Irena, and their daughters Judi and Hanna. It was July 1944, the fifth year of the war, and they were going east, across the wide fertile plain of Poland, although Poland did not exist any more, because the Germans had swept it away in the heat and fire of their victory. Now they called what was left The Greater Government. A new name for a new country that lay beyond the limits of everything.

The thick summer heat was stifling; two old men died before the first sunset, their bodies laid out at the back of the boxcar. The living gave up their coats as shrouds. That night the train stopped, the door rolled back, and two guards threw the prisoners bread as if they were animals at the Tierpark, and then hosed them down with a pipe; but they would not take the dead away. The children drank the water first from a tin bucket. Hanna, who was always thirsty when she wasn't hungry, cried softly when the cup was taken from her lips.

Her mother gave her some stale bread, rolled into small balls, to stop the tears.

The next day they travelled on, but with less speed, as if the bureaucratic energy that had brought them together and propelled them out of Lodz was dissipating in the summer heat. Their train seemed to have lost its sense of purpose, occasionally stopping at a barren signal post, where the only sound was the wind and flies. They waited outside stations for hours, and then slipped through without stopping. The rabbi, Yitzchok, said that they were once more wandering in a desert. What was so new about that?

There was a single gap in the wooden boxcar planks by the lock on the door, and this allowed them to look out on the countryside. Some of the men pushed and shoved to see outside, and to breathe the air from the fields. By noon on the second day, when most felt their strength had gone, it was Duvos's turn to look out. He had worked in a photographic studio in Dresden, and explained that it had been his job there to mix the chemicals and develop the pictures. Duvos had small expressive hands, which moved rapidly as he spoke, and so he did not keep what he saw through the gap in the door to himself; he described the landscape moving past, exhibiting a genius for detail, for the surface nature of things.

'Two boys naked in a stream, the water's brown, like a sweating horse.' His childlike voice, light and fluting, almost broke with excitement. 'One boy is holding up a fish. It's dead, but he's making it flap by jiggling the tail.'

Hanna, six years old, listened with an open mouth, watching Duvos's lips.

A minute passed in silence and then he took up the commentary anew.

'Russian soldiers, prisoners of war, they're walking along a path beside the tracks. Most are wounded and there's a cloud of flies around their heads, so they're all blurred. Bloody bandages around their hands, and brooms for crutches. Heads down, in rags and so thin! The fat guard's eating bread, both hands full, one bite to the right, one to the left. Smell it, brothers – I can!'

Their lungs filled with their own stench from the overflowing bucket in the corner.

'Peasants in a field,' Duvos said, the next afternoon. 'A field that runs to the wide horizon, as far as the setting sun itself. Does it look flat, this land? Can I see the curve of the earth? Maybe I can. Maybe not. Either way the earth looks round, brothers – *the world's round*! Big news. Even that Pole from Krakow knew that.'

'Copernicus,' whispered Yitzchok to the little boy next to him.

'The women are picking potatoes and their backsides are facing our way,' said Duvos. 'They're as big as autumn pumpkins.'

The boxcar rattled on. The third day, the fourth; each punctuated by the nightly ritual of the bread, the hose and the bucket of water. After dark, the men traded whispers concerning the great question: *where* were they going? Stern had asked the officer on the platform in Lodz about their destination and been told simply that they were being resettled in the East. But upon these two words: *resettled* and *East*, they had built a future, a version of what lay ahead that could obscure the alternatives like a screen.

They had all heard rumours of what might await them. Stories, tellingly precise, of the massacres, the open graves, the SS officers drunk with murder holding hot pistols, the barrels glowing. Some brothers, escaping from the transports, had seen for themselves the camps, the wire, the huts, the distant chimneys. They whispered at night, in their hiding places back in the ghetto, about what they had smelt on the wind.

For four years the Jews of Europe had boarded cattle trucks at unnamed stations and gone east. Now the last trains carried the last Jews.

But hope had to have a name; and the name they gave it was *The East*. Fathers told their children of bustling towns with thriving markets, studded across great plains of wheat, beside wide green rivers upon which laden barges slid towards the sea. They talked to the children about the colours: the golden crops, the red and green and gold of the fabrics in the market, the brown and white feathers on the chickens. Blue eggs.

This idyll was in sharp contrast to the barren plain over which they travelled. Passing a hamlet, Duvos struggled to describe it because each cluster of shacks appeared to be identical, as if the railway track had been laid in a ring, and they were doomed to circle for ever the same farmhouses in brick, the same outhouses in wood, the same mean thorn trees. A land, it appeared, of hovels and black earth, baked under a Polish sun.

'Old men looking over a high wall beside the track,' said Duvos, one morning. 'They've got whiskers like cats.' He drew the whiskers in the air with his hands. 'Three have pipes – clay pipes, yellow and long. One of them is spitting at us.'

The voice of one of these old men followed them in the trundling boxcar: 'They're going to make you into soap, Jews!' The men had heard this insult many times, but the women fussed with the children, hoping they wouldn't ask questions.

For six days they travelled south and east, until, finally, Duvos's voice registered surprise. 'A signal box,' his face pressed to the gap by the lock. 'A man is pulling one of the bronze levers, smoking at the same time, there's a cloud round his head. We've passed a station. We're taking a branch line into the woods.'

Stern, who had been sitting with his eyes closed, sat up. Then, slipping a small travelling chess set into the pocket of his overcoat, he stood and stretched his sore joints. The sounds outside the boxcar were all new: voices shouting, an engine labouring, dogs barking and the lilt of music.

To travel is to live, Stern thought, but now we have arrived.

The sickly sway of the waltz made Stern nauseous, so he knelt down and leaned his forehead into the nape of Irena's neck. At thirty-eight years, his wife was ten years younger than him, her skin still soft. Her neck felt damp and cool against his face. He had been resigned to life as a lonely doctor in a small Bavarian village until the day she'd come to his surgery, walking all the way from the foot of the mountain to answer an advertisement for a part-time secretary. Stern gave her the job because she appeared efficient, although it soon became clear that she was a dreamer by nature. He'd noted that she didn't strike a pose like the women from town and often ran with the children in the village orchard when the leaves were falling.

Their daughters were dreamers too; Judi was reading a small book with dense print, while Hanna was using a blue crayon to embellish a wave-like line on one of the wooden slats of the boxcar.

The eldest girl put her head on one side. 'Real music, father, not a gramophone,' she said, always the calm observer. Her mother nodded, thinking to herself that the child had inherited her maternal grandfather's musical ear.

Stern considered his daughter. 'How do you know it's real music?'

'The beat changes. It's getting quicker.' Judi closed the book she had been reading and put it in her bag. At home she'd always chosen clothes with pockets big enough for her books. Irena, the family storyteller, had once made up a tale about a girl born with a pocket in her stomach like a kangaroo.

Irena spat on her handkerchief and gave it to Judi. This was a small family ritual. Her little sister had got crayon on her face and even her teeth, and dust mixed with sweat on her forehead. Judi cleaned the child fiercely, telling her not to cry, but to be brave.

Aside from their shared dreaming nature, Hanna was her sister's devoted opposite. A permanent hoarder of crayons, she left scribbled lines everywhere. Watchful, she seemed to monitor the adult world. 'That child has been here before,' her grandfather had said on her second birthday, not entirely kindly. Since the family's violent eviction from their home in Bavaria, Hanna had been locked in a form of episodic withdrawal, intermittently mute.

Two government officials had broken down the door to the Sterns' house in the village of Weissenstein, in the Bavarian Forest, at just after midnight one spring night in 1942. An SS trooper appeared with a lantern at the bedroom door, shouting for them all to get up: orders had arrived, he said, authorising their resettlement by train. The time had come. The time was now!

While Irena rushed to pack their bags in the few minutes they had been allowed, Stern had tried to reason with the officials, explaining that he was a doctor, that he had even worked for the health ministry in Berlin, that he had been assured he would not be rounded up as so many others had. But he had no documents, just the promises of friends in high places. The officials were unmoved. The Führer had decreed that the Reich was to be *judenfrei* – so they must leave.

It was Judi who discovered Hanna's empty top bunk. A perfunctory search failed to locate her. This was no surprise to the Stern family, as the child was an inveterate hider, with the gift of simply disappearing. The house, laid out over three floors and a basement, was a warren of chests, drawers and cupboards, and – up a single vertical ladder – an attic crammed with a lifetime's clutter. If she decided not to show herself it could take hours to find her.

Stern explained to the SS officer in charge that his daughter would not come out until she was hungry or wished to show her sister her latest drawing. Judi said she would stay behind and wait for her sister to appear. But the officials were adamant: there was a truck waiting outside, and there was to be no delay.

Blank, bureaucratic intransigence of this kind had become part of their lives. What was new was the casual, brutal violence. The Sterns' neighbours – old man Proll and his timid wife – were roused from their beds and forced to drag two bales of straw from their barn into the doctor's house, where one of the soldiers set them alight; the first in the stairwell, another in the cellar. Irena, who had begun to scream for her child, was pushed out and loaded into the back of the waiting truck. Stern pleaded desperately for more time, and was allowed to stand in the yard and call out Hanna's name, but when there was no response, he too was forced to climb over the tailgate of the truck. While the officials completed the documentation for the driver, the Sterns watched their home burn down under a cloudless, star-scattered sky. Stern's eyes ached with staring into the flames, because at any moment he expected his child to appear, a flailing vision of burning limbs. As they were driven away to Regen, Stern could think only that Irena would not survive the parting, and that his family would shatter under the loss.

Seven hours later, the door of their cell under the Rathaus opened and Hanna stood before them: an apparition in ash, a ghost in dust. She had been dead to them, and her rebirth stood as a family miracle, for the facts failed to offer any other explanation: the village air-raid warden, who was the teenage son of the local blacksmith, had been left to watch the embers of the fire at the Stern house. Once the truck had gone, he'd fetched a kitchen chair and a bottle of cider. Hanna had touched his hand to wake him up shortly after dawn. The house was a pile of ashes. They had no idea where she had been hiding, and she would not answer questions. In fact, she hardly spoke a word, withdrawing into a sullen coma of introspection. Irena, who had occasional insights into the psychology of her children, felt that while Hanna's body had escaped the fire, her mind was, perhaps, still hiding.

Chapter 10

The train slowed, lurched, then stopped. Irena ran a hand through Hanna's hair. The engine let out a long, final breath; the signal for the boxcar doors to be thrown back. The air outside buckled with heat, creating a series of mirages, so that nothing seemed fixed, or even real. The Stern family blinked this new world into a picture.

Duvos, first out on the platform, filled his eyes with more pictures, his hands dancing in the warm air. The station clock, set in a small wooden tower on the ticket-office roof, stood at 4.15 p.m. precisely, while the ticket window was open, and a sign, a painted arrow, pointed the way to Platform 3, and trains to Minsk.

The station sign itself said: BOREK – FOR MINSK.

Dr Stern was six foot tall, with white hair like a shaving brush, and limbs slightly too thin, perhaps, to take the everyday strains of walking, or carrying his suitcase. Irena, who knew that her husband sometimes used his natural air of authority to indulge a streak of laziness by simply monitoring the work of others, often sought to pester him with questions that drew him back into the everyday responsibilities of the family.

'Leo. The girls are thirsty. What can we do?' She tugged at the sleeve of his once-white shirt. Food and drink had become her obsession. After leaving Weissenstein, the transit camp at Regen and the two labour camps en route to Lodz had provided only bread and water. The ghetto had been its own city, with food for those who could pay. Luckily for them, doctors were scarce, and Judi worked in a paper mill, so there had been food on the table in their tenement block, if only potatoes and bread, cabbage and milk. But since they'd left the Radegast station they'd had only bread and water again. The thought that they might be given a meal here at the station, perhaps even hot soup, had set Irena's heart beating erratically. Hanna was in the dust, hunting for seeds, crumbs or leaves that she would investigate with her lips. The child foraged like a chicken.

But Stern didn't hear Irena's question, because he was trying to estimate the size of the crowd on the platform: three hundred perhaps, or more. Most were Polish Jews or Hungarians, with a few Germans, and no doubt there were ragged bands of what the Nazis called 'asocials' too – communist politicos, or deviants, even gypsies. At the far end, the little orchestra played, the elbow of the violinist sawing the air. The music had lost its lazy rhythm, as if the musicians were hurrying towards the last note.

The voices they had heard shouting orders on the platform were not German, but Slav. A savage tongue to Stern's ears, but employing distinctly German words:

Badehaus. Entlausing. Essen.

They'd all heard the rumours in the ghetto, that the Germans forced Ukrainians subjugated in the bloody onslaught against Moscow and Stalingrad to work for them as guards. The Jews were no friends of the Slavs, over whom they had held sway in the centuries of the Settlement of the Pale, that state-within-a-state, crowded with shtetls, under the ultimate power of the Tzar. History, thought Stern bitterly, had reunited them here, at a dusty Polish railway halt.

The guards dragged the bodies of the dead out on to the platform, taking the first boned flesh they could find:

a foot, a hand, or a skull below the chin. The foot of an old woman caught in the gap between the boxcar and the platform and Stern looked quickly away, although he heard the fragile bone break; the sound was indelible, an audible glimpse, perhaps, of the hell towards which he feared they were all falling.

Stern held his own case in both hands, across which he had carefully painted his address.

L.E.L. STERN
2377 Castelstraße
Weißenstein
Regen
Bavaria

Irena had scolded him for leaving off the 'Dr', insisting that the Germans would need doctors in the new settlements of the East. They hadn't been completely honest with each other since they'd left their home in Weissenstein. Both had realised, by a kind of emotional telepathy, that if they confronted the truth about their fate in the East, they'd have to be honest with the girls too. Most of their friends had been taken away, and the promised letters had never materialised. The inevitability of what lay ahead remained unspoken. In their own way the children understood much more than could be said, but they would only survive if they could keep these two versions of reality apart: the said, and the unsaid. Irena was right, of course. They would need doctors in the East. But how much, they both privately wondered, would they need doctors' wives, and doctors' daughters?

A group of men appeared from the far end of the platform and began helping the guards remove the bodies. They wore the yellow triangle of the Jew – but also red armbands. Slave workers, thought Stern, *Sonderkommando*, Jews organised into a work squad. They must live here, at Borek, and help run the showers, and the delousing.

Among these new faces Stern recognised a friend from the ghetto.

'Stay here,' he said, touching Irena's arm. 'I can see Carl Lichtenberg; do you remember, the carter from Adastrasse? One moment and I'll be back.'

They'd lived for more than a year in the ghetto. The few German Jews had congregated together. Lichtenberg had suffered from a badly set broken leg and paid for the drugs that dulled the pain by delivering turnips and potatoes with his cart. Weaving through the crowd, Stern was very close to Lichtenberg's face before the carter recognised him.

Lichtenberg embraced his friend.

'What should I know?' asked Stern quickly, shielding his eyes from the sun. 'Where are we going?'

Lichtenberg glanced towards the station sign. Two SS officers were stepping up on to a large wooden mounting block. One was a small man, slight, despite the uniform with its peaked cap. Stern knew the SS ranks by their insignia and this man was an Obersturmführer. Behind him stood another lieutenant: much bigger, broader, with blond hair. The clock above their heads still said 4.15 precisely.

'The small one we call The Puppet,' whispered Lichtenberg.

Stern thought it was one of the joys of Yiddish, this genius for naming things.

'Stay away from him,' Lichtenberg continued, adjusting his red armband. 'He's out of control. He kills when he wants to kill. The Ukrainie are thugs, but they are prisoners too. If the Germans are not watching, they can sometimes be trusted.

Look, Leo, the time is bad. There are visitors, bigwigs from Berlin. The Germans are like this …'

He made a knuckled fist of his hand.

'Everyone is on edge. You need to tell them you're a doctor, Leo. Tell them quickly. You won't get a second chance, not today. It'll be clear on your papers, but they don't bother with them until it's too late.' His eyes flicked back through the crowd. 'Your family?'

'Here.'

'Listen to me.' Lichtenberg's voice was flat and workaday. He looked into Stern's face. 'Leave them, Leo. It's best.' Then he fled before he could face any more questions.

Stern, alone with the knowledge of what lay ahead, bent his head down and covered his face for a moment with his hands. When he looked up, he saw the two SS officers more clearly. The one Lichtenberg had labelled The Puppet had a stiff leg, and a pale face, the left cheek of which carried a red duelling scar. His hair was thin, cropped, but clearly a sandy auburn in colour. He turned his head rapidly from left to right as if exercising a stiff neck.

The eyes distinguished him above all his other features. They were light green and Stern's scientific brain registered the facts: this shade of colour was usually confined to the Nordic countries and the Celtic fringe, and even then to just 1 or 2 per cent of the population. It was even more unusual for such a pigment to be matched by red hair.

The SS lieutenant's eyes were in fact remarkable; *clinically* rare. In some situations these observations might have given Stern some satisfaction, especially as such a combination was typically non-Aryan. But what made Stern's heart race was not this small triumph of academic observation, but a mixture of fear and sudden hope, for he had seen these eyes before.

The Puppet held a white linen handkerchief to his mouth as a slight wind lifted more dust off the platform. Even so, Stern could still see those eyes, and they were the most important thing in the world to him, because ever since they'd left the ghetto Stern had been haunted by the idea that God would give him one chance to keep the promise he'd made on the Umschlagplatz – outside the Radegast station – that he would hold his family together, and even keep them alive. This, he knew, was that chance.

The eyes were, unmistakably, those of a young man called Jonas Keuper, who had left Stern's village to join the SS in the year before the war. A teenager then, a man now, but always a boy to Stern. He'd watched him grow up, the son of the local tax collector, Johann Keuper, a friend of the Sterns. He had delivered the child into the world on the Regen road one winter's night in the winter of 1918. The child's mother had been returning home from town with her husband when their battered Adler ran into a snowdrift. The anxiety of the situation had induced contractions. The tax collector walked up the mountain to fetch Stern, and they'd gone back down the road together, Johann lighting the way with a lantern. Jonas had been delivered on the back seat and Stern, counting the toes and fingers by the flickering light, had noted the slightly crooked left leg. The mother had lost a lot of blood, and as they helped her up the track to the village, she left a trail of crimson spots in the snow.

The child had cried in the frosty air. That same voice rang out now, twenty-five years later, on the platform at Borek. Despite the show of authority, there was still something plaintive about the tone.

'Silence!' Keuper tugged at the uniform collar around his throat and steadied his feet, each shoe set as wide as his shoulders.

The prisoners baked in the sun while the officers enjoyed the shade of the station awning. Keuper let the silence stretch out, demonstrating his hold over the crowd. Still at last, the travellers felt many things that their usual, bustling motion helped to disguise: the itch of lice, the sores on their skins, the stinging dirty feet, but most of all the ache of hunger, the rasp of swallowing in dry throats. Many of them, suddenly dizzy, clung to each other.

Stern felt a hand slide into his and did not have to turn around to know that it was Irena. She wore two rings on one finger – her wedding band and her engagement ring. He turned his head so that his lips touched his wife's ear. 'The SS officer – the small one – it's Jonas Keuper, from the village, Johann's son.'

Irena's eyes widened and she dared to smile at her husband.

The closeness between the Sterns and the Keupers had survived even the first months of the war. Johann's enthusiasm for the Nazi cause was always muted, and he never mentioned Jonas again, or sought to shun the Sterns in the street. Stern had suspected that it had partly been the tax collector's influence that had kept the SS from their door for so long.

Keuper was reading a single sheet of paper held in a gloved hand, his lips moving slightly. The prisoners waited to be told what to do. Stern tried to calculate how he could get close enough to Keuper, at the right time and in the right place, so that he could plead for his family, and seek special treatment. His chances of success would be seriously reduced if he had to do this in public. Forcing the issue in front of Keuper's fellow SS officers would be a disaster. By far the most promising scenario would be one in which Keuper recognised *him*.

'Listen now,' said Keuper, folding the piece of paper into two, then four.

Stern had worked, briefly, in the morgue at the university hospital in Munich, and he could envisage Keuper's skull stripped of flesh and gristle, revealing a predator's bones – a fox, perhaps, dead in a ditch.

'Who is a goldsmith among you?' asked Keuper.

Hands were raised. The two officers smiled in an identical way, and the guards laughed too; not at the prisoners, but at each other.

'Who is a barrel-maker, who is a carpenter, who is a furrier?'

Hands waved.

Keuper's head jerked up and Stern caught another glimpse of his eyes. A splinter of memory came back: those eyes looking at him from the pear orchard one summer's evening, when he'd caught the village boys stealing fruit.

Weissenstein had several apple orchards, but the Sterns' six pear trees, dotted across the green hillside, were prized. With the memory came the powerful scent of the fruit itself. Hunger, a physical flexing of the palate, made Stern feel light-headed.

'You have trades,' said Keuper. One of his gloved hands smoothed the lapel of his SS uniform. 'Your leader …' He indicated a man standing to his right on the platform, the elder elected leader of Transport 573. He looked ill; his mouth hung open, and he held one hand over his heart. Shaking, one of his legs gave way at the knee so that he stumbled forward before regaining his balance.

'Your transport leader says that some of you *fear* …' Keuper stopped at that word, as if the mere idea of it were unthinkable. 'Yes – are *afraid* – that when you reach your destination you will be put to work in the fields, or in mines, or quarries.'

There was a murmur of agreement. Yes: this was what they feared, thought Stern, but really it was a hope, that they would live long enough to have such fears.

'Nonsense!' Keuper bounced on his toes. 'All those with trades will be encouraged to use them. We will respect these skills. In your new home, The Greater Government, do you think there are no towns? No shops? No bakers? No brewers?'

Applause rang out along the platform. Two men in front of Stern clutched each other's hands in celebration.

'In time we will take down the relevant details. There will be documents. Borek is a transit camp. You will be given fresh clothes, but you must leave behind useless baggage. Hoarded gold and silver must be given up for the war effort. You will not be here long. As you leave the platform you can take a postcard and fill in a message to your loved ones. Address the letters carefully. If they have gone before you, use the official number of their transport and that will suffice. Then you must go quickly to the bathhouse.

'After you are clean there will be a meal. Food and water.'

The words enslaved them all. Most of the women pressed their hands to their lips. Applause broke out again from the men. Irena bent down and kissed Hanna, telling her in a whisper that they would eat soon.

As soon as Keuper stood down they heard shouts behind them: 'Move along! Quick now. Move along!'

They all clutched their suitcases to their chests and shuffled forward. A mother straightened the jacket of her son and brushed back his hair. An old man tripped and one of the Ukrainie helped him to his feet.

At the end of the platform the dead, dragged from the boxcars, had been laid in lines. The slaves wearing red armbands – the red squad – had carefully placed all the heads at one end, the feet by the edge of the platform, and turned the faces away from the crowd, so that they looked back down the line towards Lodz and the West, to the ghetto and the lives they had left behind.

Chapter 11

The living filed past the dead and then turned right under the brick archway into a square, at the centre of which were hundreds of abandoned suitcases, many gaping open, revealing exotic linings of silk, damask, striped calico or simple hessian. The cases, and the trunks and carpetbags, were marked with the owner's name in chalk or white paint. Around this pyramid of abandoned luggage were piles of objects removed from the suitcases – books, trousers, canned food, bottles, hats, boots, underwear, shirts, coats, belts, socks; amounting to an open-air market, a street bazaar. Slaves, this time with blue armbands, were sorting out the goods and throwing anything worthless on to a fire, the fumes from which made the whole scene buckle like a mirage.

Irena knelt before Hanna, spat on her handkerchief, and tried to clean her face. The child's eyes were blank, brown glossy mirrors reflecting the pile of luggage. Tending to the children was Irena's vocation, and no minute passed now in which she did not touch them, but she accepted that this helped allay her own fears of what lay ahead.

On three sides of the square, which was about the size of half a football pitch, stood the barracks of a military camp. The fourth side comprised a fence topped with barbed wire, through which they could see the woods beyond. A single Ukrainian guard stood on the open ground, holding a dog by a short lead.

A large painted sign, nailed to a post, stood by the suitcases and read:

Der Gepackecke
[Left Luggage Corner]

Stern glanced down one of the avenues of grass between the barrack huts to his left. In the mid-distance the pattern was broken by a garden, with a picket fence and beanpoles standing in neat lines. A flag, bearing the swastika, flew from a pole in front of a small bungalow built in the German colonial style. An old man in a white shirt tended the garden. Even from a hundred yards, Stern could see that he wore a leather gun holster around one shoulder, and that he worked slowly, as if tending a coral reef.

Keuper had followed the Jews into the square and now mounted a second wooden block set down by one of the Ukrainie. In his fluting voice he told them that they must leave their suitcases here in the square, but that first they should extract their documents, any small valuable items, especially jewellery, and their toiletries: soap and towel. Their belongings would be sorted and any good clothing fumigated. The rest would be burnt. They must pool their resources.

'You must share, not hoard!' he ordered.

Irena had all the family's documents in her suitcase. She gave Leo and Judi their papers, keeping those for herself and Hanna. Then she whispered in her husband's ear: 'Do it now, Leo. Speak to Keuper while you can. Who knows when there will be another chance? What do we have to lose?' she said.

Stern noted that this précis of the situation had omitted the possibility that Keuper would just cut him down. What had Lichtenberg said?

He kills when he wants to kill.

Besides, Keuper had turned his attention to an old man struggling to open a suitcase, which then broke open, so that they could all see it was full of shoes: polished, with smooth leather soles, which had never stood on the ground.

'Leave them,' ordered Keuper.

The man scrabbled to collect the precious goods in his arms.

Keuper took his pistol out and fired a shot into the air.

The percussion was deafening, and Stern's hands went up to his ears. Everyone started screaming and clutching at each other in alarm. The cobbler, panic-stricken, leapt to his feet and Keuper cuffed him with the pistol-butt, so that he sprawled back in the dust.

The crowd wailed, whirling slowly, as the bullet-shot echoed back off the woods, the barrack huts and a brick latrine.

Two SS officers appeared immediately. The blond-haired officer, who had stood beside Keuper on the platform, led the way, followed by another lieutenant; a tall soldier with small round glasses. The first officer ran to Keuper and grabbed him by the lapels of his uniform. This confrontation astounded everyone, including the slaves of the blue squad, who stopped working to watch.

The officer with the round glasses pushed himself between his comrades.

'Not here, Rolf. Consider the circumstances,' he hissed quietly, one hand on the blond officer's tunic. 'Remember our visitors from Berlin. Do they need to witness this exhibition? Keuper knows the rules, no gunshots, and no arbitrary killing. This infringement will be dealt with, Rolf.'

'Yes, you must follow regulations, Meyer,' said Keuper, in a playful voice. 'Listen to your good friend Sandberger. I'm sure he has your best interests at heart.'

Meyer's face was very close to Keuper's, his eyes on his brother officer's narrow features, although he inclined his skull away, as if he found his comrade's breath unbearable. Unlike Keuper's fox-like skull, Meyer's head was a knuckle of bone.

The peace-maker's voice hardened. 'Is this the image they will take back to Berlin, Rolf? Two SS officers brawling in the dust? Is this typical of our brotherhood here at Borek? Rolf – you have duties here with the suitcases. Jonas – you are needed in the next square. Go now.'

Meyer, who had taken hold of Keuper's lapels, let him free.

The cobbler's wife knelt beside her husband, dabbing at a wound on his skull.

Stern was in shock. He found violence on an individual level intolerable. A career in medicine had in part been an attempt to alleviate pain in others, because he found it intolerable in himself. Seeing the wounded cobbler in the dust clutching his bloodied skull reminded him that the sweeping panorama of history was in fact made up of millions of personal confrontations with violence. He clutched Hanna's hand, at the wrist, and felt her warm body against his leg.

The Ukrainie, perhaps sensing that they might be blamed for the interruption to the routine processing of the prisoners caused by the gunshot, began to rip suitcases open, urging everyone to be quick. Quicker. *Schnell!*

Stern found that he was standing next to Liff, the watchmaker from their tenement block on Sattlergasse in Lodz. Several of the families in the block had been summoned for the same train. Liff was in his late twenties and had worn his eyeglass so often that it appeared to have distorted his right eye, which looked larger than the left.

Liff was reluctant to part with his suitcase, on which he had engraved, in a neat Gothic chalk script:

Tobias Liff

Watchmaker.

Pocket Watches a Speciality

Stern prised the handle out of Liff's long fingers. 'They want you to leave this Liff – take a few valuables, and documents, your soap. Leave the case.'

Liff didn't seem to understand. Stern opened the case and saw that it was full of watch mechanisms and bits of clocks. Nothing else. Not even a winter coat. *Idiot*, Stern thought. When the snows come, if we live to see the winter, some fool will have to give him a blanket.

From his pocket Liff produced a small wooden box, which flipped open when he pressed something hidden in the metal edge. It held tools – miniature files and screwdrivers and stelli.

'I want to work,' said Liff.

Liff, who had struggled to make a living in the ghetto, had often shared their food. His tragic story had bewitched Judi, who dreamed of writing books. The watchmaker had lost his fiancée in a bombing raid over the Ruhr. The bombs had destroyed a dam and they'd found her body, when the waters subsided, lying in a field on a hillside. Hanna was fond of Liff too, for his innocent devotion to clocks and watches, a toy-like world of mechanisms and springs. She often held his hand when her parents were busy.

'Take the tools with you,' said Stern. 'Leave the rest. Your name's clear.'

Irena gripped Stern's shirt in a tight fist. 'Leo. The Keuper boy has gone. Ask one of the guards to take a message. Leo, you must do this.'

Stern put a hand on Hanna's head and looked at his wife. 'Patience. Keuper will be back. Trust me. If it comes to it, I'll send a message if I can. For now, wait and tend to the girls; they must choose what to keep and what to leave.'

Stern opened his own suitcase to extract some valuables, including a notebook, and his copy of the siddur. Then he extracted his towel and a toilet bag that held soap and a razor and a small bottle of cologne, which had been a gift from his children. The glass was yellow and the stopper gold, and the Gothic script read: Farina of Julichplatz.

All that was left in the case were a few of his favourite books, some spare clothes, a travelling microscope he'd bought as a student, second-hand, in Munich, and his doctor's bag, sewn into the leather interior of which was a series of pouches holding glass bottles of drugs: pills, liquids and powders. Many of the phials had come with him from Weissenstein, but he'd been able to add some penicillin and cocaine, purchased on the black market in Lodz. Most of the bottles were green glass, but one was Prussian blue, two ochre, one black. He closed the suitcase, sliding the locks, and put it on the pile with the rest, and then approached a slave who was stacking empty suitcases, a stocky bullish man with the Star of David tattooed on his forearm.

Stopping short, Stern bent down to signal an apparent interest in a cigar box of old photographs.

'Brother,' he said, flicking through the pictures with a manic intensity. 'Listen. There's a case with my name on it: Stern. There's a medicine bag inside. Take it to your own doctor if you have one.'

The slave continued to search the lining of a suitcase he'd picked up.

'Where?' he said, then straightened up, a hand to his back.

'Just here by the carpet bag and the leather trunk.'

Stern walked away quickly, free of the burden of the medicine bottles.

The Ukrainie began to work their way through the crowd, picking out the very old, and anyone who was agitated or crying. These people were led to a small hut in the far corner of the square, decorated with a large red cross painted on the whitewashed wood. Behind it was a stockade, a screen of close-set wooden poles with pointed tops.

Outside the hut, a man in a white coat sat on a camp stool. There was something about the fluid grace with which he smoked that suggested to Stern he was drunk. The wind was blowing from that way and the smell was appalling: not really a smell at all, but a taste, as if the air was putrid.

A man Stern and his friends recognised, a teacher who had set up a mathematics class on the doorstep of the tenement block, had started talking loudly to everyone at once: 'They're going to kill us brothers and sisters.' He said this again and again, the accusations growing louder with each repetition. Then he swore very badly in Yiddish and a lot of the women tried to cover the ears of the children.

'Kill us like pigs – that's the smell. Dead pigs. Human pigs. That's us,' he shouted. The words were becoming blurred because his mouth appeared to be filling with saliva. When the guards got to him, he collapsed before they could knock him down. They dragged him to the Red Cross hut and his feet left a trail in the sand like a railway.

Yitzchok, the rabbi, tried to calm everyone down. 'It's a lazarette, a sickbay. They don't want anyone weak to go out on the next train. It's for workers. Maybe the sick will follow on. There may be many miles still to travel. It is a journey for the strong.'

This vision of the future seemed to quieten the crowd.

Meanwhile, a trestle table had been set up by the slaves in the shadow of the railway station building, and behind it stood Meyer. Some suitcases, selected by the slaves, were placed on this table for examination. The officers made notes on a clipboard as these were unpacked.

Sandberger, who had intervened in the confrontation with Keuper, had returned and now stood ten feet from Meyer, smoking. His glasses caught the sun and the flash of light as he rhythmically turned his skull from side to side made him seem like a human lighthouse. This elaborate pantomime set Sandberger aside as an outsider, an observer who did not want to take part in the scene around him. Stern sensed a close bond between him and Meyer, because they talked together without looking at each other's faces.

A dull shot sounded from the lazarette.

The bullet from Keuper's pistol had been ear-splitting and brittle, but this sounded distant, almost soft, and no one screamed, although many of the women clutched their husbands and children. Stern was standing beside Tomma and Esther Boniek, the couple who lived in the back room on the same floor as the Sterns on Sattlergasse. Tomma was a glass-blower and the constant inflation of his lungs had given him a great barrel chest.

He spoke into Stern's ear: 'That's a side-arm, with a silencer,' he said.

Esther, who was pregnant, didn't flinch when another shot sounded. Stern noticed that while many of the women showed their fear, Esther was calm. Her eyes darted around the square appearing to memorise its exits, the barrack blocks, the white-washed fence of the lazarette.

They all heard a voice raised beyond the picket, then three more shots, followed by several others, like fireworks heard from a distance, crackling. A woman who'd given her child to the guards to take to the lazarette clutched her stomach with circling hands, her voice beginning to keen.

The black-uniformed guards had formed a sickle-shaped cordon behind them and now started shouting that the prisoners should move on. They wielded whips and staves but, Stern noted, no guns of their own. The way ahead lay down a narrow alleyway between two barrack blocks, beside which Sandberger now stood, clicking a mechanical counter.

Judi and Hanna clutched their chosen treasures: a book, and three crayons, respectively. Irena had her purse, and a small locket that contained a picture of her father. In the end she had been forced to abandon a painted plate that Stern had scolded her for bringing. He had pointed out from the start how heavy it was and how easily it would break, but it had been Irena's grandmother's and was decorated with pictures of a village in the forest: a woodcutter's cottage, a church, an inn with snow on the roof. As a little girl she'd woven stories around the scene; a whole childhood's worth of imaginings.

Stern turned his back on the suitcases. He'd decided that he'd never get his belongings back now. There was an unexpected relief in leaving his suitcase behind. He'd carried it out of his house and across Germany, through labour camps and transit camps, constantly checking its whereabouts, so that he was strangely elated to be free of it. He felt more buoyant, less real. As with many burdens, he did not realise it was such until it had gone.

Looking back, he saw two slaves approach Meyer's table, carrying a suitcase, which they hauled up and stood on its end. Stern's keen eye noted immediately that it was Liff's, with its chalk advert for the watchmaker's skills, and that the SS officer began making a careful note on his clipboard.

Chapter 12

Another sign, by the same hand that had crafted LEFT LUG-GAGE CORNER, pointed the way forward to the second square and read, in a display of Teutonic irony:

PARISER PLATZ

Leo knew the real *platz*, Berlin's finest, east of the Branden-burg Gate. Before the war he'd advised the government's health department on the treatment of childhood disease, a task that brought him to the capital, and afforded time to enjoy its luxuries. On one corner of the square stood the Hotel Adlon, the city's plushest meeting place, famous for its coffee and cakes, certainly, and its slightly racy clientele, including several prominent Jews, but – most of all – for its silver-mirrored barber's shop. Leo always treated him-self to a daily shave when he had the chance, watching the world go by outside, the great crowded *platz* the very heart of the city.

In contrast, this square rang with the echo of something just lost, like an empty stage. Stern loved the theatre and was sensitive to this quality of resonance; as if the air had been chemically altered by the dramas enacted before the audience. All that emotion: love, hate, terror, anxiety, distrust – in one space, each night, repeated. Faux emotions it was true, but nonetheless real to that part of the audience able to suspend disbelief. He'd even wondered if, in the so-called real world, this was the scientific root of the phenomenon of the ghost: that by the ferocity of their emotions, the dying leave behind them images burnt into the very space in which they blazed so brightly.

This square was like the first in that it was open on the right side, giving a vista of the woods beyond the wire, but ahead was a metal fence, about the height of two grown men, with razor wire at the top, and the mesh itself was draped with pine branches, which obscured the view beyond. The branches had gone yellow. Sheets had been hung on this fence too, and quilts, curtains and blankets, just like those they'd left behind in the last square.

All the men stood looking at this fence. The sound of a digger was very close. Fumes – sickly gaseous fumes – painted Stern's lips so that he could taste the fire he could not see. The smoke, in contrast, was impossible to ignore, rising in a twisting oily column, like a section of the gut, powered by the unseen flames below.

There was a gate in the fence, a wide entrance about twenty feet across, with a metal arch. Through this they could see shadows and a sandy path, beside which trees shivered in a light breeze, their upmost leaves catching the sun. It was clear this would be *the way*. Did it really lead to the bathhouse? Stern thought he had rarely seen anything so terrifying.

A new group of slaves stood watching them. They wore no armbands, neither did they keep their heads down, nor move in sinuous paths to avoid the guards. They wore belts and had shoes. They must be the *kapos*, Stern thought, the captains chosen from the slaves to be their leaders. In Lodz they'd called them 'court Jews', privileged servants to the Germans.

One of the kapos had brought a wooden crate on which to stand. He was a short, muscle-bound Pole, with rickets. He set it down on the ground but then stood back so that another kapo could step up. This young man was very unusual to look at. He had vivid red hair, cut back to his scalp, but nonetheless revealed by the amber dots of the stubble, and wore glasses, with a cracked lens. The most remarkable thing about him was his height. He must have been six foot one or two, but the effect was accentuated by his extraordinary shape: narrow hips, sloping shoulders and a small skull combined to make him appear like a reflection at a travelling fair, glimpsed in a distorting mirror.

He spoke in Yiddish. 'My name is Kopp,' he said. 'Here at the camp we need carpenters, a plumber and a scribe. There are many of us here who help run the camp. Goldsmiths too, we need. And a dentist. Doctors – we always need doctors. Even a few labourers, but not weaklings; we're looking for great arms, tree trunks for legs. You'll get food, and a bed.'

The crowd became restless at the mention of food. Had they not *all* been promised a meal? One of the Ukrainie, sensing the air of rebellion, cracked his whip.

'Life is not bad here for those who work,' finished Kopp. 'We can take sixteen of you now. Just sixteen. There is no choice. If we need you, then you must come with us.'

Stern wondered when he had started saying 'we', and why he did not articulate the alternative to be chosen to work for the kapos as a slave. Presumably, that lay beyond the fence, through the archway, and down the path.

The kapos moved among the crowd searching for the craftsmen they needed, cross-examining each volunteer. If a man said he was a plumber then a particular kapo would ask him questions about pipes, and taps, and cisterns. If he said he was a goldsmith they questioned him about the market value of gold by the ounce, the chemistry of solder, the regulation of metallic purity.

For the children – and to comfort each other – those overlooked by the kapos fussed among themselves, talking about the bathhouse, getting on a new train, and going further east. They all took their roles as if in a play.

The kapos found a liar, a man who said he was a carpenter but did not know the difference between mortise and tenon. The guards waded into the crowd and beat him with wooden staves, then dragged him back through the narrow alley towards the lazarette.

The casual nature of the violence marked a further step in the journey they were all taking. So far, but for Jonas Keuper's attack on the cobbler, each punishment had been meted out in response to a crime, or at least an infringement perceived as such. But the two Ukrainians who dragged the 'carpenter' away laughed hysterically, and when they shouted they slurred their words. Sensing a loosening of civilised bonds, the prisoners edged closer together, the family groups re-forming, lovers holding hands.

Stern looked at his shoes. Despite Carl Lichtenberg's advice, he knew he couldn't tell the kapos he was a doctor. He'd be taken away, and Judi, Hanna and Irena would be lost to him for ever. If he kept quiet, Keuper, he felt sure, would return, and God would give him another chance.

One of the kapos had spotted Tomma.

'You with the great chest. What do you do, brother?'

'He's a glassblower,' said Liff, without taking his eyes off a watch mechanism he'd taken from his case and held in his hand. In Lodz, in the ghetto, the watchmaker's inability to engage in the real world around him had constantly drawn the attention of officials. If Liff went out, Stern usually sent Judi along with him to make sure he kept out of trouble.

Tomma glared: '*He's* a watchsmith.'

'Just the glassblower,' said the kapo.

'What for?' replied Tomma. 'You need crystal here? For fine claret? For Riesling?' he asked, trying to keep his voice as light as he could. Tomma had worked in a factory that produced drinking glasses. He'd described each model to them on the journey, from the flute to the *Gluhwein*.

'Don't be a fool,' said the kapo. 'We need your muscles, your great lungs. Be nice or we'll send you down the path for a bath.' At these words, the kapo leered. Stern had guessed the truth: that the opposite of working for the kapos was death, that his life could end here at Borek, or perhaps the next station down the line. What he feared was the moment when even the girls understood.

'I want to wash, eat the meal, and go on,' said Tomma stoutly, clutching Esther, who held both her hands against his face.

The kapo had red-brown-stained teeth and his lips seemed too thin to cover them. Irena thought it looked like he had maggots in his mouth. He pushed Esther aside, took Tomma's face in his hands and whispered in his ear, loudly, so they all heard: 'You don't want to go on, brother.' He then unfurled a massive fist and took Tomma by the collar. 'And you heard. There is no choice.'

Tomma stood his ground effortlessly, bracing his thighs against the kapo's weight, who released his grip only gradually. This movement, this slow-motion retreat that simply suggested the reserves of power unused, was the most threatening thing Stern had seen since they'd got off the train.

'The strong man proves me right,' said the kapo in a loud voice. 'His muscles are too hard for me. Muscle is what we need, brother. There is no choice.'

'I'll look after Esther,' said Stern quickly. 'We'll write.'

Stern instantly regretted his words, knowing that he was given to rash promises, like the one he'd made in Lodz, in the square by the railway station, to keep his family together.

'Go,' added Duvos. 'Before they find someone else.' And then, in a fierce whisper: 'For God's sake, take your chance

Tomma. Look at the fence. *Smell* it. Imagine what we cannot see! We'll look after Esther and her child, when the time
comes.'

Tomma, tortured by the decision he faced, seemed to sway
on his feet, his great fists hanging loose.

Esther suddenly pushed him away, and the strength in her
thin arms was so unexpected he fell backwards to the ground.

The kapos laughed, while two of them put Tomma back on
his feet. He threw them aside and stood looking at Esther. The
kapo who'd selected Tomma was given an iron bar by one of
the others. It was about three feet long with nails knocked
through drilled holes. He let it hang from his fist.

'Walk brother. The woman knows what must be. Don't
fight it now, not on my watch.'

Tomma let out a single breath, and began to walk away,
backwards, never turning his face away from Esther, so
that Stern could see his mouth stupidly open, his face wet
with tears.

Stern felt sympathy for Tomma because he could see how
much he wanted to live. He wondered what Tomma thought
life was – at this point, in this second, what he thought it *en-
tailed*, and what, therefore, he was in danger of losing. Life,
Stern felt, was questions worth asking, a need to know the
future, because you were going to have to negotiate a way
forward. Who was the white-shirted gardener tending his coral reef? What was so interesting about Liff's suitcase? Would
Keuper come back? That was life.

But with each step they took, each minute that passed, such
questions became less important.

Esther waited until he was gone from sight and then
sank to her knees. Irena knelt down beside her with Judi
and Hanna, and while she caressed her friend's hair, she
thought how selfish this was, to distract herself with the
pain of others.

In total the kapos took sixteen men and women, as they said they would. A few shouted promises that they would meet their loved ones up the line.

One man held both arms up with the fingers of his hands outstretched.

'I'll write. Keep safe.'

The kapos looked at their boots.

Chapter 13

Once the kapos had left the Pariser Platz, the prisoners regrouped, families crowding close, everyone waiting for the next order. A teenage boy with a cap tripped into the square wheeling a barrow, circling the prisoners, picking up litter. He kept his eyes down and used a pointed stick to skewer bits of paper. Another slave, without an armband, swept the alleyway that led back to LEFT LUGGAGE CORNER, so that all the footprints were wiped away. No sign that the crowd of prisoners had ever walked this way remained.

Then Keuper reappeared, strolling down the alley, his footsteps following a narrow line.

It was, Stern felt, his last chance.

Letting go of Irena's hand he walked quickly through the crowd to intercept the German. Barring Keuper's path was out of the question, so he judged a sidling approach, inclining his body like a waiter about to offer a plate of canapés.

'Excuse me, Lieutenant. Herr Keuper. I wanted to make myself known at this point. My name is Leopold Stern, the doctor, from Weissenstein? The *family* doctor.'

Keuper's pace did not slow, so Stern was forced to walk with him. The doctor had spoken softly and thought at first he had not been heard. He kept his eyes down, so that he never knew the blow was falling. A sudden heat filled his skull as he blanked out, although consciousness returned before he hit the ground.

Looking up at the sky he found Keuper bending over him from the waist. The German was blinking very rapidly and his hand was on the pistol in his holster.

'I'd get to your feet, Dr Stern, or you may find yourself in the lazarette. Did you think I had not seen you already? For now, we will overlook the fact that you have failed to declare your qualifications. I think we can struggle on without yet another Jew doctor.'

Stern scrambled to his knees and then stood, the image of the square distorted in his head, turning about him like the view from a carousel.

'Do not approach me again,' said Keuper, turning away.

Irena and Judi ran to Stern and helped him to stay on his feet. Irena wiped a trickle of blood from his forehead.

'It's all right, Leo,' she said. 'It's done.'

Hanna appeared then, looking up at her father with wide eyes, transfixed by the sight of blood on his skin. Judi put an arm around her father's waist, and was shocked to feel his weight shift, so that she had to put out a leg to help hold him upright.

'I am not hurt,' said Stern.

'Just rest for a moment,' said Judi. 'You're too pale, father.'

Keuper, offered a fresh wooden mounting block by one of the slaves, took a second to set his uniform straight.

'Hand in your valuables and papers – men to the left, women and children to the right – and we will issue you a ticket for the bathhouse,' he shouted. 'Once you have a ticket you must take off your clothes and queue for the barbers.'

Two small huts stood on a concrete base in a corner of the square, each with an open hatch, as if they were ticket booths. Within each sat a white-shirted official with a pencil behind his ear, the wall behind them covered with lists and printed sheets and calendars. A light-bulb in an iron cage hung above each clerk's head, as if both were waiting to be blessed with an identical, brilliant idea. To Stern, the German love of petty bureaucracy was almost comical, even in this hellish place.

'Keep the ticket with your towel,' continued Keuper. 'Keep nothing else. Do not try to hide anything within your bodies; this is degrading and unnecessary. All valuables will be returned. The bath costs one zloty – put the money in the metal bins provided.'

Stern was still shaking from the blow he had suffered, but he managed to extract the right coins from his wallet, giving three to Irena.

'You tried, Leo,' whispered Irena, and kissed his shoulder.

Stern joined the end of his queue, aware that he was in shock, blood throbbing behind his left temple, where Keuper's blow had fallen. The clerk in the hut took Stern's valuables and sealed them in an envelope, writing a number on the white paper with a fountain pen beside his name. The zloty coin echoed in the bin. His documents, he noted, were set aside in a wicker laundry basket, unread.

The time had come, Keuper announced, for them to go to the barbers', and then to the baths. 'And, after the bathhouse, food! Fresh bread and soup. A broth, yes, but with some mutton. Each will get a bowl.'

To the left of the square stood a long hut. When they'd first arrived it had been shuttered, but now the windows were revealed, and the glint of etched mirrors within. Beyond the reflections stood the barbers, watching, some in leather aprons. They could hear a whetstone being used to sharpen scissors, perhaps, or a blade for shaving. Dimly, Stern discerned the joke: here was Borek's version of the glittering luxury of the Hotel Adlon.

They all began to pick at buttons and string belts. The rabbi raised both hands as if to indicate that this was the final humiliation. A few women began to remove their children's clothes. Irena quickly undressed Hanna, while Judi took off her own clothes, although she blushed fiercely, and her eyes filled with tears. Irena then took off her own dress and underclothes. Because she'd been made to do this, she felt no shame, and she didn't care if anyone else could see her – anyone else but Leo. She looked at her grey marbled skin and stood behind the girls.

Stern worked at the button on his shirt. He couldn't stop the thought forming that this might be the last time he did this; the last time he worked with his nimble fingers to slip the little padded buttons out through the sewn eyes. Or undid his belt. Or slipped the neat double bow on his laces. He'd spent his life being a student and now he'd learnt a great truth: that there is a last time for everything.

Once naked they would do almost anything asked of them. They had learnt this in the ghetto when the Germans searched the tenements and made them stand naked in the street. Without clothes they were children again. That was the cruelty, the dark genius at the heart of their enforced nakedness; that they were allowed to feel young again, and to hope that their lives were back in the hands of people who loved them. It made them trust in fate.

'Women and children to the barbers' ...' shouted a guard.

Stern touched his daughters again quickly, hoping they did not notice, Judi behind one ear, Hanna at the top of her spine below the hairline. Irena touched him on the forehead as she often did. In the moment, he didn't touch her back and – clutching instead at the air where she'd been – he regretted it as she walked away.

Now that they were separated from their families, Stern noticed that most of the men stood apart, avoiding each other's eyes, lost in private thoughts of what lay ahead. Across the sun-baked square edged the shadow of a brick water tower. Otherwise, there was no respite from the heat, except along the pathway ahead into the shadowy trees. Tipping his head back, Stern saw a black-winged kite, a honey buzzard, and four kestrels on the wing. He knew these birds because they flew over the hills of his village. All of them were low in the air, turning in the same lazy thermal. Then he let his eyes focus higher and he glimpsed vultures: circles of birds, hundreds of them, almost beyond his vision, and perhaps beyond number. They turned in a single clockwise spiral as if someone had stirred the sky.

Feeling a moment of despair, Stern turned to a favourite memory. He was standing in the shallow water of the Chiemsee, the great Bavarian lake, on one of the family's annual summer holidays. He'd first come to the village of Graben on the shore with Irena on their honeymoon. Their courtship had revealed a common passion for swimming; in Weissenstein this was restricted to an icy pool further up the valley, which Leo had visited for years. But here the lake stretched to the hazy blue horizon, offering Irena the opportunity to employ her rhythmic, stately breaststroke to swim out to a group of small islands half a mile from the shore while Leo, less adventurous, waited to applaud her return.

But this particular memory was of a day many years later, after the girls were born. Under the water he held Irena's hand. They were about thirty yards out from the sandy beach. The lake was warm but spiced with occasional cold currents, melt water from the high Alps, the shock of which made them clutch each other for warmth.

At this remembered moment he and Irena were studying the distant beach where a few families sat on picnic blankets. Nobody else had entered the water. The Sterns were famous for this, swimming every day that they came while others took the sun or adjourned to the wooden café built on piles that stood in the shadows at the edge of the woods. (Since the *No Jews!* signs had appeared on other beaches, trade here had flourished.) From the water, they could smell lunch on the shore, the aromas of grilled pike, sardines, lamb chops, veal cutlets floating out just above the lake's surface.

On the beach Stern had laid out their picnic blanket for the girls. Judi, engrossed in a book, looked up every few seconds to make sure her parents were still in sight. Hanna was entranced by a sandcastle her father had built, and was decorating it with the beach's many strange, identical, clam-like shells. It was the first time, perhaps, that Stern had seen his youngest child as entirely outside the ambit of his own consciousness, the first fleeting signal of independent life. It filled him with a real sense of selfless joy – an emotion so particular it had no doubt helped imprint the moment on his memory.

He and Irena only had a few minutes together away from the children, so they parted quickly to initiate a small ritual, floating on their backs. Stern, who thought science was beautiful, had told Irena many times the specific forces at work on their bodies at this precise point – principally gravitational attraction, and the differential pressures of water and air. These forces would, inevitably, draw them together, as if they were two boats drifting, like painted ships, on a painted ocean.

To Irena the forces at work were simply Romantic.

They would lie as still as they could; drifting, waiting, their fingers splayed out, their feet extended, their whole bodies tensed for the moment of contact. If the forces of science were inexplicably inactive, Stern would very smoothly ripple the arm furthest from Irena; once, twice, no more.

A few seconds, a minute, and it would happen as it always did: a fingertip to a toe, or Irena's floating hair brushing his leg. Irena would cry out, they'd stand up, and Judi would look up from her book, Hanna from her castle, laughing with them, as their parents launched two fountains of water up into the sky, full of diamonds.

Chapter 14

While the women and children had their heads shaved in the barbers' shop, the kapos returned with a group of sixteen bedraggled slaves. Stern thought that this was typical of the Germans; that there would be a rigid system in place, that those earlier chosen to work in the camp exactly matched a predetermined number already deemed too old, or too ill or exhausted to be of further use. These men and women looked spent, half dead: one boy, only a teenager, tried to stand still, but the effort made his legs shake. Kopp, the leader, gestured to the group to take their clothes off, and they instantly complied, although he looked away as if embarrassed, removing his glasses to clean the broken lens.

Beyond the high fence of blankets and dead wood they heard the machine again, revving, grinding. David, the plumber from their tenement block in Lodz, was standing beside Stern. His family name was Todt but the boy was known only as David, a sign perhaps that despite being seventeen he had yet to mature into manhood. His mother and father had been taken away to the Radegast station on one of the early trains for the East, leaving him alone in the family's single room.

David, Stern learnt, was fascinated by the way machines worked, especially pipes and wires, laid out in systems and networks. The ghetto council had organised a school – just three hours a day – but David had been a brilliant pupil, and Stern had told him many times that if he worked hard he could become a scientist one day.

'The noise you can hear – not the diggers, the other one, the new one. Tank engine,' said David. Stern concentrated on the palette of sound and detected a lighter, arrhythmic note. He had long suspected that the boy's obsession with all things mechanical helped divert a feeling of helplessness.

'A captured Russian tank,' said David. 'No doubt the T-34. Twelve-cylinder engine. Idle, stationary, just ticking over, do you hear it? It needs looking at.'

The engine coughed and backfired as if in reply.

A dull shot came from the direction of the unseen lazarette, and then for the first time they heard dogs. Looking towards the shady trees, they saw them, Alsatians with black dirty snouts being pulled along on leads by a squad of Ukrainie into the sunshine of the square.

At the entrance to the barbers' hut the queue was almost gone. One of the last women waiting ran a hand through her hair. A guard said something to her and pointed at her face, knocking the soap and towel from her hands and reaching out a hand to her ear, ripping something away. The blood on his fingers was arterial-red as he held up an earring to the light, a jewel catching the sun. The woman screamed, and this seemed to signal the beginning of the end. A keening had begun among the women who had been shorn, but now the note changed, and one or two began to beat at their own heads with their fists.

Only the children were now innocent of what was about to happen.

Through the entrance, under the metal arch, Stern could see more guards approaching with dogs.

One guard in a sweat-blotched black uniform got behind them. 'The water is getting cold in the bathhouse!' he shouted.

The women with shaved heads ran to join the men, relieved to be reunited, but afraid of the dogs. Irena, with the girls by the hand, emerged from the crowd, her face a mask of stretched white skin. Stern felt utterly helpless, reminded of the crushing burden of responsibility he bore for his family. His held his wife's head for comfort, noting that its new shape was not ugly at all – it was very round, and noble, without the bulges of bone at the back that disfigured some. Stern thought that it was sad to discover something new and beautiful about her now.

'The bathhouse, the bathhouse!' The cry went up, like a chant among the guards, and the dogs began to strain at their leads.

A shout behind them brought silence with its authority. 'Stern! The Jew, Stern. Where is he?'

A Ukrainian guard with a smart uniform was already just a few steps away, his eyes locked on the family. He looked the doctor up and down, as if matching the physical reality to an abstract description.

'Leopold Stern?'

'Yes,' said Stern.

The guard clamped a hand around Stern's upper arm, and pulled him off his feet, dragging him away.

Looking back, shouting Irena's name, Stern saw the shock on Judi's face, as she clutched her sister. Hanna, her arms hanging down limply, stood watching, her face registering the moment of unexpected loss. The rest of the crowd was being herded through the gate along the path.

By the time the guard had dragged Stern to the alleyway between the barrack blocks, the doctor was on his knees. For a moment he heard only the harsh breath of the soldier, then a whiplash fell across his back, making him leap to his feet and run forward.

The first square was now empty except for the pile of luggage, and the neat lines of food and clothes, books and shoes. To one side of the mountain of suitcases the fire was burning fitfully.

Beside the flames, upwind of the smoke and heat, stood Jonas Keuper.

Chapter 15

It was immediately clear to Stern that Jonas Keuper was a different man when not acting out the public role of an SS Obersturmführer. The ramrod back, the slightly jutting chin, the pivot at the hips; all were gone, as if some unseen puppeteer's strings had been cut. His crippled leg was now apparent because he was not making the effort of holding the twisted limb in line with its undamaged partner. Smoking, the cigarette held loosely between the lips, his natural voice emerged an octave lower than the one he'd used to harangue Transport 573.

'Ask the question you wish to ask of me, doctor. The one you were trying to ask in the second square.'

'I hoped only that you might be able to find jobs here for my wife and daughters,' Stern said, deciding that honesty and directness were the only ways he might win Keuper's support. And there had to be hope: why else had the German sought this meeting?

'I see. And yourself, no doubt?'

Stern forced himself to answer in a loud voice. 'Yes. For myself, but lastly for myself.'

'Do I owe you anything, doctor? Why should I do this? An appendicitis, I think? Ritter that time. Yes, we used the Jewish doctor – we all did. You were a good doctor. But you were well paid for this.'

Keuper paused, remembering. 'And my mother; she had shingles, which you treated, and Father had a hernia and then Mother had varicose veins – and so on. The life of a small German village. The life of its doctor. So much, and so little.'

'And I tried to reset your leg,' said Stern. 'After the visit to Munich.' Stern had no idea if this is what he should have said, but Keuper's intellect appeared so cold, so *procedural*, he felt that the truth could not be a mistake.

'Indeed. Munich. That was my stupid father's decision, of course. To send his son to a butcher surgeon in the city to cut into the twisted leg and straighten the bones. And yes, doctor, you tried to redress the damage.'

He tipped his head to one side. 'But without success. A shame. Now *that* might have won you all a reprieve. But I am not bitter about your failure.' He laughed sourly.

'You only have to look at our noble Reich Minister for Propaganda. You know that he too is a cripple?'

Stern shook his head in a lie. The image of Joseph Goebbels was indelible, standing at a microphone, speaking to the nation, saluting from a cruising car. But everyone gossiped about the limp, the metal cage on the left leg, and the clubfoot.

'Yes. A halting figure. But he has risen above ridicule, has he not? Power has done this, Stern. Men see only the leader beneath the uniform, or the sharp suit. Very sharp suits, in his case.'

Again the smile, immediately curtailed. He checked his wristwatch. 'You want to live? You want your family to live?'

The dogs howled.

'Yes, I want them to live. I want to live.'

Keuper began a series of small nods, as if agreeing with an internal inquisitor. 'There are three squares in all,' he said. 'In a moment you can join your people in the final one. I wanted to ask a question before you completed your journey; it won't take up much of the time left to you, and it is just possible that the right answer might save the lives of your daughters.'

Stern brought his palms together in a gesture of thanks, but perhaps Keuper saw it as a symbol of a greater hope, for he held up his own hand. 'Not you, I'm afraid, Dr Stern. Or your wife. Just the girls. It's a question about the past. A question about the village.'

Stern would die with his wife: the fate he had long expected was confirmed. He felt no grief or fear, and this was no time to dwell on death, because the fate of his daughters still hung in the balance.

An SS trooper approached with a wad of forms for Keuper to sign.

'One moment,' said Keuper, smiling at the doctor, tipping his head by way of an apology. The trooper looked dumbfounded by the politeness shown by an SS lieutenant to a Jew, but Stern saw the gesture for what it was: exaggerated deference designed to emphasise the extent of Keuper's intellectual sophistication.

Stern heard screaming from the second square, the voices of women and children, and then the manic barking of the hounds. The thought of his family passing beneath the metal archway to tread the path beyond without him was unbearable.

Keuper signed the last form and gave the papers back to the trooper, who saluted and left. He then produced from the black leather pouch carried by the smartest of SS officers, the white envelope Stern had handed in at the little hut on the Pariser Platz. He slipped out Stern's notebook and then emptied the rest of the contents on to it, holding it horizontally, like a platter. Stern noted that his hand was very steady. He reminded himself of the rage with which Keuper had pistol-whipped the defenceless cobbler. Which version of Keuper's character was real: the cruel and brutal anti-Semite, or this diffident, methodical officer? Here was a scientific issue of professional interest to Stern: whether two personalities could coexist, or whether one was a screen for the other.

Keuper tipped the items back into the envelope but held the book out at arm's length. 'What is this, precisely?'

'A notebook, for observations,' said Stern, impatient to know the question upon which so much now relied: the lives of Judi and Hanna. 'There's a sketch of the castle at home I think, from memory.'

The distant barking of dogs reached a crescendo and Stern turned away to look back. The vista, through to the second square, was blocked by the barrack buildings, because the alleyway between them was set at an angle. When he looked back, Keuper was turning the pages of the notebook, taking a childish joy from the sketches: the interior of a walnut, a sycamore seed, an earlobe, a neat, scribbled note on the life cycle of the mosquito.

'No diary?' he asked, the face transformed, all emotion falling from its lines and folds.

'No.'

'Letters?'

Stern shrugged: 'Who to? Who from?'

'Don't try to be clever, doctor. To your friends and family. You had a great number of friends I recall. The parties in your orchard were a great feature of village life, under the awning in summer. And you must have a teeming family no doubt – a biblical tree of Sterns, spread across Germany, and beyond.'

'They've gone before.'

'Friends still in Weissenstein?'

'No. None.'

Stern saw that the German still held the gold ring he'd put in the envelope, which had been his mother's.

The sun caught the dull glint of the metal and a memory came to Stern of his mother's hands, moving towards his face with a rough cloth to wipe away food. He could have drawn those hands in his notebook – every line, each nail. And he could smell her, the family flat in Berlin: his father's tobacco, boiling sheets, potato water. He had never rehearsed this memory, it came now to him for the first time, and he couldn't help concluding it was an intimation of his own death. For the first time since he'd got off the train, he thought he would cry, and he felt his bottom lip bow upwards to fight it back.

'Tears, doctor? Why tears? Why now?' asked Keuper. 'Not for yourself, I hope. What awaits you and your wife will be swift and merciful compared to the fate of your people before these camps were built. Believe me. We wielded pistols for hours beside festering pits. Many of us are veterans of *that* campaign, for which there will be no medals.'

The SS officer lit a cigarette, then retrieved the siddur, the prayer book from the envelope, glancing at a few pages before tossing it to the ground. Stern had memorised the prayers he loved and was comforted by the idea that the *word* would endure. He wondered if Keuper had any idea of the extent to which the Jews could survive without the things they'd had to leave behind so many times.

'Where is your suitcase?' asked Keuper. 'Is there a diary there, perhaps? Or papers, documents. Please, find it. Quickly.'

Stern retraced his steps around the pile of luggage and found the spot where the group of Leszno Street residents had left their suitcases. He searched for a minute, no more, but was quite sure his case had gone. What did Keuper want? He'd said he had a question, but why the obsession with letters, diaries and notebooks?

'It's not here,' he said. 'I don't think any of our cases are here, not just my family's, the residents of our tenement block too. Someone has taken them away. Or they have been burnt already.'

'Did you paint your name on the suitcase?'

'Yes.'

'Very well. I will have a proper search conducted in due course.'

Keuper held out a hand, inviting Stern, with a slight bow, to walk on. But the doctor saw through this small piece of theatre, because Keuper stumbled slightly, and had to clutch at the twisted leg. This vulnerability revealed the German to Stern as yet another individual: a third personality to complement the other two.

He's afraid. He's consumed with fear, just as I am.

Keuper appeared to make an effort to push aside the idea of the missing suitcase. He began to stroll, indicating with his hand that Stern should join him, as if they were taking the air on an elegant terrace.

Keuper lit a fresh cigarette, offered one to Stern, which he took, although in any single year he smoked – perhaps – three cigars.

'So. *The question*,' said Keuper.

They walked on in a torture of silence. 'Tell me the secrets of our village, Stern. Tell me the best gossip.'

Keuper paused and lit the doctor's cigarette. Stern had begun to shake, unnerved by the constant alternation between menace and civility.

'What secrets could we have? A hundred souls on a hillside in Bavaria?' asked Stern, the nicotine making his eyes swim.

'If you want the girls to live, tell me the secrets of Weissenstein.'

Stern had no doubt Keuper was serious in the bargain that he offered.

'There's always gossip,' he said, coughing. For a terrifying moment the village seemed a lost lifetime ago. What could he recall? He tried to think of all the people, in their houses, and at their various trades.

'Eugen, the carter, did he have an affair with the baker's wife?' he offered. 'And Klaus Faltermeyer at the inn, they said he tried to touch the children when he made ice cream. Other stories … When they built the new barn by Mann's Yard, they say they found bones in a pit but they kept it quiet. And there's a ghost in the orchard below the castle.'

All this tumbled out of Stern's head. He took a deep breath, this time drawing the cigarette fumes down his throat and into his lungs. The surge of nicotine in his blood made him feel idiotically hopeful.

'Tell me about the ghost,' said Keuper, inclining his head politely.

'A child, a pale child, sometimes in the forest, sometimes in the orchard. Singing sadly. The children say he's there at dusk sometimes. So they keep away.'

'I don't remember that story,' said Keuper.

'It began just after the war started. You had left then?'

'Yes. I had. Has anyone talked to the ghost?'

It was an odd question, but Stern made himself consider an answer with the upmost seriousness. 'Never. It is just the stuff of fertile minds. Anxious minds. The war makes us all think of the dead.'

'And this is all there is? The secrets of Weissenstein? Did my family not have any secrets?'

'Your brothers?' asked Stern, too quickly.

Keuper stopped walking and turned. He tried to smile but his eyes were murderous.

He hates me now. The brothers; this is about the brothers.

'There was Christoph,' said Stern swiftly. 'A wonderful child. An innocent. And Ritter. A fine boy.'

Keuper spat in the dust. 'Platitudes. Ritter fights for his country. I am a proud brother. Christoph was an imbecile, but loyal. What did the village say about him, doctor? No, what did *you* say? You were the village doctor. What, Herr doctor, was your diagnosis of Christoph?'

'He suffered from epilepsy.' Another mistake, he saw, because so had Jonas. 'But most seriously there were signs of microcephaly – an undeveloped brain.'

'And what did the village say happened to my little brother in the end?'

'That he was taken away to the hospital in Regensberg. A panel of doctors was appointed by Berlin to judge each case. The Führer wished the race to be cleansed of those who might contaminate the nation. Some lives, he proclaimed, were not worth living, and in wartime they were a burden on their families when everyone was striving for victory. Certain cases were earmarked for sterilisation. They were taken to care centres. One was in Austria, a place called Hartheim, where there is a schloss with high walls. Christoph died there.

'As his doctor I saw the death certificate. It said pneumonia was the cause.'

Keuper seemed to come to a decision: 'Bravo. A secret after all. The Führer's own doctor ran this programme of course. It had a code name, yes?'

'Aktion T4,' said Stern.

'Indeed. Tiergartenstrasse 4, the Berlin address of this noble enterprise. But you have not told the complete truth, doctor.'

'No. Many died. Not just Christoph. None came back, in fact,' said Stern. 'And they all died of pneumonia. Every doctor in Bavaria had compared notes on the death certificates – every doctor in Germany in fact. It was a silent scandal.'

'Indeed,' said Keuper. 'The state killed them. This was the law, but yes, a secret nonetheless. But not the one that will save your daughters.'

Fatigue, pain, and now despair crushed Stern's spirit, and he was unable to stop himself sinking to his knees. For the first time in his life, he sought death as a way to end his own suffering.

'I'm begging you to show sympathy for my family – not me. My daughters, my wife. Give them jobs.'

Keuper turned away, embarrassed by this show of abasement.

Stern shut his eyes, wove the fingers of his left hand into those of the right, and raised both hands in an act of supplication. He was aware that this was not the right thing to do: the right thing – his one chance – had passed by. There was something in the past that might have saved the girls. Keuper wanted to know if he shared the secret, if he'd committed it to paper even, in a diary or a letter. But the moment had gone. Instead, Stern would beg for their lives. And he would be rebuffed. But he could tell Irena that he'd tried, and at least she would think he'd done all he could.

When Stern lifted his head, Keuper was beckoning with his hand to someone unseen.

A very small boy appeared at his elbow with a glass of water. With a dull shock Stern realised the child had a withered leg and wore an iron cage from his hip to the ankle.

Stern could see ice inside the glass, capturing the sunlight, so that a shard of rainbow fell on the sand.

'This is over now,' said Keuper, draining the water and tipping the ice on to the ground. 'Go and join your family.'

Chapter 16

Stern ran free back down the alleyway into Pariser Platz and under the metal arch towards the trees, desperate to find his family, noticing a painted sign on a stake by the path:

DIE HIMMELSTRAßE

[THE ROAD TO HEAVEN]

The Jews were waiting, guarded by the Ukrainie, their dogs lying in the shade. A lot of the women were crying, all were shorn, and several had smears of blood where the scissors had grazed their scalps. Some of the men tried to quieten the women by holding their heads to their chests so that their lips moved against skin and ribs. Most of the children were crying too, clutching at the unfamiliar naked flesh of legs and thighs.

Stern's arrival seemed to be a signal, for the Ukrainie started herding them on again, down the path. Irena and the girls ran to Stern. Irena was shaking very badly, and hugging Hanna tightly with both arms.

'Mama's cold,' said Stern to the girls, kissing his wife on her newly shaven head.

Judi put her arms round Irena's middle from behind. She was already as tall as her mother and so she kissed her on the back of the head.

'Keuper won't help us,' he said to Irena, trying not to sound desperate. Judi could hear everything now, but then Stern felt she knew the truth already.

'Not even the girls?' whispered Irena.

'No. He won't.' He knew it would come to this. 'I begged. On my knees.'

'To the bathhouse!' the guards shouted, beginning to herd them down the path, away from the Pariser Platz, and deeper into the dappled sunlight of the trees, which were birch, bone-white and architectural, creating a strange green half-light beneath the two-tone leaves.

The path wound onwards, every square inch of the sand imprinted with the heel, ball and toes of those who had gone before. Once they were all moving forward, the guards dropped back, leashing the dogs, so that the prisoners could stumble ahead. Judi held her father by the arm, supporting him, while Hanna walked beside her mother, clutching her naked thigh, which was cool and a comfort.

The view through the wire fences on either side of the path was very different. To the left they could see sunburnt grass running up to an outer perimeter wire and the forest. To the right the fence, although laced with pine boughs, gave fleeting glimpses of open ground stretching to the apron of trees. It was here that the digger was working. If they looked, they could now see that it was lifting bodies out of pits and dumping them in piles. Towards the edge of the forest other pits had been dug, and over these, concrete girders had been placed in grids, on which the dead were burning.

At this sight, some of them began to shout and swear, turning back to face the guards and their dogs.

A young man, his face wet with tears, shouted out: 'The Russians will come! They're a hundred miles away but getting closer every day. Soon they will be here and, when they are, you will beg to be with us on the fires. But,' he spat, 'you'll die slowly, pig shit. They'll make you squeal.'

An old man knelt down in the sand and raised both his arms to the sky as if in prayer or addressing the dead: 'The

Russians will avenge us, Mother. We'll look down and watch, you and I.'

A teenager got close to one of the guards, a Ukrainian who was sweating so badly there was a drip under his chin. 'God sees you, fuck-face! Right now, this second, he knows your name.'

'They're going to kill us. Don't be fooled any more!' The man who said this looked round at his neighbours as if they didn't know the truth themselves. 'Say your prayers! Kiss the children!'

The guards were trying to keep their grins wide, but their eyes betrayed them; flitting back and forth, bright with fear for their own lives.

'Cowards!' a woman shouted, spitting at their feet. 'Think of your own sisters, your own children. You think the Russians will pass by in the night?'

Judi brought her face very close to her father's.

'Who will punish them, father?' she asked. It wasn't a cruel question, Stern knew, because there was no note of accusation within it. But her life had been reduced to this, a shady path in the Polish woods. Even now, within a few yards, perhaps, of the end of the journey, she was still curious. The fact that she believed there would be a just reckoning broke Stern's heart at last.

And then the pathway was at an end. Before them was what looked like a temple. A long, low stone building with a row of metal doors. Lettering, scrawled over the fine ashlar block over the door in chalk, read:

THE HACKENDORF FOUNDATION

At one end of the building they could see the chassis of a tank, the gun barrel swaddled in blankets. A soldier with thin blond hair, standing beside it, was drinking something from a tin mug. He was licking his lips as if he couldn't remove a taste from them.

One of the guards shouted: 'Hackendorf – say hello!' All the guards laughed, letting the dogs snap at the prisoners.

The soldier waved wearily. Stern noted this man's oily fingers, and the way that nicotine had discoloured his meagre moustache. Beside him stood a slave – a woman – who refilled his tin mug with liquor from a green bottle. Her hair was long and black, and brushed to a sheen. It was a remarkable sight in this strange world where all the other women had naked bony skulls.

A Ukrainian guard they had not seen before stood on the top of a set of stone steps that led up to the doors of the chamber. Although black and worn, his uniform looked as if it had been washed and ironed. There was some kind of silver insignia on his epaulettes.

'The water in the bathhouse is getting cold,' he said, but without feeling or intonation of any kind. He didn't look directly at them when he spoke, addressing the words to his fellow guards instead. The tank at the far end of the block was silent, and Hackendorf had gone, but his woman was sweeping the steps, singing quietly, her voice as liquid as her long black hair. The song, a soft Hebrew lamentation, had calmed them all. Stern could see that lots of those around him were now whispering prayers to themselves.

The Ukrainian guard began to open the doors. Stern saw now that each had a peep-hole set at eye level, and that the interior of the chamber was bare concrete, the ceiling studded with showerheads. The far side of the chamber, which he could just see, was also full of doors, again each one studded with a peep-hole.

'Into the bathhouse!' cried the guard. 'Into the bathhouse.'

The prisoners stood their ground. Stern thought it was an oddity of the human condition that the value of dignity should rise so quickly with the imminent arrival of death. As the moral worth of the killers fell, so the intrinsic value of the victims rose, a shifting equation that made of the moment an unexpected miracle.

A voice shouted: 'Halt!'

The Ukrainie retreated, just a few feet, reining in the dogs. Stern thought they must live like this now, as if they were a single organism, electrified by their own fears, seeing the world out of the corner of a common eye.

The German officer Meyer stood, hands on hips, on the path behind them, holding Liff's suitcase. Jonas Keuper was beside him.

Keuper's hands were behind his back and Stern, who felt now that he knew something of his adult character, guessed that this was because they were shaking.

Meyer stepped forward, holding a piece of paper upon which there were typed words, and a crest: a swastika in red. He said something in the Ukrainian's ugly language and the guards walked away, back into the shade of the trees, dragging the dogs with them.

Hackendorf's woman stopped singing.

'My name is Obersturmführer Meyer. I have a short announcement to make.'

Keuper turned his head away from his fellow officer, looking at the dust beneath his feet.

'Which of you is Liff?' asked Meyer.

Liff stepped forward, both knees giving way, so that he stumbled and had to scramble back to his feet.

Meyer unclipped the lock on Liff's suitcase and it fell open to reveal the clockwork and wires.

'The Gestapo have been informed of the contents of this suitcase. A week ago, near Lublin, a bomb exploded on a transport train. The device was made by Jews. Polish partisans were part of the plot. They killed the German guards.

'The prisoner Liff will be taken to the cells, and all those who travelled with him from 87 Sattlergasse as listed on the manifest. Step forward.'

Stern took his daughters round the waist, and his wife followed. David clung to the doctor, his soft hands on his back, Duvos was in tow, and finally Esther emerged from the crowd.

Keuper's head jerked up and he said something to Meyer, speaking into the gap between his fellow officer's broad shoulder and his ear. The movement seemed designed to be casual, but Stern thought there was something pleading in the inclination of his upper body.

Meyer shook his head.

This unleashed Keuper: if he'd been a mechanical man, it was the moment the pent-up energy held in the internal spring was set free, transferring its latent power to the metal limbs. He moved forward very quickly, his elbows held out for balance, the knees high. The limp in his damaged leg was disguised to perfection.

Meyer went to follow, but then appeared to decide that it was best to hold his ground. Instead, he kept his body in an attitude of authority; stiff, with the shoulders back. But his blue eyes were moving quickly across the faces of the prisoners.

'This is not seemly,' said Meyer. 'I am quite determined to follow procedure.' He paused, to fill his lungs, adding: 'Obersturmführer. I must remind you of the regulations.'

Keuper had come to a halt ten feet away from the prisoners. His left shoulder jerked forward, his knee gave way, and his tongue worked in his mouth, as if he had been overcome with thirst.

'Keuper,' said Meyer. 'Consider this action.'

Keuper fumbled with the catch on his leather holster but managed to extract the gun. It had been polished to an almost liquid, slippery shine, and for a moment Stern thought he might drop it.

'Red tape. More red tape.' Keuper said this very loudly. 'For sabotage the military code makes it quite clear that the punishment is death and that summary execution is entirely appropriate.'

'Keuper!' Meyer snapped the sheet of paper in his hand, a quite distinctive sound.

Keuper raised his own voice. 'I too have examined the suitcase of the watchmaker Liff, and interviewed his accomplice, the doctor Stern.'

The pistol came up quickly, levelled at Liff.

'A saboteur,' said Keuper. 'The watchmaker manufactures the trigger with his wires and clockwork. Summary execution is in order.'

Meyer seemed to relax, giving up, throwing his head back, as if he too wanted to watch the circling vultures.

Keuper cocked the trigger, then swung the gun round quickly towards Stern.

'But the doctor provides the explosives, no doubt secreted in the missing suitcase. You are the leader, not the idiot Liff. You should die first.'

Stern could see the dark eye of the gun barrel and the little silver ring of the tip. The girls turned their heads away. Irena's nails dug into his palm. All this in a second punctuated by a tumbling heartbeat.

Keuper's narrow arm shook as his fingers took the pressure of the trigger.

There was a gunshot.

That part of Keuper's skull that held his right eye flew away. The half of his face that remained intact registered frozen shock.

Irena screamed, falling to her knees.

Keuper's nervous system must have shorted out because he sat straight down – collapsed, as it were, into his own body, so that his spine appeared to support only his upper skeleton, and he ended up sitting among his own senseless legs. His head still held quite steadily on the spinal column.

Shouts and cries filled the air, and the dogs barked wildly.

Then – after another second in which Stern's heart did not beat at all – the German's skull tipped back. The teeth, top set and bottom, clashed, his shoulders dropped and the remaining eye closed. His body fell into the dust, but in falling his fingers tightened on his pistol and he fired a last, random, shot.

Meyer's holster was open, the arm that held his gun held slightly away from the body like that of a gunslinger. The German's face was drenched in sweat. He fumbled with the gun in trying to return it to its holster.

The sound of the sharp pistol shots, quite different from the dull percussion of gunfire from the lazarette, circled them, echoes returning from the trees.

They heard shouting almost immediately. The guards were suddenly around them, a cordon of yelling dogs on strained leads.

Meyer went to speak to the head guard but his voice failed.

He took a deep breath. 'These few prisoners must be interrogated. Take them to the cells by the station.' The guard didn't move, so Meyer repeated the order in their own guttural language.

Keuper's body made obscene noises and one of his legs kicked out.

Stern, finally, was able to look away.

Then, more gunshots, and two SS guards and an officer ran out of the shadows. The officer was Sandberger and he went directly to Keuper's body and used a boot to tilt what was left of the head.

He turned to Meyer. 'Well done, Rolf. You do this today? Of all days?'

Taking off his glasses he held them loosely by the metallic arm. He was disappointed in his friend as a parent might be in a child who has under-performed on sport's day.

'These prisoners must be interrogated,' said Meyer. 'The watchmaker is a saboteur. There is a request from the Gestapo at Lublin.'

He offered his fellow officer the sheet of paper.

Reading it with a single glance, Sandberger turned to the guards. 'Take this group of prisoners back to the square and wait for me. Escort Obersturmführer Meyer to the mess.'

Finally, he looked up at the Ukrainie officer on the steps. 'Continue as if nothing has happened. The bathhouse is ready. The water is hot. The Jews are dirty.'

The flies had already found Jonas Keuper's body.

Hackendorf's beautiful slave, her face a mask, began to sing again.

Chapter 17

Hanna swam Olympic lengths in the green water, overseen by two ten-foot-tall Prussian soldiers, hewn from stone, standing guard either side of the entrance to the pool. Always backstroke, so that she could count the iron ribs of the arcing roof and reach out at just the right moment to touch the tiles, tumble, kick and find her rhythm anew. Two summers ago, she'd swum with Peter at the Lido in Venice, effortlessly carving an Adriatic mile across the grey sea. Last summer they'd climbed the wooden steps behind Swan House to the high river, and tasted the salty water on their lips, because the great sluices were open to the distant sea. The pool here reeked of military efficiency – chlorine and its associated gases – which hovered just above the shimmering surface of the water. Peter was making his own waves, his butterfly strokes a series of fluid explosions in the far lane.

Touch, tumble, kick and she settled again into her sinuous breaststroke. Did her body lie strangely in the water? She thought of the child turning sluggishly within her, floating within her, as she floated within the waters of Andrews Barracks. Weightless, she felt free of the burden she carried each waking hour. The appointment at the clinic off Harley Street was six days away. Her body had not betrayed her yet, and only Vanessa shared her secret still. She'd used more of Marcin's money to get herself a return train ticket, propelled here to share with Peter the mysterious letter claiming her father was still alive, posted from the Soviet Sector, Berlin. *Der*

Springer was a talisman, and she had it with her always – even now, tucked away in the locker with her clothes. Who had sent it to her? Why could they say no more? Was her father here, in the beleaguered city? Was the chess piece a clue?

She reached the far end of the pool, noted that the hands on the numberless stone clock had reached noon, and hauled herself out of the water, begrudging the moment when gravity took back control, her bones settling, her shoulders aching. She found her towel on a marble bench and sat down as two GIs plummeted from the diving board, watched by a staff sergeant with a clipboard. Through the tall windows she could see snow falling on the barrack blocks and a dismal parade ground, while the pale light lay across the pool in white, bloodless, splashes. Although frosty outside, the air inside was moist and fetid, and left her skin damp however hard she rubbed her face with the towel. The sense of claustrophobic compression reminded her of listless afternoons with Vanessa, sketching orchids in the hothouse at Kew.

Peter hauled himself out of the water and sat beside her, their skin not touching.

He examined his hands, ridged by the water, and she noted the black paint caught beneath a fingernail. This was their third day at the pool, each day's swim preceding a visit to the Berlin Document Centre, a mile south, and then a return to the gallery.

Hanna closed her eyes. 'I'd die if I couldn't swim,' she said.

Peter nodded, rubbing roughly at his face with the towel. 'Next life we'll be fish, Han. You and me. It's elemental – one world swapped for another. A sense of freedom. Big question is – will we be in the same pond, same river, same sea?'

He looked away, not expecting an answer. Hanna took off her swimming cap and dried her hair. They sat in silence watching the GIs climbing back up the metal stairs of the diving board, then plummeting expertly into the pool.

Peter checked his watch, brushing aside the drops of water on the face. 'We better shift. There's ten canvases arriving this afternoon, all paid for by my new best friends – the US government. I'm a kept man now. The ambassador in Bonn has asked for a private visit. Pierce – the guy from the State Department you met at The Nut Tree, right? – he's the fixer, he says the *Trib*'s sending a critic to the opening, and the guy from *The Atlantic*.'

Zum Nussbaum was Peter's favourite bar. He'd only been in the city three weeks but already knew all the waiters by name.

'You'll stay for the private view?' he asked, slinging his towel over his shoulder.

'I'll stay. I want to see those pictures on a gallery wall. And there's always the free champagne. Then I have to go, Pete. Lydia's weak.'

Lydia's health had in fact improved quickly after the floods, but her aunt's great age afforded a constant excuse to return to Long Fen.

In the fug of the narrow changing booth, she thought about Peter – the *new* Peter, calm, patient, oddly watchful. The ground rules of their relationship had been set on her first night. Officials from the US Mission had found him an attic studio a minute's walk from the gallery. He'd dutifully set aside the bedroom for Hanna while he used the sofa in the loft. They'd spent three days being polite, treating each other like old friends, although he'd casually told her he'd never had time to make that trip out West, to Artesia, to see his lost son. And sometimes she caught a look in his eyes, a suspicion lurking there that something was remaining unsaid. She could see hope too, in those same eyes, encouraged by her visit, her decision not to cut the emotional thread between them.

Weighed down with Marcin's old coat, and a woollen hat, she met him on the snowy steps outside, and they marched together through the snow to the guardhouse, a stout brick block, adorned with the Kaiser's arms in stone, an echo of the barracks' imperial past.

A US soldier slid back the glass window and offered Peter the logbook so that he could sign them both out, next to a blue stamp that said Congress for Cultural Freedom – 1961. His ID card for the Allied Sectors was returned to him from a pigeon-hole.

'Klaus here says it won't stop now,' said the guard, the accent Mid-West, a farm kid perhaps. He nodded to a man in overalls sweeping the back office. 'He says it'll just get colder, and colder, until the lakes freeze. You two skate back home?'

Hanna's face brightened. 'If it's cold enough you can't stop us.'

'I'm from Nebraska. I was born on skates,' added Peter.

The guard took back the pen and nodded towards a framed picture of the new president on top of a TV set.

'You see it?' asked the guard.

Peter shook his head. Kennedy's inauguration had been in January and the bars on 18th Street had shown the pictures, but the usual babble had drowned out the words, although he'd read them later in the papers.

'We reckon he's gonna sort out the Ivans. Heard the latest?'

Berlin was a city that lived on gossip.

The guard leant closer. 'Khrushchev's sent in missiles – nukes – to East Germany, but he left the locals to guard them over winter. The fuel was in bowsers. So, these guys get thirsty OK, and they have a sip. It's 92 per cent ethanol, that's 184 per cent proof.'

Klaus whistled, leaning on his broom, enjoying the tale.

'So they drank the lot,' said the guard. 'Took 'em three months. They mixed it with soda and called it Blue Danube!'

Peter struggled to get his gloves on after signing the log.

'They've been out cold ever since!' concluded the guard, feeding the city's prejudice against the East Germans, the *Ossies*.

'I guess it *was* rocket fuel,' said Peter.

The guard blew out a plume of breath, clapping his hands, then slid the glass closed.

Out here near the city limits the bombsites were intermittent, so that the tram approaching seemed to emerge out of a canyon of brick and overhead wires, clanging past, to leave them walking in the quilted silence. At one spot, beside a ruined church, Hanna glimpsed a desolate stretch of rubble, beyond which lay a flooded crater, a film of ice forming a mottled pattern. A woman bound up in coats picked through the ruins, one of the dwindling band who'd cleared the city in the years after the final battle. Whenever Hanna saw one of these women, she was overcome by the feeling that she was watching a ghost in broad daylight, completing some sentence set for those in Purgatory.

The search for news of the Stern family had brought them to this wasteland each afternoon. Peter had turned for help to his old commanding officer at Camp Ashcan – Major Clarke, currently heading up the Berlin Military Mission, at Andrews Barracks. (He'd got them the permit to use the Olympic pool.) Clarke knew Secretary Pierce – Peter's liaison officer at the State Department. They were all part of a tight-knit group of shadowy players representing the city's four governing powers – the US, British, French and even the Soviets; a club that everyone called the 'Berlin mafia'. Between them Clarke and Pierce had been happy to open doors in the search for the Sterns, meaning that Peter had been able to check the city archive, sift through the Nuremberg papers in the Justice Department library, and had access to the Borek files at the Berlin Document Centre. Pierce had asked to see Hanna's mysterious letter with its SOVIET SECTOR postmark, and offered to pass it on for 'expert analysis', which Peter said was 'spook-talk' for the CIA.

But so far, his efforts had drawn a blank, save for the original manifest of Transport 573, buried away in the BDC files. All that was left were the tapes.

Reaching a street corner, they saw the sign for the BDC in the teeming gloom, and turned down a street of deserted five-storey flats. There was a café on the corner, with misted windows, but Hanna could see two old men playing chess. Since she'd arrived at the railway station, she'd been studying faces, especially the chess players of Berlin, looking for the echo of her own broad cheek-bones. Peter agreed that *der Springer* must be a clue of itself, not just a random gift. He'd contacted the organisers of the city's chess league and put a note in their newsletter asking for news of Leopold Stern. He'd also made a flyer and visited local chess clubs. But there had been the familiar sullen silence. Clarke had contacted his opposite number in East Berlin and asked them to circulate Leo Stern's details to clubs and bars – another Sisyphean task Hanna felt was doomed to fail. The sudden hope she'd felt when *der Springer* had fallen out of the envelope in Marcin's office that night on Long Fen now seemed like an echo of a past life.

Ahead, along the street, not a single footprint or car track broke the snow, which lay a foot deep. At the far end, a concrete bunker blocked the way forward, its entry ramp a shadowy mouth, angling down into the earth. A single yellow bulb shone in the gloom of the entrance. As they approached, a man appeared, climbing the steps, rising from the subterranean depths. As the stranger passed, he lit a cigarette with a match, and Hanna caught the distinct whiff of sulphur.

Finally, two sets of iron doors brought them to a marble desk, at which sat a soldier in immaculate white cuffs. 'We're booked in,' said Peter, giving him the card. Hanna recognised the young soldier from their previous visits, but she'd already learnt, in the great bureaucracy that was Berlin, that a smile was not always welcome.

The guard swung round an entry log, and asked for passport, sector ID, and introductory letter of confirmation. Peter produced them all. Hanna noticed a line of perspiration on his forehead – each droplet a sphere reflecting the neon light above. She felt guilty, subjecting him to this private hell. Last night she'd heard the familiar cries of nightmare from his bed in the studio.

The guard picked up a phone.

'It's all ready,' he said. 'Booth 24, in the basement.'

He pressed a button under the counter, which produced a loud mechanical click from one of the three doors that led further into the bunker.

A concrete slope led down to the floor below via a single zigzag. There, three men sat on chairs smoking, one drinking coffee from a flask, while the other two simply watched them pass, their bodies exhausted, eyes dead.

Booth 24 was a soundproof room, with two chairs and a desk.

There was a typed note on the blotter.

WITNESS TESTIMONY: BOREK: TAPES 0001-0006
Mr P P Cassidy. US State Department.

You asked specifically for BOREK. The number is limited, as it is for the other camps. The Germans wished to leave no witnesses to what they had done. There was an uprising by the Jews in the final hours before the Germans left and the Red Army arrived on July 3rd. Several hundred prisoners got over the wire, but only a handful escaped to freedom, and only six of these gave taped interviews. Most of the others died in the woods around the camp, tracked down by guards with dogs. Before they left the Germans killed any other prisoners they could find. After your last request we double-checked the files and there is no record of any member of the Stern family among the survivors. If your interest is general you might consider Majdanek, which was liberated by the Red Army before many witnesses could be shot.

Peter sat down and lit a cigarette, his notebook open in front of him, three pencils sharpened. Hanna could hear each and every breath he took now, the air whistling in and out.

The tape machine was on the desk beside the pile of round cans.

There were two pairs of headphones, but Peter put them aside. He'd told Hanna once that the pressure on his ears, during the long shifts at Camp Ashcan, had added to a feeling of imprisonment, a sense in which he was being forced to share the visions of those on the tapes.

Hanna moved her chair closer to Peter's and slipped her arm through his.

'It helps that you're here,' he said, but his voice sounded far away.

There were six cans of tape.

The first five provided broadly synoptic accounts: each of the survivors had been chosen to join a *Sonderkommando* – a work squad – rescued briefly from the line of prisoners being taken to the gas chamber. These lucky chosen few would live a little longer, working for the Germans. The rest were dead before nightfall on the day they were delivered by train. To be chosen implied the survivor had a skill: a goldsmith, a tailor, a strong labourer, a cook.

Hanna listened, her body rigid, expecting at any moment to hear mention of Leo, Irena or her sister Judith.

Peter flinched twice: once as a survivor who'd climbed a tree in the forest began a vivid account of an execution when a group of Ukrainian guards caught up with six women who'd climbed over the wire. They'd set the dogs on them, and Peter lunged for the tape machine, stopping the voice as it painted the scene; and again, earlier on the day of the rebellion, a man – a woodcutter – described having to endure the brutality of a guard wielding a rifle butt on a prisoner who had collapsed while hauling a log. It was not the scene that proved intolerable – the witness had closed his eyes – but he did describe the sounds of the attack.

Hanna moved her chair closer to Peter's and offered him a *Gitane*.

After the fifth tape, she could see his hand shaking as he stubbed it out.

'We don't have to go on, Pete,' she said. 'Not today, or even ever, if you don't want to.'

'Last tape,' he said.

He picked up the tin marked TAB/06 and threaded the tape through the heads as he had done so many times at Camp Ashcan. His finger hovered briefly over the button marked *ABSPIELEN*, as if unable to release the disembodied voice within. But then the tape was engaged, and the crackling soundtrack filled the room.

'This one is a Rachel Perel,' he said, reading the file as he had done the others. 'It says in the file she gave evidence for the Borek Trial at Nuremberg, held at the Palace of Justice in 1947, between the hearings dedicated to Auschwitz and Treblinka. Her profession is listed as hairdresser. In 1944 she was nineteen. It says her statement was given at the headquarters of the international military tribunal in the Kammergericht – the supreme court, here in Berlin.'

Hiss, hum, silence.

'I was a slave working for the man who ran the gas chamber.'

The voice was pellucid, light and airy, and gave the impression she could hit a tuneful note at will.

'I tried to be merciful to my brothers and sisters. There was no escape. I cannot forget their faces. Thousands, looking at me, beyond me.'

Peter lit a fresh cigarette, straining his skull back until the neck cracked. Hanna, for the first time, had to fight the illusion that the witness was talking directly to her, answering unspoken questions. Her heartbeat picked up.

'All I did was take this man his food and bring him his drink. He forced me to sleep with him. He liked my hair, and my voice. I sang while he worked. He always thought the music was for him, but it was for those about to die. In the end, at the revolt, they beat him to death.'

There was a loud thud – possibly a leg nudging a table.

'And this man's name please, the man who operated the gas chamber?'

Peter leant forward. 'That's the "whistler",' he said. 'We got to know all the interrogators' voices at Ashcan. He smoked throughout. Hear that?'

A thin nasal wheeze was just audible.

'Hackendorf. I was to call him this always,' said Perel.

'No first name?'

A silence. 'For the tape, please.'

'No. Never.'

For several minutes Perel was invited to sketch the command chain as she had seen it: the SS officers, the Ukrainie, the kapos, the guards. They'd followed such patterns of question and answer in the other tapes. The questioners seemed interested only in the perpetrators and the crimes, not the victims. Perel was quizzed about how many prisoners the gas chamber could hold and how often it was used, but she made it clear her time at Borek was lost in a hellish confusion. She survived the final hours of the camp by hiding and was eventually rounded up with others by the Red Army. The list of survivors she knew did not include the Sterns.

There was a pause on the tape and a fresh match was struck.

'Did anyone cheat the gas chamber? Were some reprieved?'

Hanna leaned forward: for the first time the 'whistler' had asked the question she would have asked.

'Once or twice an officer would take away a pretty girl. And some died on the Himmelstrasse – they cheated the gas chamber, but not death. If anyone was alive when the bodies were taken out of the chamber, Hackendorf had a pistol.'

There was the sound of papers being shuffled. 'We have this, a Gestapo memorandum, which records an incident three days before the revolt. An SS officer at Borek contacted the Gestapo by telegraph to inform them that a group of saboteurs had been identified at the camp. They were being processed that day. An emergency order was given requiring them to be held for interrogation. Here …'

Hanna imagined the document being handed to Perel. She knelt down on the concrete floor so that she was closer to the tape machine.

'Yes. Of course,' said Perel. 'Can I?'

They heard the sound of water being poured.

Perel coughed. 'There had been a bomb on the railway line and these people were suspected of being involved in sabotage with the *Armia* – yes?'

'The Polish Resistance – the *Armia Krajowa*?'

'Yes – the Poles. This is what frightened the Germans. That the Poles would join with the Jews, and then the Russians would arrive. So, yes, they took some prisoners away. But this was a nonsense; they were innocents. Even then there was a fight over this …'

'The Jews fought?'

'No, no. One officer wished to follow the Gestapo orders, but one of his comrades wanted to kill them there – the so-called saboteurs. The first officer used his pistol to kill the other. That was the first sign that order among the officers might be lost. It gave us hope. Three days later the camp was in ruins.'

Hanna touched the machine. 'Stop the tape, Pete. When is this? I'm lost.'

Peter wound back the tape and they listened to the key passage again.

'So – this is three days before the revolt,' said Hanna. 'That's the day on the transport manifest when we arrived at the camp.'

'This could be you,' said Peter.

A light glimmered in the darkness that had been Hanna's past: the dusty camp, the concrete chamber, a line of prisoners being led away from the rest, and a six-year-old girl holding her mother's hand. Did she see this, or did she conjure it up?

'This killing – one officer of another. Is this possible?' she asked.

Peter shrugged. 'Maybe. Sounds like it could have been a feud. Maybe it's what saved your lives.'

He let the tape play on. Hanna struggled to hear what was said. Each word was so important she struggled to leave it behind, so that she was still considering the implications of one, before the next was gone. She wanted so much to believe, but she was also wary, afraid of a trap or a false path.

The 'whistler's voice had been flat, formal, even bored; now there was a note of genuine interrogation.

'Why do you say *innocents*?'

A match struck, a chair creaked, and Hanna imagined the 'whistler' leaning back.

'There were children – two small girls, a pregnant woman, an old man with white hair. A thin man with half his wits. A few others. They clutched each other – yes, I remember, they were all from the same address. Jews from Lodz. So friends, family, neighbours.'

'And these officers who fought. Do you recall names?'

'We called one The Puppet – although his name was Keuper. The other Meyer.'

'Did you see any of the saboteurs again?'

'No.'

The interview ended. The tape clattered free of its spool.

Hanna dared not speak.

'Let's go over it one more time, Han,' Peter said.

'We don't have to, Pete.'

'It's fine now. It's the fear of what *might* be said that's difficult to face. And I need to take a better note; it's important that we have a record.'

Hanna listened in a daze. Peter kept stopping the tape, his pencil scratching at the paper of the notebook.

And then it was over, and the spool turned until it stopped.

'It's you,' said Peter. 'Don't you feel it?'

She put her hand on the cold metal surface of the magnetophon.

'I want to,' she said.

'There's an address,' said Peter. 'Look.'

He gave her the file.

Rachel Perel

Block 3
Flat 5 10B
Schmucker Straße
Friedrichshain
East Berlin

November 6
1949

'How far is it?' asked Hanna.

'We could walk in an hour. Or take the U-Bahn – there's a station, Warschauer, I think.'

'But it's in the Soviet Sector?'

'Sure. But it's easy to cross to the East,' he said, gathering up his things. 'Even easier to walk back. Thousands do it every day. There's rumours of a new visa system, of a crackdown. But we can go tomorrow. I'll check with Pierce – we may need a visa, but it won't be a problem.'

He took both of her hands. 'Nothing's nailed on here, Han: war's chaos – you can't trust names, least of all dates. But the 'whistler' missed a trick – he never asked what happened to the innocents. And hell – it sounds like this woman, this witness, saw you and your family on that day. Imagine what she might tell us if we ask the right questions.'

Chapter 18

The Stern family and their neighbours stood expectantly under the showerheads. This room, which was longer but narrower than the gas chamber they had glimpsed through the peep-hole doors, was covered inside with white tiles. Half-pipes laid in the floor ran to a drain in one corner. They stood together in the middle and waited. Outside the sun was setting in the treetops and the light that came in through the high windows was the colour of butter. Two of the windows were open.

They looked at each other's faces to avoid their bodies. But they didn't make eye contact. Shock held them all in a bright trance. They were different people now: survivors, once certain of death, they'd been given this strange antiseptic life. They were strangers to each other, at least until they could speak, because with them stood the ghosts of those they'd left behind.

Water gushed out over their bodies.

Stern shook his head, the white hair darkening. 'It's hot!' he shouted. 'Don't worry – it's hot.'

'Use the soap!' shouted the bathhouse slave, who had short black hair and flushed cheeks, which looked wet. His flesh was shiny, and stretched to fit, as if he lived in the shower room. He sat on a little wooden chair watching them shower.

'What is your name, brother?' asked Stern.

'Ephraim,' he said, studying his naked, wet, feet. 'This is the Germans' shower house – not the officers' bathhouse, but the foot-soldiers',' he added, apparently eager to share his knowledge of the camp.

They realised then that David was crying, standing naked outside the cone of water that fell from his showerhead.

Stern stood closer. 'We must be clean – it's an order,' he said, gently edging the boy under the falling water.

'I won't see my family now,' said David, covering his eyes, ashamed of his tears. 'They were on Transport 566, ahead of us. They must have ended their journey in that chamber, with the rest.

'I didn't want to walk away,' he added, in a whisper.

'I'm sorry,' said Stern. 'We had no choice.'

For a minute nobody spoke, but Stern took Irena's hand, and Judi washed Hanna's feet.

Ephraim shrugged. 'The killing will end one day, one day soon,' he said, his voice conspiratorial.

'Why?' asked Stern.

'A lot of the other camps are closed already. The Reich will soon be *judenfrei*, as Goebbels says, so they've sent us Italians, and communists, and Gypsies. But the trains hardly come now – yours was the first in weeks.

'If it's the last they won't need me. They won't need anyone. It will be the end, brother. All that's left to do is cover their tracks – dig up the dead and burn the bodies, give Borek back to its forest.'

'Where are we to be taken, do you know? Will we get food?' asked Stern, trying to lift his voice with optimism.

'They want you taken to the officers' mess. Nobody's mentioned food.'

'Can they really think we are saboteurs?' said Duvos.

Ephraim shrugged again. 'They're taking no chances. Last year, when they closed a lot of the camps down because the trains stopped coming, the slaves rose up. Most died, but some got out. So it's not impossible.

'But it's the Poles they're really scared of,' he said, his voice dropping again to a whisper. 'At night we hear them. The

Armia. They say the partisans are communists and they seek an alliance with the Ivans. God help them. I'd rather share a bed with a wolf.'

Ephraim spat eloquently on the floor, then stood up, edging forward until he too was showered, but in the lightest of falling water. In a low voice he went on: 'The Russians are sixty miles away. Work parties go out into the woods from Borek and they talk to the local peasants. The Poles wait for their moment. You can see why the Germans are afraid.'

'What will they do to us?' asked David, washing his tears away.

'They will ask questions. For hours, maybe for days,' said Ephraim, looking directly at Stern. 'About this watchmaker, about the journey, about the suitcase, about the street where you all lived on the tenement block. They will want names. *Give them the names of those who went before you.* They will be dead anyway. So give them names when they ask.'

Irena tended to the girls, her hands still shaking. Using a bar of soap, she scrubbed Hanna's scalp, while Judi was told to work on her feet quickly because they might have to go soon and they were filthy. Irena washed the water over their bodies with a dreamlike motion, as if she were storing the memory. That they were all still alive seemed like a bitter miracle.

The door opened and a guard told them to finish and be silent.

The water turned to a string of drops.

Once dry they put their towels in a wicker basket and followed Ephraim through a door into a smaller room that had only slit-like windows, too high to offer a view. On a wooden, scrubbed table, three metal bins held various white powders.

They began to pat the powder into their armpits, on their heads, between their legs, and over their scalps.

'All over,' said Ephraim. 'When you're clean they'll march you to the laundry and it's fresh clothes for all of you. Maybe they're going to line you up in front of the top brass from Berlin.'

'Why are they here?' asked Duvos.

Ephraim looked around as if they might be overheard. 'They're lawyers – SS. The commandant, Brigadeführer Eigrupper, is on trial.

'He's an old soldier, but he's not senile,' explained Ephraim. 'He set up the camp in '42. They say – gossip only – that he has been stealing the gold taken from the prisoners instead of sending it back to Berlin. Watches, jewels – but most of all teeth. Anyway, there is a shortfall in the accounts, and, well, this is a business after all.'

The powder was thick in the air and made them into white shadows. Stern thought of the men, women, and children, they'd left on the gas chamber steps. Soon their bodies would burn over the fires on the forest edge.

'This trial is today?' asked Stern.

'Yes. Maybe. There has been an investigation for months. Eigrupper has been restricted to his bungalow where he tends his plants. They've been searching for the gold here in the German compound. That's the only reason they haven't given up and closed the camp down already – why leave the loot for the Russians?

'When they do find it, they'll head back to Berlin – everyone knows it. Then we're for it. They won't leave anyone alive.'

Irena put an arm around her daughters, pulling them close.

Ephraim leaned in towards them. 'Ebner's running the camp while the trial's on – he's the deputy: you can't miss him, he's tall, blond, looks like an albino. He's a cruel man. It will be bad for us if they take Eigrupper away. Or hang him here. They say the judge who sits in this court has done this before; that a commandant of a camp in Germany was put on trial for fraud and they hanged him in Berlin.'

The white powder had begun to settle on the floor.

'You must go now,' said Ephraim, almost reluctantly. Stern realised then that he was lonely, of course, because his job was to clean up after the Germans.

Five minutes later they were outside – not in the dirt – but walking on duckboards across dried mud and grass. Ahead of them strolled an elderly guard, apparently unconcerned if they followed. They had to leave the towels behind so they were completely naked; eight spotless prisoners walking in the sunlight of evening, still very pale from the delousing powders. It made Stern think there might be another line walking in the evening dusk, strolling away from the gas chamber towards the woods, the dead in single file, but that this line would not end.

Chapter 19

They were marched to a tailor's hut to choose clothes and shoes, and then onwards until they reached a drill square. In the centre of this open space, two German officers played *pétanque* with rusted metal balls in the dust. A third watched them, holding a small fox on a dog lead. A chamber orchestra sat on chairs in one corner of the square, the musicians in a semi-circle around the conductor, the very same ensemble that had greeted Transport 573, although Stern thought they looked different now, and they certainly sounded different, for the music had a real melody, as if it came from the heart, the languid rhythm constant and serene, not hurried, or anxious. It occurred to Stern that it must be a torture to play Berlin waltzes for new arrivals at Borek; brothers and sisters who hoped they were stopping to rest and wash, but who were actually just an hour from the gas chamber. It was an aspect of the genius of those who ran the camp that they had been able to enlist the innocence of music to tell a lie.

The SS guard who had marched them this far without a word, led the way up a short flight of wooden steps and into what looked like an officers' mess. From a hallway they were able to see, through a series of interior windows, a bar, with large leather armchairs and small tables. A gramophone played discreetly, the sound meshing atonally with the orchestra outside. Behind the bar they could see bottles, and glasses, each one capturing the reflection of the evening light outside the windows. A man in a white shirt cleaned ashtrays, flicking a bar towel at a persistent fly.

A rank-and-file SS soldier appeared through a door, and they glimpsed a kitchen beyond, while he was brushing crumbs from his uniform. 'I have to take over from here,' he said, to their guard. 'They want you back at the station.'

He was very young, with freckles around his eyes, and soft skin that looked like dough.

'Sure you're up to it, Brunner?' said the guard, smiling as he turned to go. 'Isn't your bedtime soon?'

Their new guard blushed, gripping his rifle.

An officer came up the steps from the drill square, flicking dust from his cuffs.

'It's true?' he asked the boy soldier. Stern looked at the newcomer's lapel badges: an SS captain.

He didn't seem to expect an answer. 'Christ. Clean Jews – all dressed up too. Don't let them use the glasses or cups in here or there'll be a riot.' He straightened his uniform and wrinkled his nose. 'This is not going to end well,' he declared to nobody. 'They still stink. The waters of the Rhine could flow over them and they'd still reek.'

The young soldier's eyes stared straight forward, his face immobile.

'And don't gossip with them, Brunner. They've been summoned. They have been given a reprieve, but only for a few hours.

'They don't need to know anything more, do you, Jews?' His face began to disfigure in disgust.

This question was met with silence. 'Well – do you?' he repeated, speaking as if to children.

Stern shook his head. They all followed suit.

The captain swept past them into the bar and flopped into one of the chairs. The sound, of good leather crackling, made Stern feel the weight of his old bones. It had been the longest day of his life and the sun had only just set. He imagined the sensation of his weight leaving him, bleeding away, as he too sank into an armchair.

'Just wait,' said Brunner, unnecessarily. 'Sit if you want.'

They crowded on to a polished wooden bench.

Stern felt dizzy with relief, but also a familiar despair prompted by the German officer now in the comfortable armchair, who had revealed again the Nazi capacity for casual cruelty, treating his prisoners as sub-humans, degraded souls. They had all seen the extent to which the SS attracted sadists and perverts of all kinds, and those whom Stern's generation of physicians might describe as suffering from 'mania without delirium', or what the modern school called 'psychopathic inferiority'. To what did these words amount in real life but an enduring tendency to anti-social behaviour, restricted empathy, a lack of remorse, and poor behavioural control? Stern wondered if the SS captain would recognise the diagnosis.

He closed his eyes, feeling sleep steal over his skull, recalling a debate he had entered upon with the rabbinical community in Regen: an academic dispute with a group of elders held, rather unfairly Stern had felt, within the confines of the synagogue itself. It had been December 1938, and they were still in shock after the coordinated attacks that had swept the country. The windows of their own synagogue in Regen had been broken, a small fire set, shops attacked. By the standards of the vicious violence of the cities, they had escaped lightly. Nothing had happened in the village of Weissenstein at all. Nonetheless they were left with a profound sense of dislocation and insecurity, and a kind of mannered panic. They met to discuss what to do in defence: to send the children abroad, to leave for Palestine, to collect arms, to send money to New York or London or Paris.

As the chief rabbi spoke, tiny splinters of glass fell from the shattered dome above. Typically, the discussion had become philosophical. Most of the older men wanted to know why the Germans acted as they did. Stern had sought to dispel the notion, unsuccessfully he had to admit, that the Teutonic race contained a very high proportion of those capable of psychopathic action. On the contrary, there was little doubt that all societies contained such individuals, and to something like the same degree, he said. What had happened in Germany – Stern had argued – was the construction of organisations, both military and civilian, in which such individuals might thrive. No – *would* thrive. Indeed, Stern explained, some members of the Nazi Party and its affiliated organisations had actually taken on the behavioural traits of psychopathy in order to gain advancement, even against their own moral natures. This was because the state required its agents to create an atmosphere of fear and terror. Sympathy for the victims was a hindrance to good government. Empathy was treason.

Stern's message of comfort was that these men – and yes, they were *men* in almost all circumstances – were very rarely the leaders of society. The character defects involved in such a personality made it extremely unlikely that anyone encumbered with such abnormalities could rise to positions of real control. No: they were the tools of those above, or in Hitler's case those below; damaged men let loose to wander the borderlands of human nature. Outcasts offered a home, or a leather armchair.

Chapter 20

The single door in the corridor on the opposite side to the bar swung open, pushed by a civilian in a grey suit, who told Brunner to bring his prisoners through. The room, which was empty, was panelled in polished mahogany. The wood had clearly been torn down and brought to Borek, as several of the panels did not fit neatly: two or three overlapped, and the ones round the doors and windows had been sawn to fit. There were carved heraldic devices where the wall met the vaulted wooden ceiling, most of which involved images of swans, several with intertwined necks.

The room's principal feature was a triple-arched window at one end, beneath which was a desk, nearly eight foot wide, decorated with carved scenes of a battle, a group of horsemen crossing a shallow lake, swords held high. Again, swans cruised on the rippling water. The late evening light falling through the windows reminded Stern of the Ark at the synagogue in Regen, the doors open to reveal the Torah. He was holding Hanna by the hand and it was clear the child was struck by the triple arc of light, as if by a vision.

The prisoners clung to each other as they were shepherded to a line of chairs and ordered to sit down.

There was one modern item in the room: an office desk in chipboard, on top of which was a typewriter and a stenotype machine. David, always alert to the mechanical, whispered to Stern that the typewriter was a Triumph Perfekt – a fine new model – and that the stenographer's machine was made by Alpina. The eight chairs on which the prisoners were directed to sit were set to one side. In the centre of the room were three rows of ten chairs. Two smaller desks stood facing forwards.

'It's a courtroom,' whispered Duvos. 'See the gavel?'

Stern hadn't seen it: the wooden hammer, a wooden base, set on a silver disc, with an engraved edge made up of interlocking SS symbols. The court began to fill with officers, two hanging back in the corridor by the door, smoking.

Stern was confused; were they going to try Liff, here in this splendid court? Surely not. But then who? The watchmaker himself was oblivious to his surroundings, engrossed in examining the stitchwork on the cuffs of the shirt he'd been given to wear.

The heraldic decorations, the dignity of the bench, gave the doctor hope, in that they were in themselves the trappings of civilised men, the physical representation of a judicial process. He suddenly felt elated, unable to suppress the idea that here, at the most unexpected moment, they had been brought into the presence of justice.

A side-door opened, and three officers came in to sit behind the great, decorated, desk. The clerk ordered everyone to stand. The officer in the middle sat first while the other two remained standing.

'This SS Military Court of the Krakow District is now in session. Judge Georg Johl presiding,' said the clerk.

Stern recognised the two officers flanking the senior judge. One was Sandberger. The other was an albino with invisible eyebrows who Stern guessed, from the bathhouse slave's description, must be Ebner, the deputy commandant.

So: Sandberger, Johl and Ebner.

How quickly this alien world had become Stern's own.

The three panes of glass above the judge's head were darkening quickly towards dusk, the first stars fidgeting in the sky. There was a distant view of the square in which they'd had to abandon their luggage, a fire still smouldering. Stern found it hard to believe that they had only arrived at the camp that morning, less than ten hours earlier. The passage of time had been chaotic, a headlong fall into a different world, and he had yet to come to rest.

David, who sat in the middle of the line of prisoners, knew the patterns of the zodiac but he did not recognise the constellations he could see emerging outside. This couldn't be true: they hadn't changed hemispheres on their long journey, although it might feel as if they had. No – he must be confused, disorientated. It made him feel far from home, and for a second he experienced a thrill of despair. Even on the steps of the gas chamber he had not felt this strange sense of a void into which he was about to fall. His eyes filled with tears, and he sat very still, hoping none of the others would see his face.

The clerk spoke again. 'Will the defendant – Obersturm-führer Rolf Meyer – step forward to the dock.'

So, it wasn't Liff the bomb maker accused, but Keuper's executioner. Meyer walked to the dock, rising slightly as he took his position.

'Rolf Edwin Meyer, you are charged with murder under Section 102 of the German Military Code. Do you at this point wish to plead to the charge in front of the tribunal?'

He nodded.

'How do you plead?'

'Not guilty.' Meyer ran a hand back through his fair hair. There were whispers in the courtroom, and someone clapped.

The clerk and the senior judge exchanged some paperwork.

Johl, the judge, wore glasses made of heavy plastic, in black, which he took off now and set beside his gavel. Stern guessed he might be forty-five years of age, possibly younger, his thinning hair without a trace of grey.

'The court has been convened and we have heard the defendant's plea,' he said. 'We will reconvene at 8.00 tomorrow morning. A few small items before we adjourn ...'

He adjusted a sheet of paper on his blotter, his fountain pen suspended in a pale, pudgy, hand. Johl's face was very large, with fleshy jowls, and was devoid of any kind of aura, or charisma. The attention of the court was focused on him because he sat in the principal seat of judgement. Otherwise he could have been a nobody; less, a petty bureaucrat glimpsed each day through a post-office-counter window, or railway station ticket booth. There were a million Germans just like Johl – thought Stern – and all of them were sitting behind a desk or a counter.

'Minor matters, but *extraordinary* nonetheless,' said Johl.

The clerk's hands softly played on the paddles of the stenograph.

'The death of Obersturmführer Keuper occurred approximately four hours ago. The SS court investigator here at Borek, Sturmbannführer Raeder, has visited the scene. In due course, following the procedure set down in the legal code, he would have assembled a list of witnesses and a file on the case and passed it to the court prosecutor. This court would have sat a matter of weeks after the event – several days, certainly. But here we are, in session, within a few hours.'

The fingers of one of his plump hands flexed.

'This is because in the last two days an extraordinary SS Military Court has been in session in Borek to try another matter. This required a bench of five judges and all the usual administrative support. This does not concern us now. That verdict has been handed down. Sentence will be carried out in Berlin.'

He paused here and Stern was convinced he did it deliberately to create a silence, a challenge to anyone in the court to disagree with his summary of events. No one did. The court had sat, the court had reached a verdict. The fate of the commandant, Eigrupper, was sealed. It sounded very much as if a firing squad awaited the hero of the Great War.

'Outside, darkness falls,' said Johl. 'We were looking forward to our final meal here at Borek before returning to Berlin. However, I am here; the administration of the court is here. I can see no virtue in delay, especially at such a time. We are not – yet – in the frontline of our heroic war. But we are close. A confrontation looms. If time defeats us, we must adjourn to Berlin. Better still, we must be swift in our justice.'

Johl looked over all their heads as if trying to see a great distance. Stern wondered if this final, rather florid, phrase had been written down in the notes he had before him.

'I am grateful to the defence for agreeing to an expedited process. If they had requested a later date, I would have been duty-bound to agree. They have asked only one thing in return: that the eight witnesses are available to give evidence if required. I should remind the court at this point that they are the *only* witnesses to the death of Jonas Keuper other than the accused. The Ukrainian guards were some thirty yards distant in a copse of trees. They have been interviewed by their own commander and insist they saw nothing, but specifically *heard* nothing – and besides, their testimony would have had to be translated for the court. So, we are left with the Jews.'

Johl poured himself a glass of water and sipped it.

'Jews, of course, do not normally appear in any of the courts of the Reich. Due to racial impurity and inferiority, their testimony is not acceptable. In some extraordinary cases the court investigator would cross-examine a witness if their testimony was deemed vital, and then report that evidence to the court second-hand, as it were.

'However, the defendant argues that their evidence is crucial, in that they heard what was said before the fatal shot was fired. Also, time is short. I'm minded to grant the request, but it must be limited. There is no need for such a crowd ...'

The prosecutor stood.

'Funk?' asked the judge. He was a small man with very large lips – fleshy and wet – as if he had been struck in a fight and they'd swollen; bruised and slightly blue.

'The request is unfortunate. The smell ...'

There was a murmur of laughter.

'And what credence can we give such testimony,' continued Funk. 'The mental capacity of the Jews is crippled by inbreeding and vice.'

Johl put his glasses back on. 'Indeed. What fun you will have exposing their inferiority, Funk.'

Funk was taken aback. He decided this statement was a joke and sat down.

As he did, his opposite number stood, as if they were connected by a counterbalance, so that the weight of one descending propelled the other to his feet.

'Weiss?' asked the judge.

The defence counsel looked fit and young, although he had a shadow of stubble along his chin and under his nose, and held his left leg stiffly.

'The accused, Rolf Meyer, begs the court's indulgence. He wishes to be released from custody. He offers his word as an SS officer that he will attend the court as directed.'

Johl didn't even look up from his legal pad where he was making a note.

'Granted.'

Weiss sat down.

'Now. Which one is Liff?' asked Johl. 'Which one Stern?'

Stern stood, taking Liff by the arm, edging him forward, into the space before the bench.

'The Gestapo has possession of the prisoner Liff's suitcase and they wish to interview him tonight,' said Johl. 'Later, possibly, the prisoner Stern too, if his suitcase can be found. Liff is released into their custody now, Stern will remain with the rest until required,' said Johl.

Outside the door, someone gently stroked a dinner gong.

Ebner readjusted his belt as if anticipating a feast. Outside, through the triple window, Stern saw a cloud of sparks rise in the dark, presumably from the suitcases burning on the square.

'Court dismissed,' said Johl, and he tapped the gavel playfully.

Chapter 21

Brunner, who had acquired a lantern, led them away from the officers' mess. In his oddly rustic accent he explained that the cells they would sleep in that night comprised the camp 'cooler' for German rank-and-file and Ukrainie guards; a lock-up for those tempted by the local vodka, or driven mad by the boredom of camp life.

'We're very hungry,' said Stern. 'The children especially.'

'Just wait,' said Brunner, abruptly. 'Meal times are meal times. We all have to wait.'

Ahead of them was the brick water tower they'd glimpsed from the Pariser Platz. While from a distance this structure looked circular, it was in fact octagonal: two high-ceilinged floors of brick, supporting an iron water tank, the steel, riveted sheets of which were rusted red. Against the stars they could see the radio mast on top, and the steam klaxon that marked the hours.

The ground floor of the building housed a generator and an area set aside, behind a wooden half-partition, which looked like a makeshift telephone switchboard. At the end of the desk stood a single teletype machine, a broad ream of paper hanging out, crowded with words, but torn across in a jagged line.

A circular metal staircase rose like a corkscrew to the upper floor. At its base a captain's chair was set beside a pot-bellied stove, a bunk-bed, and a desk that held nothing but a black phone. This was presumably Brunner's guard post. His chair was surrounded by wood shavings, and on the seat lay a carved chess piece, the knight, whittled from a soft wood. On a wooden shelf other pieces crowded: a queen, a pawn, a bishop.

Turning to the prisoners, Brunner brandished a ring of keys. 'I'm the gaoler. I guard the radio mast. It's an important job,' he added, lifting his chin. 'And I make the rules, so don't fuck about.'

Stern thought the German was very young to be given such a responsibility. He wondered if he felt any personal guilt or empathy for their fate. The guard glared beyond Stern at Hanna, who had slipped her father's hand, reaching for the carved knight. Roughly, Stern gathered the child up.

'I'm sorry,' he said.

Brunner nodded, then led them up the stairs, into a windowless, hexagonal room, off which were six, numbered, cell doors. Weary, dizzy with fatigue and hunger, and feeling suddenly older, Stern longed for an open door to reveal a bed.

'Schirach is often drunk, and they put him in here,' said Brunner, throwing back a cell door marked No. 5. 'But they don't turn the lock. For the Ukrainie we bolt the doors, because they're animals, and they'd slip a knife in your guts as soon as whistle.'

'Thank you for your kindnesses,' said Stern to the guard.

Brunner blushed.

'Your food is coming, it comes through here,' he added, flipping up a metal flap by the keyhole to demonstrate how the feeding hatch worked. 'There will be water,' he added, for Irena. She'd asked him three times already for a drink for the children.

'I will be here at all times. Any trouble, I've been told to shoot you. The court doesn't need you that badly. Remember that. If you try to escape, they'll hunt you down and bury you upside down in a sand hole to see how long it takes you to stop breathing. Believe me, I've seen this.'

Judi took a step back and Irena hugged her quickly. Hanna simply stood listening.

'Can my family stay together in one cell?' asked Stern.

'Mother and children can have one cell,' said Brunner. 'You, doctor, can go next door. They may come for you later if they finish with the watchmaker. If you must talk together, I won't hear until lights out. After that, silence.'

He went and stood by the stairs, taking out a tobacco tin. 'Choose a cell now. I need to lock the doors.'

'This one for me,' said Duvos, entering a cell facing east over the forest. 'And look,' he added, coming back out holding a small piece of red chalk. 'I can draw. Is that all right?'

Brunner shrugged.

Duvos had also found a small piece of white chalk, which he tried to slip into Hanna's hand. In the boxcar the photographic chemist had watched the child clutching her crayons. Hanna's eyes widened but her fists remained closed, so Irena took the gift herself.

The klaxon sounded on the roof, its echo captured in the water above their heads so they felt its long half-life continue after the alarm stopped, diminishing until it faded away as a single note.

'Time,' said Brunner, shaking the key-ring. 'Your food will be in an hour.'

The Stern family hugged each other.

Behind his locked door Stern listened to Brunner plodding down the stairs to his stove.

'Are my girls there?' he called softly; then he held his hands to his face, ashamed that he'd felt a distinct sense of relief at the parting, at the closing of his cell door, in that it had separated him physically from his direct, active, responsibility for the lives of his family. Stern also felt overwhelmed by a sense of fear. The next time the cell door opened it might mean the Gestapo had come to take him away for interrogation.

In the next cell Irena had engaged the girls in their favourite game, in which they had to guess what their neighbours at home were doing at bedtime. They'd started playing it in the transit camp: each night they'd imagine the sounds and smells of their sleepy village home. But Weissenstein seemed a distant memory now, so they tried instead to remember their one-room flat in the ghetto in Lodz, which in a way had been their home too.

'I'll start,' said Irena.

But there was a silence, so Stern took up the thread. 'I can hear the Nowaks arguing – there! Another plate in pieces. And a glass! They'll be playing tug-o-war with that poor child.'

The tenement block was five stories high with paper-thin walls and echoing stairwells. At night Irena said she could hear their neighbours breathing in their sleep.

'I can smell dinner,' said Irena. 'It will be Frau Hahn down-stairs – she's got black pepper from somewhere, and juniper berries. And that sizzle is oat cakes.'

'There's Zuzanna,' said Judi, who loved dogs. 'She's got stewed cabbage in her bowl, but she wants sausages.' Mr Fischer worked night shifts in one of the ghetto's many factories, where he had to make knives for German soldiers. His wife had died on a transport train and so the dog was left alone after dark on the ground floor.

They moved on to include their neighbours on the same floor.

'That's Liff pacing up and down his room,' said Judi.

They fell silent, hoping the watchmaker would be back soon, or at all.

'I can hear Esther creeping down the stairs, trying not to wake us, off to work at the bakers',' said Irena.

'How is the child, Esther?' called Stern. They hadn't heard her voice for a long time.

'She's kicked twice,' came the voice. Esther had decided the baby was a girl.

'And there's a cockroach on my windowsill. And flies, three, circling the light.' They heard the bedsprings creak and imagined her hauling herself up on one elbow. 'I just hope Tomma's all right. Where do you think he is?'

'In one of the barrack huts,' said Duvos. 'I can see them from the window, lines of them, penned in by wire fences. Ephraim, from the bathhouse, will tell them all you're alive. Tomma will know, Esther. Tonight, he'll be told. Trust me.'

An hour passed in gossip and then they heard footsteps outside. Heavy boots clattered on the steel steps, and there was the sound of something being dragged up the corkscrew stairwell.

'Holy Mother.' The voice of Brunner. 'He needs the doctor.'

'They're not bothered,' said another voice. 'He's a watchmaker from the Ruhr. The Gestapo man was in a hurry. Raeder knows his business, so they finished quickly. They know as well as we do that he's no saboteur. He'd have pleaded guilty to anything. They know the truth. They won't bother with the rest. They want to get to the feast.

'Take him. He's yours.'

Stern said a prayer of thanks that he'd been spared, until his door rattled and the little hatch opened to reveal Brunner's face, just the eyes and nose, which made him look even younger, like a child.

'Here.' He pushed in a piece of bread and what looked like a small section of smoked sausage, and then a mug of water. Stern's mouth flooded with saliva as he lunged for the bread, his jaw crushing the crust, his tongue savouring the wheat and flour. The water, sweet and cold, cleared his vision. His family was alive tonight; it would have to be enough.

But as the guard drew back, Stern glimpsed a little of the cell opposite. Liff was standing by his bunk-bed. One of his eyes was a mess of dried blood and blue, bruised, flesh. He had a small, prim, mouth but the lower lip hung down to reveal some childlike shattered teeth. His right arm carried his left, which was clearly broken below the elbow. Then the hatch was closed.

After the silence, in which they all ate, they started talking again, their voices transformed, and full of hope. They called out to Liff. Was he all right?

'Yes,' said a voice, but they did not recognise it.

Then at ten the lights went out. Something chattered in the forest. The generator whirred below.

'There's still lights in the slaves' huts,' said Duvos. 'Candles, I think, because they are very faint. And I can see people out, moving between the huts. They run their own little world these brothers.

'Wait. A wonder! Seven lights flickering. They have a menorah!'

The image of the menorah was like a spell. They were silent, picturing the seven-branched candlestick, remembering the glitter of gold, or silver, and rich jewels. It made them think of feasts, and dancing, and flushed, excited smiles. Irena conjured up her family, the faces of her mother and father caught in the shimmering light.

'It's the truth,' said Duvos, as if they wouldn't believe him. 'We can carry everything we need, my friends, for we are a travelling people. The branches of the menorah will unscrew – I've seen it done. It's what we do best, brothers and sisters: we pack. Or do you think they made it here out of scrap metal? That's it perhaps: the kapos will run a smithy. They run their camp, the Germans run this. I bet there's a Talmud too; a big fat one. They'll have burnt many but kept one.'

They heard the springs on Duvos's bed creak. 'The menorah's on the move, from window to window.'

Irena held Hanna up to the window to see, but after a few seconds the watchtower searchlights came on, and the candlelight was lost.

Irena, trying to reclaim the sense of hope, began to tell everyone a story.

It was the tale of Rabbi Onias, who travels to Jerusalem in a time of war, saving his basket of dates in case he meets someone on the way who needs the food more than he does. On the edge of the city, he sees a man planting carob trees because his vineyard has been destroyed. With trepidation the rabbi climbs the hill, in fear of what lies beyond, and gazes down on Jerusalem in ruins. Despair overwhelms him so that he lies down with his camel and sleeps, his dates spilling out of his basket and on to the earth. When he wakes he is in the shadow of a great palm, amid an orchard of fine carob trees. Running to the brow of the hill, he looks down on the city again, and sees it now restored, with its golden domes and minarets, and flights of birds swinging between towers, and knows that he has slept for a hundred years.

Chapter 22

A noise woke Stern, so that when his eyes opened he saw the door of his cell ajar, framing Brunner, who held up the storm lantern. A golden crucifix hung outside the German's tunic, catching the light. Placing a finger across his lips, he beckoned with his free hand for Stern to get up and follow.

With an effort the doctor swung his legs over the edge of the bed and, bending down, held up his boots. Brunner nodded.

Stern was afraid; the Nazis only came in the night when they were ashamed of what they planned to do: they'd take him across the sleeping camp to the cells by the station, then ask questions that had no answers, so that he'd have to give them the names of innocent men who were already dead. Had Liff given them *his* name?

As he struggled with the laces on his boots, he saw Brunner put the lantern down and take a bundle of Reichsmarks from his pocket, counting them quickly. The banknotes looked grubby, slightly oily, their edges torn and curled. Stern wondered what it was he'd been paid to do, and his imagination constructed the scene that might lie ahead: a glade in the woods beyond the station, moonlight on tree stumps, the flash of a rifle.

As he stepped out into the corridor his knees buckled with fear and he sank to the floor, so that Brunner had to haul him up on to his narrow feet. In the silence Stern heard David crying, each sob accompanied by a rhythmic intake of breath, while Esther turned her heavy body on its crib, the rusted springs creaking.

Stern sensed that Irena lay awake, listening. She'd presume he was being led away for questioning and fear the worst. Hanna must be asleep because he could hear the rattle of liquid in her throat, which had been with her from the first night of her life. The sound lifted Stern's hopes because in a way it meant that the child *had* escaped, even if it was only temporarily, into a dream world, despite the locks on the doors.

'Goodbye, children, wife.' Stern whispered the words, almost to himself, but Brunner's eyes shone with anger. 'Silence,' he hissed. 'You'll get us both shot.'

Which didn't make sense. What were they doing that it could lead to the death of the guard?

Outside, the night was almost cold, the sky clear. The column of smoke still rose from the pits beyond the gas chamber, but now it was a lazy, grey, pillar, dividing the star-scape in half. Stern felt like a wild animal, emerging from a burrow perhaps, his nose twitching to track subtle scents on the night breeze.

Most of the camp was in darkness, although the watchtower searchlights blazed outwards, or along the wire, which made it harder to see where they were going, because of the stark contrast between the pearl-white beams and the black shadows. Coming to a spot beside the perimeter wire, Brunner put the lantern down by his boots, indicating that they had in some sense *arrived*. Sweat stood out on the guard's forehead, while a single bead trickled across his cheek. Stern's ability to see in such minute detail seemed to be related to the adrenaline pumping round his body.

'Go back, Brunner.' The words came out of the dark.

Three brisk strides and a German officer stood before them. Rolf Meyer, Keuper's executioner, bent down and took up the guard's lantern.

He checked his watch. 'We'll be back by two,' he told the young guard. 'Do not worry.'

Stern smelt alcohol on Meyer, and cigarettes, and Eau de Cologne. There was something about his easy, fluid movements that Stern sensed was reckless, as if he'd abandoned any respect for the razor wire, the watchtowers, even the machine-gun behind the beam of light.

Although he had been dismissed, Brunner still stood, hesitating.

'I said I would return with Dr Stern. You have my word. If you are worried, count the cash …'

Brunner turned back, shouldering his rifle.

'Doctor,' said Meyer. 'Follow, please.'

His studied manners left Stern wary.

'You'll need these,' said Meyer, giving him a coat and a woollen hat.

'Why?' asked Stern.

'I can't save the youngest girl,' said Meyer. 'But the other child maybe – I'll try. Is that enough?'

'What do you need of me?' asked Stern. He said it quickly, hoping to strike the bargain, but felt immediately the weight of his own guilt, to have so swiftly set aside the destruction of his youngest daughter against the life of her sister.

'You will see,' said Meyer, stopping at a point equidistant between the two nearest watchtowers.

'Two minutes,' he said, looking at a pocket watch. In front of them was a mesh door in the wire with a large padlock.

'We're about to discover the true value of the Reichsmark, doctor. Officially it buys you two zloty but I'm not so sure. We live in difficult times. I suspect the Reichsmark is a depreciating asset. Rubles eh? That's the future. Or gold. There's a lot of talk about getting back to good old gold. Just ask the commandant.'

Meyer laughed at his own joke but Stern was shocked to see that his face was bathed in sweat. Perhaps he cared for his life more than he wished the doctor to know.

J. G. Kelly

'Where are we going?' asked Stern.

'Patience. All your questions will be answered. I'd be inclined to enjoy the evening that unfolds. If I can live like this – from moment to moment – if I have to live like this, so can you.'

Meyer turned to look down the wire to one of the watchtowers.

'This may be the last minute of our lives, doctor. Even with so little left before us it still concentrates the mind, does it not? Make your peace, whatever Jews do. I hear that you are good with death, you accept it as inevitable. To us it is a surprise. Every time. So much for the master race, eh? Perhaps we will overcome death in the crucible of total victory. Somehow, I doubt it.'

He took out the watch and studied it again.

Stern took several lungfuls of air. His ears had begun to pick up sounds from the forest: a chattering that might be a fox, wings flapping against leaves, little showers of pine needles falling. He thought of the Polish forest then as an endless canopy of life, surviving, breathing, exuding gases into the air, drawing in oxygen. The trees were like a vast crowd, edging up to the camp, each one a sullen witness. Stern thought of the long line of the dead leaving the gas chamber, threading their way into the shadows, even now wandering in those same woods.

'Now,' said Meyer, snapping shut the watch. Then, with a broad smile: '*Meine Ehre heisst Treue.*'

He took out a circlet of iron holding a steel key and opened the padlock easily.

'Quick – follow me and don't stop,' he said.

Opening the gate he stepped out into No-Man's Land. Stern's eyes were blinded by the searchlight. There was no doubt that they could be seen from both watchtowers, but there was neither a shout nor a shot, although they stood in plain view. Shadows moved on top of the watchtower, making the light flutter. Meyer had already reached a door on the far side identical to the first, where he worked with the keys, the turning of his wrist becoming violent. Finally, the lock gave, the door swung out, and Stern ran to join him.

The gate locked behind him, Meyer stood, listening, chest heaving. A further twenty-five yards across open grass and they were in the shadow of the forest.

Meyer's face was lost in darkness. 'You see, doctor. In Borek you *can* buy anything. And relax, they only have half their money. We will return.'

Stern saw that Meyer had hidden the lantern beneath his heavy coat so that a circle of light lit his polished boots. The German led the way further into the trees until they reached a path parallel with the wire, which they followed until it met the road that ran out of the camp through the main gate. Keeping to the far side of a ditch, they turned away from the gates, the light from the flickering fire the guards had built at the checkpoint fading rapidly away.

After half a mile the road bent to the left, then back again to resume its arrow's flight. A track led into the trees, which they followed to a clearing. Here three cars were neatly parked; two SS Mercedes: black and polished, glittering like forest beetles, and a small sports car, with luxurious leather seats, which looked slight by comparison, its paint-work pale in the dark.

Meyer plunged ahead.

Stern's heart was pounding within a few hundred yards. He saw now why he'd been given the heavy coat. The path zigzagged through blackthorn bushes, and nettles, ivy and thistle. At one point Meyer stopped, and taking up the lantern turned it down to a blue pinpoint flame. They both listened to the night for a full minute. A door slammed in the far distance, or perhaps a branch fell.

Ahead they reached a crossing place, where several tracks met, marked by six wooden tree stumps. A single beer bottle stood on one, with the stone stopper hanging out on its wire cradle.

'A rest perhaps,' said Meyer, putting one boot up on a stump.

Stern sat, his breath slowing, his head down. After a minute he looked up. 'Will the court find you innocent of murder?' he asked. He was a curious man, a scientific inquirer, and refused to accept that he could not ask questions; and besides, he was bewitched by Meyer's whispered promise, that he might be able to save Judi's life. Why was the German risking so much when in all likelihood he would walk free of the court?

Meyer lit a cigarette. 'The proceedings are not what they seem, doctor. Johl finds the case of intellectual interest. His cause – if I can put it like that – is a simple one: to illustrate that the letter of the law applies even here, in Borek. Each and every German, he believes, lives under the law, at home, at the front, even here. A civilised country does not allow the law to lapse. And there is a greater purpose, do you not think? That by considering this single case of illegality the court emphasises the *legality* of what goes on each day – the killing of the prisoners, in thousands, in hundreds of thousands. So, the judge serves the law and the law serves the state.

'In my case there are complications. Johl, I think, is fascinated by the interplay of authority between the SS and the Gestapo; he wishes to make clear the supremacy of the first over the second. So – maybe a formality, as you say. But we will see.'

'Why are we here?' asked Stern.

Meyer threw his cigarette into the dark. 'The answers lie just ahead. Along this very path. Come. Or do paths through the woods hold an enduring fear?'

At this, Stern felt he had to speak. 'For the women and children who took the Himmelstrasse, who were beaten if they did not, who were set upon by dogs, it can hold no enduring fear. They are all dead. Fear came, fear went. Does this make German soldiers proud?'

The moon was shielded by clouds and so he could not see Meyer's face, but for the first time his voice betrayed weariness. 'I am a simple soldier, doctor. The Ukrainie command the path. War makes us all hard. I do not contemplate the fate of women and children, although I see them arrive, and I see them walk down the path. Final destinations are for others to appoint.

'Now, walk on, if you wish your daughter to live.'

Almost immediately, music came to them on the air. After ten minutes they stumbled out of the roots and leaf litter into a wide clearing, and ahead of them, against the sky, stood a three-storey building: a sawmill, built of crude stone slabs. A set of rail tracks ran out from the main structure and into the forest. A few logs stood in a storage bay. A cone of sawdust ran down a low hill. Beyond the main building a series of wooden sheds had been built into a low slope, at the centre of which stood a bunkhouse.

Meyer, holding the lamp up, smiled at what he saw: a door opening in the bunkhouse, a wedge of red light falling over the clearing, music blaring out into the night. Stern studied the German's face, which for the first time was truly animated, as if a man who has spent a long time on a weary journey in a hostile land comes in sight of home.

Chapter 23

The man who had appeared at the open door was wearing military trousers, with his shirt off, the braces thrown over his bare shoulders. He was well-built, but not in a labouring sense. Stern felt he looked like an acrobat, or a Greek athlete depicted in an ancient frieze, cradling a discus.

'One more night of freedom, Rolf?' he called at Meyer as he emerged from the shadow of the trees.

The two men embraced. The *bonhomie* dissolved when Meyer's comrade caught sight of Stern. That fine, cultured face registered instant disgust, as if he'd had a plate of rotting meat held up to his nose.

'You bring the Jew here? Why, Rolf?'

Meyer killed the flame in his lantern and set it down.

'Welcome to our home from home,' he said to Stern. 'Excuse the stench of vomit. Everyone uses the front step when they've had too much, especially Anton here, who cannot hold his wine. And has also forgotten his manners.'

Placing a hand on Anton's shoulder he looked at his comrade's face. 'Just forget what you see, friend. As I have forgotten so much on your behalf.'

A single corridor ran away from the front door with rooms to either side. The walls were rough plastered board, the floors covered in a collection of rugs. The house was full of light and music: a gramophone played, there was the clash of glasses, and from the upper storey the buzz of a harmonica.

Meyer swung his coat off like a cape. There was a silver ice bucket on a stand by the door, out of which stuck several bottles of wine. The door to the room on the left was open and Stern saw a naked woman lying on the rug amid a nest of cushions. A man was on top of her, his movements irregular, his bare buttocks blotched and sagging. Beyond them, on a sofa, two other women sat talking to each other, ignoring the spectacle, sipping from cocktail glasses.

In the opposite room were several German officers in armchairs. One of them had a naked girl on his knee. She had very dark hair and was painfully thin, with jutting ribs. A ladder led to the upper storey and they could hear the sound of laughter over their heads, and then a door slamming.

'Welcome to the whorehouse in the woods,' said Meyer. 'If we knew where the commandant had hidden his gold we'd go to the hotel in town, which has fine linen, fine wine and even finer girls. But times are hard. Are you shocked, doctor?'

One of the German officers got up from his armchair and stood in the door. He had thinning grey hair and a pair of spectacles with a single lens in the left eye. 'Christ, Rolf. What is this madness now?'

'There is no risk, Bertolt. The doctor has a daughter. He wants her to live.'

Stern rearranged his feet, and thought of Irena, holding the girls in the unlit cell.

A cry of joy came from the woman on the floor, and a brief flurry of applause from the girls on the sofa.

'The radio says Himmler is still in Krakow,' said Anton. 'If they find you guilty, he could sign the warrant tomorrow. You'll be dead the next day. Is there any risk then? Any risk to *us*?'

Bertolt put an arm round them both. 'Girls, girls. Anton's too harsh,' he said, the single lens of his glasses catching the light. 'The court will not find you guilty, Rolf – the code is clear, and Johl knows nothing if not the code. And we should be thankful ...'

He playfully pushed Anton in the chest. 'Rolf has rid us of that cocksucker, Keuper.' He mimicked Keuper's narrow hips, a hand on each of his own, turning and pivoting. He made a pistol of his hand and pressed it to Anton's head, pulling the trigger. 'Gone. Just for that we can give Rolf another night of sin; his *particular* sin.'

The three Germans embraced. Stern felt the physical echo of his last embrace with his own family.

'And meanwhile, Anton, you can go back upstairs to your *particular* sin,' said Bertolt. 'Have they sent you a nice boy from the village tonight?'

'Fuck yourself, Bertolt. Is it my fault you have passion only for your ridiculous motor car?' Anton turned away and climbed the ladder to the loft with startling dexterity, like a spider ascending. They heard laughter, the scratch of a record taken from the turntable, the sudden swelling of the gramophone, delivering a great sweep of orchestral sound.

'And that's Anton's real secret,' said Meyer. 'Mahler. The Jew. The rest of us play safe with Beethoven and Wagner.'

Meyer drank wine from the neck of a bottle. 'But we treasure Anton. A member of our rowing team in '38; yes – an Olympian, here, in the woods of Borek. The newsreel ran in all the cinemas whether we wanted it or not. The triumph of German youth over the barbarian hordes of Jews and socialists! Perhaps that was not popular in your street, doctor?'

Several of Meyer's comrades laughed. 'But Anton and his comrades had not read the whole script, you see. The final was on the Langer See, and Hitler came to watch. Our brave lads were leading with one hundred yards to go and then – *whoosh* – the Americans slipped past, even the Italians. So, no golden moment for Anton. No ambassadorial role, touring SS youth meetings with stories of victory. How he will have missed those!'

Bertolt leered.

Meyer dunked his bottle back in the ice bucket and walked away down the corridor, beckoning Stern to follow, until they reached a door, with a frosted window set in the frame, cracked from corner to corner. A large cockroach stood out in silhouette against the glass.

Beyond lay the kitchen; a stone set of sinks, several trestle tables, and a wood-burning range in rusted iron. Two girls sat smoking, regarding a pot of tea, lit by three candles set directly on the wooden tabletop. They both wore smudged make-up. A birdcage hung in a corner on its own gilt stand, within which three songbirds shuffled.

'Where's the car?' asked one of the girls of Meyer. She had a harsh Polish accent to her German. 'It's late,' she added.

'Ask Ernst: he's on top of someone in the parlour, but I think he's finished. It looked like Natalia but it's difficult to tell when Ernst's in the way – they're all fat, Prussians, but he's fat even by their standards. He's got an arse like two pigs at the trough.'

The girls smiled, leaning back in their chairs, examining Stern.

'What's this?' asked the peasant girl. 'A Jew. It smells like a Jew. Nothing personal,' she added. 'We have Jew girls here, of course. But they have to be *very* beautiful, don't they, Rolf?'

Slurring her words, she burped, using the back of her hand to wipe her lips.

Meyer ignored her. 'This is Doctor Stern, Leopold Stern,' he said.

Stern's empty stomach groaned, his nostrils full of the aromas of bread, red meat and a sweet hint of melted butter.

The other girl had a very fine face, like a china cup. She wore only a flimsy silk slip. Her body was very small, petite, but she had long legs, which were elegant, as her knees and ankles did not interrupt the smooth line between her toes and hips. She held her cigarette as if she were in a Berlin café, the smoking tip away from her face. Her eyes were exceptional – multi-coloured, like a Catherine wheel – and slightly out of focus. Stern had glimpsed, as they entered the kitchen, that she had been holding a newspaper close to her face as if she was chronically short-sighted.

'The girls appreciate their lift in the car,' said Meyer to Stern. 'It never fails to drop them by the bridge before dawn so that they can discreetly creep back into their moth-eaten beds.

'Do you think anyone in the village cares?' he asked of the girls. 'Do you think anyone in the village *doesn't* know?'

The peasant girl looked away. 'And we need our money.'

'Bertolt will give you your money. Polish zloty that you can hoard and use to buy bread off the Russians when they arrive. Although I suspect they will want payment in kind.'

Meyer turned to Stern. 'Bertolt is our money man. Bertolt is organised beyond belief. Once he ran his own business designing the dullest of things – roads. Not any road, of course, but our great autobahn. The world's first, knitting together our modern, industrial Reich! He travels still in a fine car; did you see it in the trees, doctor? But the glory days are over for Bertolt, so for now he doles out pay-packets to whores.'

'At least we do an honest day's work,' said the sinuous girl. She spoke German perfectly but in that way that indicates it is not the language of first choice. She held her chin at a certain angle, predetermined by training. Poise, thought Stern, even deportment.

Meyer went down on one knee. 'Forgive me, Natasza; the word whore is an ugly one for so beautiful a girl. And self-deception is so important. Are you still living, then, in a house with servants, a mansion with stables, so that you can contemplate the swans that glide on the lake? Olga here tells me that there were a hundred rooms in this house of yours. And it is not far away – thirty miles, or less? That must be tantalising.

Although I don't expect your family rules the roost now, eh? Pity. Now you share one room with Olga. What a comedown! Is that where you go in your head, Natasza? To the house of the white swans?'

'I didn't mean to say so much,' said Olga, taking her friend's hand.

'Is it all true, Natasza? Is that where you go in your pretty head when Ernst is on top of *you*?'

Meyer, still on his knees, poured himself another glass of wine from a rose-coloured bottle. Natasza's face was completely emotionless.

'Olga does not fill her head with dreams, do you, Olga?' asked Meyer. His voice was still light with humour but his eyes had hardened. 'Instead, she stuffs herself with pilfered Jewish food. That's why she's getting fat. She better watch out. One night the car won't come to pick her up, let alone take her home. She'll be out of a job.'

'You'll have a Red Army bayonet through your heart by then, Rolf.' Olga was proud of this remark and helped herself to a bite of sausage meat. But her neck flushed red.

'Don't let us keep you, Rolf,' said Natasza.

The girls nudged each other and began to giggle, and Olga drew back the kitchen curtain so that they could see outside. There was a light about twenty yards away, across a backyard.

'We enjoy the sounds of passion,' said Olga, and gripped Natasza in a fierce embrace, laughing out loud. 'But not tonight, eh? Tonight we listen for a quite different sound.'

Chapter 24

Meyer opened the kitchen door, drawing back a bolt, and Stern followed him down a path through what had been a vegetable garden. The rows of plants were clear to see in the light that fell from the open upstairs windows. Halfway down the path they met a man: a peasant, with string for a belt, standing to one side with his hands held like a supplicant.

'The patient?' asked Meyer.

'No better, Herr Meyer,' said the Pole.

They'd paused on the path, but before they could take a single further step, they heard a gunshot in the distance, the sound muffled by the trees.

The bunkhouse fell silent, the gramophone needle screeching as it was roughly lifted from the turning vinyl.

The pinewoods were still too, but Stern imagined the front line of trees edging a foot closer.

'Partisans,' explained Meyer. 'They march past. They keep going. I have to admit there is a tacit level of collaboration. We let them pass. They leave us to our pleasures. It will all end one day of course, and there will be blood, and most of it will be ours.'

The music began again at the beginning.

At the bottom of the kitchen garden was an outhouse, built of brick, one-storey only with a door and a single window, and a corrugated iron roof.

Meyer opened the door and stepped quickly inside, holding it just wide enough for Stern to follow.

Inside it was very hot. The window was covered in a wall hanging and there was a drape, which Meyer pulled back to cover the door. A low light showed a single bed in which a woman lay sprawled on top of the blankets. She was heavily pregnant, and the nightdress she wore, unbuttoned, revealed her belly, the navel standing out like a crab apple. Stern thought she'd been beautiful once, maybe just a few hours before this moment. Now her face was distorted with pain, her eyes focused beyond the room, beyond, even, the forest.

Then she said one word – *daktoyrim?* The inflexion indicated a question, the language plainly Yiddish.

Her face streamed with sweat. The whites of her eyes were bloodshot; the right one badly enough to impair her vision because she was looking at Stern with her head held awkwardly to the left. Her ankles were swollen, by so much in fact that at first Stern thought she wore pale, bunched, night socks.

Meyer went over to the bed and knelt down. He put his hand on her forehead and then let it run back into her hair. There was something perfunctory about the movement, nothing tender, as if he were checking the condition of a cow in the barn.

'Yes,' he said. 'I promised. A Jewish doctor.'

'Something is wrong,' she said, her eyes looking wildly around the room. 'Have I told you this?'

'Many times.' Meyer stood. 'This is Freida Klumbacher, doctor. She says she's dying. But then she talks nonsense, constantly. It's my child. I want you to save their lives. The SS court will sit for two days, perhaps three. Each night I will bring you here. It is safe – besides, the visitors are distracted by the hunt for Eigrupper's gold. When the verdict is given you will go back to the slave camp and the Himmelstrasse. I will save the life of your elder daughter. I promise this on the life of my unborn child, although such a promise is worth nothing to you. In truth you have little choice. At least this way there is a chance.'

He put his hand on Freida's belly, but she pushed it away.

From under the bed Meyer pulled out a drawer and from it took a suitcase. Stern read his own name and address on it before realising it was the one he'd been forced to leave behind in the square.

'You'll need this,' said Meyer.

Chapter 25

While Freida slept, Stern sent Meyer back to the house to prepare sweet tea, while he took the opportunity to examine the room, throwing open the window to allow a breeze to enter. The bunkhouse lights stood out in the night; a man now sat on the window ledge of the upstairs windows, naked, a white thigh like a bolster. He turned back to say something to someone unseen, and there was a woman's laugh, light, but badly slurred.

Above Freida's bed, tacked to the wall, was a single black-and-white photograph of two children, both girls. One was perhaps ten or eleven, while the older girl, whose face was the ancestor of Freida's, was fourteen or fifteen. The girls stood in the yard of a building, a tenement block, and above them stretched several lines of white linen shirts and sheets. A wind was blowing and Stern could almost hear that heavy, damp *thwack!* of the sheets cracking on the line.

Freida had the wide-set eyes of the Slav, with matching cheek-bones that stretched her skin. Such faces are often marred by the inevitable wide nose, thick at the bridge, but Freida's was short, narrow, and turned up slightly at the end. This accentuated the extraordinary width of the face. Such faces are only millimetres away from being ugly. If the eyes had been a hair's breadth further apart, if the nose snubbed by a few more degrees, she'd have looked like a malevolent creature out of a woodland tale.

With a shock Stern saw her eyes were open and she was watching him. For a second he thought she was dead. Time stood on crutches; then she blinked, with just the left eye, the one clear of blood.

'Can you save the child?' she asked. As she spoke the small muscles in her face twitched on the left side. Her hand sought out the tremor and massaged the skin.

'If I can save you, yes.'

'Rolf loves the child. It's all he lives for.'

And then: 'Are you a doctor?'

'Yes.' She'd been told this already and he noted the confusion, the possibility that her memory was disturbed.

Klumbacher sat up quickly, automatically, and vomited into a porcelain bowl, falling back as if she'd done it a hundred times.

Stern was supporting her head when she spoke to him again. 'Rolf wants a boy. He says he wants a boy, but he tells lies and I think that's one of them. He wants a girl. I can feel it. But the Germans love their Fatherland. We Poles love our Motherland. Rolf is a surprising man; he hides everything he feels. Or feels nothing; it's impossible to tell.'

She closed her eyes. The intermittent periods of lucidity and hallucination were striking.

Meyer returned with a samovar and bread with jam, and hot water in a bowl, and a piece of torn, clean, linen.

'What's wrong with her?' he asked, before he'd even set the tea down. 'Will she live?'

Stern cleaned his hands. 'Leave the door ajar; there's nothing lethal in the air of the night.'

'Will she live?' repeated Meyer, taking a seat on the window ledge.

'She's confused,' said Stern, patiently. 'Her brain is poisoned by something in her blood. Her ankles are swollen, badly inflamed in fact, and her facial muscles betray a minor *invasion*. Does she ever suffer rigidity …?'

Stern held out his arms, straight, and tense.

'Yes. The right arm, and once her legs.'

Stern sat too. 'The baby is very small. This could mean that the placenta is poorly developed. And the child's heartbeat is irregular, which is a token of stress.'

'I don't have time for riddles,' Meyer said, an edge to his voice. 'What does all this *mean*?'

'We have evidence of invasion, and contraction. The next stage, if we do not act, may be convulsion. If this happens she is in danger of falling into a coma. The symptoms indicate that she is suffering from pressure in the blood. This is very dangerous. There is a treatment, recently published in the medical journals. It requires that I administer magnesium sulphate.'

'You have this?'

'Yes. In the Prussian blue phial in the bag you saved from the fires. At home I used it to alleviate rheumatism.'

Stern began to unpack his medical bag. 'There must be many doctors in the camp. Why did you need me?'

'The kapos control the Jewish doctors like this.' Meyer held his hand in a fist. 'There are three: I have no power over them. There is a doctor within the German compound – an SS officer – and, coincidentally, a butcher by any other name. He is sober for twenty minutes each day after breakfast, often less. He hides in the sickbay and treats trench-foot, and fever, while you all shuffle past his window to the Himmelstrasse. He's dying of irony, doctor. Very, very, slowly.

'The three Jewish doctors are better, certainly. But if I go to the kapos, cap in hand, they would know my secret: that I have taken a Jewish woman, and I have given her a child, and that this child will be born. What kind of life would I have then? The kapos would inform my superiors – or worse, my subordinates.

'So, going to one of the Jewish doctors in the slaves' compound was a risk I did not wish to take, but I was close to taking it today, before I was brought your suitcase.'

They fell into a silence and the chattering of wildlife in the woods swelled to fill the void.

'And this is why your comrade had to die?'

Meyer stood, brushing dust from his trousers: 'I admit it was not difficult to kill Jonas Keuper, although it was not a premeditated act in any way. I took my chance, doctor. He was not, you see, one of us. Not for him the house in the woods. We survive here in Borek. He *thrived*.'

Freida let out a short, high-pitched cry.

'I must prepare the infusion,' said Stern, standing.

Meyer looked at his watch.

'The child will not come tonight,' said Stern. 'But Freida's labour is close. The child must be born, even into this world.'

Chapter 26

Stern watched the first sunlight touch the bars of the cell window. The hours before dawn had been punctuated by gunshots in the woods, and a plane had flown over and dropped a flare, prompting the siren to wail. Duvos, awake at his window, had described the frantic patrols of guards along the wire, the sweeping lantern beams of the search-lights, the straining dogs on leads.

Now, at last, there was silence, broken finally by Irena, whispering: 'Leo. Day is here. Where did you go last night? Are you hurt?'

His wife's voice floated over the partition.

'How are the girls?'

'They're asleep, Leo,' she said, impatient for an answer.

'I have a present for Hanna,' said Stern. Brunner had led him back from the wire to the water tower and had seemed keen to be friends. 'The guard gave me the chess piece she wanted, the knight. He says he can make one in a few minutes because he has good hands. He tried to be kind. I wonder why.'

'Leo ...'

'Irena, listen. Meyer, the German who shot Jonas Keuper, says he will save Judi's life. He promises that he will do this if I can help him. He needs a doctor. I've agreed to help.'

'How?'

'Just know this, Irena. I can do no more. Brunner will be here in a moment.' Stern could hear the wood burning in the guard's stove and the rattle of a coffee mug. In truth he was reluctant to outline the deal he'd struck, and the implications for Judi.

'But how will this save *Hanna*?' whispered Irena. She knew she was being cruel but could not stop herself.

Stern's eyes filled with tears and he could not speak.

Irena relented. 'The German agreed to save Judi. God bless you, Leo.'

On their way back through the forest, Stern and Meyer had paused in the clearing of tree stumps to devour food they'd taken from the bunkhouse kitchen. The German explained that he often ate at this spot in the woods because he'd discovered that his meal tasted better outside, and that this was a truth often overlooked by Prussians, born and raised in the mist and damp of the northern plain.

Meyer had sat on one of the tree stumps eating pickled fish from a can and drinking wine. Watching, Stern had felt there was something of the condemned man's last meal about the way he savoured the food and drink; as if he suspected the court's decision, when it finally came, might lead to a firing squad.

Stern forced himself to ask the question that troubled him: 'If I help Freida, and the child, will my daughter come here, to the bunkhouse? She is only fifteen. Will she be a whore with the others?'

Saying the words out loud made him feel physically sick.

Meyer filled his lungs with the scent of the woods, tilting his head towards Stern, although his eyes were constantly examining the shadows between the trees.

'Yes. It is safer than the camp.'

'She's a child.'

'Did you have a childhood, doctor? Where …?'

Stern didn't answer.

'Well?' There was a note of genuine anger in Meyer's voice, and with a flick of the wrist he threw an empty tin of smoked oysters into the leaf litter on the ground.

'I was born in Berlin,' said Stern. 'My father was a cobbler in Scheunenviertel. Outside the old walls, but still ... We played in the streets around the cemetery. Yes, a big family. Four brothers, two sisters, aunts and uncles ...'

'And because you and I had childhoods you think that this is the natural order of things?' said Meyer.

'She's so young,' said Stern, laying the fact down like a trump card. 'In our village the boys were all younger than her or gone to the war. She knows nothing of men.'

'Then she's an innocent,' said Meyer. 'And that is not a good thing to be, especially at her age.'

Meyer drank savagely from the bottle, then tossed it aside.

'Before the camps we killed Jews with our pistols,' he said.

He took the gun out of his holster and turned it slightly to catch the light.

'Thousands died in one day, under the blue sky, beside a cool pit. We did this many times. We only stopped when the pistols were too hot to hold, or the chambers jammed.'

He shook his head. 'I stopped once, when it was not allowed. A girl was before me, like your daughter no doubt, an innocent. She had brown eyes, and missing teeth. Of all those killed ...'

Meyer's throat made a strange sound: 'Of all those I killed it is her face I have carried to this moment. I hesitated. My comrades watched. Keuper watched, *his* revolver glowed, doctor. It was a torch.

'It was unthinkable that I should not do my duty, as they did their duty. And so the girl fell into the pit.'

He stood, straightening his uniform.

'Now you wish me to consider the innocence of this daughter of yours, just fifteen, who must confront the horrors of the whorehouse in the woods. She will have to grow up, doctor.

This will take one night. And that surely is the luxury you seek for her; that she will have the time in which to become old. Forget the single night, think of the days, the months, the years that may follow.'

Meyer raised the lantern. 'There are no childhoods left in the world.'

Chapter 27

Hanna was fifteen minutes early – knowing Peter was always late – and his usual table, on the kerb of the Ku-Damm, was free. She took a chair, arranging herself carefully, knowing this would be how he saw her when he came ambling out of the hazy city fumes. The pavement outside The Nut Tree was dappled by the linden trees, the wide boulevard stretching away down into the blue distance, past the ruined bell tower of the old cathedral, and beyond to the Tiergarten, where a gold-winged angel stood on a stone needle, just showing above the treetops. The summer heat was like a deadweight, making the cityscape buckle and weave in a constant mirage, so that when the waiter asked, she ordered a jug of iced water, and lit a cigarette, feeling sweat start out on her forehead. She wore a light print dress – one of Vanessa's designs – so the slight breeze cooled her skin.

Out of guilt for her husband's lies, Lydia had paid for the flight, a return from Croydon to Tempelhof. Since Hanna's last visit, they'd been left trailing Rachel Perel, their witness to the final days at Borek. The address they'd uncovered in the BDC files had proved hopelessly out of date. Only one couple in the block recalled her – according to Major Clarke's account – and they reported that she had married a man, possibly called Hans, and moved west, towards the heart of the old city, and that she'd run a small hairdressing business. The East Berlin authorities had promised to track her down, but no news had come to Swan House for more than five months.

Peter's telephone calls had become less frequent, undermined by the sense that they were building separate lives. Then, five days ago, his latest letter arrived in the Fens.

She'd read the key passage out to Lydia.

I've got good news. They found our lost witness – Rachel Perel. Clarke wouldn't divulge the exact details but apparently she still cuts hair for a business, so that's how they tracked her down. She's called Rachel Vogel now – her husband owns a cinema near the Frankfurter Tor, beyond Alexanderplatz. I've included a map – the red cross marks the spot. Clarke says the East Germans went round and asked if I could come and see her to talk about the camp. Report back said she'd refused point-blank. Clarke says he called in a few favours and the police basically told her she has to talk – but there's a catch. It's got to be you she talks to; you're a survivor of the camp, and British, which helps. Clarke says they can't be seen to bend the rules for Yanks, although I can go along. She must know what happened to you – to the family. Everyone's jumpy here; the Ivans are gearing up to introduce visas, strangle the checkpoints. So time is short – can you come Han? If you need money let me know.

Hanna sipped her ice water and kept an eye on the distant street corner. She felt light-headed, her joints ached, but her sense of smell was getting sharper by the day. The thought of seeing Peter, and what she'd have to say, made her heart beat faster, and so to distract herself she unpacked the aromas around her: coffee beans, custard tarts and sugar-coated nuts, and somewhere close by, apples – schnapps perhaps, or a pastry. Even the trees smelt of luxury, the scent of almonds pungent when the two-toned silver-green leaves shimmered overhead.

And then there he was, fifty yards away, walking in the road to avoid the crowds at the pavement cafés, wide shoulders tapering past non-existent hips to the leather-booted feet, which always seemed to be treading a narrow line. She felt joy then, the familiar giddiness of reunion.

'Han!' he called out, the smile blinding even at a distance.

She made herself stay in her seat, but held out her hands, so that he had to lean in and kiss her neck.

He took a seat, edging it closer. 'I'd have met you at the airport for Christ's sake.'

And then a waiter was there and he was ordering a beer, a wine for her, more iced water.

'You look …' He struggled for the right words. 'Different – I like the hair.'

Vanessa had insisted on a visit to a salon in Chelsea to raise her spirits. Her friend had always complained that she hid behind the chaotic hair, fussing with the clips. She'd emerged with a stylish bob that revealed her neck.

'And your eyes look different,' said Peter. 'And your skin. I guess the Fen light suits you, right? Luminous – that's the word.'

Han nodded, the moment overwhelming her.

'There's a reason for that,' she said.

She hoped he'd work it out, so she gave him a few tumbling seconds, but his face – slightly older now that she saw it in the shade – was absolutely immobile. Her eyes caught such details these days, a kind of hyper-reality. His black hair was still thick but there was a thread of grey at the right temple, which suggested ageing would suit him.

'I'm pregnant. It's due next month – six weeks away.' She hadn't stood up, but – in Lydia's view – she didn't really *show*, which meant it was a boy according to Polish folklore. And Vanessa's recommended wardrobe was loose and free.

Peter went to speak but she held up her hand.

'Listen to me, Pete. This is important.'

She was crying, but it didn't interrupt her breathing, so she just carried on.

'We made a mistake. I don't want a child – you know that, you've always known that, right from the start. Not now, maybe never. When I came to see you in the winter I'd decided on an abortion. There was a clinic off Harley Street. I had the money – Marcin's money. It was my decision. 'Nessa came with me in the cab. But then we sat on a park bench and fed ducks. We talked. I talked, about my family. About finding them. About the letter. It changed things – I don't know why.

'I want the child to have a life, Pete, but I don't want to share it. So, we made a different plan.'

'You and 'Nessa,' said Pete.

'Yes. This isn't easy, so please don't make it impossible.'

He leaned back in his seat, the beer bottle held to his chest.

'I want the child to be adopted. The child *will be* adopted. There's an agency – 'Nessa found it. There's a private hospital – it sounds grand but it isn't. The parents will take it away. They have to prove they have means. I don't know what life will be like after that. But this is the future I want, Pete. I'm sorry.'

'What about us?' he said. It was the question that stopped her crying because she'd rehearsed the answer.

'I don't know, Pete. I'm telling the truth. I don't know about us. I can't ask you to wait, but I don't want you to go. It's unfair, I know. When we said goodbye – outside the National – it wasn't just about family.'

She took a gulp of the wine and felt better.

'All I can see ahead is the hospital. I went, with 'Nessa. There's a garden with hollyhocks, and a ward with screens, and I keep thinking about this door – the one I came in through – but I'll walk out one day and then the rest of my life begins. That has to be enough, Pete. I'm sorry.'

The tears began again, but they were for him, because she knew she'd changed his life with a few sentences.

She pressed on quickly. 'If you give me Vogel's address I can go alone. You don't have to do this for me. Any of it. I'm here because finding my family is another thing I have to do. There it is.'

Peter's eyes narrowed into the blue distance of the Tiergarten. 'But you weren't *going* to tell me.'

'No. I knew what you'd say. And it would have been cruel to let you see that – a future that wasn't to be. You'd have tried to make me change my mind. And you're good at that, so it was a risk I didn't want to take.'

For a minute he pretended to read the menu card and sipped his beer. The sounds of the city crowded back in; the constant car horns, the threads of jazz, a radio blaring a sports' commentary. Hanna listened to her body, the blood rushing in her ears, and as she straightened her back she felt the baby turning inside her.

Peter took out an empty packet of Lucky Strike. 'I need a refill.'

There was a kiosk on the other side of the road, and he jogged across, avoiding the creeping traffic. Hanna thought that he'd either walk away now and maybe she'd never see him again, or he'd come back, and be reasonable, and calm, and hope that the unseen future held something for them both.

He came back, sat down, and they ordered food. Hanna asked for bread too, because when the morning sickness disappeared in the third month it had been replaced by an almost constant hunger.

'It's OK, Han. Let's go see Vogel. See where that takes us.'

Hanna recognised this for what it was: the declaration of a ceasefire, but little else. She was grateful nonetheless, because articulating her feelings, laying them out for others, was a particular torture for her, and he'd cut it short.

He started to tell her about art in the Neue West, the clubs and the bars, the way the *Ossies* came over from the East to gawp at shop windows, marked out by their drab clothes and worker's boots.

For half an hour they went on chatting, eating their food, letting the city wash over them.

'When we go over, you'll see. It's time-travel for real – just backwards not forwards,' he said, eating quickly. Hanna thought that this was how it would be for a while. He'd radiate a mood of almost manic enthusiasm; everything would be in a rush, so that there was no time to consider the unavoidable reality of the child.

The first sign that something was about to happen was the sound of a glass smashing further down the street, then several dogs – which Hanna hadn't seen – began to bark under tables. She could see concentric circles on the surface of the water jug, radiating, the frequency rising, and then the distant rumble of approaching aircraft suddenly loud. A woman screamed with excitement, and a few men with cameras stepped out under the awnings to scan the sky.

'Hold on to your glass!' said Peter.

People all around them started counting out loud as if watching a rocket launch from Cape Canaveral. *Zehn, neun, acht, sieben …*

The visceral rumble made the bones in Hanna's ear vibrate, and then came the *boom!*, and a series of echoes, and the tinkling of cutlery, and then the smashing of more glasses on the hot pavement. The plates on the table buzzed, and all the windows in a car parked on the far side of the road disintegrated, as if a bomb had gone off inside.

The baby flexed a limb inside her and she clutched herself.

'Welcome to Berlin,' said Peter. 'You OK?'

'What happened?' she said, drinking more water.

'It's the Soviets rattling sabres,' he said. 'They fly fast at the border from an angle and then pull away as they break the sound barrier. It's a neat trick. It's designed to frighten the capitalists, but it only makes them drink more.'

The high contrail of the fighter began to emerge in the evening sky. Peter got out his lighter and lit a candle on the table, then a fresh cigarette. A big Ford Mustang in lipstick-red cruised by and heads turned. Live music began to leak out of the basement clubs.

Peter drew on his cigarette and leaned across the table. Hanna could smell his aftershave, and the turpentine from the studio. She studied his face, noting how it was increasingly defined by the fine bones beneath.

She realised then that in some ways Berlin was a trap, but it was too late now.

'When do we see Vogel?' she asked. The thought of talking to the witness brought Hanna one step closer to touching those she had lost. Since Peter's letter had arrived at Swan House she'd imagined the conversation many times, and where it might lead.

'Tomorrow. It's all been cleared and I've got the papers.'

He put a small, passport-sized picture on the table.

'That's her,' he said.

She'd been beautiful once, with a narrow face and dark eyes, but most of all the black shining hair. But the eyes told her story: the traumatised stare of the survivor. What disturbed Hanna, though, was the grainy black-and-white picture itself, which had clearly been taken from a distance, and caught Vogel in slightly blurred profile.

Peter held it closer to the candle so she could see it clearly in the evening light.

'Be careful,' said Hanna, staying his hand. 'Where did you get this, Pete?'

Peter's hand went to his throat. 'Clarke, Pierce, everyone's really keen to help.'

'But why, Pete? Why help us – help me? What's in it for them?'

He held out his hands, palms up. 'I guess their orders are to keep me sweet,' he said. 'But you're right, there's something else, something they're not telling me. I don't think it's the Stern family they're interested in. I think it's the camp. Clarke told me straight – we get anything on Borek, on the last days, he gets to know first.

'And he's in a hurry. The city's on the brink – there's hundreds pouring through the checkpoints each morning and not going back. They're losing doctors, engineers, bright kids who want an education. The latest rumour is that the Soviets are moving tanks west.

'So we go tomorrow before it gets worse.'

Peter lit a fresh cigarette and pulled his face quickly away from the cloud of sulphur.

Hanna felt she was being pushed, even manipulated. There was something about Peter's determination to help her that seemed desperate, headlong, and he was clearly too close to Clarke and Pierce, and the malign influence of the Berlin mafia.

'And there's this,' said Peter. 'I'm not sure this is good news. But it's certainly news.'

He produced the anonymous letter that Hanna had brought to Berlin in the winter, with the envelope that had contained *der Springer*.

'Clarke had the CIA pointy-heads crawl all over it. Look.'

He held it up to the flame of the candle.

There was a faint indentation in the shape of a circle.

'Clarke says it's a stamp mark. Someone's used an official punch on a page and the mark has gone through to the one underneath.'

He held the paper even closer to the flame. 'See? See the letters? They put it under a microscope – some gadget anyway – and apparently it says: *Schild und Schwert der Partei*. Shield and sword for party: the motto of the *Staatssicherheitsdienst* – the Stasi to you and me.'

Peter's eyes caught the candlelight, and Hanna was unsure if their brightness was due to excitement or fear. 'So it made Clarke wonder, why would someone in the East German secret police send you a handmade wooden chess piece?'

Chapter 28

Peter had cast himself firmly in the role of tour guide, with a map, a new camera, and a pair of Aviator sunglasses. Hanna was hot, and the journey, on a crowded U-Bahn train, was sweaty and sullen. The weight of the child made her knees swell. But the border crossing was hardly dramatic, they simply arrived at the Alexanderplatz, and emerged blinking into the Soviet Sector. The carriage had been half lit by a sickly orange glow that flickered with the motion of the train; but at pavement level there was too much light, so that the streetscape looked like an over-exposed photograph. The West was no postcard once you left the buzz of the Ku'Damm, but it was Paris by comparison with its poor Eastern counterpart.

A half-mile from the ruined grandeur of the old city the crowds began to thin, but the buildings appeared to swell, promenades of Soviet precision leading the eye out to vanishing point.

Peter's disdain for the Soviet zone was clear: the 'sights', as such, were either uniformly bleak – the still-ruined relics of the lost Reich – or they comprised the newly built monuments of the post-war era. These combined 'egomania and servitude', a phrase Peter had clearly practised, and provided a distinct echo of the Nazi super-city they were supposed to succeed. For an artist of the West, and that is how Peter now clearly saw himself, the city was a freak-show of the ugly.

Hanna liked it. The streets had been designed on a different scale to the people. There was a lot of room, which held her innate claustrophobia at bay. The Fen girl was never at ease in the city. After half an hour walking in the humid sun she turned back and was shocked to see the distant outline of the Brandenburg Gate. Odd, she thought, to see it from its reverse side, as if she'd entered a mirror-world. History – and possibly *her* history – lay in this unfolding series of images. It might be brutal, but it looked like the past.

The wind caught her dress, and Peter struggled to unfold the map.

It was Hanna's second day in Berlin, and their relationship had been re-established, within the clear boundaries set during her winter visit. She slept in the bedroom on the fifth floor, Peter in the attic studio above. Nonetheless, they'd drunk a lot of wine after the food at The Nut Tree and collapsed on a threadbare sofa in Peter's studio where they'd held each other in a cool embrace, and their arguments had been repeated, as she knew they would. She said she'd fly back to England in two weeks. Peter suggested he could be with her for the birth, but Hanna had said she'd rather be alone, and that after it was over she'd recover at Vanessa's flat in Kensington. Peter had gone to the kitchen to make coffee, smoking as he watched the stove-top pot boil. No more words were said. In the night she'd lain awake, but the attic above was silent, and there was no sign of the usual nightmares.

By breakfast time, back at the café, he'd regained his ebullient mood, and was eager to show her the city.

He stood now looking ahead, the open map flapping in the warm breeze.

'That way,' he said, at last.

Their destination was the side-street cinema – a *'Kino'* – the home of Rachel Vogel, née Perel, survivor of Borek.

The city here was flat, the streets so wide that pedestrians rarely ventured across; hardly streets at all as much as runways, waiting for aircraft to lumber into view. There was so much space – bombsites, scraps of park, fields of rubble – and the roads themselves, what were they *for*? Occasional cars trundled past, but for minutes the tarmac lay untouched, as if red ribbons, beyond sight, had yet to be cut, releasing lines of patient drivers. Obedient crowds in shapeless coats crossed at distant lights, streaming this way and that, then bleeding away down side-streets, which led, inevitably, to acres of forgotten rubble.

They were on a boulevard called Stalin Allee, which ran in the far distance to a pair of circular modern towers. The crowds dwindled to groups of pedestrians, making their way across pavements wide and empty. Peter said so many *Ossies* had simply walked out of the Soviet Sector and not come home that some suburbs were deserted. East Berlin was the city of the left behind.

At Frankfurter Tor, the old city gate now marked by the twin Soviet towers, they stopped. Peter bought a fresh packet of cigarettes – f6, East Berlin's finest, branded to inaugurate the new decade. The drift of smoke on the air was acrid as they stood in the shade of the kiosk.

'Christ,' he said, flicking ash into the gutter, examining the cigarette. 'These are all the rage. They're made of horse dung and tram tickets. They're worse than the coffee, and that's saying a lot.'

He took a lungful of air. 'Right,' he said, 'the *Prinzessa*'s over there …' He pointed across the four-lane highway.

A sudden bank of clouds slid before the sun, dark shadows running in geometric shapes over the acres of concrete. Dots in the distance were ambling cars, ant-like. A light tank had emerged from a side-street a mile to the east, its turret cranking round to look back at the city. A policeman stood on a pedestal at the junction in an immaculate uniform, his buttons catching the light, the semaphore of the white gloves delivered with military precision. A platoon of pedestrians waited for permission to cross.

Peter ditched the f6. 'Let's dodge traffic,' he said, grabbing Hanna's hand. She'd been grateful that since he'd seen her pregnant, walking slightly stiffly to his flat from The Nut Tree, he'd treated her as if the baby didn't exist. Such outbursts of energy were typical, and often thrilling. But she felt running was a bad idea, so Peter pretended to tow her across, helping her climb over the low barrier on the central reservation. The distant policeman, hands at a quarter past noon, watched them with a basilisk gaze.

Hanna, laughing, felt the baby move; not the random sudden flexing of a limb, but a slow fluid turn.

The right-hand side of Kreutzigerstrasse was complete, the left broken by a bombsite, pitted with stagnant pools. Peter took Hanna to a doorway where they could just see the cinema. It rose up narrow and ornate, an attempt to mimic one of the city's teetering opera houses, although the fussy neo-Baroque scrollwork, once white, now bore the scars of shrapnel and bullets. Like all the city's old cinemas, the auditorium within would be long and narrow, the screen a diminishing rectangle of light. Peter, always with an eye to spatial form, said that some had a screen halfway along, so that part of the audience faced backwards and watched the film as if in reverse, which reminded Hanna of the mirror-world of the Brandenburg Gate.

A banner on the façade of the cinema read: *Kriegsgericht*. A frieze of artwork depicted a courtroom, a uniformed officer leading an animated cross-examination during a court martial.

There was no foyer, just a ticket office, and set to one side, a cloakroom. A spiral staircase led up to a mezzanine landing. The ticket booth was closed, a card propped up in the window, next to a coffee cup, read in German:

Hauptmerkmal zeigt

Hanna rang a bell and they waited. She was suddenly anxious, convinced that Vogel would refuse to see them after all, but Peter now had lost some of his nervous energy, and was studiously examining a set of framed certificates issued by the Institute of Cinematography to Hans Karl Vogel: the series, starting in 1936, was repeated in 1939, 1947 and 1957. The signature was overlaid with an official stamp in the form of a fine German eagle.

Hanna rang the bell again.

The soundtrack of *Kriegsgericht* was waxing, the action enhanced by an orchestral score.

'Wait there,' said Hanna, touching Peter's arm.

She began to climb a spiral staircase, but halfway up had to stop to let a moment of dizziness pass. It felt to her, since her arrival in Berlin, that she had been falling towards the lost past, and that if she didn't hold on to something, she'd come to earth at Borek, in the camp itself. The proximity of the truth, or at least a version of the truth, was real for the first time. Sympathetic pains ran through her arms and legs as she imagined the thudding fall that would finally deliver her into the dust, from where she would look up to see a line of prisoners, perhaps, shuffling towards the gas chamber.

At the top of the stairs there was a landing and a door, within which was set a circular porthole window. Stencilled on the glass was a sign: *PRIVAT.* Beyond she could see the projector, its beam cutting through the smoke-filled auditorium, before lighting up the distant screen. The film itself was mirrored on the metallic surfaces of the equipment.

The projectionist, a fleshy man with grey, thin hair, was perched in a seat that seemed to make him part of the machinery, as if he'd been slotted into place many years earlier and had since grown to fill the niche allotted. Two small miniature images of the film played out on his round, wire-framed spectacles. Cigarette smoke leaked from a butt held in his left hand, as if his fingers were alight. He licked his lips, making a minute adjustment to the focus by leaning forward a few inches and rolling thumb and forefinger around a burnished metal knob. Then he subsided back into his chair, seemingly exhausted.

Hanna thought the scene could be captured in a picture; a pencil study perhaps, of the machine itself, with the man insinuated, almost hidden, among the cogs and levers. Some element of this scene seemed important, but elusive, and she felt the need to record it, even if only in memory.

'Hanna!' Peter's voice came from below, but a woman was already on the stairs.

'This is private,' she said, in German. 'The sign,' she added, pointing. Her manner was firm.

'My apologies,' said Hanna. Her tutors at Swan House had given her a grounding in German, but she lacked Peter's fluency and subtle ear.

They were led into a back room where a counter gave a view of the cloakroom. There was a sink and a mirror, and a large chair of the kind used by barbers, and a shelf with cosmetics and hairspray. The windows were all open, so that they could hear the trams on Stalin Allee clanking over points. The cloakroom was almost empty in the summer heat, except for a few umbrellas, but still reeked of damp wool and cigarettes. A shelf held children's books, read to destruction, the spines splintered.

Peter presented his passport, a letter of introduction, and other documents.

Vogel did not read them. 'I've been informed of your visit by the authorities. Ask your questions,' she said.

It was clear that the interview was being granted under duress.

Vogel stood by the counter, one elbow held by one hand, a cigarette in the other.

According to the documentation she was thirty-six years of age. *Thirty-six?* Hanna thought this was difficult to credit.

Her face was etched with deep lines, and her movements were oddly stiff. And the eyes seemed focused beyond the walls that surrounded her. Only the hair projected youth, a glossy jet-black, so dark that the individual hairs were lost in a light-less stream. Hanna thought she was frightened, and that this might be a constant state.

'I made it clear,' she said. 'I can't really help.'

There was no doubting the musical, youthful tone of her voice. This was what unsettled; the juxtaposition of old and young in the single, compressed body. Time was out of joint for this woman, an impression enhanced by the surreal rumblings of the film in the auditorium.

'Please,' said Peter. 'Can't we sit …?'

Hanna was standing now as she often did: one hand on her slight bump, the other at her back.

Vogel fetched a seat.

'I know,' she said, with a small smile. 'This time is the worse. You can't wait for it to be over.'

Hanna thanked her for the kindness of the seat, although for the first time she admitted to herself that she did not *want* it to be over, she wanted time to stop still, she wanted the freedom to be herself.

'You gave evidence to the tribunal,' said Peter.

'Yes.'

'We'll be brief,' he said.

'Please. There are three intervals and I have to sell ciga-rettes.'

Peter took out the packet of f6 and lit up, expertly leaving the silence for his witness to fill.

'What can I say?' said Vogel, accepting a light. 'If you've read the files you know as much as I do, possibly more. I try to forget, and the years help.'

The night before, lying awake in his bed, he'd read the Stasi file on Rachel Vogel passed on by Clarke. It was brief but brutal. She had registered for a passport in 1948. Her affidavit to the court stated that she had been found hiding under a barrack hut at Borek by the Red Army. She had been repeatedly raped, and made to travel west with the Soviet forces, before eventually being released on the outskirts of Berlin. She took refuge in a cellar where she met her future husband, Hans Vogel, a German soldier, and a remnant of the city's defence force. Her affidavit had been overlaid with a circular stamp that read: NOT PROVEN. This was not unusual, Peter had seen it many times, and it did not imply the authorities thought she was lying, but it did make it clear that, but for her husband, her story had not been corroborated. The Stasi seemed satisfied, although they had maintained a watching brief.

Hanna opened her leather travelling bag and retrieved the photographic copy of the manifest for Transport 573.

'This is a list of all those on a particular train to Borek who were murdered: processed – you know this word?'

Vogel nodded.

'My name is on this list, Frau Vogel. How can this be? I am listed with the dead. This was a few days before the Germans fled.'

Hanna wanted to reach out and touch Vogel's hand, not to make physical contact with their witness, but with the past.

Outside they heard the clanging bell of a tram.

Vogel shrugged. 'Perhaps there was a bureaucratic error. The Germans made many but admitted to none. Your family gave your name. But perhaps you were not there. Do you remember?'

Hanna shook her head. 'Someone won't let me forget,' she said, recovering control. She produced the chess piece from her bag. 'I was sent this. A note said it was a gift from my father and that he was alive.'

Vogel looked at *der Springer*, and then at Hanna. 'I cannot help,' she said.

Peter produced a folded file from his jacket pocket. 'Your taped testimony mentioned an incident when a group of Jews were taken away by the Gestapo for questioning. This was a few days before the revolt, before the end.'

'A short-lived reprieve,' said Vogel, eyeing the file. 'They were accused of sabotage – of working with the Polish resistance, which was in the woods. One officer was so incensed he wanted to kill them there and then, on the steps of the gas chamber. A brother officer had to shoot him dead because the Gestapo demanded that these prisoners must face questions. It was the first sign order was breaking down. In a few days the Germans had fled.

'This is all I remember. But there was a family – with two girls I think. One a child – perhaps five or six years of age? So, perhaps …' She drew deeply on her cigarette, but looked at Peter only, and Hanna wondered then if she was telling them the whole truth. Her fear was palpable. It was as if she was not skin and bones at all, but china or glass, so that she might shatter at any second.

The pipes, connected to the sink in front of the barber's chair, gurgled, spitting brackish water out into the bowl. Vogel moved too swiftly, with clear relief, wiping the porcelain clean. When she turned back, having tightened the taps, her face had lost its stricken look.

'Why do you say it was just a short reprieve?' asked Peter. 'What happened to them?'

'They were taken back to the square where the hair was cut, but then – later – to the German compound – a camp within the camp. When the revolt began, all the Jews there were shot – we heard this – and none survived. Everyone who escaped came from the slaves' camp, not the compound.'

Hanna's shoulders fell, and Peter took her hand.

'I am sorry,' said Vogel. 'You should know the truth, however bad.'

'But how did *you* survive?' asked Hanna. She felt desperate, aware that, after all, she might be the sole survivor of her family, and aware that the question sounded like an accusation.

Vogel's dark eyes hardened. 'When the appointed day arrived, and the slaves broke down the outer fence, we were left behind, in our own compound beyond the gas chamber.

'We heard the sound of it, the machine-gun fire, the bells ringing at the station – that was the signal, that the fence was down and that the way was clear. By dusk it was quiet.

'And then the officers came. I heard one of them shout out that it was like a chicken shoot. They roamed the compound, hunting, and killing.

'They said there should be no witnesses. I found Karol, my friend, and she was covered in blood, so I dipped my hand in it and smeared my neck, at the back, and lay down.

'A soldier stood by me and I heard a match strike. Then he walked away, talking to his comrades, saying they'd be back to make sure no one had survived.

'I crawled away to a woodpile. After an hour I went to Hackendorf's hut and found bandages and ointment and some money, for he took his cut when the gold was sold. I was afraid they would be back. I hid.

'At dawn the Red Army came. A new hell to replace the old.'

Vogel drew on her cigarette and said no more. All they could hear was the soundtrack of the film.

'So how did *I* survive?' asked Hanna, almost to herself.

Vogel shrugged. 'As I say – a bureaucratic error. Or perhaps you left *before* the end, with the Germans and the gold.'

'What *gold*?' asked Peter.

'The interval is coming,' said Vogel, shaking her head.

'Please,' said Hanna, struggling to her feet. 'One minute more. You have been so helpful. Please – a minute more.' The idea that now, at the last, they would be denied the truth, was intolerable.

Vogel was already standing. 'The Germans took our gold – from the luggage, from our hands and ears and wrists – even from our teeth. This was sent back to Berlin in lorries. But the commandant – Eigrupper – was suspected of hiding away a secret share in the camp. So the SS arrived, a few days before the revolt, to search for it.

'They were desperate because the Russians were coming, and the Poles too, in the woods. It was said that Himmler wanted the gold at all costs. They found it the day before the uprising. They feared an ambush on the road, so they left at night in a convoy. The Gestapo too. We heard them drive away.

'Perhaps they took their prisoners with them.'

At this point, Vogel began to cry, although she seemed otherwise unmoved. It was such a surprise that Hanna wondered what other emotions she had been able to hide during the interview. Was this why she was so keen to embrace the shadows of the *Kino*?

'The Germans took the gold with pliers, but we stood by waiting, and then we dragged the bodies away to the pits, and later – when they feared their victims would be found – we dug them up and put them on the fires. These were our tasks. We had no choice.'

Peter filled her a glass of water from the sink.

'I am always guilty,' she said.

For the first time in her life Hanna felt glad she couldn't remember.

A red light flashed over the door to the auditorium.

'The interval is a minute away. I must go,' said Vogel.

She produced an usherette's 'counter' from a store cupboard, already holding cigarettes and sweets, and threaded a ribbon supporting the tray around her neck. From a shelf she took down a small paper hat with the word *Prinzessa* in gold and red. She stubbed out her cigarette. She had completely recovered her brisk efficiency.

Peter said they were grateful for her time, and that if she remembered anything, perhaps she would send a message. The Congress for Cultural Freedom had printed him calling cards, and so he left one on the counter.

'I wish you well,' said Vogel, not even looking at the card, but pushing open the padded door and stepping into the auditorium, the darkness woven with drifting cigarette smoke, and sliced cleanly by the penetrating beam of the projector.

Chapter 29

After the shadowy interior of the *Kino,* and the final glimpse of darkness within the auditorium, the street outside was a furnace of light. They left the *Prinzessa*'s clientele to the de-nouement of *Kriegsgericht* and set off south, away from the glaring expanse of Stalin Allee. The district was poor, dot-ted with bomb craters full of stagnant water, iridescent with motor oil. The pavements were covered with wooden 'eaves', designed to stop rubble falling from the decaying walls of ten-ement blocks. Only a week earlier the radio in the West had slyly reported the death of an eighty-year-old crushed by a falling iron balcony. The subliminal message was clear: the East was rotting, and in a state of slow collapse.

They emerged from a maze of backstreets, following Peter's map, into the Opernplatz, the once grand heart of the German Empire. Around the flagstoned piazza stood the landmarks of the pre-war capital, neo-Classical façades pock-marked with shrapnel. Hanna and Peter crossed the square, easily avoid-ing the few vehicles that circled, including a convoy of army trucks, tyres rumbling. In the centre, an iron lamppost stood on a stone island, decked out in imperial eagles, which looked as if they'd melted in the heat of the final battle for the city.

'That's the library of the university,' said Peter, pointing at a rather stolid building, peppered with bullet holes. 'St Hed-wig's … the Opera …' he pointed out the rest. All the stone-work was fire-damaged, the dome of the cathedral a broken eggshell.

'And that …' he added, sniffing theatrically, 'that is the smell of East Berlin. Soft coal, full of tar, and oil – the Trabis have two-stroke motorbike engines, so they mix it with the petrol. They're spark-plugs with a roof. I want one but I'm told it's unpatriotic.

'It was here they burnt the books,' he said, lightly tapping his right shoe on the cobbles. But she could see the anger in his eyes. Peter had the artist's virtue of being able to empathise with the misery of strangers, even strangers from the past.

'Twenty thousand volumes. Goebbels gave a speech, right on this spot, by the flames. Then they started on the art.'

His face was animated, cheeks flushed, eyes bright in the sunshine. Berlin seemed to suit him: *Voices!* had been lauded by the critics and drawn the crowds. At first Hanna had thought his ebullient mood was an emotional screen, designed to obscure his anger over the unborn child, but now she wasn't so sure.

'You're happy here,' she said.

He spread his arms wide, encompassing the city.

'The voices are fading, Han. It was bad, back in the winter, at the BDC, but as I get closer, see faces, see the ruins, the voices seem to still. And meeting her – Vogel – just now, was like a revelation. A face to match a voice. The images at Camp Ashcan were disembodied, but now, I don't feel they're ghosts any more, trapped in the machine.'

He retrieved a package in greaseproof paper from his jacket containing a pastry and a piece of sausage he'd bought at a kiosk in the West. They ate in silence for a moment, circled by traffic. Hanna felt exhausted by their encounter with Vogel, as if she'd been physically dragged back through time to Borek, to the heat, the dust and brutal violence.

'So what did Vogel really tell us?' she asked eventually, taking out a paper bag of sweets from her pocket. Berlin had been in a love affair with candy since US pilots had dropped chocolate bars on handkerchief parachutes during the airlift when the city was cut off from the West. More than a decade

had passed, but everyone still thought chocolate was democratic.

Peter lit a cigarette. 'It looks like she saw the Stern family.
The two girls, they're the right ages, it's the right date. It's
not certain, but I think we have to believe it was them – and
it was *you*.'

'Yes. I believe it,' said Hanna, turning her face to the sun,
closing her eyes, trying to see the moment. 'Which means
we were taken away into the German compound, which was
thick with SS and Gestapo because someone was pilfering
Berlin's gold.'

'It's the gold. I bet you that's the heart of it,' he said, although Hanna thought he was trying the idea out, because he
didn't sound certain. 'At least it would explain why Pierce and
Clarke are so eager to help.

'What if the gold was found in the camp but never got to
Berlin?'

An army convoy, of two trucks and a tank, rumbled past
along Unter den Linden, the civilian traffic pulling over to let
them pass, pedestrians stopping, watching with blank faces. It
was the second column they'd seen in a few minutes.

'What shall we do next?' said Hanna. She'd opened a door
on the past, but where did it lead, and how could they follow?
'Do you think she sent the letter and *der Springer*?'

Peter shook his head. 'Why start us on the trail and then refuse to speak to us? And how did she get to know your father
– why would she make such a promise? It doesn't add up. And
I think we can agree she's unlikely to be Stasi.

'Although I'm not sure I believe everything she told us.'

Hanna shook her head. 'I thought it was fear. But you're
right, the story seemed twisted, out of shape.'

Peter ground a cigarette butt into the cobbles. 'On the tape
she was asked point-blank if anyone got pulled out of the line
at the gas chamber and she said *never*. It was only when she

was told other witnesses had put forward a different story that she changed her line. And she had to be prompted today. How could she have forgotten that?'

They set off across the cobbles to the pavement by the Opera.

'I'll report back to Clarke,' he said. 'He wants chapter and verse, so I'll tell him about the gold – see how he reacts – and then I'll ask him to talk to his chums and have another look at Vogel and the *Prinzessa*.

'I'll go back to the BDC too – get that list of the survivors from Borek. Now we know about the Gestapo and the gold, we know what to ask.'

'But I've only got two weeks, Pete. Less,' she said, overcome with a sudden weariness, her back aching.

He reached out suddenly and took her in his arms. She knew him so well that she instantly saw this for what it was: a piece of theatre rather than an emotional misstep. But still she held him tight, finding comfort in the embrace.

'Don't look now, Han, but when you can, over your right shoulder, there's someone by the newspaper seller on the corner. He's carrying a rolled-up newspaper and an umbrella and he's really interested in his own shoes.'

Hanna ran a hand through her hair so that she could glance back, and saw a man with defeated shoulders, in an old raincoat, rummaging in his pockets, the umbrella hooked over his arm.

'Maybe it's just the State Department keeping tabs on us. Maybe not. He was outside the *Prinzessa* an hour ago,' said Peter. 'He was on the U-Bahn when we got out at Alexanderplatz. He was also opposite the flat, watching us in a shop window. He's our shadow, Han. Which, in Berlin, is bad news.'

Chapter 30

Hanna felt dizzy climbing the step to the flats, so she went straight to the bedroom, turning down Peter's offer of caffeine. The pillow yielding, she listened to the litany of the espresso machine from the kitchen: the tapping of the filter, the tamping down of the grounds, the hissing of hot water, the clink of china. Peter was a slave to obsessive routine. The window was covered in a rattan blind, and so the light was yellow and soft, the sounds of the city thickening in the heat of the late evening. The physical relief of lying down swept through her like a drug, as much as the comfort of familiar things: Peter's leather satchel in which he carried his notebooks, a denim jacket hanging on the back of the door, a camera on the bedside table.

She closed her eyes, confident that her sleep would be untroubled despite the disturbing presence of the man they had already christened *Der Shatten*, who had faded into the crowds on the Alexanderplatz, but might well have followed them to the west. She always tumbled out of the day, the familiar descent into oblivion over in a few heartbeats. Her subconscious life was as deeply buried as the past.

When she did awake it was dark, and her body felt rested, but she was aware that a voice had spoken.

'You've been out for hours, Han,' said Peter. 'You need to listen to this.'

The light came on and he placed his transistor radio on the bedside table.

The pips marked 2 a.m. Outside, car horns were blaring.

'This is Radio Free Berlin. This is Radio Free Berlin.

'Officials at the headquarters of the Kommandatura are unable to comment on reports that Volkspolizei of the GDR have closed several crossing points into the Soviet Sector. The action commenced at midnight and continues. Several streets have been blocked. Our own staff report barbed wire across Invalidenstrasse and Friedrichstrasse. Sources at the Allied Control Council have urged caution over a claim by the Mission Militaire Française de Liaison at Potsdam that concrete blocks are being used to erect a barricade at the Brandenburg Gate. It is unclear if the remaining checkpoints will remain open. Queues have been noted at several points as shift workers try to return home to the East. Student Action Berlin has demanded immediate demonstrations of support for freedom of movement under the Four Powers Agreement. The US Embassy in Bonn is also unable to comment.'

For the first time Hanna realised the car horns were coordinated to a regular, insistent beat.

'What does it mean?' she asked.

Peter shrugged. 'Sounds like the start of something.'

Chapter 31

The vultures circled lower over Borek as the witnesses were led back to Georg Johl's courtroom. Stern sat between Esther and Irena, who had Hanna on her lap, while Judi had slipped into the seat next to Duvos. They'd left Liff in the water tower because he couldn't stand up, and his wounds still bled. The panelled room looked different in the glare of sunlight, which projected the three arches of the windows behind the judges' bench down on to the wooden, polished floor. Outside, dust rose from Left Luggage Corner as the first transport train arrived. The sound of suitcases burning was a constant audible backdrop.

The judge was about to speak when Deputy Commandant Ebner whispered in his ear. Johl nodded, forced a thin smile, and readjusted his heavy glasses. He looked along the line of witnesses until his eyes rested on Hanna, who was trying to sit still, although her narrow thighs jiggled slightly on top of her mother's, a game she liked to play, and that Irena had hoped would not catch the attention of the court.

'Can the child step forward?' asked Johl.

At first Stern thought the judge had a sneer on his face, but then he realised with a shock that it was a half-finished smile, as if he was tempting Hanna with a Christmas Eve parcel, or a sweet.

'Can she step forward please …?'

Hanna stepped forward, her hands hanging dead. She stood in the splash of sunshine projected by the three arched windows.

'How old are you, child?' said Johl. There was something about his perfunctory manner that suggested he was playing out a pre-arranged drama.

They were all too scared to speak. Hanna had begun to shake.

'The mother?' suggested the clerk.

'Yes, yes,' said Johl. 'Is the child's mother here?'

Irena stood. 'I'm her mother.'

Her voice was very strong and clear, and for the first time they all heard a slight echo in the room. Meyer, in the dock, was watching the child with an unblinking stare.

'What age is the child?'

'Six years, one month, three weeks.'

Someone said something in the body of the court and there was laughter.

'Does she speak?'

'Yes, Sir. In Yiddish, with a little German.'

Johl managed the full smile this time. 'I've bent the legal rules to allow Jews into the witness box. I'm not breaking aesthetic ones by allowing them to mouth Yiddish.' He poured himself more water. 'I said yesterday we must dispense with some of the witnesses. This is an SS court, not a pantomime.

'The child will be returned to the jurisdiction of the deputy commandant ...'

He nodded towards the two guards at the courtroom doors.

'I don't want to be separated from my child,' said Irena.

Her level tone had gone, and Stern could see his wife's hands shaking.

The guards froze on the edge of the pool of sunlight.

Johl blinked, then turned his head to Ebner, and they had a brief conversation.

'Very well,' he said. 'Mother and daughter both. That's saved me a job.'

The defence lawyer, Weiss, rose to object, but Johl glared and he subsided, casting a look of apology at Meyer.

'Is this *just*?' asked Stern, getting to his feet, his voice filling the room.

Irena turned quickly, holding up her hand. 'No, Leo. Let us go together. You must stay for Judi.'

Johl slammed the gavel into its block.

'Silence!'

Stern subsided into his seat.

'The witness *will* be silent. I have been persuaded by the arguments of the defence to allow the witnesses to sit in court. Do not try my patience. Take the mother and her child away.'

Irena jumped forward and took Hanna in her arms, heaving her up once, twice, until she sat on her hip.

The two guards stood aside and began to corral them towards the door, which took them past the line of seated witnesses. Irena took Stern's hand in an awkward tangle of fingers and squeezed his flesh and bones tightly, but let go quickly, so that she could touch Judi – a finger to one cheek, to brush away a line of tears. Stern, paralysed, had almost let them go when he reached out with his free hand, in which he held the carved knight, and gave it to Hanna, who clutched it quickly to her chest.

Irena looked back when she reached the doors, letting her eyes slip from Leo to Judi, her lips saying something unheard: possibly 'Goodbye', possibly 'God Bless You'. The door closed behind them, but bounced on its hinges, so that Stern had a second, final, vision. Irena was smiling at Hanna, with a sudden and fierce joy, which said that the worst of her nightmares, which had existed for just those few seconds when she thought her child would be taken away, had not come true: the girl would not die alone.

The court was called to order. Stern was in shock, unable to take his eyes from the empty chair beside him. The personal loss, of wife and daughter, was a fatal wound, too raw to contemplate. He felt his own life spilling out, draining away, and any concept of the future collapsed into this single despairing moment. Judi saved him: she was in his care now, as Hanna was in Irena's. He had to function: to listen, to watch, to take his chance. So he pushed aside the sudden void; which left him with a sense of injustice. Outside, kicking up the dust, a thousand Jews were walking to the gas chamber. Here, in the courtroom, the fate of one German officer, guilty of a single murder, was to be afforded the full panoply of the legal code, while Hanna, a child, would be propelled from this world to the next, because her presence was inconvenient. The child, his wife as well, were to be destroyed, as thousands had been destroyed. What would be lost was memory, everything that they held in their heads: for the Sterns perhaps, a collective vision of a lake, a beach, a shout of joy. Who would know about them when it was over, when all their memories were lost?

There would be an answer to Judi's question on the silver path: *Who will punish them, father?* And the answer would be no one.

His mouth hung open, and his old heart laboured, but he could not cry.

Johl, meanwhile, bobbed slightly in his seat, scanning his courtroom. The SS investigator, Raeder, began to outline the agreed facts in the Meyer case, a legal preliminary demanded by the military code. The judge hardly listened. The previous night he had read the depositions in bed and committed the salient points to memory.

His impatience to get on was mixed with a feeling of general anxiety. The gunfire in the night, the single plane overhead, the anti-aircraft fire, had all conspired to rob him of sleep. (In the mess, over coffee, he'd been told that the camp's gun store had been broken into during the raid. Had the partisans breached the wire?)

Unable to get back to sleep after the raid, Johl had set the dispositions aside and re-read by candlelight the latest letter from his wife: stolid, bleating prose, deftly hinting at the wider chaos gripping Germany. The military machine was burning itself out under a hail of bombs. Civilian life was in ruins. There were critical shortages of coal, iron, petrol and food. The army fought endlessly on all fronts. The Americans and the British were at the gates of Paris. People talked secretly, to those they could trust, of the end. But, ludicrously, they talked also of one more fighting season. Johl, who despised self-delusion, saw a very different scenario. The war would end in the streets of Berlin. And then the victors would judge the defeated.

Many of those in power, Johl included, now feared retribution for their crimes. And here lay the real source of his unease, for, according to the private letters he received from his colleagues, these were not to be classed as crimes against German law, or even English law, or American law – but against *Humanity*. Johl noted the abstract capital H he had inadvertently imagined. Charges would be laid with reference to laws as yet unwritten. His job, in contrast, was to follow the code set down by the state. Whatever his personal opinion might be, the Führer's word was literally the law.

Johl had met Hitler once, in Berlin, at a reception a year before the outbreak of the war. They had shaken hands. He recalled with relief now that their brief physical union had not been recorded by the official photographer. What did he remember of this historic moment? That the Führer's skin had the tension of a week-old party balloon and that his teeth were unnaturally small. That was Georg Johl's window on history. Also, the Austrian's hand had been slight, and damp: but nonetheless the very hand that had set in motion the great events that had brought Johl here, to a makeshift courthouse in a forest in Poland, to listen to the sordid facts in a tawdry case of military indiscipline.

Vaguely moved by this insight into the random nature of world events, he forced himself to pay attention.

The killing of Obersturmführer Keuper by a fellow SS officer would hardly cause a stir in Berlin. But in disentangling the jurisdiction of the Gestapo from the SS he was faced with a neat legal knot. Besides, the precise motives of Meyer and Keuper still eluded him, as did the rationale behind Meyer's insistence that at some point the defence would call the Jew to give evidence. There were hidden layers here – some of which Johl had already glimpsed – and he was determined to uncover them all.

Which was distinctly more enticing than the prospect of sitting through another day of evidence in the case against the disgraced former commandant, Max Eigrupper. The arrogance of the Prussian officer class was jaw-dropping. The fool had not only embezzled gold; he'd kept records that clearly showed, after a cursory inspection, the magnitude of the theft. Only two questions remained: where the loot was, and who had helped him steal it. A thorough search of the entire camp was still in progress. As to the question of which officers had helped in the fraud; well, the answer might be all of them. If they found the gold, more heads would roll, Johl had promised himself that.

'Those are the agreed facts in this case,' Raeder said, raising his voice slightly, to counter the noise of the distant tractors working on the field of the dead. Raeder was sweating badly. His face was scarred by a very large port-wine birthmark that entirely surrounded his left eye and appeared to make it shine more brightly than its partner.

Johl sat upright and shot the cuffs on his uniform.

'Very well. Let us hear now from the defence.'

Through the window behind Johl those in the body of the court could view a new consignment of prisoners, filing into Left Luggage Corner. Dust, drenched in sunshine, drifted in the air. The judge picked up his fountain pen and held it poised over his yellow foolscap pad.

Chapter 32

The Sterns had whispered together in the nights many times since their brutal eviction from their home in Weissenstein, and a lot of what they'd said on their tortuous journey to Borek had been in the form of a disguised, protracted, farewell; so as Irena, still carrying Hanna, followed the guards she did not feel any crushing sense of loss. Everything had been said, so the arrival of the actual moment was strangely empty, as if it was already a dry narrative chapter of the family history: a footnote perhaps, in some other, greater story. And there was a sense of guilty relief, because now she was responsible only for Hanna. Leo and Judi would have to look after each other.

The nightmare, the dark shadow, had always been the fear that they would be separated from the girls. And so there was an unexpected release of anxiety in Irena's fluid movements: her hands, her purposeful step, to which the child responded, demanding to be set down on her feet, taking her new, carved, toy horse from her smock pocket, holding the head erect, performing a series of small hobbling, equine steps.

'It's a gift from your father,' whispered Irena, touching her hair, creating a memory.

They were taken to a brick-built hut with a wooden roof and several iron chimneys, to one side of which stood a line of metal bins. The smell of kitchens as they climbed the steps was overwhelming: fried eggs, and potatoes and cabbage boiling, and the cloying aroma of yeast. Hanna, overcome with frustration, began to cry out that she was hungry and that her stomach ached.

Panelled in dark wood, the mess room within held a single large table, in fine oak, with carved legs and a deep, layered, polish. A long hatch in one wall opened into the kitchen beyond, revealing three cooks, with their backs to the hatch, washing up plates, banging pots and ladles on the hobs like percussionists.

The guards left Irena and Hanna saying they would be back on the stroke of the next hour, when the klaxon sounded.

Irena and Hanna were given bread and water. The cook who brought them the crusts, and two metal cups, set their plates down kindly, edging one closer to Hanna, her large doughy hands fussing. Irena judged that the hunk of stale bread was more than the ration they had been given by Brunner, and there was even a smear of butter on one side. Hanna's small hand held the bread fiercely, chewing each mouthful. Irena saw the bread for what it might be: their last meal. Then she smiled at Hanna and understood how powerful it was, this knowledge, that this might be the final day of their lives, and that they would spend it together.

Outside, they heard a heavy engine approaching, gears crashing, and then the wrench of a handbrake. The door of the canteen opened and an SS officer in a freshly laundered uniform came in reading a clipboard. He asked one of the cooks who stepped forward why the two 'peasants' were still eating; the breakfast hour had long passed, and they had been instructed that the canteen must be empty by ten o'clock when the klaxon sounded.

'The mother and child are waiting for the next transport to arrive,' said the cook with the fussing hands. 'They are under special orders.'

'Get them out,' said the officer. 'And then the hut must be cleared – all of you, out. Now.'

Irena sat on the baked mud outside, Hanna between her legs. They let her take the water and some more bread with her, so with her free hand she was able to roll the dough into pellets and press them between the child's lips.

A platoon of soldiers began to climb over the tailgate of the half-truck, unbending stiff limbs as if they'd just finished a long journey. All wore the black uniforms of the SS. One or two had tied handkerchiefs around their faces so that they could breathe through the material.

After a few minutes the cooks came out too, in a line, and stood in the sunlight, their smocks brilliantly white. Talking in stage whispers they discussed events: apparently these soldiers had been drafted in, from outside the camp, to speed up the search for the commandant's stolen gold.

'It's a treasure hunt!' said a thin cook with a shaved scalp, wiping her hands across her stomach, and bending down to deliver this good news to Hanna. Irena, smiling indulgently, sang softly in the child's ear, a Yiddish nursery rhyme this time, about a dancing snowman from the Russian woods.

The officer splayed an architectural plan on the bonnet of the truck. It showed the camp, each of the barrack huts, and the interior details – chimneys, drains, urinals, stairs. Choosing six of the soldiers, he ordered them to crawl under the canteen hut. Reluctantly, they dropped to their knees, then their stomachs, edging forward on their elbows, as if negotiating barbed wire on the Western Front, as their fathers might have done. One of the soldiers got stuck and had to be pulled back out by his boots, his uniform grubby with dirt and filth. The search awakened a stench of rotting, discarded vegetables. Irena saw that soft, rotting potato peel was smeared on the soldier's knees.

'Christ,' he said. 'I stink of dog shit.'

The officer laughed. 'Well done, Ells. It's an improvement. You normally stink of your own shit. Get used to it. There are six barrack huts left, and then there's the Jews' huts beyond. Another twenty.'

One of the other soldiers had lit a cigarette. 'We'll be in this hole for a week – more. Two nights ago, I was in a beer hall in Bremen. Can you believe this?' He spat in the dirt. 'Why can't the Jews do it? Or the guards?'

'Because we are trusted,' said the officer. 'This is not bad news, is it? When the time comes, perhaps this will weigh in the balance. The top brass will remember the hard work and dedication of our unit. They do not trust the local guards. And remember, the top brass, at least some of them, are here. We must be diligent in our duties, boys. Just search the fucking huts.'

Two of the soldiers went inside the kitchen carrying a step-ladder, torches, and what looked like long wooden vegetable canes. The officer circled the building making notes. Irena could tell that one of the soldiers who had gone inside had climbed into the roof space because they could all hear him through the thin felt and rafters, calling out, edging towards the gable-end.

'Nothing. Nothing. Nothing.'

'Every corner, Cripps. No slouching,' shouted the officer. 'If the commandant's gold turns up in one of these huts, and we missed it, they'll be turning *you* into soap, not the Jewboys.'

He turned to Irena. 'Or the Jewesses and their livestock.'

Hanna examined the officer as if he was applying for a job.

Inside, they could all hear the clatter of pots again, and crockery, and knives. A plate broke, then another, and the cooks began to protest: 'Careful! They beat us if we break anything. Be careful, please.'

'Silence,' said the officer, and he flipped the buttoned hol-ster on his belt open, as if he felt threatened by this battalion of cooks. 'Outside Minsk we shot ten thousand Jews in a day. You think I can't manage half a dozen fat Poles in my spare time?'

The soldiers clapped this witticism.

Irena stood up, holding Hanna, and told her a Yiddish tale, choosing Leo's favourite – about the lazy Hershele Ostropoler, who never worked, not ever, so that one day the family did not even have money to buy a chicken for Shabbat. Scolded by his wife he went into town and, standing in the square, announced that he would take people to the next town of Leitshev for half price. People queued up to buy a ticket because everyone thought the official coach and horses was over-priced. Hershele told them all to follow him. 'Where are your horses?' they asked. 'Just follow me,' said Hershele. And they did. Out of the town, down the road, over the hills, and all the way to Leitshev. It took half the day. Everyone was angry and wanted their money back – they'd had to walk! But Hershele kept the money, pointing out that he'd told no lies. He said he'd take them to Leitshev and he had. He'd never mentioned how.

'And walking's not so bad,' said Irena, swaying at the hips as she spoke, dipping with each turn, a motion that the child had always found comforting. 'Your father loved walking,' she said, hearing in her words how quickly Leo had become a hero of the past. 'We used to walk to the fair in Regen and buy ice cream.'

A sound of splintering wood came from within the roof space.

'I can't get into the end space,' said the disembodied voice. 'It's too narrow. But I can see. There's nothing there. I'm using the cane to poke about; there's nothing there. There won't be anything there – will there? He'll have buried it in the woods. He's not stupid.'

The officer threw open the door into the canteen and Irena saw him go to the foot of the ladder and shout up, gripping the rungs.

'Cripps, listen to me. Get your lousy head into the roof space – crawl man, poke about. You're good at that – remember that whorehouse in Neuberg.'

All the soldiers laughed.

'How do we know he hasn't left a little gold here, a little there?' asked the officer. 'It's billions of Reichsmarks' worth. You think that's all in one place, in a pirate's treasure chest marked GOLD in Gothic script for poor dumb Cripps to find? And use the torch, light up all the dark corners of this shit hole. Then we can go home. A week, less if we're quick.'

'All right, all right,' came the soldier's voice.

They heard wood shattering and the sound of material tearing.

Five minutes later the soldier came down the ladder and walked out into the sunshine. He was black with grime. A nail had gashed his forehead so that he had blood in one eye. The back of his uniform hung loose, torn from shoulder to shoulder.

He opened his hands for the officer to see. 'This is what I bring you. Gold? No. Bird shit. And here's the bird.' He held out the desiccated skeleton of a crow.

Chapter 33

Left Luggage Corner, by the railway station, was full of a new consignment of prisoners, and Irena and Hanna were pushed roughly into the crowd, their guard exchanging words with the kapo in charge of the suitcases. Several people looked at their shaved heads with open curiosity. Irena, wilting under scrutiny, held Hanna's face hard against her own cheek, pointing out things of interest in the milling, dusty crowd: a fur coat, a gilded bird cage, a child trailing a spinning top in the dust. These were very different people from the ones who had arrived on Transport 573 from the Lodz ghetto. They were all dressed expensively; the fur coat she'd seen was – it soon appeared – one of many, despite the heat, and the men wore suits with long overcoats of fine wool. To Irena they looked like film stars; exotic, and languid, as if they were merely changing trains *en route* to Cherbourg, and a liner to New York.

They talked incessantly in French, of which Irena understood half a dozen words. She watched a man stop and take out a silver cigarette case and was astounded to see him offer one to a woman, who took it with her fingertips, and having lit it, held it near her mouth with her arm bent at the elbow. One man was carrying a suitcase so heavy he had to put it down every two or three steps. Others used horsehair brushes to wipe away the grime of the journey from their long coats or held handkerchiefs to their noses to counter the smell.

The Ukrainie were not behaving as they did with the transport from Lodz. They stood back, silent and wary, letting the new arrivals stroll around the square. The excited sound of conversation from the prisoners was notable, springing perhaps from a lively interest in their next destination: Minsk perhaps? When Irena caught the eye of a girl Judi's age, she smiled and the child smiled back. Insanely, she found herself sharing the sense of optimism, as if she did not know what lay at the end of the path.

The slaves with the blue armbands, who waited to sort through the luggage, stood in one corner of the square. They were mostly Poles and Germans; they did not talk at all to their French cousins, and the new arrivals did not talk to them. There was something openly predatory about the slaves on this particular morning. When the Sterns had passed through the square they had sorted through the suitcases with little enthusiasm. Today, the expectation, the *greed*, was palpable. By comparison with the new arrivals the slaves resembled brigands, in their ill-fitting clothes, their heavy boots and socks, chosen with the aim of surviving a winter in Borek, not a summer's day.

An SS officer stood on a mounting block and shouted: '*Attention!*'

The swirl of prisoners stopped dead. Irena wondered what they'd been told out on the platform. Had promises been made, as they had been to the Lodz train? The officer continued in French and whatever he said produced a visible shockwave through the crowd. Irena caught only the French for suitcase: *valise*. Children moved closer to their parents. One man, perhaps fifty years of age, with a neatly trimmed beard and hair, approached the German officer, only to be pushed roughly back by one of the Ukrainie, so that he lay sprawled in the sand.

The white-coated 'doctors' from the lazarette moved among the crowd and led away several invalids, mostly elderly men, to the whitewashed stockade in the corner of the square. Three women walked after them carrying crying children. Irena set Hanna down and told her to stand still. Tense, expecting the dull percussion of the pistol shots, she was surprised as the silence stretched on; this time, perhaps, the Germans were trying harder to keep up appearances for the French, fearing what might happen if they guessed what lay ahead.

There were also many more German guards here than for the Lodz transport. No doubt they too were keen to see what the French had brought with them, and to make sure nothing of any real value fell into the wrong hands. The kapos, too, stood watching, overseeing the slaves, calculating *their* share of the spoils. One kapo picked up a miniature gilded bottle and, screwing off the top, offered it to an SS officer, who sniffed the contents; they both laughed, the kapo shrugged, and then pocketed the vial. Irena sensed a parity between them as the officers and kapos joked together, pointing at a bottle of cognac, a box of cigars, a small brass orrery – its miniature planets catching the light.

Given the order to move on, a queue formed to go down the alleyway into the second square. Irena fell into line behind a woman with three children. There was a boy, the age of Hanna, and two older girls. The children were playing, immersed in acting out some fantasy with two cotton dolls, although they cast quick glances at Irena's shaven head.

Once they were all in Pariser Platz, Irena stood and closed her eyes. She did not want to see again the barbers' shop, or the leafy shade of the Himmelstrasse. Her lips moved as she recited a prayer, feeling her courage begin to fail. She missed Leo so much it felt as if she'd been winded, the air in her lungs useless, stale. She felt afraid, and trapped, because she could not show her fear to Hanna.

The two small kiosks for documents were open for business, and the queues formed, but she hung back. Then the SS officer asked them all to take their clothes off ready for the barbers' and the bathhouse.

Hanna buried her face in Irena's fleshy hip.

'Close your eyes, now,' she told the child.

Irena slipped off her clothes, and the child's, and left them in a neat pile, folded, still slightly stiff with starch.

The French woman with the three children came up to her and made it clear she wanted Irena to hold the boy's hand while she went to the barbers' shop. She spoke French, then a kind of laboured Yiddish, pointing at Irena's shaved head. She touched the little boy and said his name – Auguste – then fled towards the barbers' hut. The child stood with one hand in Irena's, and his eyes on his father, standing in the queue for documents. Feathers began to fall from the vultures flying overhead and Irena gathered up one or two and gave them to the boy to examine, which he did with exaggerated curiosity, perhaps sensing that this was what this strange woman expected of him.

The French were not as compliant as the Germans and Poles. Two of the women had to be dragged to the barbers' by their hair, kicking up a trail of dust. The Ukrainie brought the dogs down the Himmelstrasse to help hold the male prisoners in a tight circle. Irena felt a fight might break out at any moment. She let her face fill Hanna's field of vision, trying to focus the child's world into this small picture of her mother's mouth and eyes. She was aware now that these were among the last images her child would see of the world.

'We all love you very much,' she said.

A hand touched Irena on the shoulder.

Kopp, the red-haired kapo who'd addressed their transport the day before, stood in the dust. Several of the other kapos were with him, and a group of slaves who must have been chosen to be returned to the Himmelstrasse; broken men, their heads down, bleeding tiredness into the ground on which they stood.

'I'm sorry,' he said in Yiddish. 'This has to happen. Today, now, there is no choice.'

Irena misunderstood him. 'I'm not afraid. I was before. Now I just want it to be over. Will you help my husband if you can? Tell him you saw me and that we're at peace. Tell him it's over and he doesn't need to worry about us any more.'

The French woman returned and took Auguste's hand.

Kopp stared both women in the face, alternately, almost theatrically, as if making a choice. Irena saw that the right lens of his glasses, which had been cracked when they'd first met, was now completely gone. The blue iris of this one eye seemed to shine with a sudden cruelty. He grasped Irena's arm roughly and twisted it so she fell to her knees.

He bent down and spoke into her ear. 'Trust me for these few minutes. We have seen your papers. *A doctor's nurse: unqualified.* But you may pass muster, and we have no choice. Give the child to this woman. Do not make a fuss.'

Kopp was flanked by two other kapos. They got their muscled arms around Irena, and then Kopp pulled Hanna away, pressing her on the French woman, who took her, and tried to smile at Irena.

Kopp spoke again into Irena's ear. 'Don't speak. If you speak we could lose everything. You could lose everything.'

Around them the other kapos were picking out prisoners who said they were carpenters, and silversmiths, plumbers, and tailors.

Irena couldn't breathe, but she turned to look at the French woman and memorised her face: brown eyes narrowly set, pale skin, black hair cut to a stubble, and wide made-up lips, smudged with coral. She had fleshy earlobes with piercings.

An SS officer was strolling towards them and Kopp said, very clearly, to another kapo: 'I've found a nurse at last for the sickbay. Now the doctor can leave us alone and concentrate on the bottle.'

Irena could hear someone shouting, and realised the voice was her own.

She caught Kopp's eye just before he hit her; a cuff, with the open hand, but more than hard enough to knock her out. The world slewed drunkenly from left to right, and she saw Hanna one last time, her hand examining the French woman's face.

Chapter 34

Tomas Boniek sat opposite Hanna and Peter in the canteen of the Hertha Works, a factory on the edge of the French Sector, in the old working-class district of Wedding. Behind him an interior window offered a panorama of the factory floor, with its serried rows of glass furnaces, from which the molten fiery 'metal' flowed out in angular rivers, to be fashioned by machines into test-tubes, retorts and scientific glassware.

They'd been given tea in metal mugs, and the glassblower cradled his as if for warmth, despite the sweltering heat. The factory manager fussed with chairs and ashtrays. Hanna's spirits were low. It was three days since the border had been closed, the city outside was in turmoil, but here the workers seemed untroubled, going about their tasks of servicing the great machines. They'd seen three more witnesses from Borek – all, by luck, in the West – but none could recall the Sterns or anything about the commandant's gold. Rachel Vogel was to be re-interviewed by the Stasi, but Hanna suspected that whatever secrets she harboured she would keep. The last days of the camp were chaotic and bloody, but each survivor seemed to have lived through their own private version of hell.

The fate of the Sterns was lost in the smoke and dust. Boniek was their last chance.

'What will you do now?' asked Peter, offering the glassblower a cigarette. Boniek's file, obtained from the factory manager by Clarke, listed the glassblower's address as Kaulsdorf, in the Soviet Sector.

'They let us sleep here,' he said. 'They say the checkpoints are open if you want to go back. But then what would we do? They're not letting anyone *return* to work.' He looked around as if he might never see the factory again. 'I've worked here for ten years,' he added, examining his large, rough hands. 'I know of nothing else.'

Clarke had set up the interview, through a contact at the United Jewish Appeal, telling officials only that a relative of a family lost at Borek wished to speak with an eye-witness to the final days of the camp. Boniek – it was explained – had often spoken out about the camp on behalf of those who had been murdered in the gas chamber.

'You are a survivor of the camp at Borek ...' said Peter, a gentle opening gambit.

Unbidden, as if by rote, Boniek described the day of the revolt – 12 July 1944.

The Red Army was approaching, the Germans were loading the last of the lorries, the slaves had got guns and breached the wire to escape into the forest, but the Ukrainie were in pursuit, with dogs. For nearly twenty minutes he painted the scene in vivid detail and Hanna wondered if with each re-telling the story had become more rigid, an unchallengeable version of history. Breathless, he paused at last to take a gulp of tea.

Hanna took her chance. 'Forgive me, Tomma, we've read the transcripts. We wanted to ask you about something specific – about the fate of one family: the Sterns. My family.'

She touched her chest.

'The Sterns?' repeated Boniek. He rocked slightly in his seat.

Hanna leaned forward.

'Yes. Leo; and Irena, and Judith ...'

He nodded. 'And little Hanna,' he said, beaming, and holding out a hand, palm flat, to indicate the height of a child.

'Yes. Little Hanna,' she said. The moment tied the past and present together. Peter took her hand. The thought that her past was here, in front of her, *alive*, seemed to collapse the time that separated her six-year-old self from the woman she'd become. Vogel's story had seemed second-hand, distant. Boniek's was immediate, as if he saw it now, before his eyes. It was the moment she'd imagined might one day arrive: she'd landed in the dust of Borek.

She went to speak but cried instead, sudden tears falling easily.

'You are family?' asked Boniek, nodding with sympathy. 'I can see Irena's face in yours. As plain as day. A niece, perhaps?'

Hanna shook her head. 'No. *I am Hanna*, Tomma, I survived the camp, but I do not remember how. I do not remember at all.'

She struggled to get her breathing under control. 'I must remember because the others may be alive too – as you and I are alive.'

Boniek held his hands to his face and began to rock slightly in the canteen chair.

'Leo's child? It is not possible.'

Leo. To hear someone use her father's name brought him almost unbearably close, so that she repeated the word with her tongue, silently, feeling the two syllables tumble together.

'It cannot be true,' he said.

'But it is,' said Hanna.

She set *der Springer* on the table. 'I was rescued and taken to an estate in Poland, then to England. Five years ago, someone wrote to say my father was alive – they were forbidden to say more. The chess piece was in the envelope.'

Boniek held the knight in his bowl-like hand. 'Leo played chess, he played well – in the ghetto, on the train, he played your sister. A very clever man, and a fine doctor.'

'A doctor?' asked Hanna. 'My father was a doctor?'

All the things she'd ever imagined about her lost father were suddenly cast in a new light. She could see so much more: a surgery, patients in a waiting room, books, instruments, hats raised to a figure of importance. In the void of her memory a man now stood, and she strained to hear his voice.

'I had no idea,' she said.

'You were too young. Your only interest was to play. And to watch us all with those great brown eyes. And you had your crayons. Always drawing, lines and circles … And looking at the world. But not in surprise; as if you had *been here before*. A wise head. This was what your father said: *as if you had been here before*.

'You kept close to your mother,' he added, welding his two hands together in a clasp. 'As one.'

Then, as if to bring himself to a stop, he held up his arms, embarrassed by this tender picture.

'Did he survive because he was a doctor?' asked Peter.

'No. He hid his profession, and his doctor's bag. He did not want to be separated from his family, from you, Hanna. They would have taken him away.'

He fumbled for a cigarette, and so Peter took up the questions. 'We need to find out how Hanna survived, Tomma. We've discovered that a family was taken away by the SS guards to be questioned by the Gestapo. A few days before the end?'

Tomma was laughing now, brushing away his own tears. 'Not a family – all of them, from the house in Lodz. The Sterns, yes, but my wife too, and Liff the watchmaker, and Duvos the chemist.'

'Where were you?' asked Peter.

It was an innocent question, and out of his mouth before he could weigh its implications.

Boniek's mouth hung open for a moment in shock, then he hurriedly lit his cigarette, but Hanna felt he was suddenly diminished. 'I had been picked out for a *Sonderkommando*. A work party. The woodcutters. They wanted strong men. I had no choice but to go.'

Hanna heard it then, the edge to the voice, which made it sound like a plea for forgiveness. *He feels as guilty as I do.*

'If we were all taken away then perhaps others survived too,' said Hanna.

'My Esther did not survive.'

'How do you know?'

'I went back.'

'*Back?*' said Hanna.

'Yes. We woodcutters had a plan. We had marked a copse of pine trees with our axes in the days before the revolt, knowing we would need to fool the dogs. When the fighting began, we met in the forest and climbed up into the canopy and waited for the Ukrainie to pass. We had a map. We wanted to reach the San, and use the logs to ride downstream to the Vistula. But we had to hold our nerve.

'We let them pass beneath, and then we came down, and the rest escaped in the dark. Esther had been taken with you all into the German compound. I thought she might be alive, so I went back through the wire.'

Boniek was sweating now, and his breath came in shallow whistles. The glassblower's face had achieved a strange fluidity, the emotions rippling just below the surface.

'The camp was lifeless. Those who had tried to climb over the fence were shot. In death they hung on the wire …'

It was such a precise image that Hanna suspected he'd used it before.

'The station, the square beyond, all was silent. The dead were everywhere. My brothers and sisters, the kapos, the Ukrainie, even the German guards.'

Boniek's lower lip was wet and blue.

'I walked on and found my Esther. She'd been shot in the back; I know this because I could see no wound. She lay facing the sky, and her eyes were open. I didn't touch her.'

He stopped then and his chin fell on to his chest. Hanna stood up and went round the table and, kneeling beside his chair, awkwardly embraced him.

'We always thought of the baby as a girl,' he said, his face wet now and glistening. 'I was frightened that if I touched her I would feel the child's pulse, so I walked away.'

Outside on the factory floor a siren sounded.

Hanna let him get his breathing under control.

'I am sorry they died, Tomma. They would have been proud of you – you survived.' She said this to comfort him, but she found solace as well, because she too was a survivor.

He mopped his face with the sleeve of his overalls. 'After that, I went back into the woods, where I met the rest down by the river and rode the logs. Many drowned on the way. Then we walked, the long march through winter to the gates of Berlin. I keep their memory with me.'

Hanna took both his hands. 'But how did *I* survive, Tomma? We spoke to another survivor; she said the Sterns – and the rest – may have been taken to Berlin to face questions from the Gestapo? She said they thought we were saboteurs, that there was a great plan to join forces with the Poles, with the *Armia*, to steal the German's gold?'

Tomma shook his head. 'What? Liff the idiot watchmaker a saboteur? No, no, child. This is not why you were kept alive. No. Your lives were spared because you were *witnesses*. A German officer tried to take you away, as the Gestapo had ordered, but a comrade – a tyrant we called The Puppet – wanted you all executed on the spot. He wanted Leo executed on the spot. Shots were fired. The Puppet died.

'An SS court was convened that very day, yes – in the camp itself. The officer faced a charge of murder. The SS judge was the same one who had already found the commandant guilty of hiding Berlin's gold. You – and the rest – were the only witnesses to the killing. The only witnesses to what was *said* – this was the key. This is what we slaves heard.'

Tomma sat forward, his voice regaining its authority. 'The court met every day, Hanna. But perhaps it did not reach a verdict. The Red Army was coming, the partisans were in the woods, and the Germans were ready to abandon the camp. If the case was adjourned to Berlin, perhaps they took some of the witnesses with them?'

Chapter 35

Rachel Vogel was in the playground, watching her daughter Elka run in circles while the doors of the District Six school were still shut. Since the closing of the border with the West, the mothers had stood each day in animated groups discussing *der Notfall* – the emergency: would there be a war, would there be food shortages, when would the checkpoints reopen? Rachel stood apart, as she always did. For a few moments she took her eyes off the child and pretended to admire a banner made by the children at Christmas, and strung along the railings, celebrating the safe return to earth of *Vostok 1* and Comrade Gagarin. It was decorated with stars, and planets, and the bulbous metallic features of the spaceship, alongside a pair of poorly executed portraits of President Pieck and First Secretary Khrushchev. Elka's contribution, a map of the cosmodrome at Baikonur, had been completed with Hans's help at the kitchen table in the flat above the *Prinzessa*.

The school stood on the edge of a bombsite, distinguished by a flooded crater, out of which protruded the rusted turret of a tank. Despite the years of reconstruction District Six was still scarred by war. Rachel had stood on this spot for the first time sixteen years earlier, in the bleak days after the fall of the city. The memory was clear, and certainly more real than the colourful image before her of playing children. On that day the smell of death among the rubble had been sweet, the muffled crump of collapsing masonry the only interruption to the silence. Smoke had drifted from the ruined buildings that still stood, their interiors exposed to reveal the private lives of the dead: wallpaper and bathtubs, pictures, beds, and severed pipes. The time, for Germany, had been decreed: it was *Stunde Null* – zero hour – the start of a new age of which she had never felt a part.

Fear, she knew, was like a colour upon her, because she was haunted by what had gone before. The cruellest echo was the school itself: a low stone block with doors to each classroom, which closely resembled the gas chamber at Borek. The first morning she'd seen it, she felt that someone – the builder, the architect, the stonemason – someone *knew* and she was about to be exposed; that she would sink to her knees and the other mothers would hurl rubble and clods of oily earth from the bombsite. And then they'd cut off her hair, and tar and feather her, as they had done to so many in those first weeks when the Russians stood back and let the city tear itself apart. And then they would turn on Elka.

In a plain pediment of the school block the letters had been etched with a flourish of craftsmanship:

Bezirk 6

As she stared at the letters, they rearranged themselves, and she saw Hackendorf's sweating face, and heard the dull litany of the Ukrainie officer, addressing the new arrivals from the upper step. This inversion of present and past was – she knew – an indulgence, a failing on her part. She swayed slightly on her feet, petrified that to faint would betray everything. She had never fainted. Not once.

But this morning there was a new fear. The post had brought a brown envelope stamped Staatssicherheitsdienst SSD – from the Stasi's central office, less than half a mile away in Lichtenberg. The street on which the building stood was Ruschestrasse, visible from the tram that ran past at the junction with Stalin Allee. Berlin folklore insisted that you never saw a pedestrian on that street. Not one. The black Zil limousines came and went. But it was a street without footsteps.

The letter comprised two paragraphs of terse bureaucratic prose informing her that in the interests of the process of denazification she and her husband were to attend for yet another routine interview, the date and time specified. The SSD wished to review her testimony, given in 1946 to the war crimes tribunal. (It was not the first unwelcome reprise. She had been re-interviewed by a French officer in 1948, and a British diplomat in 1949.) She had no doubt this summons had been prompted by the unwelcome visit of the Stern girl, and her American.

And it was hardly a surprise. It had been quite clear for some time that they were being watched, and Hans had discovered a small 'bug' attached to the chandelier in the living room. But this was not a problem because they had always talked as if overheard. Only outside, in the street, did they tell the truth, or speak of the hidden past.

The school bell rang, and the children ran to form seven separate queues for the first class. The scene echoed the past: in the week after the war ended she and Hans had joined the line here waiting to fill a bottle at a water tanker. The night before they'd slept under the trees in the Tierpark. The schloss was a ruin, within which fires flickered, but they kept their distance. Rachel had searched the branches at dawn for a sign of blossom, but there was none. The city's lampposts were bent, distorted, the hanging corpses a rare vertical motif in a city that had been flattened by Allied bombs. The line for water was a hundred yards long, more, but orderly, unlike the crowd they'd seen on the far bank of the Oder, which had swirled, clawing at an open lorry full of stale bread.

It was at that moment, on this spot sixteen years ago, that she noticed it for the first time: the dull, soft, cushion-like acoustic that was to be Berlin for her, for ever. Never again would she hear a clear sound, a crisp bell, the high treble of a child's voice, the whistle pip of a bird's call. The city was lost beneath a deadening carpet of white-grey ash, which swallowed all its echoes. On the bombsites it lay a foot thick, on window ledges it settled like lagging, in the street it was compacted by wheels and footprints. Her own clear voice might have broken the spell, but since her arrival in the city she had never sung again.

Every day, they'd returned to the spot designated by the Soviets as a distribution point to buy bread. Hans hid their money in an old punctured iron tank in the ribcage ruins of a gasometer. For that was what they'd brought to Berlin: Reichsmarks (traded for rubles), and a pistol, which Hans kept in the large pocket inside his greatcoat. For a year, perhaps longer, they hoarded the money because there was nothing it could buy, and to brandish it drew thieves and robbers.

The bomb-crater lake survived but the reflections changed. They built District Six, a line of high-rise flats, where they'd secured their first home, at the north-west corner, so that they could look to Treptow Park, and even the distant forests. (This also meant their windows were clear of the three monumental banners of Marx, Lenin and Stalin, which, when they fluttered, obscured so much light for their neighbours.) By moonlight, from Flat 9c, they'd seen the rats, like a river, flowing through the street below.

They lived there for five years and each night she imagined it would be their last, that they'd be bundled into a waiting car and taken to Ruschestrasse. The Stasi had an official on the ground floor, but the Guttman family next door were widely suspected to be agents too. Below lived the Furhmanns, party luminaries, who, because of their position by the stairs and the lifts, no doubt made regular reports.

But Hans insisted that their secret was safe, and after all, it was a very *specific* secret. How could anyone know? How could anyone even guess the right question to ask?

But Rachel couldn't sleep, imagining the people around her, above her, below her, all listening through the thin walls. When they finally used the money to pay the rent on the *Prinzessa*, a mile west, she noted the old caretaker's flat over the auditorium. Hans had – reluctantly – paid the necessary bribe to secure permission to live above the cinema, and so they'd moved out of the block. But District Six was not finished with them yet. Elka had been born at precisely the moment they began construction of the school, which stood beside the old flooded crater, now known throughout the suburb with East German irony as *der Spa*.

And so Rachel stood this morning, watching Elka fidget in the line, unable to escape the suffocation of this daily torture in which she had to watch her child disappear inside the chamber.

When one of the other mothers spoke, a woman she knew only as Clara, she jumped, dropping her daughter's lunchbox.

Clara clasped her hand, her touch unwelcome. 'Your hair, Rachel, always a marvel. You look well. Is it going to be good for business then? The Wall? No more trips for us to the Ku'Damm to see the latest from Hollywood.'

Rachel smiled and looked away to watch Elka running into class.

'See you this afternoon?' said Clara, for some reason applying lipstick. 'You haven't forgotten? I wrote it in the book. The children too. We all need a trim, and Ernst is taking me to the Institute.' She pulled a face. 'Dancing in the workers' paradise. But I can't pick and choose … I still want to look my best.'

Rachel's hair had been an irresistible advertisement for her skills, although she suspected that many of her customers expected her to impart a biological component for the price of the cut. In those first weeks in Berlin she'd kept it all under a cap. The Ivans raped women at will. Hans said he'd use the

pistol, but they both knew that would simply imbue the act
with an additional violent charge.

All the children were finally gone.

The mothers dispersed, waving and chatting, heading for
the shops at the foot of Tower Havel, or the tram stop. Inside
each classroom the children sat, invisible below the high sills
of the windows.

Rachel always contrived the same manoeuvre, one of many
that allowed her life to move forward in the shape expected by others. She walked briskly towards the east gate, then
turned back across the playground in a wide curve as if she
had changed her mind, so that she came within twenty yards
of the window of Elka's class. Registration required each child
to jump smartly to their feet in response to their name. By
the time she was in position the teacher was moving briskly
through R, S, T, U and V.

She'd pause, begin the little ceremony of lighting a cigarette, drawing out the first inhalation, until she saw Elka stand.

Shaking with relief she left by the west gate, her eyes down
cast, knowing that she must not look past the school to the
wide bombsite beyond the flats. If she did, she would not see
the swept earth, the islands of rubble, the ruptured pipes. She
would see instead the field of the dead at Borek, the pits, and
beside them the fires over which the bodies burnt on their
concrete platforms, the oily smoke twisting up into the sky.

Chapter 36

Two days after their interview with Tomma, they walked to Potsdamer Platz, once the busiest square in Europe, and one of Peter's favourite places, because it was usually deserted, except for a single *brati* stall, providing a puddle of lurid light in the darkness of a neighbourhood that still lay in ruins. But tonight, a small crowd, two or three hundred strong, stood in the far distance, just short of the checkpoint into the East. A single floodlight showed the barbed wire, and lurking a hundred yards beyond, the geometrical shadow of a tank, the barrel pointing west.

A tram crossed the square, its wake marked by twin tracks, the lit interior bleak but crowded with reinforcements for the demonstration, placards pressed to the glass. The city was in the throes of a crisis, but the world seemed to be looking the other way. There was still no official word from the Americans, or the British or the French. The TV showed pictures of women and children jumping from windows on Bernauer Strasse to be caught in blankets, while an East German guard with a map was pictured carefully painting a white line across the road at every crossing point, a task that reminded Hanna of her crayons and the walls of Swan House.

Hanna and Peter waited for their food in a cloud of greasy condensation as the demonstrators, mostly students, called out for freedom, for the Americans to come and clear away the barrier, for Free Berlin. In the gaps between the orchestrated chants, people shouted out the names of family and friends on the far side. But in the East, nothing moved, except for a pair of border guards smoking cigarettes and watching the crowd with professional indifference.

Peter shook out an f6, rolling his shoulders, trying to edge the slight chill of midnight out of his loose-fitting jacket.

'There was a crowd in the gallery this afternoon from Bonn – Brits mainly,' he said. 'Word is, it took them days to get through to Kennedy – he was out at Cape Cod. So everyone's catching up. They reckon Khrushchev's bluffing, but that doesn't mean we'll take 'em on.

'Maybe it'll blow over, but maybe this is for keeps. I hope not. I kinda liked this place as it was, ghosts and all.'

Peter had taken her to a photographic gallery on the Ku'Damm to see an exhibition on pre-war Berlin: the platz in its heyday had been the centre of an empire: a jigsaw of metropolitan life, all controlled by the Traffic Tower, with its nightmare shades of Lang or Orwell: a mathematical construction of steel, thirty-foot high, displaying red and green signals. And what traffic! Peter was ready with the numbers for her: thousands had criss-crossed the square every day, in buses, trams, cars and on bicycles. In a glass room at the top of the tower, a policeman, omniscient, pushed the necessary buttons, and pulled the levers, controlling everything.

The war had left behind a bombsite, stranded where the three Allied zones met the Soviet Sector. Hanna thought about what lay *beneath* the dust and rubble: the tramlines (partly cleared), the tunnels leading down to the forgotten U-Bahn stations, the flowerbeds and statues: all lost – the café tables reduced to matchwood, the beer halls in rubble. But, like Peter, she could feel the people, the ghosts moving along the paths that lay hidden, controlled perhaps by phantom signals from the Traffic Tower.

Which made her think about Borek.

Vogel's and Boniek's testimony had opened a door to the past, but they couldn't step through it. There was no record of the Borek gold after the war, no *official* record certainly, and no paper-trail leading back to the trial held by the SS. Clarke had made enquiries – in Berlin, Paris and London, with the library at Nuremberg. There was nothing. Everything had gone up in flames at Borek as the Red Army approached. So the question remained: how had Hanna gone from there to here: the steps of the gas chamber, to the Potsdamer Platz?

She wondered if Borek felt like this: a wide clearing in the forest perhaps, the grass gone to seed, haunted by the pathways beneath. The camp had come alive in her imagination; she *felt* closer, not just to the past but to her mother and father and sister, but only thanks to borrowed memories. Which made her feel despair again, as she had that night at Swan House; a physical void in her chest, as if she might implode and fall to the ground, so slight she'd fail to leave a mark in the city's dust.

The tram clanked out of sight behind a streetscape of rubble.

She sat down on a low ruined wall, on the edge of the island of light, while Peter went to the stall. Another tram entered from Bellevuestrasse, the overhead pantograph showering sparks down into the gloom. It ran, bell tolling, across the wasteland, trailing miniature thunderbolts.

'So what do we know?' asked Peter, coming back with bottles of beer and two trays of chips and sausages smeared in curry sauce. She knew then that her despair had betrayed her. She felt physically smaller – shoulders hunched, her arms held close, cowering in her coat.

He answered his own question. 'Many things, Han. That they – you – might have left for Berlin in the lorries with the gold, or as witnesses for the unfinished trial. Or – like Vogel even – you somehow survived and escaped after the revolt.'

He swigged his beer from the bottle.

'But where did my family go, Pete? Why am I alone? If they're alive, why are they hiding from me?'

She clutched herself. 'What if it is only me. What if they all died at Borek.'

'But the letter,' he said.

'You said yourself – this could be about the gold, or the trial. The letter was on Stasi notepaper. Maybe we're just being used. Do Clarke and Pierce think we can find out what happened, where they've failed?'

Overhead they heard a helicopter circling, a single beam of light swinging briefly over the vast open space, searching for the small crowd.

They ate and drank in silence.

'One last try, then,' said Peter. 'But this time we look somewhere new.'

'Where?'

'Clarke came to the gallery today – just before we closed up. He brought Pierce. He was in a five-hundred-dollar suit. He offered me a three-month extension to my contract, so I can paint here, so there'll be Berlin pictures, a legacy they can hang on the wall.'

Peter ate, the vivid red sauce smearing his lips.

'What do they want in return?' asked Hanna.

'Good question. Like you say, they're good at hiding what they're really after.'

'So what did you say?'

Peter held up a hand, screwed up the greasy tray and took it to a bin by the stall, buying two more beers.

They clinked glass. 'I said I'd stay if they helped try and find your father. Tried harder, tried faster. We're in a dead-end now – Vogel, Boniek, the witnesses. We tried, we failed, but that doesn't need to be the end of it.'

He lit an f6. Hanna wondered if this was one last effort to find her father, or one last effort to keep her in Berlin. She was due to fly back to London in seven days. It was a return ticket and she'd already booked the taxi to Tempelhof.

'I want them to ask questions in Poland, at the estate at Łabędzie. Get someone there – an agent, police, I don't care. That's where you and Natasza fetched up. It's only fifteen years ago – it's not some kinda lost legend. You were there, Natasza was there, Hasard was there, briefly at least. Someone must know their story, your story. The count wrote letters, sure, used the channels, pulled strings. That's not enough. Someone needs to ask the right questions …'

'Is it possible?' asked Hanna, looking across the platz at the checkpoint. Poland lay beyond, embedded in the Eastern Bloc. Despite her misgivings she felt that there was hope, however distant.

'Sure it's *possible*,' said Peter. 'They're the Berlin mafia – they can call in some favours.'

Hanna put a hand on the baby.

'I can't stay for ever,' she said. 'A week, Pete. Then I'm gone.'

'I told them the clock was ticking.'

Chapter 37

The prison stood on an island where two roads divided, and so the traffic, oblivious to the individual dramas within the walls, streamed past on either side. Marcin had made Hanna a medieval fort as a child, with just the same double-turret façade, the portcullis waiting to drop, the drawbridge over a dry moat. Paying the cab driver, she turned and looked beyond the crenelated walls to the central block, with its serried rows of barred windows, roofs patched, the brickwork decorated with that peculiar pattern that had become a *leitmotif* of Berlin's suburbs: the gun spatter. All this, she thought, for three prisoners.

They'd driven into the British Sector from Andrews Barracks, trying to avoid the crowds, but getting stuck fast, just west of the Tiergarten where the radio said a million Berliners were lining the route in from the West, waiting for the US Armoured Brigade, and for the limousine carrying Vice President Johnson. The city had gone 'LBJ' mad, the crowds waving the stars and stripes, while the Wall got bigger and stronger every day. There were tanks now at several crossings, and they'd shot a man in the Humboldt Canal, trying to swim to the West. At the checkpoint on Friedrichstrasse, two Red Army tanks faced two US Army tanks. If the world was a bomb, that was the fuse.

Colonel Maxim Krikalev met them in the gatehouse and watched, smoking, as they completed the necessary bureaucratic requirements at a counter overlooked by a large framed portrait of Stalin. The Four Powers shared the duties of guarding Spandau on a rota basis. As they'd crossed the drawbridge, they'd noted the Red Flags flying. But the entrance hall, and the first corridor, didn't smell very Russian. The French had gone overnight, and left behind a trace of polish, fresh coffee, and – somewhere – they'd baked bread, because the sweet aroma of melted butter was hypnotic.

'Definitely the French,' said Peter, sniffing the air, as they followed Krikalev, a remarkably thin-boned comrade, with a light step, and a small round head set on a slender neck. The Red Army uniform was immaculate, but Hanna thought there was something louche about the colonel's body language, as if he had another life, far removed from military regulations.

Krikalev was one of Pierce's contacts, and he knew Clarke too, so they were wary. Peter had pressed for help on getting questions asked at Łabędzie, and this had been the result after three days of silence: a one-line typed pass into the world's most infamous prison.

They hadn't asked for a tour, but the celebrity status of the prisoners, and of the gaol itself, was clearly taken for granted. They were escorted upstairs and along a corridor that had windows on one side giving a view of a courtyard. The colonel stopped and threw open a window.

'The infamous garden,' he said, his English polished. 'Prisoner 4 is the mastermind here. The architect of the Third Reich now plants his favourite flower: the daisy.'

'Speer?' asked Peter.

'Only numbers here,' said Krikalev.

There had been eight prisoners after Nuremberg: now there were just three, including Hitler's architect and munitions minister. Handsome, urbane, even modern, but reduced now to designing the parterre.

'There's a particular pattern?' asked Hanna, reminded of the hidden paths of the Potsdamer Platz.

Krikalev nodded. 'Yes. Prisoner 4 says he wishes to keep his mind trained – honed, for the day he walks free. Which will be never. He has a programme of study: mathematics, aesthetics, geology. And a two-week holiday each year: a holiday of the mind. For this he reads travel books: he picks a country – perhaps India, or Peru – he studies the maps, plans an itinerary, an imaginary walk. He acts out the hike in the garden. He estimates his achievements. We are told it is now nearly ten thousand kilometres. He walks the imaginary world in his head.'

Krikalev shrugged. 'He tells his guard this is therapeutic. Personally, I hope that is a lie. He should have hanged in this very yard, where the gallows stood, alongside the rest.'

Hanna struggled to follow the colonel's words. She felt sick and nauseous, and her joints ached as if she'd had to scale the walls of Spandau, not stroll over the bridge. The prison seemed to be bleeding her dry of energy: the puddles on the floor, the carcass of a dead bird, the cells to the right, doors open, each the same: whitewashed, a rusted bunk-frame, a bucket. Every detail seemed to weigh her down.

Peter took her arm. 'Hanna's tired,' he said to Krikalev. 'A glass of water?'

The colonel's eyes considered her face, then the hand on her belly. 'Of course. We are nearly at the office.'

Krikalev strode along a corridor, leading them on into a block where they could hear the staccato gunfire of a typewriter from behind a door.

Unlocking an office, pausing on the threshold, he nodded down a corridor in which three guards sat on stools, facing each other, rifles at attention.

'The prisoners. For one hundred dollars you can see one, any one. Even his Imperial Lordship is available – but then we don't need his permission. He is unwell these days. At night he shrieks and cries, which is sweet music indeed. If I had a tape machine, I'd make a record and sell it on Mother's Day.'

Krikalev closed his office door, placed his cap on a peg. 'The French let him out for walks, on the street, and take him to a restaurant – a British restaurant – so perhaps it is a form of punishment after all ...'

Rudolf Hess, the one-time Deputy Führer, was Spandau's *raison d'être*. Despite her anxiety Hanna registered the moment: they were twenty steps away from a man who had helped make her world – all of it: the lost childhood, the missing parents, the dislocated life on Long Fen. Like Hackendorf he had been an operator of a machine, only on a vastly more lethal scale.

Hanna took the chair and a glass of water. The prison's cloistered silence, so deep despite the city outside, was pressing down on her. On the desktop she noted an edition of the *International Herald Tribune* that carried a large picture of Adolf Eichmann in the dock at his trial in Israel. Perhaps he'd once had an office as mundane as Krikalev's.

The colonel placed a hand on the newspaper. 'The jury is out. But we know the verdict, do we not? There will be no appetite for pleas for clemency there, I think. Our dull pen-pusher will hang by the neck.'

He took his seat, straightening his uniform. 'I'm talking to you in the interests of denazification. I was a member of an intelligence unit that reached Borek a few days after its liberation.'

For a moment Hanna processed the thought: the revolt was over, the Germans had fled, and then within hours, emerging from the great wastes of the Pripet Marshes, came the Red Army. But what in reality had they *liberated*?

'I understand you think your father, and possibly other members of the family, survived the camp, as you did yourself, although you were a child, and the memory is lost. I have been directed to help if I can.

'But I have to tell you I, we, have our own motives in this – what shall we call it? This quest? Along with Major Clarke and Secretary Pierce, we are of one mind. Your father, you see, is not the only missing person.'

Krikalev had their complete attention, so he took the moment to produce a silver cigarette case, and taking one, threw it down casually, so that they could help themselves.

'Two officers remain unaccounted for from the camp garrison: lieutenants by the names of Meyer and Sandberger.

'They did not leave on any of the German convoy trucks and their bodies were not found – either by us, or their own comrades. At least this is the case if we believe the account given by the acting commandant, Eisner. He stood trial at Nuremberg, after the Borek hearings, and he escaped the rope, so perhaps we should be wary of his testimony. Until now we simply assumed their bodies lay hidden in the chaos of the camp with the other dead.

'Now, it seems, there is another possibility. You are alive, Miss Stern. Perhaps also your father. My question is: are they?'

Hanna, revived by the cold water, nodded.

'All this to track down two SS officers of minor rank,' said Peter. 'There must be hundreds, thousands, like them.'

Krikalev steepled his fingers. The mannerism spoke again of a more cerebral role: a KGB officer perhaps, of unknown seniority.

'When we reached the camp, the dead had been dead for days. It was high summer, and the heat and flies were impossible. The Ukrainian guards had fled back to villages in the woods, a few cabins in rough clearings. We rounded them up and they dug fresh trenches.'

He sucked nicotine deep into his lungs.

'In the German compound we found a few dead soldiers, still in uniform, rank-and-file SS. The commandant, shot in the revolt, had been buried with honour, on the drill square.'

Krikalev smiled. 'We dug him up and threw him in the open pits beyond the gas chamber.' He flapped a languid hand. 'A minor lapse of discipline. Emotions were high. It had been a long march. We had seen many dreadful things, but to see this place was a revelation. Is this the right word? Perhaps.'

Krikalev shrugged as if this was his burden; a kind of grim enlightenment.

He had to relight his cigarette. 'The Germans had destroyed much evidence. Fires had been fed with documents. The corpses of the dead dug up and burnt. Even the bones. But, in a small shack, we found something of very great significance. It was a tally house, and the tallyman was Sandberger. You are right. Meyer is inconsequential, although he was the confidant of Sandberger, and it is Sandberger who kept the numbers. He counted the prisoners off the train, he counted them as they progressed through the squares, he counted them at the gas chamber. Each night he went to the tally house and chalked up the numbers. Later, Eigrupper – the old commandant – would come to inspect the figures.

'When we found the tally house, we expected to find nothing left. Sandberger had been ordered to destroy everything: this order, from Eisner, was given on the evening of the revolt. But Sandberger disappeared, and the chalk board in the tally house still held its numbers when I entered it three days later.'

From under the desk he produced a leather satchel, and a notebook. Hanna noted the Cyrillic script, and the carefully etched numerals.

'There had been no transport trains for twenty-four hours. The complement of slaves in the camp on the morning before the revolt was one thousand and seven. We know now that while many escaped, only forty-two survived the war. The most important number was on the board: the cumulative total of the dead, over the two years of the camp's operation. This was 342,315.'

A pair of dusty pigeons landed on the windowsill and scuffled, scratching on concrete.

Hanna, her breath shallow, imagined again the view from the dust, the prisoners walking towards the gas chamber.

'Why do we wish to find Sandberger?' asked Krikalev. 'Because it was his duty to communicate these numbers to Berlin. That is the line we wish to establish: from the tally house in the woods to the Führer's office in Berlin, and then – finally – to the bunker in the Prussian woods to the man himself. The Führer, of course, is beyond our justice now. But the intermediaries may be alive. Several are at liberty, many of them thriving no doubt, in the West ...'

The colonel placed two passport-sized photographs on the desktop.

'Meyer here,' he said, touching one. 'And Sandberger here ... Take a moment. It is best to keep them in your mind. There is a trick to this. You keep these faces, of the young officers, and you rotate them in your imagination, see them from all sides, and then you add the years, and then one day you see a face in a crowd ...'

Hanna studied the pictures, which were black and white, and no doubt the work of an official photographer. Both men were without expression, but in immaculate uniforms. It struck her that in her unremembered life she had probably seen them before.

Peter looked too, but then decided that the time had come to press on with their own agenda. 'I asked Major Clarke about Łabędzie – the estate, in Poland?'

Krikalev stiffened, and then smiled at Hanna. 'Colonel Clarke tells me that you recall nothing?'

'Nothing of the camp, or the estate, except for the last year – a few images, nothing more. Before that my life is a blank.'

'If you went back to Łabędzie perhaps there would be – what shall we call it – an awakening?'

'Is it possible, to go back?' asked Peter.

Krikalev stood, opened the window, and shooed away the pigeons.

'Efforts are being made. But the situation is volatile. The Americans wish to *appear* engaged with the process of denazification. But they must balance the interests of their allies. On our side the precise relationship between Moscow and our friends here in the GDR is nebulous.

'Frankly, there is chaos. But at least it is bureaucratic chaos. So there may be a chance. You should be ready if Major Clarke calls,' he said. 'This is a matter of utmost importance at the highest levels. We must explore all avenues open to us.'

'I fly back on Friday,' said Hanna.

Krikalev nodded, lighting another cigarette. 'Until then you will no doubt continue your enquiries. We have taken a further look at the Vogels by the way. They seem innocent. We will conduct a formal interview, but in all probability their file will be closed.

'Boniek too. He has returned to the East. We were wary of his determination to defend one version of the story. But he is harmless.'

Krikalev closed the file with the hand that held his cigarette.

'The situation in the city, in the wider world, is deteriorating quickly. Our ability to cooperate may be drastically reduced.'

He stood and offered his hand to Hanna. 'If you remember anything, Miss Stern, about the camp, about your escape, tell Major Clarke. Tell him quickly.'

Chapter 38

The clerk of the court read out Stern's full name, and the address he'd given in the ghetto. His medical degree was cited but he was not addressed as 'doctor'. Stern was still in shock, seated beside the now empty chair where his little daughter had so recently jiggled her legs on her mother's lap. The absence, the sense of a permanent void, drained him of energy, and a feeling of exhaustion was deepened by the heat of the day. There was a large electric horizontal fan attached to the central light that turned lazily over his head and made him feel worse, creating the illusion that the fan was stationary while the room was spinning.

For several hours after they'd taken Irena and Hanna away, he'd sat and listened to the proceedings. The rest of the witnesses, including his elder daughter, were sent back to the water tower at lunchtime, while Stern was given bread and water in the corridor, sitting on the polished bench beside Brunner. Various officers came and went in the witness box. Funk, the prosecutor, tried to project Meyer as a Jew-lover, with a personal grudge against the punctilious Keuper. But the morning had not gone well. The defence had patiently stuck to the facts, pointing out that Meyer had sought to follow regulations.

It was clear that the case would turn on what had happened on the Himmelstrasse, especially what had been said between Meyer and Keuper. Stern's evidence would be vital because he was clearly seen as the leader of the Jews who had been present at the killing. This gave him a degree of power, over both the outcome of the case, and more importantly, its length. His life, all of their lives, depended on a protracted trial.

At last, Stern was called to the witness stand, but, stumbling, he had to grip the lectern, and so Johl ordered a chair. The relief when he sat down was like a drug, so that he thought he might swoon, but he decided instead (and it did feel like his decision) to remain conscious. The heat, the lack of sleep, his exertions in the woods, combined to produce an oddly elevated mood.

Funk's tactics were quickly clear. He would get to what was said on the Himmelstrasse soon enough. First, he wanted to depict Keuper as a diligent officer who had spotted Liff's suitcase, and its suspicious contents, and then dragged the doctor back to the square to try and find his suitcase, because he suspected he was in league with the *Armia*, and that he too was a bomb maker.

'He knew you were a saboteur just like the watchmaker Liff. Isn't this true?' asked Funk.

The court looked at Stern. Since taking the stand the doctor had felt his fear dissipating. He felt a peculiar sense of ease. He'd been given a role within the administration of justice, while, outside, his brothers and sisters trudged towards their deaths in the gas chamber. He felt an almost crushing weight of responsibility to them, an urge to voice injustice. This, he felt, was his opportunity.

'No, it isn't true. Jonas Keuper didn't suspect me of being a saboteur.'

Stern's contradiction of Funk brought complete silence to the room.

Funk looked to the bench for support, but Johl's watery eyes were on the witness. Then the judge made a note, as did Ebner. Johl used a fountain pen, the deputy commandant a pencil. The sound of the dual scratching of nib and lead was like a piece of experimental music.

Funk had no choice but to ask the next question. 'How do you know this? Can you read the mind of a German officer?'

Stern saw the fear in Funk's eyes: not the everyday fear of the camp – the brooding sense of violence, a physical, visceral alarm. This was a *forensic* fear, an anxiety entirely confined to the courtroom. Stern knew the lawyers' golden rule. On his feet, in front of a judge, a lawyer should never ask a question to which he does not already know the answer.

Stern's blood drummed with a sense of power.

'No, I cannot read minds. He never mentioned sabotage. I was his family's doctor at home in Bavaria. I was a friend of his father. He told me to look for my case – he thought I might have a diary, or papers. It had gone. Then we talked of other things.'

Johl brought his gavel down with a sharp crack.

Like most bureaucrats the judge advocate was clearly irritated by the unexpected. 'The witness is telling the court that he had a conversation with Jonas Keuper shortly before his death? A *private* conversation?'

'Yes.'

Johl spoke in a whisper to Ebner, then Sandberger, their faces betraying nothing but bureaucratic concentration. Stern was aware that his testimony threatened the due process of the law; a turn of events that might cost him his life.

'I see. A surprising development …'

'A recess perhaps?' asked Funk, out of turn.

Johl slowly removed his glasses. Funk sat down.

'We will continue for now. We are hardly blessed with time to waste. Let's get to the heart of this. Just ask the questions, Funk.'

Funk went back to his desk and tipped open a file.

His neck was bright red and Stern could see he was playing for time.

'Perhaps you can enlighten the court as to the content of this private conversation. Or is it just a fabrication?' asked Funk.

Stern was now in complete control of the cross-examination.

It was hot and his lips were dry.

'Can I have a glass of water?'

Brunner brought him a tin beaker, ignoring the glasses and decanter set on the clerk's table.

Stern drank, gulping, allowing the noise of his Adam's apple to echo in the courtroom.

Finally, he was ready to answer the question. 'It is not a fabrication. We had a conversation of about five minutes on several matters.'

There was silence in court.

'Go on,' said Johl, taking over Funk's duties.

Stern gave a brisk summary of his encounter with Keuper, starting with the SS officer's demand that he be told a secret about Weissenstein – their home village. Stern said that finally he *had* offered up a secret of sorts, certainly a scandal: the story of Keuper's young brother, Christoph, an imbecile taken away by the state, and his sad death from pneumonia.

At this allusion to Aktion T4 the atmosphere in the courtroom became tense.

'But the truth was that Christoph, and all the others, was murdered by the state,' said Stern, finally.

Several officers jumped to their feet; Ebner stood too, one fist in a tight ball, staring at Stern.

Johl raised his voice. 'The programme of state-controlled euthanasia has, of course, been discontinued following an order – a direct order – from the office of the Führer,' he said.

Stern hadn't finished. 'Yes. But the biggest secret is that the programme continues. Illegally.'

Above the uproar Stern's voice went unheard. 'Many of the methods perfected then have clearly evolved into what we see today. Out of that window.'

Stern raised a hand in accusation and pointed just above Johl's head.

One of the officers in the front row took a few steps towards Stern, as if ready to drag him off the stand. A senior officer stood up and walked out of the court, but as he went through the doorway he turned back. 'They should take the bastard out and shoot him; but why waste the bullet?'

Johl's face had reddened. He smashed the gavel down hard and missed the silver holder so that the hammer struck the top of the oak desk.

Gradually the room fell silent. The guards outside the courtroom had come in and cocked their rifles.

Johl cleaned his glasses and then leant back in his seat, then forward, clasping and unclasping his hands.

'Do not repeat this again. Ever. The programme of euthanasia for mental defectives and the deformed has been suspended by government order. That is the legal position.'

Stern made an effort to relax his shoulders.

Johl was collecting up his papers. Ebner sat down but was looking through the doctor, as if he was already a ghost.

'We will adjourn,' said Johl. 'The court will sit tomorrow. The witness can stand down, but he will be recalled because he is to bear witness to what was said by the defendant before he fired the fatal shot.

'When he returns he will mind his tongue or pay the consequence, as will his family and friends. The court will not allow insubordination again. Not one word.'

Johl was studying a piece of paper. 'But first, a detail. What is the witness's full name?'

There was a peculiar lilt to his voice, a combination of menace and playfulness that made Stern's mouth suddenly devoid of spit.

'Leopold Emanuel Lasker Stern.'

'Precisely. L.E.L. Stern. How satisfying. Thank you.'

Without any explanation Johl led the three judges out of the court.

Chapter 39

Liff had been laid in his cell on his bunk and Duvos, who wouldn't cross the threshold but had kept an unbroken watch on his injured compatriot, said that his breathing had changed, his thin chest rising and falling, rising and falling, in an ever-shallower rhythm.

'He's dying,' he told Stern. 'Not that you need *me* to tell you that, doctor. But they'll want him in court eventually, right? They'll have to get him on his feet.'

Stern shook his head. 'They're finished with our watch-maker. They're only interested in me, Duvos. So relax. The trial will last another day at least.'

Judi struggled up the stairs with a big bucket of water. 'This is from the horse trough, but it will have to do. I've scooped the scum off the surface.'

Leo took the water into Liff's cell and filled the tin mug. The watchmaker drank three lots, then said he'd had enough. 'That will do,' he said, as if it was the last drink he'd ever take.

They washed Liff's face, revealing under the dried blood a blinded eye.

'Raeder, the SS investigator, left me to the Ukrainie,' said Liff. 'But they didn't show the necessary brutality. They're just victims like us. So Raeder took over. He said I might not be a saboteur but I'd made him miss the soup course. He said I'd never fix another watch and he was true to his word. You can't do the intricate work without stereoscopy. The mechanism has no depth, it looks like a diagram, not a living watch.'

David joined them. The teenager looked older. His clothes defined the shape of his body, not the other way round. In his hand he had a metal bracket Stern recognised as part of a bunk-bed. The boy twisted the door handle on Liff's cell, then stood on the edge of the bed to test the bars on the window. Reaching over to a pipe attached by bolts to the ceiling, he tested his weight on it to see if it was firmly fixed.

Then he sat down on the floor and embraced his own knees. 'I'm very worried about dying,' he said. His face began to crease, to fold, tears trickling down his cheeks.

'I've been trying to understand the plumbing,' he said, wiping his face, making an effort to sound workmanlike. 'How it all fits together.' He looked up at the ceiling and the maze of pipes, which clearly provided a diversion from the wider world. 'I wish they'd let us drink the clean water, then there'd be a point to it all.'

Stern placed a hand on the boy's head. 'We are just men born at the wrong time, David. This is a German world, and then it will be a Russian world. I don't think we've got much chance in either. All you can do is watch, and wait, and who knows, God may save us after all.' Even Stern didn't sound as if he thought this was likely.

A slave appeared with Brunner to take away the toilet buckets. The guard took up his usual seat at the top of the stairwell. He sat quietly, his hands cupped on his lap as if in prayer. The heat was stifling now under the weight of water above their heads, and Brunner took off his tunic and sat naked from his belt up. He had a strong body, muscled, with white skin. On his upper biceps was a tattoo of a cross, with Christ's body in agony.

Stern sat on the floor, his back to a wooden partition. The German un-cupped his hands from his lap and Stern saw that he hadn't been praying at all. He had a lizard in his hand, frozen still, petrified.

'If the Americans come will you say I was kind?'

'The *Americans*?' In the ghetto they'd heard snippets of news from the outside world, picked up on the many illicit radios in the tenement blocks, for which the Germans searched with dogs and guns. But there had been no news from the West – and Brunner's tone implied this was already *old* news.

'We shouldn't listen to the radio but we do. Berlin says nothing, Warsaw nothing. But one of the men who cleans in our hut can speak Russian. He listens for us. Moscow says the Americans have landed in the West – in France. If they come they'll find this place. It doesn't matter about the fires. Even if we burn all the paperwork it won't help. The partisans know what's happening.'

Stern steepled his fingers to indicate the taking of an oath. 'If I'm alive, and the Americans come, I'll say you were kind, Brunner. But if the Americans come, will there be anyone left alive? Why leave witnesses breathing, when so many have died?'

'And I made that toy for your little girl,' said Brunner.

Stern said nothing.

'We're running out of Jews, it's true. Three trains today, from Hungary and the East, one from Bordeaux. Most of the other camps have shut down. They say Budapest is *judenfrei*. Berlin soon. If the trains stop, they'll kill all the Jews – the slaves too. We don't need them if there's no work left to do. That will be the end. Then we can go home.'

Stern lowered his voice. 'Brunner, will you do something for me if you can? Another favour you can add to the list. In the second square the prisoners leave their spectacles in a heap. Could you bring me a pair, maybe three? It's for a friend. You won't get into trouble.'

'Glasses for reading?'

'Yes.'

'I'll try. It's a kindness after all.'

Brunner stood, quickly pulling on his tunic and buttoning it up. 'It's time to sweep up downstairs.'

Stern could see what the young soldier would look like if he ever got to live his life. A kindly father, perhaps, if he was given the chance.

'I must lock the cells, you should all rest.' He took a step closer to Stern and whispered: 'I will be back at eleven to-night, doctor. Be ready. And the girl.'

Stern went to his own bed and lay down, thinking of Irena and Hanna. He felt very strongly that they were still alive but was aware that this idea – that they breathed, and talked, and walked – might be an illusion, in that they had always existed so strongly in his imagination.

When he awoke, someone had come into the cell without disturbing him.

A small battered table, made of mahogany, and once inlaid with mother-of-pearl, had been set by his bunk. On it, the pieces in place and ready to start a game, stood a chess set. Oddly, the chessmen were not black and white, but red and white. The workmanship was very fine, certainly beyond the skills of Brunner. There was something disturbing about the clandestine gift, as if it were bait in a trap.

Chapter 40

Georg Johl was tired. As soon as he left the courtroom by a side-door he felt the fatigue of the day. A tumbler of brandy, a bath, some fresh cologne, a cigar – these were his goals, but first he had to report to his temporary office. He walked to the commandant's bungalow in the evening sun and said a courteous good evening to Eigrupper, still under house arrest. The old man aged by the day. He sat rigid in his chair, in his habitual white shirt, reading in the shade of the covered terrace. Johl tried not to react to the commandant's arrogant posture: the straight spine, the level jaw, shoulders back.

Eigrupper's bedroom and sitting room were to the right of the entrance hallway; while to the left an anteroom had been set aside for a secretary, beyond which was the commandant's office, both of which had been requisitioned by the SS legal department for the duration of the court sessions.

Beatrice Padberg, the commandant's secretary, was in her mid-twenties. At the end of the working day a car took her back to a hotel in town. She had a signed photograph of Joseph Goebbels on her desk. Johl wondered how long the snapshot of her hero would remain on the desk once the sound of Russian tank-fire began to rattle the windows.

'Good evening, Beatrice,' he said.

She stood at Johl's arrival, her shorthand pad held against her chest. She wore a plaid skirt that dropped to just below her knee. She always wore stockings and Johl noted they were never laddered.

'A call, please. Can you try to get me to the SS switchboard in Krakow? I want to relay a call to Berlin, to my office.' Johl

checked the clock, which read 5.08 p.m. Ingrid, his private
secretary, left at 5.25 p.m. precisely.

'Brandy?' asked Padberg.

'It can wait. The call first if you please.'

He went into Eigrupper's office, leaving the door open, and
took his seat, to wait for his call. The current case worried
him. From the opening statements he had begun to harbour
doubts about the true motives of Rolf Meyer. The answer to
that riddle lay here, at Borek. The more he discovered about
Meyer, the more questions remained, and the more he heard,
the less he trusted what he heard. But it was Keuper's motives
that were his current preoccupation. His headstrong attempt
to murder the Jewish doctor looked stagey, melodramat-
ic even. What was the precise relationship between Keuper
and Stern? Their shared past in a small Bavarian village was
a worrying coincidence. Johl felt a little background research
would help.

Absolutely nobody was going to make a fool out of Georg
Johl.

He needed to make that call. Impatient, he stood and went
to a large globe in a wooden, circular frame. With his finger
he traced the long arc of the Frisian Islands, where he owned
a chalet and had spent the summer months in the years before the war with his wife and children. At this scale the coast
of England looked very close. The borders of the Reich had
been inked in at their 1941 extremities – a cruel commentary
now, as the Russian armies drove westwards, and the Americans and British, eastwards. Johl, who had read history at university in Hamburg before taking up the law, imagined that in
the years and even decades to come, after Germany had lost
the war, zealots would treasure maps produced during this
brief interlude between blitzkrieg and retreat: a cartographic
snapshot of the Nazi high tide.

'Krakow is on the line,' said Padberg, appearing at the door.

Johl sat and picked up the receiver. A crackling voice asked what he required. 'A Berlin number please: 5657.'

The sound of an open telephone line was, thought Johl, multi-layered. He could hear at least three conversations, one distant, two quite close, and all in German. Then, periodically, the whirr of interconnections, as the call made its way in zig-zag fashion north from Krakow to Berlin. Then total silence, but not a dead line – that would have sounded final, echoless, whereas this was like a moment of electronic free-fall. Johl thought the chaos on the line reflected perfectly Germany's condition: armies on three fronts losing battles, civilians starving in between air raids at home, all held together by the brittle routine of a bureaucratic state.

A single metallic click, and then a voice: 'The office of Sturmbannführer Johl.'

'Ingrid,' he said.

'Herr Johl.'

He heard the distinct sound of a ringed shorthand notebook being flipped open.

'Ingrid. I am in the commandant's office at Borek. I need you to take a request for information down to records. I'm interested in a family called Keuper.' He spelt the surname. 'From Weissenstein, near Regen, in the Bavarian Forest.

'There were three sons in this family, Ingrid: Ritter, Jonas and Christoph. Jonas was an SS Obersturmführer here at Borek. The father is named Johann, a local tax collector with the state government in Munich. Also, a magistrate, so there should be references in our records. If not, ask them to try the Gestapo, and then the central office. I'm afraid I need information tonight – or tomorrow morning. I am sorry, Ingrid.'

Outside, in the camp, Johl heard the klaxon mark the hour, but there was an awkward silence in Berlin. He felt it was his duty to ask for the latest news in the capital, but he hesitated. While the radio broadcasts were upbeat, he knew the reality was very different. Life here, on the far edge of the new German empire, felt precarious enough without evidence that the Reich's great city was in chaos. His wife and family were on the coast, but his home was in the suburbs.

'How is the situation?' he asked, carefully.

'They've taken to leaving the dead in the streets,' said Ingrid, her voice catching. 'It takes several days for them to be cleared away to the cemeteries. They burn them there, which leaves a cloud in the sky all day.

'At night we go down to the U-Bahn. There is no point waiting for the air-raid warning. It is frightening and everyone is tired. We come out at dawn and go home and wash and then come to work.'

'Yes. I see,' said Johl. He thought an upbeat assessment of the war against Russia was called for at this point, but the energy required to fabricate the lie flooded away.

'I'll let you get on,' he said.

But then the dismal tone of the conversation seemed to demand decisive action, and that in turn made him realise he'd made a mistake typical of what his brother officers called the *Herrenrasse* – the master race: they were prone to ignore the dangers posed by those deemed less than human.

'One last thing. Do we have a man in Regen?'

For a moment Ingrid consulted the files.

'Yes. A staff officer – Hauptsturmführer Jurgens.'

'If you can raise him on the phone get him to drive out to Weissenstein tonight. He should inform the family that Jonas Keuper is dead. He died in action. The family need to know no more at this stage. Then, as I said, I want to know about the family. But most of all I want to know about their relationship with the village doctor, a man called Leopold Stern, a Jew. This is most important, Ingrid. I want to know about the Jew.'

Chapter 41

The sickbay at Borek had eight beds, only one of which was in use, by an SS trooper who had broken his leg hunting for Eigrupper's gold. Up in one of the barrack-hut attics the planks had given out beneath him and he'd fallen through the ceiling, driving his thigh bone into his pelvis with such force that the leg had shattered like a champagne flute struck with a blacksmith's hammer. Irena knew that the pain must be very bad because when she wiped the sweat from his forehead, the water was icy cold.

The trooper's name was Eric Carstens. Irena had told him her name, and that she had come to Borek with her husband, a doctor, and their two daughters. She was alone now. She'd told him all their names too, even though it was clear he did not care.

'They didn't need my youngest daughter. She's six. So they took her away.' She wanted to cry out these words, but instead all she heard was her own voice, distant and calm.

'She'll be ash with the rest,' said the trooper through his teeth. 'Good riddance.'

These words fell like a blow on Irena. She carried Hanna's absence as a void in her chest, which threatened to drain her body of the slightest energy. The separation had occurred less than five hours earlier. Part of her mind was constructing a screen, beyond which it was increasingly difficult to glimpse the final image, of her daughter staring into a stranger's eyes.

Carstens wasn't paying attention. Despite the pain he was far too happy to listen to anyone else. The injury promised a ticket home to a hospital in Germany. *Germany!* Tears of excitement and joy welled up in his eyes.

'Tell me again,' he said. 'How long will it take to heal? Months, you said?'

'It's a multiple fracture and the cast will have to embrace the hip. Dr Lange will make the decision of course, but perhaps eight weeks, six at the very least.'

They had given Irena a white smock and a nurse's fob-watch, which had a cracked glass but worked nonetheless. She still felt like a fraud, for her medical qualifications were non-existent. What she knew she had learnt in the years she had assisted Leo in the surgery at Weissenstein. But they needed a nurse urgently, Kopp had told her, and for this reason she had been picked out by the kapos. No: not *only* for that reason. Kopp wanted her to carry out a task that had nothing to do with her medical skills. In return, he would tell Leo that she was alive, and working in the sickbay.

Carstens' lips parted in a smile, revealing teeth clamped together to stop himself crying out with the pain.

'Fuck me, I'm a lucky pig. They sent Sig home and that was only for three weeks. I'll be going out on one of those trains. Home.' The word alone brought fresh tears to his eyes.

When Kopp had brought her to the sickbay, the doctor had asked her to list the symptoms of internal bleeding, the outward signs of gangrene, and to explain how to evaluate blood pressure using a sphygmomanometer, explaining the significance of both readings.

She had answered as best she could, but her performance was perhaps not entirely convincing because Lange had contrived a fourth question: what were the specific symptoms of *gas* gangrene?

Irena was in luck. Leo had been called out into the forest one summer to attend a labourer who had fallen into a thresher several days earlier. His wounds had been poorly washed, leaving traces of the rich dark loamy soil on the flesh. His thigh had been swollen and covered in blisters with a foul-smelling red discharge. Leo had treated the wounds by debridement – the removal of the dead skin – using maggots. He'd then taken half an hour to sketch the presentation of the blisters in his notebook, while the man slept and Irena changed the dressings. Gas gangrene: a classic case. She'd even remembered the technical term: myonecrosis.

Lange, satisfied, laid out her duties. She was to tend to the soldier and bring the doctor coffee on the hour. She was forbidden to leave the sickbay except when the food bell rang. At night she was to go back to the slaves' compound, where she was allocated a hut, and a bed. Her place would be taken by the woman who cleaned the sickbay, and then slept in one of the bunks. If any patient needed urgent attention, she would fetch the doctor. Irena must report back for duty after breakfast at 7.00 a.m.

The doctor had fled to his office leaving her alone with her patient.

'How long 'til the next pill?' he asked, his back arching with the pain.

'Soon. Drink water if you can.'

Carstens swore, his body stiffening under the sheet.

She had taken a cast of the leg and hip, but she would wait until the next morning to set the limb. At the moment the patient was too agitated. She went to fetch the drug from the locked cupboard in the store and re-filled the pitcher of water.

'Time,' she said, returning and producing the pill. He thrust his tongue out.

'Lie still. It will take a few minutes to work,' she said, as he gulped water with the morphine.

She knew it would not bring relief as quickly the next time he took the drug, and this knowledge, that his pain would linger a little longer each time, gave her a thrill of revenge.

Carstens' eyes closed, the retreat of the pain allowing him to slip into unconsciousness.

The door opened and an SS officer came into the sickbay. He was tall and well-made and carried himself with an aristocratic stiffness, swinging off a loose greatcoat and throwing it into Irena's arms.

'Tell Lange I'm here.'

He looked at the soldier asleep.

'Wake up, Carstens!' he shouted. 'If you hadn't actually broken that useless leg I'd have had you shot. You've been looking for a way back to Berlin since you were posted.'

Irena was hanging up the coat.

Turning back, she found herself just three feet from the officer. 'When he comes round tell him he will stay here for the duration. Right here. If the Russians come they can bayonet him in his bed. Tell him that. All leave is cancelled. And if there's no leave for us, we're not sending idiots like Carstens back to Berlin to lie in a bed. He can fight the Russians on crutches.

'Now, tell the doctor I'm here. I don't have hours to waste. Or is he drunk?'

Irena was unable to answer the question. She'd taken him coffee an hour earlier and he'd been asleep at his desk, the vodka bottle by his elbow.

'Drunk, eh?'

He marched past her and kicked the door open with his boot.

Lange jumped to his feet and a glass fell to the floor but didn't break.

The SS officer unbuttoned his tunic and threw it on to a chair, before pulling a vest over his head to reveal a heavily muscled back, like a side of beef off a butcher's hook.

Lange was hastily washing his hands.

'The spine, Lange. I'm in agony again. I come every day – either you're a quack or my spine's fucked. I don't care which.

Put me out of my agony or I'll make sure you never taste
vodka again.'

He slammed the door shut in Irena's face.

She went back to the peg on the wall where she'd hung his
coat. Her hands were shaking, and a dizziness made her fear
she might fall down. She had to examine the officer's coat to
ascertain his precise rank. Kopp had said she would get one
chance to find the right man. She might have to wait a week
for the moment to come. The thought had been a comfort to
her because she had not been able to imagine living a single
day, let alone a week's worth of days. Such a span of time offered up the hope that she might see Leo and Judi again; but
the instant this small joy was born she felt a crushing sense of
shame, for having left Hanna alone to face the Himmelstrasse.

She examined the officer's coat. The epaulette was embroidered with what she feared to find: two oak-leaf clusters.
Kopp had been very clear: if she saw these insignia, she had
found her man. She must act. This was her one chance; the
task for which she had been selected. If she did what they
wanted, she might see Leo again.

Irena slipped her hand into the pocket of the coat and carefully retrieved a large bunch of keys, perhaps twenty on a single iron ring. She studied each, found the smallest, and detached it quickly, before slipping the ring back into the deep
pocket, and then hanging the coat back on the peg.

From the treatment room she heard the retort of joints
cracking, the sound travelling through the flesh.

The SS officer let out a gasp.

Chapter 42

The SS staff car, newly waxed, briefly caught the reflection of the pencil-thin chimney of the town brewery before it swung across the tramlines, turning off the main road out of Regen towards the hilltop village of Weissenstein. In the rear-view mirror the driver caught sight of refugees on the Munich road: a straggling line of carts and horses that had been threading its way into town since dawn.

Hauptsturmführer Marc Jurgens lit a cigarette, his elbow resting on the open window, and ran a hand back through dark hair, distinguished by a single streak of grey that had its roots at his right temple. He was very glad of the ageing hair, as, without it, people might have thought he was a malingerer who should have been on the Eastern Front, or crouched behind a hedge in the Norman bocage. Jurgens was forty-eight and had fought in the Great War on the Italian front. The ribbons of the several decorations he had been awarded were carefully sewn into his SS uniform.

On the seat next to Jurgens was the notepad on which he'd taken down his orders. The name of judge advocate Georg Johl was reproduced in capital letters. His task represented simplicity itself: a routine inquiry, a bureaucratic mission. But Johl's reputation went before him, and so he must be alive to stupid errors, and he must be thorough.

As the car snaked up the side of the valley, he caught sight of the low, humpback of the Grosser Arber. Last winter he'd taken his only son skiing on the slopes. Now this very son – Reinhardt Eugen – was 'missing in action' in Finland, and life at home was intolerable. Jurgens wanted no news, but his wife lived for it. Jurgens had told his wife that a whole army was lost, and that 'missing in action' was a euphemism that covered an entire theatre of war. But in his heart Jurgens was almost certain his son was dead. His wife had taken to their bed to await news, making the upper storey of their house into a convalescent home, a series of rooms in perpetual half-light.

Now he was glad of the sunlight in which he drove up the mountain. The rock on which the castle of Weissenstein stood came into view, topped by a flagpole, from which flew a Nazi banner. The ruins were a landmark in the hills of the Bavarian Forest, a fairy-tale bastion, perched on a precipice. In a landscape of modest mountains and soft woods, it provided a rare note of Romantic drama.

Jurgens brought the limousine to a stop outside the inn, The Castle, where three cars stood in the shade. On the far side of the building a terrace looked down into the Regen valley. This was, according to gossip, one of the few eating places that could still offer decent food. In the town the cats and dogs had disappeared from the streets and the mayor had ordered a guard to watch over the smallholdings by the railway station each night. Everyone was living on soup, disguised with herbs, especially fennel and forest garlic. In the evenings fishermen stood a few paces apart along the banks of the river. But, mysteriously, a few country inns could still serve boar, rabbit and pheasant. Jurgens suspected that an army of poachers stalked the woods at night.

He had planned to visit the inn first before walking up to the house. The SS uniform was usually enough to extract gossip and rumour, and it was often best to conduct interviews from a position of a little local knowledge. But as he stood by the car, he changed his mind. The sun was still an hour from setting and he thought it best to return later, for the dying light, and a glass of beer.

Climbing the short incline that led to the tunnel under the old drawbridge, he found a stone staircase leading up to a house built into the castle walls. According to the council directory, Johann Keuper, the tax collector, was also warden of the ruins. A small metal sign on the gate read with admirable modesty:

CARETAKER

An old man answered the door. Jurgens was struck by his expression, which was of polite inquiry. In Germany now this was very rare. Jurgens spent his life at half-opened doors looking at fear in the faces of people who were desperate for life to be dull, to be full of anything but strangers at the door.

Brandishing his SS warrant he explained that he had official news concerning Obersturmführer Jonas Keuper. The old man nodded and stood back. The house had high ceilings, painted walls and a stone floor. The kitchen, at the back, was very cool, and through the open doors lay a courtyard surrounded by the ruins.

Keuper was joined by his wife, a small woman with loose flesh and bad teeth. It struck Jurgens forcibly that tax collectors in Bavaria did not appear to be paid very handsomely.

'Can we sit down?' he asked.

They sat around a table black with age, the planks split, so that Jurgens could see the sunlight on the stone floor beneath, spilling in at an angle through the door.

He told them their son was dead, that he had fallen in the line of duty and that they would get a written statement from his commanding officer in due course. The news appeared to have very little impact on the old couple. They asked several questions about the exact circumstances, which he was unable to answer but deflected with kindness. After a few moments Jurgens was offered cider, which he accepted. As the father went out into the yard to get the drink, his wife looked around the kitchen. It was a big house, and Jurgens thought it must feel bleak and empty to her now. Perhaps the ghosts of children filled the room: at the table eating on Christmas Eve or running out into the yard, or lifting the wooden trapdoor in the stone floor to play hide and seek. These old houses always had capacious cellars, used for wine, beer and cider. It only occurred to Jurgens much later, when he was filling in his official report, that the old man had gone out into the yard to fetch his drink.

'You have other sons,' he said, taking a glass of the cloudy brew.

The mother fetched a picture of three boys from the dresser. As she handed it to Jurgens her breath was so laboured that he looked up into her face, and there, saw hatred in her eyes. Was she picturing her son's killer? What did she imagine? A partisan ambush perhaps, in the woods near the Polish border, or a sniper in the trees, a Russian scout, a few miles ahead of the Red Army?

Jurgens took the picture. The boy on the left, the eldest at perhaps sixteen, was dark and strong and had composed his features for the picture. The one on the right, Jurgens guessed, was Jonas. He wore long trousers, although his brothers were in shorts, but this did not entirely mask that his left leg was in irons, for just above the foot the cloth was rucked and split to reveal the base of the metalwork. The brother in the middle was clearly a simpleton – mentally retarded – for the mouth hung open, the facial features strangely undeveloped, so that the iris of the right eye was almost lost in the upper lid.

'This is Obersturmführer Keuper?' asked Jurgens, indicating the child with the twisted leg.

Neither of his parents appeared to hear the question. He asked others instead, about the son on the left, and learnt that this was Ritter, a major, currently serving under Reichsmarshall Kesselring in Italy. The old man showed Jurgens a postcard sent from Rome. It said simply: 'Dreaming of home.'

'And this?' asked Jurgens, pointing at the boy in the middle. The question was unkind, but he had a job to do.

The old man had begun to nod, rhythmically, and now tears were falling into his lap.

'A stronger drink, perhaps?' suggested Jurgens.

The wife fetched apple schnapps in a stone bottle, this time from a cupboard. It was cool, but nowhere near icy. Jurgens knocked back his glass in one, while the old man sipped his.

'The third child?' he prompted.

'Christoph,' said Johann. 'He was taken away in 1940, by bus, from Regen to a medical assessment centre in Munich. He suffered from a spastic condition. But he was very happy, joyful in fact, and a great friend to his brothers.'

The old man threw back the remains of the schnapps and refilled his own glass.

Jurgens shifted slightly in his chair and for the first time noted the crucifix on the wall and a niche holding a Virgin and a night-light.

'And your family doctor was Leopold Stern – the Jew?'

'Yes. We knew the Sterns. They were our friends. And Irena – and the girls, Judi and little Hanna.'

Jurgens admired the old man's courage, even his loyalty. He too had counted some Jews as his friends. But the affairs of men were like a pendulum, Jurgens felt, and the Jews had enjoyed the good times, and now they must endure the bad times. It was all part of a societal mechanism that was beyond his remit to police.

They talked about the Stern family, about the Jews of Weissenstein, and of Ritter's unit in Italy. Every few moments one of the Keupers would buckle under the grief, assailed by the reality of the news they had just been given, only to fall silent, so that the other would be forced to take up the conversation. Jurgens could not help but feel that the dominant emotion in the old kitchen was tension, not grief. It made him feel ill; light-headed, and feverish. They clearly wished to be alone, and he, just as clearly, wanted to go.

Standing abruptly he told the Keupers again that they would hear in due course from their son's commanding officer. The sun was waning, he explained, and he should drive back to his office to make his report.

Above all he wished to communicate to them the condolences of the SS. With a smart salute he left them to share their grief.

Chapter 43

Once he'd stepped outside the Keuper house, his duty done, Jurgens felt his spirits unexpectedly soar at the sight of the sunset, which had bathed the wooded hills in a golden light. It was hypnotic, the way that the creeping dusk swelled the canopies of the trees, decking them with heavier, lusher leaves, layered in shadows. He ran a gloved hand along the black paintwork of his car outside the inn, thought briefly that he might – after all – drive home for supper, but instead walked on, and through the door of the inn, which stood open. He felt the coolness at the heart of the old building, and the smell of a stew from the kitchens – possibly rabbit, or even hare. He walked in through the restaurant, which was empty, and out on to the terrace at the back. Here were set a dozen tables, with checked cloths, at which a few people sat drinking, averting their eyes once they'd noted his uniform. Voices fell to a whisper. He asked for a menu from a waiter who smelt quite badly of sour sweat, and took the end table, which gave a view of the castle on its rock.

One official task remained: he had been instructed to ring the judge advocate's office at eight the next morning to make his report. A written confirmation, by telegraph, was also required, sent direct to Johl via Krakow. Such a communication needed to be brief, factual, insightful and professional, constructed with a sharp intellectual precision and care, despite the fact that he had discovered nothing of note. He asked for paper, a pencil and a beer.

Scratching out his brief, forensic report in the last light, Jurgens found his concentration wandering. He could not put aside the image of his son's body in a shallow grave of ice and snow. With a supreme effort he continued to manipulate the words of his report, crossing out phrases and finding sharper, more pertinent replacements, but it was no good. He recalled his son running towards him, across a school field, clean limbed, winning a race over one hundred metres. He'd felt at the time that the boy ran with such determination that all the spectators must be able to feel what he felt: the thudding of his bare feet in the grass.

When he looked up from the paper, he saw that dusk had suddenly deepened. This was a further trick of the light in the Bavarian Forest. The sun held the hills until late, but the moment it set in the valley, the shadows rushed out from beneath the trees. He could see the castle against a dark blue sky, with the first stars above, and the black silhouette of the rock below. From the ramparts a stone staircase dropped to a meadow, where he'd seen cattle earlier. And there was an orchard. His eyes, which had been focused on the white paper for so long, shifted now to night vision.

His son had loved the final hour of the day, being one of those children who could go mad with joy if the conditions were right: a strong wind, snow. Eugen would run, zigzagging, in their garden, and his father would chase him.

There were tears on the white paper.

Blinking more away he looked up and saw, in the shadowy orchard, a figure. The vision made his heart break, as if he'd conjured Eugen up from the dusk he loved, from the past, or even from that shallow icy grave. Was it a child, a boy perhaps? The face was white, the shirt and shorts pale linen. A pale ghostly figure running between the trees in the half-light.

Jurgens stood and strode to the end of the terrace and then down a set of steps to the garden. In fifty yards he had reached a low picket fence designed to keep the cattle out of the orchard. The wraith-child was at the back of the field, but as Jurgens raised a hand the figure turned and careered down the hillside, running from side to side, touching the boles of the apple trees.

'Eugen,' he called, almost sternly.

The child laughed and ran at him, stopping a few yards short of the picket fence. The clothes were deceptive because it wasn't really a child at all, but a young man, with slim bones, and the carefree fluid movements of youth. The iris in his right eye was half obscured by the lid, while the mouth hung open stupidly. It was Christoph Keuper.

Chapter 44

The journey was due to begin after midnight on the wide pavement of the Ku'Damm. Despite a sharp shower, which had cleared the pavement cafés, the 'Times Square' effect was still oddly convincing, the advertising signs flashing, the cool blue and cherry lights reflected in the flooded gutters. Yellow cabs, another New York echo, swished by, blank windows catching reflections of BAR and NIGHTCLUB, NACHT GEOFFNET, JAZZ, GIRL SHOW. Now that the East was behind barricades, the West was even more determined to flaunt its energy. Further west she could see the beacon on the summit of the Funkturm radio mast pulsing with a white signal, ghostly in the dank air.

Krikalev had moved swiftly. Less than forty-eight hours after their visit to Spandau a man in a visor and leathers had climbed the stairs to the studio to deliver a note: they were to be outside, ready to travel east, with all their documents, at midnight. If the roads were clear, Krikalev promised they'd be back in Berlin the following night, or early the day after. Hanna complained that if there were delays she might miss her flight. Then Peter found her packing her bag, and that had sparked a long, tortuous low-energy row, which had started on the stairs, her sitting two steps below him, the ashtray between, and now continued on the damp pavement, beside a café table pooled with water, as they waited for the car.

'We don't have to go,' said Peter, lighting a cigarette, pacing the kerb.

'No, I want to go, Pete. But it's the last throw of the dice. Then I'm going home.'

'You know …' He turned to face her, his features lit alternately by red and green neon. 'This child – our child – it won't have a past either. You've thought of that?'

'*Thought of that!*' She let her hand drop at her side, the energy flooding out of her body. 'You think I haven't *thought of that*? Listen to yourself! I'm the one standing here with the child inside me.

'I have to give birth to this child and then watch them take it away – her, him, that's all I'll ever know. And you think I haven't *thought about that*?'

Her voice had risen and a lone couple at a table under an awning had fallen silent.

Peter took two steps towards Hanna and held up his hands in surrender. 'I could look after the kid – take it back to New York.'

'No, Pete. It's wrong to use the child to try and keep us together. Life is taking us apart: look.' She held her arms out wide. 'New York – London. Success – failure. You're sorted, I'm a mess. There's a boy in Artesia who's growing up without a father – and an old woman alone in a house in the Fens. The child isn't an answer; it's another question.

'This way, the way I have chosen, the child – yes, all right, *our child* – has parents, a life, a future.

'And before you ask. I don't know what that means for us.'

She looked up into the sky. 'So let's just do this now. And then move on.'

When she looked back at Peter, she was astonished to see tears in his eyes, so she turned away. Looking down the Ku'Damm, she saw the car pulling up: a Zil, in black, with a single red hammer-and-sickle pennant mounted on a miniature pole on the forward left wing. The driver, in the uniform of a Red Army sergeant, examined their ID cards with an air of supreme boredom and ushered them into the back seat, separated from his compartment by a sliding glass panel.

They had no real luggage, but spare coats, and two thermos flasks of sweet tea, and some sandwiches Hanna had made with leftovers from the kitchen. Peter patted his pockets, locating the four packets of f6 to which he was now addicted.

The backseat of the car was capacious, and included a drinks cabinet, which was empty, a reading light, a pull-out desk, and a telephone that Peter examined in the hope of finding a 'bug'. Potsdamer Platz was now cordoned off, a no-man's land set aside, the new concrete wall, still under construction, stretching away to the north. A chicane had been constructed after a truck had driven through the checkpoint loaded with a cargo of what Krikalev would have called 'deserters'. Metal barriers had been lowered in the canals and the rivers to stop more *Ossies* swimming to the West. The vast square – still threaded with tramlines – had lost its gentle echoes of imperial Berlin. The scene was bleak and functional, suggesting that even the ghosts had fled.

They sat in silence as the car reached the barrier. The 'flag' on the bonnet should have been enough to secure a crossing, but the guards insisted on taking away their permits to be checked. There was a brief interval, in which their driver was called away to the guardhouse, and then the barrier lifted with a bounce, as if in joyful surprise. Hanna, peering out, met the gaze of a border guard, peering in. They had to stop again for the East Germans, but only to press their passports to the glass: a graceful swish of an index finger indicated that they should turn over a page – once, twice, three times – then they were waved forward. A second barrier sprang upwards, and the Zil accelerated past four tanks, a newly constructed barrack house, and a field gun on a concrete plinth, its barrel almost vertical.

East Berlin, as always, did not look like part of the same city, especially as they had reached a speed at which the buildings were a blur.

Peter, peering ahead, whispered: 'The Zil lane, who'd have thought. This is the official fast-lane of the Soviet masters – and we're in it, Han.'

He sucked the life out of a cigarette, stubbed it out, and replaced it with some gum. The sullen anger of a few minutes before had been replaced by the familiar manic energy. He started to wind down the window, until the driver – his voice amplified by an interior microphone – announced: 'Not here. When we leave the city if you like. But not here.' His Russian accent was very strong, and Hanna found it took a second or two for the meaning to emerge from the broken English.

In ten minutes they'd reached the inner German border between East Berlin and the GDR. Documents were checked again, but with a grim lethargy.

Except for a few lights glimpsed and a floodlit petrol station, the world outside was reduced to telegraph poles, railway sidings, and dusty villages, grimy with petrol fumes. Hanna slept fitfully, her head against the cold window. She'd spent the last few days dreaming of the take-off at Tempelhof. Their trip east seemed desperate, doomed. She imagined a half-ruined chateau, a dull collective farm, and the endless questions of strangers.

They stopped before dawn, and the driver told them to stay in the car. Outside was a border post, a few lights, a long road leading away into green-black shadows. Peter said it looked like a painting by Hopper – *Gas*, perhaps – with a highway leading into an unseen continent. It was still five in the morning, but the air held a hint of a different kind of heat, a soft pulse of warm earth, a presage of the thousand miles of open plain that stretched ahead to Moscow. After a twenty-minute halt, the ritual of the paperwork, they were back on the road again at a steady speed, leaving behind the border crossing with its limp Polish flags.

Hanna stayed awake, watching dawn break over the landscape. The moment of recognition was extraordinary: she imagined her eye sockets shifting, the skull creaking, in an effort
to encompass this newly revealed horizontal world. The shadows of fence posts stretched west, a steel water tower stood in
the mid-distance, a mile from the road: but in the *middle-dis-
tance of what*? A plain certainly, of lichen green, ditched and
scarred with tracks, which revealed a black earth beneath, the
damp musty womb where the heat lay. Featureless: not a spire,
not a hill, not a farm, not a river, but a landscape of missing
things. Even now, in the cool morning, the horizon buckled
slightly in a mirage. The nearest field, which was impossible
to set to any human scale, had been stripped ready for a crop
and was entirely bare soil, cut deeply by a plough, in shimmering ridges. It slid past unbroken for twenty minutes, until
there was a ditch, and the next began. It felt familiar; but possibly just as an echo of the Fens.

It was noon when they turned off the main road, just beyond a level-crossing, where a pine forest offered shadow. The
way to Łabędzie was not tarmac at all, but an endless series of
concrete slabs, so that the wheels of the Zil beat out an unsettling rhythm; not the rolling percussion of a goods train, but
a beat without an embracing song or the promise of a breath
taken in a pause. The driver had the radio on and Polish voices weaved between the airwaves. Hanna slept for an hour and
then sat up, with her face half out of the car in the warm wind.
A woman, carrying a vast bundle on her head, stood aside as
they swept past. Ahead, the sky was darkening with a summer
storm. The main road was twenty miles behind them when
they came to the estate gates: stone, embellished with the inevitable swans, the ironwork between long gone.

The gravel drive was sinuous and led lazily to the house,
skirting the reed-clogged lake. Hanna's eye fell on the façade
of the chateau and dim memories stirred of that last summer

before Mr Hasard had taken her away to Paris – a few months of harvest, during which she'd picked fruit. She recognised the grand *porte-cochére*, and the leaded cupolas much more clearly – but only from old photographs and paintings Marcin had shown her during those shared evenings behind the Imperial Red Door. He had often told her tales of life on the estate, although never within earshot of Lydia, for whom the past was too painful to re-live. But she could imagine them now, arm in arm, strolling in the grounds of their magnificent home.

No sooner had they come to a halt in front of the house than the storm broke over their heads with a dull crack of thunder, and rain began to fall. Through the trickling droplets on the windscreen Hanna saw the first child, a boy, coming out of the house and going down to wait by the lake. He was, perhaps, six or seven years of age, dressed in an institutional uniform of blue shorts and a white shirt. Standing awkwardly, he waited, looking back at the house. Hanna could see now that a crowd of boys was crushed into the porch, watching the downpour, hands outstretched into the falling water. Then she realised they were not being held back by the prospect of getting wet at all, but were slyly studying the Zil, and presumably its passengers.

The boy by the lake shouted what must have been a word of command for the rest to follow and set off clockwise round the water. Soon all of them were running, in their regulation uniforms, shouting and laughing in the rain. Each was barefoot, and they kept to the grass, souls flashing.

The driver opened the door of the Zil and Peter took Hanna's hand as they ran for cover in the great porch, which was dusty and had been used to store firewood. An older boy appeared to welcome them, so the driver handed him a document and, holding it respectfully, the child asked them in Polish to follow him into the house. It was clear that the façade was in much better condition than the interior, which had been reduced to institutional bleakness: whitewashed walls, bare boards, fine doors obscured by fireproof padding. Strip lights ran along the corridors, the wiring visible. A network of cables appeared, and then disappeared, through roughly drilled holes. All the doors were shut except one, which revealed a reception room, where desks had been laid out in ranks.

They came to a kitchen that reeked of cabbage and bacon. Three cooks, in smocks, sat at a bench chopping onions, but stopped to watch them pass with open curiosity. The boy led them into an old walled garden, with a cottage built into the corner.

Finally, a sharper memory of that last year on the estate came to Hanna. Here was the caretaker's cottage where she'd been given a bed, hidden away in a stone larder. An old man had provided food and let her sit by the fire in the months before Mr Hasard arrived. They must have ransacked the house for wood, because she remembered putting gilded wings and painted hands into the flames. They'd fed angels to the fire.

Through the door was an office; a desk with two phones, a fax machine, and a small switchboard that might have been for an internal phone system.

A man, with a mop of thick brown hair, stood up, one of the phones pressed to his ear, and shook their hands, indicating two chairs.

He cut the call abruptly, but Hanna recognised the phrase 'important visitors' in Polish.

'I am Boris Ochab, the superintendent here. Welcome.'

Peter began to explain why they'd come, but Ochab interrupted. 'I have been told your story. I will try to help, but it was a long time ago.'

The men shared cigarettes. Hanna noted that through the drifting blue smoke, the superintendent's eyes often settled slyly on her face.

'You are famous here,' Ochab said. 'Have the children been staring? They were told this morning that you were to visit. The excitement is tinged with danger of course: the Party has little time for aristocrats of the *ancien régime*. But the house is a state treasure, and without its past it is simply stucco and brick. So the legend is told and retold.

'And now they get to see you – the child rescued by our very own heroine, Natasza Mazurek.

'The story goes that she left you here, safe and warm, in this very room.'

'I remember the cottage, but little else,' said Hanna.

This seemed to please Mr Ochab very much, because a smile lit up his stern face.

'The legend, as I say, is often told,' he continued, standing up and opening the window.

'But I have been formally directed by the Ministry of the Interior to tell you everything; so I must tell not only the legend, but also the truth.'

Hanna's heartbeat skipped. Peter had been right after all: the old estate did have its secrets.

Ochab sat back in his chair. 'When the boys ask, we tell them this: that when the Germans came at the start of the war, the count – our war hero – escaped to England and flew Spitfires. The swan-like Natasza, his only child, was at the family town house in Warsaw, where she hid Jewish children destined for the camps. A heroine, indeed.

'In the closing months of the war, Natasza returned. The Germans had fled. She brought with her three Jews: one mother, and two children. She'd hidden you all away in Warsaw, until she had to flee the Russians.'

'A woman and two children?' asked Hanna.

Quickly he held up a finger. 'Forgive me. You lost your family I know, but this was not your family. You were a child, alone, although the woman cared for you, and her own new-born son.'

Ochab set one of his hands on the desk. 'The mother wanted to go further, to Berlin, with her child – a boy called Eden, another name that has survived in the legend with your own.

'Natasza took them to Kraśnik by horse and cart. She was part of a flood, an exodus west, as the Russians approached. The railhead ran to Berlin.

'On the return journey a lone German fighter pilot strafed the road. The horse bolted, the cart tumbled into the ditch, and Natasza's neck was broken.

'You remained safely here, hidden away by the caretaker for several months, until the count's man came to drive you away after the war …

'And here you are – the legend in person.'

He shook his head.

'And the truth, Mr Ochab?' asked Hanna.

'I was told the truth by a very reliable witness.' He looked around the room. 'This was our home. My father was the caretaker. I'd left to work on the railways, so he lived here alone.'

They smiled at each other, connected only by the kindness of an old man.

He indicated a framed black-and-white photograph on the desk showing a boy on a cart beside an old man. Dimly, in the bleached-out background, they could see the lead turrets of the house. The young Ochab struck a proprietorial stance, even then.

Hanna stared at the old man, but nothing stirred anew in her memory.

'So – the truth. By September 1939 everyone knew an attack was imminent,' said Ochab. 'A month perhaps, a week, a day. It was understood from the first that the count would leave Łabędzie if the Germans crossed the border. His position, in the air force, meant that he must first join a unit on a nearby grass airfield – at Polta, thirty miles west. Here the fighters – the PLZs – had been taken, leaving the military airfields for the Germans to bomb as they pleased.

'Forgive me. As a boy I found such things thrilling.

'Once at Polta a decision would be made: to fly to France, or, if the battle was going well, to stay and command the struggle here, in our own skies.'

Ochab lit a cigarette. 'The battle did not go well. The German advance from the border was astonishing. By the time news came here – by motorcycle messenger – the Germans were *between* Łabędzie and Polta. There was only one means of escape.'

Ochab stood and went to the small window that looked out over farmland. 'Out beyond the folly, and the poplars, is a field. Now there are sheep. The count had laid down grit, to make a runway. And there was a plane, a fine thing …' He shook his head. 'The latest wonder. A modern streamlined beauty. The military planes were fit for the Great War – and no match for the Luftwaffe. But this …'

He sat back down. 'Only one problem. It was a single-seater, and Natasza wasn't in Warsaw, she was here. The plan had been for them to escape together by car to Polta. It was a secret plan, because of course we – the poor peasants – were going nowhere.'

'What did the count do?' asked Peter.

'He flew away and left his child,' said Ochab, his voice flat, as if delivering a piece of disappointing news to a class of children: that rain had led to the postponement of a football match, perhaps, or that dinner would be potatoes.

'He *abandoned* Natasza?' asked Hanna.

It was an almost physical blow. Marcin's lies, his betrayal of Hanna in withholding news of her family's fate, had diminished him, but an echo of the love she felt had always been with her. Now it was gone.

'There was some room in the cockpit, but there were docu-ments, plans, codebooks. In the end the plane only just man-ages to fly …' He held out a hand, just above the desktop. 'A few feet above the trees … So no room at all for a young woman.'

Ochab shrugged. 'He felt he had higher responsibilities. There was no criticism at the time, and Natasza played her part. Her father had to save his country. Sacrifices had to be made. But the women whispered; a vain man, a man of rank, but not of substance. And what could Natasza do? She was no peasant girl. She was a prize of war.'

The bleak brutality of Natasza's fate seemed to hang in the air. Hanna considered the truth revealed; the moment of abandonment seemed to unlock the mystery of Marcin's character like a key. What she thought was love was guilt, and perhaps that is what they had shared. The count's incessant labours behind the Imperial Red Door now appeared in a very different light. He was obsessed with Hanna's story – her past – because it led to Natasza's past. He hadn't sought to find the truth at all; he'd laboured to suppress it. This betrayal was no less bitter for discovering a motive.

'Go on,' said Hanna.

'The Germans came and established a garrison in the house. We could not hide the girl for ever, so she worked in the fields. But the portraits do not lie: she was indeed a beauty, or perhaps she was betrayed. The Germans requisitioned her for their comfort. That was in 1940 – the summer – and I did not see her again. It was whispered that the SS took her to the camp at Borek, about thirty miles east, for their pleasure.'

And so, at last, Hanna saw how their paths had crossed. Natasza's story had been recast yet again. She hadn't spent the war as a wealthy Polish aristocrat hiding away Jewish chil-dren, but as a courtesan for the Nazis. She seemed to haunt Hanna's story, never quite coming into focus.

'When Natasza returned, the estate had been largely abandoned. Everyone who could work here at Łabędzie was taken by lorry to Warsaw where the Germans were organising labour camps. My father took her in with the others. The rest is true: she took the child and his mother to the railhead, and died on the return journey in a roadside ditch. The war ended. My father continued to hide you away: and a story was invented for anyone who asked after you – for the Soviets were keen to round up the elite – a story that *you too had died* on the road to Kraśnik with Natasza.

'And then one day nearly a year later the count's agent arrived, looking for Natasza, and you were taken away instead. Europe was in chaos, but the count had influence at the highest levels. The borders were no barrier. We presumed you were taken safely to Paris.'

The story finished, Ochab settled back into his chair.

Hanna felt exhausted. Her life was literally a story told by others. Yet each version seemed to take her further away from discovering what had happened to the rest of the Sterns.

Peter, business-like, took up the thread.

'Why do you tell the children the legend, not the truth?' asked Peter.

'Even a communist needs a hero,' said Ochab. 'But there is a less noble reason. The situation here was uncertain in 1945. Would the Russians stay? Might the count return? His agent, when he came to fetch you, Hanna, asked my father to repeat only the legend, so that no shame should fall on his swan-like daughter, although the only shame was his. And so the legend thrived.'

The boy who had brought them through the house appeared with a tray of coffee and some hazelnuts in a dish. For a minute Ochab fussed with the pot, and then lit a fresh cigarette. Outside, Hanna could hear a pair of secateurs patiently snipping at plants in the garden.

'We're looking for my family, Mr Ochab,' said Hanna at last.

He shrugged. 'The family agent must know more?'

'The firm closed a few years after the war with Mr Hasard's death,' said Hanna. 'The papers are lost. Besides, the lawyer was interested in his clients, and their daughter, not a little girl.'

Peter then asked if they could trace the child called Eden and his mother? They would surely know the fate of the Stern family.

'I am sorry. We know no more,' said Ochab.

'And nobody ever came looking for them or asked questions?' asked Peter. 'About Natasza, or Hanna, or the mother and child?'

'There were one or two phone calls – to the house I think.'

Hanna sat up. 'From who – when?'

Ochab held up a hand. 'I did not return from Warsaw until '49 – so it must have been soon after the war. I heard this only second-hand, perhaps even third-hand. My father said there were calls to the big house – to the commissar, sent to oversee the cooperative farm. Dreadful years, believe me. He took these calls – or at least directed his secretary to make the appropriate answers to enquiries. The story he told would have been the story my father gave him – which protected us all from reprisals: that you died on the road with Natasza Mazurek.'

'But who called?'

Ochab held up his hands.

She tried, but failed, to follow the conversation as Peter asked more questions about the orphanage, and the years since the war. Hanna was stunned: here at last was the answer to the question that had haunted her since the arrival of the chess piece and the letter at Swan House: if her father had survived, why had he not tried to find *her*? She found a strange comfort in this latest discovery, for now it was possible that they had lost each other.

The phone rang and Peter said they'd find their way back to the car but Ochab told the caller he'd ring back, and insisted on showing them out.

'Besides, you've come all this way, there is one thing you must see.'

The kitchen was now full of steam and the smell of potatoes, and the door of the classroom was closed, so Ochab held a finger to his lips as they passed.

Their driver was leaning on the Zil when they emerged from the house, and he quickly replaced his cap, but Ochab led them away from the lake along a rough path that snaked into the woods. After a minute's walk the pine trees had closed around them and then they arrived in a small clearing. At the centre was a stone block, upon which was carved the image of a swan.

'When they brought the body back, the Red Army was close, so they had to be careful,' he said. 'Aristocrats were still the enemy, even in death. They dug the grave here at night, out of sight. It's Natasza's last resting place. They found the stone in the mason's yard at the back of the house; it had been taken down for repair before the war and forgotten.'

Hanna knelt down and ran a finger over the rough image, along the curve of the wings, and the sinuous line of the neck.

'I owe her my life,' she said. She felt now regret for resenting her for so long; her perfect skin, her beauty, but most of all the love she'd inspired in others. Hanna had even once despised her for hiding her away from the Germans – an act of charity from a rich young woman that always seemed to demand that Hanna spent her life beholden to others. The truth revealed a very different Natasza: a woman of decisive action.

'She must have been very brave,' she said.

Mr Ochab made a rapid sign of the cross and turned to go.

Silently, Hanna wished Natasza peace – which was a prayer of sorts.

Back at the car, looking out over the lake, they all shook hands.

Hanna felt she should say how grateful she was that she'd come, but the words would not come. So she asked instead if there were any swans left at Łabędzie.

'All long gone,' said Ochab. 'A generation starved here after the war, and the flesh was good, if a little oily – like duck – but even more gamey, luxurious. Forbidden, even. They no longer trouble our beautiful lake.'

Chapter 45

Back at the main road they turned west for Kraśnik and Germany but stopped at the level-crossing they'd passed earlier. The driver killed the engine, so that they could hear the wind as it batted the Zil's panel-beaten chassis. The way forward had been clear, but now the signal post dropped with a mechanical clatter and read STOP.

Beside the track stood a station, built of fine bricks, with a veranda and ticket windows that had once been graceful, an echo of some imperial design. Hanna imagined a map on a wall in a government office in Minsk, or Lviv, or even Moscow, showing a network of lines like a spider's web. Outside on a bench sat a young man with a plastic cup nestled in his crotch.

A sign said: KAWA.

'We can get coffee, and food for the trip,' said the driver, although he appeared to be studying a map on the passenger seat.

At first Hanna said she just wanted to sleep, and that she'd stay in the Zil, but Peter took her hand and said she should try to eat. The truth was that she felt numb, unable to process emotions that she struggled to identify. She kept thinking about her father hearing a voice on the phone telling him his daughter had died on the road to Kraśnik. And Marcin in the cockpit of his plane, rising – only just, above the lead rooftops of Łabędzie, watched by his lost daughter.

Hanna got out of the car, leaving her coat behind, and stretched out her arms. Her bones ached now, every joint sore, as if she was being very slowly torn apart. But the warm wind blew through her print dress, and she felt suddenly hopeful for no logical reason.

The interior of the café had a counter, with an array of sweets, the brands unknown to them, and a hot-water geyser. There were a few chairs, a tiled stove and a pool table. The coffee, black and granular, tasted like roasted nuts. The young man was called Henryk, and he clearly enjoyed practising his English, because he told them at length that he was the signalman and station master as well as the café owner.

There was a TV in the bar draped in the Polish national colours.

'For the games; everyone comes here to watch,' said Henryk.

They took their coffees outside to sit on the bench, leaving their driver poring over the map with Henryk.

The view outside buckled in the midday heat.

The train, when it arrived, was a mile long and took twenty minutes to clatter past, each truck full of potatoes. Hanna imagined a circular line, which would bring it back the next day, at precisely the same time, and that their road, too, would prove inescapable, delivering them back to the KAWA sign in time to see the train pass. Which made her think of the curiously threatening property of circles: that they were the shape of being trapped.

Hanna wondered where 'everyone' came from to watch football; were there really people out there, on the edge of sight? It was hot, but the illusion was that it was not the sun beating down, but the black earth below, radiating up through the thin veneer of grass and cracked mud. She felt sweat trickling out of her hair and into her eyes.

Henryk shut the café explaining that the next train was two hours away, and climbed in the front of the Zil with the driver.

'Henryk's going to be our guide,' said the driver.

'To where?' said Peter, sharply.

Hanna sensed that the diversion had been planned, that they were no longer in complete control of their itinerary.

The driver adjusted his cap. 'I am Victor,' he said, as if the journey had begun anew.

'Colonel Krikalev said we should take a short diversion if we had the chance,' he said. 'A few minutes only.'

They trundled over the crossing and took an immediate turn right on to a dusty track.

It occurred to Hanna that the station must have a name, so she twisted in her seat and, looking back, saw it pass in a blur.

BOREK KRZYŻÓWKA

[BOREK JUNCTION]

Victor watched Hanna in the rear-view mirror.

'This is the site of the camp, yes? Borek. Major Krikalev said that if you did not wish to go, this would be acceptable. Henryk knows the site well. His father was a guide for the Red Army when they liberated the camp.'

Peter held Hanna's hand.

'Let's go back to Berlin,' said Peter. 'Han – you're shaking.'

The baby had turned over, and she felt sick, but it was utterly unthinkable that they should turn back now, when they were so close. A sense of internal panic made it difficult to speak. She had always wanted to remember, but now, on this hard road, she saw another part of the truth; that not remembering was a shield, and that she was frightened of what might lie ahead.

'It's all right,' was all she said.

'You're not alone, Han,' said Peter.

'We can go back?' said Victor, who had paid Henryk in dollar bills, which the station master was now counting. He looked in the rear-view mirror and saw Hanna shake her head.

The road quickly degenerated into a farm track of iron-hard clay ruts, which ran towards a distant brick water tower. They had all the windows of the car open now and the air was gravid with rotting peat and still water, and some species of seed or pollen, which made Peter's eyes run.

Henryk took off his baseball cap and twisted in his seat, sliding back the glass partition. He said that in the village, just unseen over the eastern horizon beyond the pine forest, no one knew what had happened here in the war. They thought it was a work camp. In 1939 – long before he was born – the Germans had come and sacked the village, and the men had been taken away to work in Danzig. A branch line had been built from the station, *his* station now, into the camp.

'This is the platform,' he said.

Victor braked, and they got out of the Zil. In the long grass they could just discern the concrete, and the footings of a row of buildings. The grass was so high the ledge of the platform was almost lost. Beyond it ran scrubland, with a few brick foundations, and finally the water tower, which was burnt out, so that when they got to the door they could see inside through the charred frame. A short piece of rope hung from an iron beam. A few sheets of rusted metal held the remains of circuits and wires.

Victor lit a cigarette and watched Hanna closely. Peter, for his part, watched Victor, certain now that like his commander Krikalev, his real role was more sophisticated than his uniform suggested.

Henryk said the tower had been the camp landmark – *strażnica* – but that everything else had been destroyed or buried, except for the gas chamber itself, which was hidden in the wood ahead. He said there was little to see, and Hanna thought his enthusiasm for the diversion, no doubt inspired by his fee, had dissipated quickly, and that he looked uncomfortable, and never met her eyes with his, but studied his smart white baseball shoes.

'Just the concrete base remains,' he said again, looking at his watch.

'I must see it,' said Hanna.

So they got back in the car and Victor let the Zil creep forward, in first gear, until they came to a copse of birch trees through which ran a path. The tree trunks were old and gnarled and had attained a sculptural complexity with age, arcing over the way ahead.

Henryk said Victor should steer right, and circumnavigate the trees, but Hanna told him to stop.

The pale path led between two fields – the one to the right behind the wreckage of a fence.

'Hanna? What's wrong?' said Peter, getting out of the car on the far side.

'Stay there,' she said, taking off Marcin's old coat and throwing it on to the back seat.

She took three steps and stopped. Everything around her was vivid, sharp and alive. The leaves shimmered and she saw every single one, and the grass, yellow and dry, blade by blade. A bird crossed the path in flight, and she registered each feather, and the light in its eye. The path was changing, widening, even though she stood still. In the silver sand she noted the marks of naked feet. She heard a crowd about her, getting closer, shouting and cursing, carrying her forward. She smelt everything – a world unlike her own: sweat, and tobacco, and hair – shorn hair, and blood, and ash, and bones. She felt hungry, and so thirsty her throat seemed to narrow and burn.

'I remember,' she said, and something mended inside her.

Then she saw them. Her father was ahead of her, with his arm round a teenage girl, and they were both naked. In this moment the girl was looking into his face, and she could see that what she was saying had made him cry, and she knew that this was unthinkable, that she'd never seen her father cry before. It made her hold on tighter to the naked leg beside her and look up into the face of the woman who must be her mother, who was looking down, and talking: the words she heard she didn't understand, but she knew her mother was promising water, and then soup.

Which is when she heard the dogs bark.

She was shaking so badly she fell to her knees and then Peter was there, helping her up on one side, while her mother was on the other. She heard horrible shouts – oaths and threats – and her mother whispered in her ear, again in the words she didn't understand, but she knew that she was loved.

Then the path twisted, and her connection with the past faltered, so that it was only Peter who helped her emerge from the trees.

Ahead was an open pasture, dotted with mounds, which ran up to the forest. There was no bird song at all, just the whisper of the pines.

Hanna heard a woman singing in a high clear voice, a sound that seemed to rise up like a lark and dissolve, and then the past was gone.

She leaned on Peter, and so Victor gave her a military canteen full of water and she drank until she felt she wasn't going to faint.

Henryk walked forward and held up his hands. 'This is it,' he said. 'Not much to see.'

There was a long concrete platform, surrounded by steps, which had crumbled and fractured.

Henryk had regained some of his authority. 'There was one chamber, built by labourers who came from Munich, so we did not know,' he said.

'The bodies here, in the field, were all burnt. A memorial is planned, but we are never told when. There is a Jew in the village now, a teacher, and she came with the children, but it was stopped, because they saw bones, after the snow cleared. The frost forces them up …'

A flock of crows clattered out of the trees.

Only Hanna heard the gunshot, which was in the past, but she started so violently Peter had to hold on to her to stop her falling in the dust.

'What do you remember?' asked Victor, but Peter shook his head.

The driver turned to Henryk. 'This was the gas chamber?' he asked, writing in a small notebook with a pencil.

Henryk nodded. Hanna noted that he seemed pale and eager to leave, increasingly uncomfortable perhaps with the story he had been forced to tell. 'They told the villagers it was a shower block. It's too far from the village anyway; even if they'd cried out, they couldn't have been heard.'

He went on nodding after saying this, hands in his pockets.

'The bodies were burnt here. But they were given a proper burial in the end and laid under the grass. The Red Army did this. My father brought his spade too. It was all before I was born.'

'There *was* a shower block,' said Hanna. The strength of her own voice made her feel confident in this version of her own story. 'But not here. We were taken away.'

It was as far as the memory went for now: they were naked, in the falling water, and she felt her mother's hands, circling, and then they all walked away in the sunlight. It was a moment of joy, and she could feel the heat on her skin.

'We walked away,' she said.

She knelt down, pushing her fingers into the black soil, which felt hot, as if the fires still burnt. She looked out over the grassy mounds. The sun was sinking, and each had a shadow, so that they could see the undulating surface, and the geometric lines in which the cairns had been left. Each one was about fifty yards long and rose up three or four feet. They looked like the graves of giants.

Henryk broke the silence. 'There is a story that the Germans fled but left behind the gold they'd stolen from the Jews. When I was a child, we all came to look for it, even though they told us to keep away. But the treasure is long gone, if it was ever here.'

Henryk looked at his watch, but Victor, adjusting his cap, held up a hand. 'If she wants to stay a moment, there's time.'

Hanna was trying not to think, to leave her mind open, so that she might remember more.

'Your father, Henryk, he brought the Russians here?' asked Peter.

'Yes. They came to our village and said they knew a camp was nearby in the woods. My father led them along the lumber road. The Germans were gone. Everyone was dead. Not a soul …'

He cut the air horizontally with his hand.

Victor turned back towards the car.

It was Hanna who asked the question on Peter's lips.

Something made her wait until Victor was out of earshot.

'Everyone was dead?' she asked. 'But there was a woman – here, she worked for the man who ran the gas chamber. She sang for us, she sang for all those who died.

'I've spoken to her. She was alive, Henryk, because the Red Army took her away. That's how she survived.'

Henryk shook his head. 'No. This is a mistake. My father has told us all the story many times. Not a living soul, even though the soldiers searched for days. It is the Borek Plantation on the map, but to us it is *miejsce duchów*: the place of ghosts.'

Chapter 46

The nurse knocked once and entered, placing a cup of coffee on the desk. A tall woman from the Fens, arthritic, with a stoop and stiff legs, she maintained the silence of a nun.

'Is it bad?' asked Lydia, glancing out the window, which was obscured by fog. The room was clammy with condensation. The weather was hot but wet and had been oppressive for a week.

'Biblical,' said the nurse. 'There's this,' she said, placing a letter on the tray.

Lydia listened to her stiff steps descending to the kitchen.

The letter was from Hanna, with a Berlin US Sector post mark she'd come to know well.

> *Dearest Aunt Lydia,*
> *I have been to Łabędzie and found the truth. And I have been to Borek and remembered the past – at least in part. Each day a little more of my lost life is revealed.*

The old woman read the letter, which ran to three pages, then closed her eyes, and took to her bed.

At noon she went to her desk and retrieved her husband's last will and testament, which ran to nearly fifty pages, and was printed in the archaic Gothic typescript favoured by the Mazurek agent, Mr Hasard-with-one-S. Aside from the allocation of the Fen estate – part of which was transferred to Hanna on her twenty-first birthday – the will represented the count's posthumous effort to establish the legend to which his life had been devoted.

It stipulated that his body was to be cremated, a funeral service held at Our Lady of Czestochowa and St Casimir in London. The ashes were to be taken to Swan House and the Polish Air Force Association was charged with a final theatrical flourish: a Spitfire would be flown over the aerodrome and the ashes scattered by the pilot. Various codicils set aside sums for other memorials, including a marble plaque of the family crest for the church in London. A bequest was made to the air force association for the writing of a history of what was to be called the *Mazurek* squadron. The sum of £1,000 guineas was to be spent on a stone column to mark the squadron's record, placed at the aerodrome gates. It would list the exploits of the Polish pilots in exile, in order of their tally. This would place the name Mazurek at the top with eleven confirmed kills, two unconfirmed.

She adjusted her glasses to the Gothic script. The will, which she had always found distasteful, attempted to ensure that the count would be remembered; above all that the family name would be sustained in its position in the nation's history. This concept of glorious memory her husband had equated with justice, because immortality was a fitting reward for heroism. Anonymity was defeat, and victory for the aggressor.

She'd always known he'd lied to her, even when he was alive. She could have demanded the truth if she'd been stronger. But there was another reason she didn't speak. She wanted to watch the untold secret diminish the man. They'd drawn apart with the years, so it was not always possible to observe at first hand the process of disintegration. It was easy for Marcin to avoid her: he had a bunk-bed at the aerodrome and the duties of a squadron leader were open-ended; when he did return to Swan House he'd march to his office, or commune with the politicians and generals, the priests and the journalists, who made the pilgrimage to Long Fen.

Marcin's struggle to live with his secret had its own pathology, a series of symptoms. Lydia noticed a distinct inability to depart: at the fen burials for those pilots mortally injured over Germany he would be the last to stand beside the flooded grave. At the burns hospital at Ely, where Lydia would accompany him on 'rounds' – the swaddled pilots in wicker chairs set in the white light of the French windows – he would linger, unable to leave the often sightless patients. The only farewell that was crisp and functional was that on the steps of Swan House each day, the staff car whisking him away without a backward glance for his wife.

And then it was Hanna he could not leave. Lydia had woken one night in that winter of the child's arrival to find Marcin had deserted the bed they still shared. She'd found him sitting in the moonlight of Hanna's room, watching her sleep, his face, caught in a moment of intense concentration, portrayed a man held in dynamic equilibrium by opposing, but balanced forces: guilt, love, loss, wonder. She saw that for Marcin the sleeping girl had become his lost child, and he was a father once again.

But the saddest thing about the contents of Hanna's letter, which had recast Marcin's memory in such a bleak light, was the revelation that the trip to Łabędzie had failed to unlock the mystery of the Stern family or bring Hanna any closer to finding her *real* father.

Lydia stood, unhooked the key from the chain around her neck, and unlocking a cabinet by her bed, transferred the contents to a string bag she used to ferry vegetables from the allotment to the kitchen. Before going out she unfolded an old Ordnance Survey map on the table. It had been Marcin's, when, briefly, he'd taken an interest in the farming of the thirty acres that came with Swan House.

She checked the forward path on the map, stowed it in her bag, fetched her coat, and opened the front door. The world outside was aquatic: the fog teemed with moisture, instantly coating her skin. Visibility was a hundred yards, the poplars by the lake wraiths, the sky, land, and water all precisely the same shade of grey-white, the boundaries between them welded so neatly the lines defied the eye.

'Perfect,' said Lydia, checking the contents of the bag one last time.

She left the door open, hearing the steps of the nurse advancing from the kitchen.

'A walk,' she called, not looking back.

She skirted the lake, suppressing a memory of standing on the ice, watching Hanna's careful steps. She'd taken a decision then, and this was her reward.

The path, memorised from the map, revealed the history of the landscape that she had come to know, with its constant flat echoes of home: hardly history at all; for once, a few generations ago, this had been open water and marsh, and nameless. Drained, the world was featureless, and so the map, with its droves and ditches, lodes and fleets, had to be embroidered with names, allocated, conjured up, to make it possible to tell one place from an identical other. Adventurers' Fen – now on her right – was of no apparent difference to Burnt Fen – on her left. The poplars of Siberia Belt, which she knew were to the north but could not see, were identical to those of Pate's Drove, except in number, which was too great to help. The ruins of Bait's Cote, where she set out across a field, were no more than a stone block, mossy green, and half submerged in peat.

For this final part of the journey she demanded one more degree of anonymity. It had been a game Marcin had played with Hanna. The child would be given a map and told to find the square that contained the fewest features. She would pore over every box – each a square mile – weighing up the thin line of a ditch in one, against the spurred motif of a line of pylons in another. One day she'd found the Grail: an empty square. Pure white. An Empty Quarter of Arabian bleakness. With a blue crayon she'd coloured it in.

The fog had begun to weep a fine rain. When Lydia finally stopped, she double-checked her location with the map, which became spattered with raindrops. She stood north of Soham Lode, which she located as a blue line, east of a pumping station, marked with a miniature cube. She must now be standing within this unmarked world of the blank square, still coloured blue on the map. Walking forward she lost sight of the ditch behind in the mist, while the high flood bank of the river was more than two miles ahead, and completely invisible. The peat had begun to clog her shoes.

Laying aside the string bag, she took out the strange metallic canister within. She'd defied Marcin's wishes from the start, despite the sporadic enquiries of the Polish Air Force Association, sensing that one day she would find a fitting place of rest. The count had lived for the pages of history. His family had been a tool manipulated to that ambition. This was her revenge for that dereliction, for his emotional absence. She unscrewed the top of the canister, picked away at the plastic bag within, and judging there was no wind, spread his ashes in a white arc before her. She didn't mark the spot with words, or thoughts, or even a simple sign of the cross. She did tap the urn against her shoe to dislodge the last ashes, and then she walked lightly away, without looking back.

Chapter 47

Stern was now aware of the series of events that had brought him here, to a well-furnished sitting room, with old High German furniture, a patterned carpet, and gloomy, smoke-dark, gilt-framed art. Georg Johl sat opposite him, a chessboard between them on a card table. Stern smelt badly of sweat and dust and the judge occasionally held a white linen handkerchief to his mouth and feigned a cough. Or, contemplating his next move, would cradle his brandy glass under his nose, breathing in only the air soaked in the high-octane fumes of the spirit.

The judge had seemed amused by Stern's evident surprise when he was led into the room.

'There was a chess set in your envelope of valuables, a travelling set,' he said. 'And then your name: L.E.L. Stern. I have books of games that I play when I have no opponent. I recalled a game from 1935 – the Lens Provincial. You played Bogoljubov. A famous victory.

'I had a chessboard put in your cell earlier this evening. I hoped it might whet your appetite. And so here we are.'

Stern returned his gaze to the board.

An electric fan turned over their heads. The apartment, an annex to the officers' mess, looked as if it had been built specifically for high-ranking visitors. But Stern was irritated by the chess set, for in his childhood the use of red pieces, in a fussy medieval Gothic style, was a sign of an amateur enthusiast.

Stern responded to Johl's move with the traditional riposte at this stage in the Ruy Lopez opening. In truth he could have played more quickly, but he was still trying to calculate his best course of action. It was late evening and Freida's labour might begin within hours. Should he win quickly, and get back to the cell block, or eke out a draw and see if he could divine the judge's motives in bringing him here to play chess?

Stern let his fingers linger on the mitre of the bishop, before finally setting it down on the fourth square on his queen bishop's file.

'Some time ago I despaired of finding an opponent of merit,' said Johl.

Was this really why Stern was here: to provide the German with a worthy antagonist?

'Despair is not too strong a word.' He smiled, blinking behind the lenses, cradling the brandy. He'd opened the top buttons on his shirt and Stern could see ample flesh; pale, with a sheen of sweat.

'If I was a rich lawyer, I could buy myself a mechanical opponent, perhaps? You have heard of this thing?'

'The Turk?'

'Yes, yes. The Mechanical Turk.'

Stern knew the story but didn't interrupt as Johl rehearsed the details of the eighteenth-century inventor who'd built a clockwork man that could play chess, seated at a sumptuous desk. Despite the unmasking of the fraud (a man lay hidden within the desk), the myth persisted that such a machine could be constructed.

Johl stood and took their glasses away to refill. Stern had white wine, a Riesling served in a Rhenish brown globe of glass. The judge replenished his own glass with brandy.

Johl moved a king-side pawn.

The wine had dulled much of the pain in Stern's limbs and he felt dangerously alive. This served, ironically, to reawaken a sense that he might after all be able to exact some kind of revenge for the loss of Irena and Hanna. The sense of injustice, which had fallen on him in the courtroom through the triple-arch of the windows, was crushing.

He responded almost instantly to Johl's move, a knight penetrating the heart of his opponent's defences.

Johl's face froze for a second, which was extraordinary, because otherwise his flesh was constantly rippling, catching the light, folding into shadows. Stern perceived his error, for by moving so quickly he was humiliating Johl, who, he already sensed after a total of a dozen moves, was a player of mediocre skills. Logical, clearly intelligent, and painstakingly meticulous, it was true; but Stern had noted a failure to grasp strategy, and a countervailing fondness for short-term tactics. Johl was, it appeared, a man who did not wish to see too far into the future; to engage with the bigger picture. He had developed an intellect that could avoid complex questions by constructing a screen of smaller, intriguing, *solvable* puzzles.

Stern, at least, could now foresee the evening ahead of him. They would play out the game, however long it took, and Johl would shimmer with the alcohol in his bloodstream. A waiter – a German in a threadbare jacket – had been told to bring them cheese at eleven. There would be a handshake to match the one Johl had offered when Stern had been brought from the cells. What would Johl gain from the encounter? A frisson, perhaps, of danger and intellectual endeavour. The judge advocate had defied convention in order to find a worthy opponent. There was something of the free-thinking intellectual peacock about Johl, the theoretical rebel, otherwise penned in by rules and regulations.

On a good day, Stern thought, his daughter Judi might have beaten the lawyer. He'd left her in her cell alone. David would not answer any questions through his door. Liff's wounds were flyblown. Esther lay on her bunk cradling her unborn child. Duvos looked out of his cell window, and, at Esther's request, kept a keen eye open for any sight of Tomma. Brunner had his orders from Meyer – to take Stern and his daughter into the woods at midnight – but the judge's summons could not be ignored.

And so here sat Stern, sipping Riesling in the judge's quarters.

Johl played the move Stern expected.

The unspecified anger grew inside Stern each time the pendulum in the casement clock swung. It was as if the contradictions in the room were being compressed with each second recorded by the swinging lead weight. He replied to Johl's move instantly, a further open insult to his host. It was a pathetically small act of revenge, but deeply satisfying.

'Will you send your mechanical men to kill me one day, doctor?' asked Johl. There was a note of disappointment in the judge's voice. He'd hoped, perhaps, for an evening of purely intellectual entertainment: two men, prisoners of forces beyond their control, seizing a moment of individual reconciliation. But the Jew, it seemed, was too bitter.

'Mechanical men?' asked Stern.

'The golem. Or an army, perhaps, of such creations.'

'Fairy tales.'

'I came to Borek from Prague,' countered Johl. 'A case of fraud, of little note, but technically interesting. My fellow officers stationed in the old town were thrilled with this legend of the golem; that out of the ghetto will come a monster to kill them in their beds, a man-made man, imbued with life by the rabbis.'

Stern took a gulp of wine. 'The golem is a parable,' he said. 'The first was Adam. If I may say so, German culture seems to have a problem with allegory.'

Johl, delighted, leaned forward. 'The *first* golem. So, this implies others. As I say, an army perhaps?'

He leant back, and then frowned, contemplating his position. They sat in silence for a minute and then Johl moved, edging his king into safety. Stern responded instantly, his queen sweeping a diagonal to the left-hand edge of the board.

Stern drank more wine, deciding that he could not become Johl's accomplice in this polite clash of intellect, this denial of the world outside the room on the field of the dead beyond the gas chamber, where his wife and child might now lie, looking with open eyes at the night sky.

The waiter brought cheese. Johl did not attempt any more conversation, but returned immediately to the game, the plate at his elbow, his hands ferrying morsels to his damp mouth. Plump fingers, bitten nails and fleshy wrists. Stern thought that you are rarely offered the opportunity to collect details about an enemy at close quarters. It was like examining a corpse.

Johl moved his king further into the defences offered by his pawns.

Stern replied immediately, the rooks doubling on the fifth file.

'Once, briefly, I worked for the German government,' said Stern. 'In 1929. A commission on the hereditary aspects of diabetes. The laboratory was in the ministry of public health. Prinz-Albrecht Strasse. Perhaps …?'

Johl sat back. 'I know it,' he said, the playful note of amiable tolerance gone entirely. 'You know that I know it; the headquarters of the SS are on the same street, as is the Gestapo's. Play one game at a time, doctor.'

Stern blinked at him. What could this man do to hurt him? Nothing. But Judi? Might Johl stand between her and sanctuary in the woods?

Pouring himself more brandy, Johl forgot Stern's wine glass, which was now empty. If Stern would not play guest, Johl would not play host.

'I have friends still at the ministry of health,' said Stern. 'Despite everything that has happened in Germany since those happier days.'

'How uplifting,' said Johl, and returned his stare to the board. After three minutes he moved, blocking the file dominated by the rooks with a knight, a sudden tangible reminder to Stern of his lost daughter, clutching her wooden toy.

'Last year,' said Stern. 'In February, my friends at the ministry watched an extraordinary thing. One morning they saw a crowd of women in the street at the side of the government buildings, in Rosenstrasse. Apparently, and this they learnt in the coming days, a house on the street was owned by the Gestapo and inside it they had gathered the last Jews in Berlin. These women outside were their wives. Brave women!'

Stern moved his bishop diagonally to remove the knight. He held the fallen piece in his hand as he spoke. 'If these men, now imprisoned in the house, left Berlin, then the city would be *judenfrei*. This was the goal of the city authorities. But why were these few Jews left in the city, when many thousands had been taken away?'

Johl blinked at Stern.

'You will know, of course. They were married to non-Jews. German womenfolk; the very ones who had gathered outside in Rosenstrasse. Do you see?' asked Stern. 'The men had been given privileged positions within the civil service; their presence was tolerated. But such clemency was now at an end. Rumours swept the city that the men were to be loaded on a transport and taken east. A euphemism of course. As we know, in the East lie the gas chambers.'

Johl blinked rapidly. 'It's bad manners to talk during the game. Very bad manners.'

Stern, briefly, found himself speechless.

'I am not an anti-Semite,' said Johl. 'Many of my friends, my family, look upon the fate of your people with sadness. Do you think I want to be here, doctor? Do you think I wish to be a witness to this? Our great state does not hear rebellious voices. There are exceptions, but they are rare, and of no importance. No, my moment of decision has passed. My role is to administer the law. The law protects many people – the weak, the disadvantaged. In the case in question, it seeks to protect officers of the state from murder. It does not protect the Jew. This is not my decision.'

Johl was breathing heavily.

'The women gathered outside the house in Rosenstrasse shouted that they wanted their men back,' said Stern, as if Johl had not spoken. 'They were threatened. A soldier came to tell them that if they did not leave the street there would be consequences. The next day there were more women. Placards now, too, demanding that their men be returned home. And there were onlookers, of course, from the government buildings, workers on the way to the U-Bahn.

'On the third day a machine-gun was placed on the steps of the house and sandbags set in a ring. The women fled to nearby streets. Then, a few bold ones returned, and there were no shots. So the rest came back too. There was then a riotous confrontation: the SS soldiers said they would shoot if provoked. The women shouted: "Murderers!"'

Stern had raised his voice very slightly. The guard, posted outside the door, opened it immediately.

Johl simply raised a hand. The door was shut.

'And then something unprecedented happened,' said Stern. 'That night all the prisoners were released, turning up on their own doorsteps to be greeted by their wives. My friend, in his letter, said that Reich Minister Joseph Goebbels personally ordered the release. It was even said that some Jews were on a train heading east when the order came through and they had to shunt it back to Berlin.

'Was this the Reich Minister's decision? No. Surely a higher authority had intervened; and there is only one higher authority. A man, I think, who identifies himself with the German people. The Volk. A man particularly alert to the dangers of dissent when expressed by ordinary citizens. Not Jews like me – we are no longer citizens, as you point out. Not the zealots within the party – they never express disquiet, because they never even contemplate defiance in their own heads, let alone on the streets of the capital. No: he listens to the man in the street. Not the beggars, but the workers, and the professional men – the teachers, the small businessmen, the notaries, the shopkeepers.'

Stern took a pawn with the first rook. 'The lawyers.'

Johl looked at the board for six minutes, according to the pendulum clock, and then stood stiffly, took his king by the crown, and gently laid it on the board in token of resignation.

Chapter 48

A boy was born at two in the morning in the caretaker's shack at the sawmill in the woods. Freida brought the child into the world with a scream that must have stopped the partisans in their tracks on the forest path. The boy howled too, for several minutes. Meyer was in the bunkhouse with a bottle of wine. When he came into the shack, Stern noted that he made a fundamental emotional error: he walked towards Stern's daughter, Judi, who held the child, and studied the face of the newborn, before turning to the mother. Freida's face was translucent, the blue veins showing in a network at her temples, eyes closed.

For a moment Stern considered the miracle he had witnessed; one life becoming two. 'Freida's lost a lot of blood and is very weak,' he said to Meyer. 'She has shown no signs of convulsions. For that we must be grateful. Talk to her if you can about the future. Paint a picture of what is to come for her and the child. She needs something to live for, then she will recover, but she is still very weak, although the child has good lungs.'

'I need more wine,' said Meyer. 'Is there a name?'

'She chose Eden,' said Stern. When he'd understood what Freida wanted to call her child, the doctor had found the moment transformative, in that she could think of paradise here, in the woods of Borek.

'It's a good Jewish name,' she had told Stern, as if embarrassed by her choice. 'Don't let Rolf change it.'

Over the years of his medical practice, he'd become a modest expert in onomastics, the origins of names. Often, at the birth, mothers turned to the doctor as a source of wisdom, and so his black bag had once carried a small Yiddish text on derivations, which he knew by heart. Eden was indeed a fine choice, from the original Hebrew for delight, or possibly lush or abundant.

Meyer simply nodded and fled, while Judi followed to fetch more water. Stern picked the child up and felt the erratic, vital, jerky movement of his legs against his own arms. The thought of Hanna's body was too painful a comparison. He fought to keep the idea of his daughter, the mere outline of her name, at a distance. Since leaving Johl's quarters he'd felt his anger crystallising into the concept of physical retribution. It was such a crude word – *revenge* – and usually he'd have thought himself above its aura of animal brutality. But in his head, he had played out an execution: Johl in his seat at the card table, Stern stuffing the chessmen into his wet mouth, forcing them down the wide fleshy throat. The sensation, of pressing the pieces into the narrow, gasping gullet, was as real as the warm, blood-tinted water in which he washed his hands.

Meyer returned with a bottle of cognac and two etched goblets of crystal. As he shut the door they heard an owl call out in the forest. It was still night and there was no hint yet of the dawn.

The German studied his son's face. The infant had a wisp of dark hair and the features echoed his: the broad, knuckle-like skull looked immensely strong, despite the fragile eyelashes and the pouting mouth.

'He has the head of a Prussian,' said Meyer. 'I don't know what the future holds, doctor, but looking like a Jew is unlikely to be an advantage. So, a celebratory drink.' He filled the glasses with an extravagant air, allowing the precious liquid to spill.

Judi came back with a cup of tea and a pitcher of water. Once she'd washed Freida's face, and the child, she sat, perfectly upright, a china cup balanced in one hand, with her eyes closed.

Stern drank Meyer's cognac. He felt immensely tired, and fleetingly the thought of lying down on the bed next to the sleeping Freida made his head swim. He closed his eyes, the glass in his hand.

'The wet-nurse from the village will come at six,' said Meyer.

Stern woke instantly, lifting the glass to his lips, not knowing if he had been unconscious for ten seconds or an hour.

'Your daughter will help nurse Freida until she is well. A week, less if the Red Army continues to move west. Then she must go to the village with the rest.'

'Thank you,' said Stern.

'The court clerk has given me notice that I will be called tomorrow as a witness. You are to be ready too. Johl has requested this, not Funk. This worries me deeply. You say he said nothing about the case tonight?'

'Nothing. It was, for him, not business but pleasure. An intellectual joust.'

'When the case is over you will go back to the slave camp.'

'Yes. I must follow my wife and daughter; they may still be alive.'

Meyer knew that Stern said this only for the benefit of his surviving daughter, so he nodded. 'The clerk says the other Jewish witnesses will be handed back to the camp authorities at six this morning. They are no longer required. I can't influence such decisions. Judi must stay here. I have made arrangements and documents have been completed. Money has changed hands. You may not see each other again. So, say your goodbyes now.'

Meyer stood, touched his newborn, and left, leaving the door ajar.

Stern took Judi's head in his hands and kissed her hair. He'd had only a few moments before they left the water tower with Brunner to tell her what lay ahead for her at the sawmill. There was a heavy price to pay for the possibility of freedom: she would have to provide comfort to men, but she might be able to stay in the shadows for a while, as she was young, and still skinny, and her hair was stubble. Judi had cried, and asked to stay with her father, but Stern had said it was what Irena wanted too – she must take her chance on behalf of them all.

He went ahead now with what he had to say because he knew he was close to tears, and that was a luxury they could no longer afford.

'Irena and I were blessed with such a daughter. Nothing can take away our pride. I may return tomorrow. If I don't, look after our memories. There is justice in this, in becoming the guardian of the story. You love stories. Keep this one. There may even be retribution and revenge one day.'

Judi embraced her father, her chin on his shoulder. 'Mamma and Hanna may still be alive,' she whispered. 'I feel that they are. I do, Father. I really feel that.'

'And I feel, just as surely, that I will see you again,' said Stern.

He held her face at a slight distance so that he could focus on her eyes. 'Judi. Listen. There is a girl in the house here, one of the whores, who is called Natasza. Befriend her, tell her you are my daughter. She loves to read too. Books, newspapers, whatever she can find. When the Russians come, she will not stay here, she will go home. Go with her if you can.'

Meyer returned. 'We must leave now, doctor,' he said. 'Have you said goodbye?'

'For now,' said Stern.

Natasza was in the kitchen, wearing a pair of the glasses that Stern had got from Brunner. She was reading a book, leather-bound, but frayed, with gold Gothic title letters. The spectacles were small, and round, while the frames were silver metal.

Meyer took bread, cold meat and a bottle of wine, and they fled the bunkhouse towards the clearing in the woods so that they could eat out in the fresh air. The night was warm, and still, although for the first time they could hear the sound of distant artillery.

Meyer sat on one of the logs. 'We don't have much time, so eat.'

They heard a single artillery shell, louder than the rest.

'Sixty miles away,' said Meyer, lighting a cigar. 'They've broken through. A week away, perhaps two. Now we'll see the whites of their eyes. The partisans only have to wait. Who knows, advance units may be in the woods already. One of the watchtower guards saw parachutes the night of the air raid.'

He drew on the cigar, until the end glowed red, and then covered it with a cupped hand. 'My mother's father died at the Second Battle of the Sambre, on the Western Front, just a few days before the Armistice, at the moment of dawn. My grandmother said this was typical because he was a farmer and all his life he'd had to get up in the dark, and he would work like the peasant he was until first light. Then he'd always stop and have a cigarette. A sniper – an American sniper according to a comrade – shot him here …' Meyer touched his right temple. 'He fell down dead on his back and the cigarette was still between his lips.'

Meyer drew on the cigar again, making it glow vividly, so that it crackled and a spark flew. This time he made no attempt to shield the light.

Chapter 49

The first klaxon sounded at five thirty. There was a raucous roll-call of the slaves down on the Pariser Platz. From the German compound came the clatter of cooks in the kitchens, then the dull percussion of the slaves dishing out food, a mug of water flavoured with coffee from a metal bucket, and stale bread. The blunt percussion of plates and cups was like a herd of goats or sheep on a mountainside. That this palette of early morning sounds had become familiar to Stern was incredible, as he was hearing it for only the second time in his life, and it was just his third day at Borek.

Liff looked dead when Stern opened the watchmaker's cell door at six. His head lay to one side on the wooden pallet and beside his eye he'd set a pine cone, very close, so that he could study the intricate pattern of the overlapping edges. Stern took a step closer and saw that beside the cone lay the body of a wasp, and the two-winged seed of a sycamore tree. Liff's hair was matted on one side with dried blood and his lip was split and dry like that of a dead animal, revealing small white teeth.

Two seconds passed and Liff blinked. Stern was relieved he was alive, although there was no doubt he was dying. The brutal beating he'd suffered at the hands of the Gestapo must have damaged his brain, or there was an infection in his blood. Liff was slipping away, and the doctor had to admit that this might be a conscious decision of the patient. Increasingly, they all lived now in this twilight world, in which the binary division of life and death, light and dark, was a thing of the past.

'Can you get up, Liff?' asked Stern. 'Brunner says you have to go back to the slave camp.'

The guard was outside in the hexagonal chamber at the top of the stairs.

'You are all freed from the court jurisdiction,' he confirmed in a loud voice. 'You must go back to the squares. Not you obviously, doctor. They want you in court again. The watchmaker, and the rest, including the mother with child, they're all going back …'

Liff couldn't stand on his own so they put him on his chair.

'They plan to bring a stretcher and take him to the lazarette,' said the guard, setting out in a matter-of-fact voice what would be the last minutes of Liff's life.

Stern looked Brunner in the eyes. 'He could try and walk.'

'Why, you think it makes a difference? The first train has arrived.'

Of the nine who had walked away from the gas chamber, this was all they now were: five – Stern, Liff, Duvos, David and Esther. Stern thought it was ironic that he'd made that promise to his family on the square in Lodz: that, life or death, they would stay together. Instead, they had flown apart, and he was alone, with these people who had once shared a house with him on a backstreet in Lodz but had otherwise been strangers.

Duvos was in his cell and he'd completed a picture on the wall in coloured chalk.

Stern sat on the bunk to admire the finished work.

'The Jewel Box,' said Duvos, his delicate hands encompassing the vision. 'That's what we call it: the Jewel Box.'

The skyline Stern recognised depicted on the plaster wall was that of the city of Dresden, Duvos's home, in the borderlands beneath the Czech mountains.

Duvos got to his feet and identified the buildings from left to right, his fingers dancing over the spires and domes until, lastly, he pointed out the grassy hills beyond the city, which he said had been coloured in by Hanna.

'When I'm dead, and God asks what kind of heaven I want, I'm going to tell him that I want to go on seeing the city,' said Duvos. 'I'm going to float above it all and watch out for everyone who is good. I'll float over Dresden. You know what I'm asking for here, Stern?'

'You want to be an angel, Duvos. It's unlikely, don't you think? Angels are beautiful. Serene. Full of light.'

'All-seeing,' said Duvos, responding to Stern's smile, with a crazy glint of hope in his eyes.

'It's time,' said Brunner. 'But paperwork first.' Brunner had a habit of talking out loud to himself, of externalising an internal conversation, which made him sound profoundly stupid, because he ended up contradicting his own statements. 'So, it's not time. Five more minutes.'

He left them, tripping lightly down the staircase. They heard a conversation below dominated by the teenager's voice. Then Brunner returned, holding a sheaf of forms, followed by an old guard with a wispy moustache who looked like he'd staggered out of a newspaper cartoon featuring the Kaiser; one of the scurrilous etchings in the papers the communists printed when they wanted a revolution.

'You have a new guard,' Brunner announced. 'He will take you to the squares. You must help Liff on his way as there is no stretcher. The boy David is strong enough at least.'

The new guard, who had only got as far as the top step, turned round and went back down without saying a word, his jaw working away, as if he was chewing sausage, or stale bread.

Brunner kicked David's cell door. 'Todt – wake up!'

The door flew open and bounced back off the wall, but in that one second the view was clear and they'd all seen that the cell was empty. Brunner swung round to look back at Stern and Duvos. There was something in his eyes that told them that despite his many kindnesses he'd kill them in a moment if he thought it would save his own skin.

'Where is he? Where's the bastard cry-baby?'

Brunner went into the cell. From the pipes above his head a sheet hung with a noose fashioned in the end. The metal bracket of the pipe had broken and the pieces lay on the floor.

'So. He thought he'd take that path,' said Brunner.

They checked all the cells but there was no sign of David Todt.

'He did not pass me,' said Brunner.

Stern could see the young soldier's finger working at the trigger on his rifle. They'd all heard him snoring in the night, so it was quite possible that the boy had slipped away. If he turned up in another part of the camp, Brunner's absolute protestation that he'd been alert all night might get him shot.

'Maybe he slipped past,' said Duvos, wide-eyed. 'He was light on his feet. That boy could have blended in with the shadows.'

Brunner looked up at the pipes on the ceiling. 'No. He must have climbed the stairs. I'm here to stop anyone getting to the water. They think the partisans might poison it, or bring down the radio mast, or the telephone lines. You think I guard this place just to keep you safe! If he's up there he'll get what he wants; I'll string the fuck-face up on one of his bloody pipes. Even I'm not allowed up there. Commandant's orders.'

There was no doubt Brunner was scared now for himself, for the boy in a uniform had aged in front of their eyes, his once bovine eyes darting from face to face. A summary court martial could easily lead to a firing squad for dereliction of duty. It struck Stern that in some ways he was not unlike his missing prisoner, David Todt: the war had robbed him of the last precious days of childhood.

Brunner went to the circular staircase and looked up. It corkscrewed twice before meeting a round iron manhole cover. He quickly climbed the steps two at a time and braced his back against the iron plate.

'He's broken the lock,' he said.

They all heard the cover open an inch, because the air pressure changed. Brunner came down and took out his holster pistol, levelling it at Duvos.

'Go up. See if he's there. If I go up, he could kill me with a single blow. I bet he's taken the broken pipe with him. And you,' he said to Stern. 'Go with him; he's too weak on his own.'

Esther stood at the door of her cell, cradling her stomach. 'David's scared. He needs the people he's lost. He can't cope with all this on his own.'

The implication was clear, that she *could*.

Duvos went first, Stern just behind, and they squeezed themselves into the narrow space and bent double under the iron cover.

'One, two and three,' said Stern.

They flexed their bodies up, up, up, until the iron manhole cover rose, reached a fulcrum-point, and fell backwards. The metal cover struck the concrete floor, and a single note rang out like a great cathedral bell: the tenor at Ulm, perhaps, turning beneath its Gothic arch.

'Christ,' said Brunner, waving the pistol. 'Wake the dead, you fools.'

The echo circled them still, caught within the water above, and the space above that, diminishing with each receding wave, but never destined to be silent. Around them light played as if floating on the sound waves, studded with flecks of sunlight, dappling the walls, so that the air shimmered. The smell of fresh water filled their noses and mouths; not brine, or stagnant slime, but the green essence of rain.

They heard heavy boots shuffling on the stairwell below. It was the old guard. 'Brunner. What's wrong? We're late. It's the captain's watch, if you make me late ...'

'One's missing,' said Brunner. 'He's gone up into the water tower. A moment. Take time to learn some patience, comrade.'

Stern led the way up the staircase. After three turns it emerged on a platform, which itself was circular, twice the diameter of the stairwell, with a guardrail running at the edge. This platform – an iron dais – stood in the centre of the water tank. From the rail hung a series of metal chains attached to large tin cups, no doubt set aside to allow the water to be tested. Around the dais was the green water itself. Light shone in through the gap between the corrugated roof, and the sides of the tank.

Close to the platform the body of David Todt floated face down. Stern wondered at what point the pipes, and valves, and taps had ceased to be an object of academic study for the boy and had become useful in this precise way – as a means of ending his own life. It was as if the young man had followed them to this death.

'Come up, Brunner,' shouted Stern. 'The boy's dead. You'll need help to get his body out of the water.'

'In the water! Christ,' called Brunner, climbing the stairs. 'They won't drink it now.' When he got to the handrail, and saw Todt's body below, Stern noted that the guard's hands were shaking.

Brunner turned to Duvos, his eyes narrowing. 'You. You were in his cell last night, talking. He couldn't have got through the metal trap alone.'

But Duvos's eyes were on the water below. He spoke, and for once his voice wasn't powered by excitement at the world he could see, but by a kind of wonder.

'Look, beneath the water; look down into the green light.'

Within the water they could see the lustre of gold. There were several metal baths sunk under the surface, standing on the base of the tank; stately baths, from a country house surely, with claw feet, and brass taps. Each bath – and there had to be a dozen or more – was filled to the brim with different gold objects, sorted by type: plain rings, rings with jewels, bracelets, earrings, pendants and watches – many of the latter still with the air caught behind their glass faces, like white tears. To one side, a large tarpaulin bag had been sunk into the water, like the baskets used by builders to move sand or broken bricks, and this was filled with small ivory pellets. The bag was overflowing, its summit breaking the surface so that they could finally see clearly what lay before them: the ivory pellets were teeth, taken from the dead, each one glinting with stolen gold.

Chapter 50

The discovery of the gold seemed to awaken Borek from its summer torpor. By the time Brunner marched Stern to the drill square by the mess, the sleepy, bored, atmosphere of the German compound had been replaced by manic activity. For the first time Stern noticed guards posted at strategic points, as well as along the perimeter fence. A machine-gun post had been set up on the empty grass space in front of the mess. German soldiers stepped quickly from hut to hut. A truck was being loaded with furniture and boxes, within which Stern could hear the clash of bottles and china. Outside each barrack hut, linen was being dumped in rough piles. At the main camp gate, four trucks waited, bumper to bumper, as guards checked documents. On the far side of the perimeter wire a platoon of Ukrainie were cutting down the barbed wire and rolling it up into cylinders.

There was no doubt the Germans were preparing to quit Borek. Not today, thought Stern, but soon. Retreating west must have seemed a bitter option for the SS authorities if it embraced the possibility that they were leaving behind a fortune for the Red Army to uncover. Now that the gold was found, the road to Berlin was open. And there was no doubt the enemy was closer. Even now they could hear the crump of distant artillery fire.

Stern was not led up the steps into the mess but had to stand in the sunlight on the baked earth, while Brunner courted the shadow of a walnut sapling.

'Can't I have some shade?' asked Stern, dizzy and thirsty.

'Be silent.'

Brunner was agitated. He kept rearranging his feet like an old man, afraid he might fall over in the dust. Stern wondered how long he had been the guard in the water tower. Was he, even now, a suspect Johl would wish to interview? The young German shook the sapling as if he could dislodge a walnut.

'They fruit after the tenth year,' said Stern.

'Just shut up.'

Stern, eyes closed, considered the events of the last two hours.

Held in their cells in the water tower they'd heard Brunner being cross-examined by his superiors. No doubt to save his own skin he'd clearly implicated Duvos in young Todt's suicide. The chemist had been frog-marched from his cell, while the rest of them were rounded up, and all led to a clearing by the inner perimeter wire. Brunner took Duvos by the arm and placed him at a spot with his back to the barbed wire. There was no post, no bindings, no blindfold. It was not an *appointed place*, in any sense of the word. It was just convenient, and in the confusion of the first moments Duvos did not even know which way to face, until Brunner marched away and began loading his rifle.

The photographic chemist entered a trance-like state. His wide eyes were open and he looked about him with an expression of intense study. This last moment of his life was clearly to be rigorously recorded in his brain, while it functioned: the cool edge of the pine forest, the rusted metal of the water tower, his own shadow. Duvos, the human camera, recording his own final scene, thankful, perhaps, that it was to take place under an open sky, rather than the cramped concrete box of the gas chamber.

The tragedy, thought Stern, was that with the sound of a bullet they'd all lose that unique back-catalogue of stored images that was Duvos's memory, a photographic library as impressive as any in Berlin, or New York, or London; obliterated in a second, as thousands had been destroyed. And this loss would be the chemist's tragedy, but also a collective one.

Duvos looked up and what he saw there caused him to let out a small cry of delight. Cloudless, still clear at this early hour before the heat could buckle the air, the sky above was full of the twirling, knotted contrails of dog-fighting aircraft. So high, there was no sound. The patterns were insanely beautiful, like aerial worm-casts, wrought in silver. Duvos raised his arms to the sight of this, as if the tableau had been choreographed to mark the moment.

Brunner shook his head, stamped his left foot and marched smartly back another few yards, checked his rifle again, raised the gun to his shoulder, and fired. He did it so quickly that Duvos was still studying the aircraft above his head. Brunner, it turned out, was a good shot. Two slaves with blue armbands put Duvos's body into a handcart.

Stern's heart pounded in his chest, but only for twenty seconds, before it began the slow trajectory of recovery to normal. Inured now to pain and loss, he was aware of the moment passing into a forgotten history. The only emotion he felt was a kind of trivial pity, in that Duvos lay twisted in the cart, so misshapen that Stern wanted to rearrange his friend's limbs and restore a sense of dignity, if nothing else.

The old guard who had come to help Brunner took command of the handcart, Liff and Esther. Stern embraced Esther stiffly and let his hand rest on Liff's bony shoulder, realising that his own life had become a series of partings, and that with each one he left something of himself behind. The feeling that he was somehow shedding his life, leaving in his wake a series of discarded skins, left him with a ghost-like sense of his own lightness. Duvos, in his cart, looked up at the sky, his eyes still full of light, his left hand stiff, the fingers extended, and, Stern noted, smudged with the blood red chalk he'd used to depict his particular version of paradise.

Which left Stern alone an hour later, standing in the deadening sunlight of the drill square, beside a walnut tree, the shadow of which he was forbidden to share. The violent loss of his friend Duvos made him feel, by one more exquisite degree, a man abandoned by his family and those who had become his family.

On the mess veranda Funk, the prosecution lawyer, and Raeder, the SS investigator who'd tortured Liff, stood and watched the sky above. The dogfights appeared endless, etched across the blue. Raeder was taking coffee, standing at the terrace rail, the port-wine stain on his face especially livid. Stern considered, fleetingly, the coincidence that both Keuper and Raeder were physically damaged in some way, and the possibility that a lot of human cruelty is a form of revenge. Perhaps that was one other facet of the genius that was the Nazi state; that it was constructed to allow each individual within its various echelons to retaliate for some perceived insult, or cruel twist of fate. In this way each zealot could redress a personal wrong by inflicting cruelty on a generic group; the homosexuals, the Jews, the Romani. Germany was an efficient machine, fuelled by bitter revenge.

A black Mercedes staff car stood waiting, its engine idling. The driver loaded a single suitcase into the boot. Finally, Raeder, mopping his mouth with a linen serviette, shook Funk's hand. He was about to get into the staff car when he saw Stern, and set off towards him, stopping ten foot short, working with his left hand to slip on his right glove.

'I don't mean to be cruel,' he said. 'You won't see your home village again, Stern. I, on the other hand, will see it tomorrow, if we travel well. The day after if not.'

His tone was light and without apparent malice.

'You're going to Weissenstein?'

'Yes. Don't ask questions; it's impertinent.'

Brunner cocked his rifle.

Raeder took one step closer. 'Yes. I must go to Weissenstein. But first to Berlin, with our precious gold.'

A lorry had been brought close to the mess and Stern saw now that a long line of guards were ferrying buckets to the tailgate. He caught sight of the gold within one – coins this time. The men sweated with the weight of the treasure.

Raeder stepped even closer, so that Stern could smell him, the soapy sharp aroma of the neatly pressed uniform, the oily dampness of the greased-back hair. Again, Stern considered a generic characteristic of the cruel: that they are often punctilious in their own dress and appearance. He wondered if it was a form of disguise, an embellishment of an outer layer, designed to obscure what lies beneath.

'I'm not complaining, you see,' said Raeder. 'My own home is in Munich. I may have been as far as Regen before, possibly. A riverside, I think? A pretty market square? This is in the valley below the village?'

'Yes. A church with a great steeple, the highest in the forest.'

'A synagogue?'

'Burnt down.'

'Shame. I just wanted to know. Is there an inn?'

'In Weissenstein? Yes. The Castle. It is very fine. The food is excellent – at least, it was.'

'You said that Jonas Keuper asked you to tell him a secret about the village, about his own family. You said you failed in this, didn't you?'

'Yes.'

'I wonder. You see, there *is* a secret, Stern. Actually, several secrets, but all of the same hue. In the short term this is very good news for you. It means you are going to live much longer than you had any right to expect. I must drive to Weissenstein to investigate further. I shall ask some questions and then I will return – or we may meet in Berlin, who knows? But we shall talk again. I had a long chat with Liff – the watchmaker. I can have a longer chat with you. Because I'm wondering if maybe you lied. Maybe you did know the secret. That would explain why Keuper tried to kill you when it looked as if you might win a temporary reprieve. These are the kind of questions you can look forward to answering when I return.'

Since his desperate interview with Keuper by the burning suitcases Stern had wracked his brains for a clue to the mystery of Weissenstein; what lay hidden there? His thoughts always came back to his friend Johann Keuper. Stern had suspected that it was the tax collector's influence that had delayed the eviction of the Sterns from the village. Had he continued to watch over them? Stern had been puzzled by the family's slow progress across Europe – the transit camp, the labour camps, and then Lodz – a ghetto for Poles with very few Germans. It had always felt as if someone was looking out for them. In his prayers he thanked God – but did He have an instrument on earth? And had Johann Keuper helped others? Was this the secret his son feared?

There was a cheer from the terrace of the mess. Looking up they saw two fighter planes wheeling, flashes of fire etched against the blue of the sky. Several officers were waving wildly, and two were drinking wine directly from bottles. Stern sensed that they had edged very close to the moment when the patina of civilisation, which was the surface of life in the German compound, would fall away to reveal something more brutal. There was a dull crump of an explosion and one of the planes disintegrated in mid-air.

Raeder had lingered to watch the battle with his comrades. Getting into the Mercedes he had a parting shot for Stern: 'I will be back,' he said. 'I'm sorry I have to go. Today will be fun. Johl's temper is short; he wants Meyer on the stand. He seems to have taken against our young hero. Perhaps he suspects his motives for pulling that trigger. He is not alone.'

Chapter 51

The barbers' hut was a hall of cold mirrors. Esther noticed that some of the glass was etched with the Polish surname Rokita, and the words *Fryzjer Buda*, which she knew meant barbers' shop. So perhaps they had simply dismantled the mirrors, and the basins, and the mock-marble walls, and dragged them here to Borek from a nearby town. The sunlight streamed in through the many windows on one side and glinted on the scissors, the china bowls, the silver behind the glass. The barbers sat in the chairs and smoked and drank tea from a samovar that was tended by a woman, who gave Esther a glass with a beautiful filigree iron holder, and a lump of bread that had been picked clean of maggots.

The kapo in the barbers' hut, a short man with a bald head but jet-black hair on his chest, arms and hands, said she could sit by the door, on a child's painted wooden stool. She was alone now: Liff had been carried on the stretcher to the lazarette and she'd pressed his hand in farewell, while Duvos's body, in its handcart, had been taken directly to the pits beyond the gas chamber. Leo, they'd left behind, while Irena and Hanna had gone before. The kapo told her she had to wait with the barbers until the next transport, which was due the following morning, when she too would walk the Himmelstrasse.

All she wished to achieve in what was left of her life was to gather news of Tomma, and if possible, send him a message of farewell and love. This ambition was limited but practical, and sustained her. The idea that she might see him, an impossible gift, she kept just beyond conscious hope.

The heat in the barbers' shop grew with the hour until it was unbearable. Esther could smell freshly cut hair, which hung like a drug on the air. This, she thought, would be her world for the final day of her life, and she was happy to wait for her chance to ask one of the men about Tomma. But as the sun rose, most of them went outside and lay in the shade of the trees that marked the beginning of the Himmelstrasse. Since the guard had left, they had not seen a single German soldier. Despite the sense of languor, Esther saw that several of the men could not lie and rest, but paced in the shadows.

The woman who had served tea took up her chair and indicated that Esther should follow with her stool. They walked a little past the men, deeper into the shade of the trees, where the sand was patterned with the feet of the prisoners. The wind rustled the silver birch leaves and made the shadows shiver.

'Where's the father of your child?' asked the woman, who was perhaps fifty years of age and said her name was Sasha. She had a slight cast in one eye, and very bony fingers, which Esther noted did not vibrate at all but were strong and still like her own.

'He works in the woods,' said Esther. 'He's called Tomma. He was a glassblower, with a great chest, and strong lungs. I think he'll last for ever, but I don't think I'll see him before I die. We did not part well, and I know this will be a lasting trouble for him. He did not want to leave me, but I made him go.'

'He's well placed if he is with the woodcutters,' said Sasha.

She explained that the green armbands worn by the woodcutters were an object of desire within the camp. These men were better fed, and in winter were given warmer clothes, and boots. They roamed the woods and knew the paths.

'I will tell you a story about the woodcutters,' said Sasha. 'You must listen,' she added, gripping Esther's hand.

Sasha's tale was told with brisk skill. Two days earlier the green squad had gone out to work by a small stream, a brook that in winter could be heard by the western perimeter wire, although in the summer it was a trickle of no account. There was a clearing there and the Germans had been directing the felling of trees to make this into a field. It was said that they intended to build a farmhouse and to clear the forest for the plough. One day they would pretend that Borek was just a farm, and that the camp, and the gas chamber, were Jewish lies.

Cutting down the trees was hard labour. One German officer had developed a way of getting the slaves to work swiftly. If he spotted a slow worker, he would demand that the man fell a tree in three minutes. Failure meant the victim was taken to the lazarette and shot. If they succeeded, they were allowed to live.

'That was the deal,' said Sasha.

But on this day it wasn't slack work that caught the officer's eye. He saw a worker, one of the new Russian prisoners called Kronrod, and this man was calmly watching the guard smoke. Men like this, caught on the Eastern Front, were beginning to arrive at the camp, but not by train, by truck. They were tough because they were soldiers and had spent years living on the land.

The guard asked the insolent Kronrod if he wanted a cigarette.

The Russian did not understand, but one of the other woodcutters had translated the question, although Kronrod said nothing in reply, itself a form of further insubordination.

Sasha had become animated by her own story. 'The guard pointed at a stout linden tree and said: "He's got one minute to cut it down. If he succeeds, he can have a smoke. If he fails, it's the lazarette."

'Once the translation was complete, they all stopped work to watch,' said Sasha. 'This Kronrod was slightly built, but the Red Army prisoners have muscles like hardwood. He used his blunt saw to fell the tree, and it came crashing down in less than one minute.

'All the German could do was clap. He had to make the best of it because the men of the green squad were all watching. So he strolled over to the Russian and offered him a cigarette.'

Sasha's face was wreathed in a smile. 'And this Kronrod, he just looked at the guard and said in Russian: "I don't smoke."'

'I don't smoke!' repeated Sasha, when Esther didn't smile.

'Of course, all the other Russians laughed, but the German was lost. He demanded a translation. Then everyone laughed. The humiliation! The German had to walk away, pretending to enjoy the joke.'

Sasha edged closer. 'It was a rebellion, do you see? Everyone's taken heart from it because it shows that the Germans have lost their nerve. And he's still alive, this Kronrod, although no one is taking bets on how long that lasts. And he's not the only Russian in the camp. There's hundreds.'

Sasha looked over her shoulder at the men. 'There are other stories too. There is hope, sister. Sometimes, I feel as if I have had two complete lives. The life before: when I helped my husband run his barber's shop in Celle. And then the life here, where I make tea for the barbers, and the sweepers. Who knows when a third life may begin?

'For you too. Maybe, even for the child in the womb. Maybe even today.'

Esther had the very strong impression that Sasha was not simply philosophising.

'Be ready,' said Sasha.

'For what?' asked Esther.

Sasha covered Esther's lips with a finger.

'When the bell at the station rings, follow me, not the men.'

Sasha stood quickly, shaking her head vigorously from side to side to dislodge leaves that had fallen in her hair. She walked away, leaving Esther and the two chairs behind.

Esther sat still, her heart beating, the child inside her turning over. The path was by her feet, the pale sandy sinuous line of the Himmelstrasse, leading towards the gas chamber. Perhaps the way ahead was not inevitable. She saw then, just on the edge of sight, something lying in the dust on the path. She went to fetch it, standing over it for a few seconds in painful disbelief. It was a child's toy; a chess piece in the shape of a horse. She recognised it as the one Stern had thrust into Hanna's hand when they took her from the courtroom. Esther thought of the little girl walking through the shadows, holding fiercely perhaps to Irena's hand, and clutched the toy to her own belly.

Chapter 52

SS trooper Eric Carstens still lay in his bed in the sickbay. His morphine-induced coma had lasted the night, and so Irena had not had the chance to pass on the comments of his senior officer; but she had the pleasure of doing it now. The trooper would not be transferred to Berlin, she said, or even Krakow, because – as the gentleman had explained – that would merely encourage his comrades to injure themselves. Instead, he would convalesce here, in the camp. And as Irena had already said, this would take between six and eight weeks. By which time the world would be a very different place.

'Perhaps he will forget to make the order,' offered Irena. She said this with silent satisfaction, because she knew that the officer in question had quite clearly been of the type who never makes such errors.

'I'll die in this bed,' said Carstens.

'The Russian guns are still far away,' she said.

'What do you know, woman? I heard them last night. Do you think my ears are shattered like my thigh bone?'

'In the hut, last night, I heard the men whispering,' said Irena. 'For a long time the sound of the guns got closer because of the wind. And then because the skies were clear. It is an illusion. There is still time before the Ivans arrive.'

But not enough time to save you, she thought.

Carstens wanted to believe her so much he felt his bowels loosen.

For twenty minutes he slept and Irena sat, her hands held on her lap, imagining Hanna's breath on her cheek; warm, cold, warm, cold, warm, cold. The child haunted her, dancing between the world of the dead and the world of the living. Sometimes she saw her, always out of the corner of the eye, scrawling with a crayon on the wall. Until she actually saw Hanna's dead body, she felt that her daughter would still exist, even if she was restricted to the world of peripheral vision.

A train, emerging from the pine forest, whistled three times. Irena roused herself, walked to the window and between a gap in the barrack huts saw the engine go past, pulling its tender, and a single goods van, but nothing else. Everyone said that when the transport trains stopped, the lives of the slaves would be worthless. The Germans would flee west, leaving behind a clearing in the forest of no note, and not a single witness to tell the truth.

For an hour Irena cleaned the sickbay. Lange was in his office drinking. Carstens continued to sleep, snoring feebly now, like a cat.

The outer sickbay door opened and a slave came in carrying a parcel marked:

ZERBRECHLICHE FRACHT

Irena had lost the habit of looking at people's faces, and so she didn't recognise this man until he walked up to her and reached out a hand towards her face. It was Kopp, the kapo, who had struck her down in the second square. Head and shoulders above her, his elongated body leaned forward, his feet anchored by heavyweight winter boots.

Irena went to speak but he shook his head and led her into a room at the opposite end of the building to the doctor's surgery; little more than a storage cupboard, its shelves were crammed with bandages, sheets and boxed medical supplies.

'I got a message. You have the key?' he said.

She wanted to smash her fist into his lips as he spoke, as he had once cuffed her to the dust, and torn her away from Hanna.

But all she said was: 'Yes. Is Leo alive, and Judi?'

They heard Lange shout from his office, just the single word he used to summon Irena: 'Woman!'

Irena opened the storeroom door, but she wasn't quick enough, because Lange was there, standing by Carsten's bed.

'What were you doing, you two?' His voice was pleasant, Irena had decided, almost tuneful, but slurred slightly by the drink. He took pills with the vodka. She'd seen a line of four blue tablets on his desk the last time she'd taken his coffee cup away. There might be a fresh supply in the package that Kopp had brought from the train. Perhaps that was why Lange had come out of his office.

'There is post,' she said.

'Then give me the consignment.'

He took the box casually, read the label, and then tossed it on to one of the empty beds.

'What were you doing?' he said again. It was clear the doctor was drunk, but there was a tightness in his limbs that spoke of pent-up violence.

'Were you fornicating in there?' he said. 'I think so. This isn't a whorehouse, is it?' His voice rose to a shout.

Irena shook her head.

'You're like animals.' He swung his body round and almost fell, so that he had to grab the end bar on the bed.

He wiped his lips with the back of his hand.

'What is your name?' he said, pointing at Kopp. 'What is a kapo doing in here?'

Irena said he'd brought the package of supplies from the station. She said that the train had only one goods van. She said that Kopp was an old family friend and wanted news of her husband and daughters. She said he'd been a fine carpenter – a real craftsman. She said too much.

'I didn't ask you,' said Lange, while his eyes never left Kopp's face. The doctor was in his shirtsleeves, his holster on, although the gun was missing.

'I know the kapo who runs the post; where is he?'

'The post-room slaves have been called into the mess to help pack documents,' said Kopp, taking off his glasses and polishing the one lens. 'Preparations are being made to evacuate the camp. They've got to close the post room. I'm making crates for the paper, but I said I'd run this errand so that I could see Irena.'

Lange's body relaxed slightly. 'Empty your pockets,' he said to Kopp. 'They're full. What have you taken from the storeroom?' He looked quickly at Irena. 'What have you given him?'

Kopp hadn't moved, but Irena could hear him breathing heavily through his mouth.

Lange took a step back when he didn't get an answer and picked up the package Kopp had delivered.

'I hope you haven't stolen anything,' he said, ripping it open. Extracting one of the small boxes inside, he took two small blue pills, then refocused his eyes on Kopp. 'I said, empty your pockets, carpenter.'

Kopp produced a wad of Polish zloty. Irena could see they were one hundred notes, wrapped in a piece of rag on which had been inscribed a simple map; the sinuous line of a river stood out, and the dark mass of a forest, and a railway line.

The second pocket was even worse for Kopp: a tailor's eye-punch sharpened to a spike, a rag wrapped around a piece of bread, a metal lighter, and a small scent bottle filled with a colourless liquid.

Kopp's eyes, for the first time, glanced at the sickbay clock.

'Stay here,' said Lange. He walked back into his office and sat on the edge of the desk so that he could watch them, then he picked up the phone.

Kopp moved very quickly, but without the slightest trace of menace or panic. Five or six strides got him to the desk. Lange's face mirrored only astonishment. 'I said stay there,' said the German, as if to a child. This was the moment the kapos had long predicted: the first moment of shock, the instant when the unthinkable happened, when the Germans, for all their guns, were openly vulnerable. Kopp knew the simple truth: the first strike must count.

He slipped one arm under Lange's chin, the other round his sternum, and hugged the doctor to his own chest. It was a strangely tender act, carried out quickly, but with no sense of haste. Lange's feet left the ground. Kopp's eyes closed and then Irena heard the crack of the spine, once, twice. The carpenter held the doctor's shirt collars in one fist and set him gently down on the wooden floor like a sack.

'I need a painkiller.' It was Carstens' voice, but it still made Irena let out a small scream.

The German opened his eyes, looking directly at her. 'I'm sorry I was unkind about your child,' he said.

Irena realised that her patient had finally grasped the desperate situation he faced, and that he might need an ally in the days to come.

'How soon can I get on crutches? Can you show me exercises that will help?'

Kopp, unseen in the doctor's examination room, searched the desk drawers and found the pistol. Irena watched him check the bullet chamber and then close the weapon with a flick of the wrist. Then he cleared his throat and said very clearly: 'Thank you, Herr doctor.'

Walking into the sickbay, Kopp kept his left arm rigid at his side. Level with Carsten's bed he took a pillow from the bare bunk opposite and covered the gun barrel. Then, moving quickly to the side of the patient's bed, he placed the pillow over the soldier's face, pressed down, and fired a shot, then a second. The bullet holes in the pillow were black, smudged with tar.

'Lock the doors and pull down the shutters,' he said.

Irena's heart was pounding, but she had no trouble moving her limbs. Kopp threw a blanket from the storeroom over Carstens' body. In Lange's office he carefully replaced the receiver on the phone, filled the glass on the blotter with the doctor's vodka and drank it in one gulp.

Bringing the bottle and glass with him into the sickbay, he poured a shot for Irena while he took another gulp from the neck of the bottle.

The clock showed nearly two o'clock. They stood in the half-light where the sun cut in through the blinds.

'We have to wait for the third klaxon,' he said. 'An hour, Irena. People have died so that I can stand here, at this time, in this place. Everything is ready. Everything is set. Now, give me the key.'

Chapter 53

Stern was allowed to sit at the side of the court, where he was given a glass of water. A glass: Brunner's nerves had fogged his brain and he forgot to fetch the tin mug, so the prisoner was instead allocated an elegant, fluted tumbler. For the first time in his life Stern recognised one of the magic qualities of glass; that it allowed you to drink water as if it were falling, flowing and untainted. The pleasure of sipping at the crystal lip made him feel oddly detached from the legal process, as if he were a spectator in a velvet chair, high above the stage in a private box.

The atmosphere within the court had changed as much as that outside in the German compound. Johl sat upright in his chair, his fleshy lips pressed together in a sullen line. The clerk fussed over papers. Weiss looked nervous and stood talking into his client's ear. Meyer sat, his face very pale, a shaving cut on his chin. Funk, for the prosecution, observed Stern as he made small spidery notes on a legal pad.

Johl brought the court to order with a single blow of the gavel. There had been developments in the case and he would provide a summary, although SS Gerichtsführer Raeder had been despatched to Bavaria to collect further information. The court would reconvene on his return – possibly in Krakow, or even Berlin. As if to emphasise the rationale for switching the proceedings from Borek, they heard aircraft overhead, droning west at a high altitude.

Johl smiled and took his glasses off. He looked at the clock on the wall as if waiting for the precise moment at which he could begin to speak.

'I felt it necessary to make some enquiries into the situation in Weissenstein – the home of Jonas Keuper, his father, mother and two brothers,' said Johl.

The judge's summation of the family history was clipped, functional, and delivered without emotion.

'So, here we have the Keuper family,' he concluded. 'Ritter in Italy, Jonas here at Borek, and Christoph dead. Meanwhile their parents have always presented themselves as good patriots, loyal servants of the state. However, as I say, due to the extraordinary diligence of the SS officer who visited the village on behalf of the court, a somewhat different picture emerged. Christoph Keuper is still alive, having spent the intervening years in Weissenstein, hidden in the cellars of the family home.'

Johl let that fact sink in, watching the overhead fan turn.

Meyer sat forward in his chair. Colour had flooded back into his face.

'The boy was not inhibited in any way when asked to tell the truth. His father had forged the paperwork relating to his transfer to Hartheim, and his subsequent death. He had lived in the cellar of the house since the first year of the war. Despite their best efforts the boy had, on occasion, broken out of his quarters to take the air in the family's secluded orchard.'

Several people shifted their weight in their chairs, but nobody spoke.

'Christoph did not live alone in the cellar,' said Johl.

The judge advocate poured himself a beaker of water.

'There was considerable evidence that the cellar had been home, over the years, to several others. Some fragmentary documentation was also discovered. According to T4 records, Christoph left Regen by lorry in a consignment of eight patients. We now believe that, at least for a brief period of time, all were sheltered in the Keupers' cellar. Their current whereabouts are unknown. One set of bones was found buried beneath the cellar floor – a small child's.

'The T4 death certificates for these children are forgeries. It seems we can add bribery to the charges. Johann and Isolde Keuper have been transferred to Dachau for further questioning. Gerichtsführer Raeder will collect evidence in the village, and conduct interviews at Dachau. We are left with some interesting questions that the court must consider, not least perhaps the possible complicity of the family doctor …

'But not today …'

Stern, head down, held the glass beaker on his knee and considered the years in which he'd played chess with his friend Johann Keuper each Thursday evening outside The Castle, or inside by the stove in winter. Why had his friend not shared this secret? In winter they had often been alone, except for the occasional ministrations of the innkeeper's wife. In summer they'd sat watching the dusk fall on the Keupers' pear trees. Had Johann seen the turmoil to come, and the fate that would befall his friend, the doctor? Had he glimpsed divided loyalties and doubted Stern's friendship? If Stern had known the secret would he have admitted it as such to Jonas Keuper?

Johl was sweating freely, pressing a linen handkerchief to his red face.

'One matter which we can deal with now. The prisoner will stand.'

Meyer gripped the wooden rail of the dock.

'Certain … What shall I say? Certain *infringements* have been brought to my attention. During the adjournment the accused will carry out his normal duties freely. We need every man. However, after dark, he is confined to the mess.

'This curfew will be strictly observed.'

The court rose.

But Johl hadn't finished. 'The guard will bring the witness Stern directly to the commandant's quarters.'

Chapter 54

It was very quiet in the commandant's garden. The old man himself, diminished since Stern had first glimpsed him from afar, worked pruning back a vine along one side of the bungalow, where the sun had just moved into shadow. He still wore the white shirt, the braces, and a pair of worn military trousers. And he still moved with the studied inertia of a diver under water. But the gun, and its holster, had gone.

Stern speculated that he was waiting to hear if the warrant for his execution would be signed by Himmler in Krakow. Perhaps he hoped the sentence would be reduced to a prison term, but more probably he hoped for a soldier's death: a firing squad, not a makeshift gallows. It was of some comfort to Stern that this old man's every waking thought had perhaps been reduced to the same narrow focus that had preoccupied Duvos: I know I will die, but how?

Johl was already seated when the guard delivered Stern. The second game of chess was to be played here; not at the front of the house, but at the back, where rows of green beans, tied to wooden poles, ran in neat lines down to the inner perimeter wire. In the meagre shade thrown by the bungalow a green baize card table had been placed between two wooden chairs, and the chess men set out on a board. Johl didn't get up or shake the doctor's hand. Stern noted with irritation the now familiar chessmen; red and white, in the fussy design.

The camp was silent at this hour, as no trains had arrived since the morning. The only sound was the commandant's secateurs, slicing effortlessly through the young vine shoots.

The judge advocate made the opening move, but said nothing, and Stern took this as a warning that the tone of their conversation at the end of the first game had been such as to cast a shadow forward, and that Stern should wait to see what mood his opponent wished to create. If the court moved to Krakow, Stern would go with it, so he also had in mind the possibility that he might have to play many games, over many hours. He had become, of course, Johl's own Mechanical Turk.

The heat was intolerable, quite literally a physical burden, so that it pinned the flies and other insects down to the ground, or to the chessboard itself. An earwig struggled to climb Stern's king's rook.

'Why do you think I imposed a curfew on Meyer's movements?'

Johl, leaning back, invited Stern to make his countermove before answering the question.

Stern shuffled a pawn forward on the queen's file. 'You do not trust the officer,' was his answer; a statement merely of the obvious.

Johl gave him a narrow look. 'The first time we met over the board I think I explained that I had recognised your name and found a reference in one of my books. I play the games out, for company and for the aesthetic beauty of the patterns. For the thrill of it.'

Thrill was an odd word for him to use. Stern felt profoundly ill at ease. There was already something unstable about the situation, as if even Johl didn't know where this conversation might take them. A strange tension buzzed in the air, independently of the judge's cryptic questions. The diggers beyond the gas chamber had fallen silent. The camp crouched in expectation of the future. Or fear of it.

'We played on the second night after your arrival, you'll recall,' continued Johl. 'But as I say, I recognised you that first day – in court, from the name. I couldn't be certain of course. But there was the travelling chess set in your suitcase. So I was confident of my identification in my own mind at least.'

He leant forward with his body tilted from the waist to make his move and Stern caught the smell of soap.

'Late on the night of the first court session I sent someone to the cell block to fetch you. Brunner had to tell the truth. You were absent.'

Stern's heartbeat had picked up and he felt profoundly thankful Judi was already at the sawmill.

'The boy soldier is easily interrogated. For a generous stipend he allows his prisoners, apparently, to walk away with any SS officer who wishes to pay the price. In this case Rolf Meyer. The accused.'

Brunner's small kindnesses now stood in a new, less innocent light. Had he avoided immediate punishment by agreeing to play a facilitating role in Meyer's nightly forays into the forest with the doctor? Had he been given a watching brief?

They heard a single shot from the other end of the camp. It was not an unusual sound in daylight. There was a slight echo from the forest cordon. But why would anyone wish to fire a gun this afternoon, when no transport trains had arrived all day?

Johl's head was back, looking up into the clear sky. 'So. This was of interest, surely? Rolf Meyer stands accused of murdering Jonas Keuper at the moment Keuper – in his turn – is about to kill Leopold Stern. That very night Meyer takes Stern from the cell block. Where do they go? I know when they return, several hours later, just short of dawn. But where *did* they go? I suspect a car awaits somewhere on the road, so the town then? Or a nearby village? Brunner says he does not know. Why does Meyer *need* Stern? This is the question, and the answer is, surely, the answer to everything.'

Relief flooded through Stern's body. The sawmill in the woods was still a secret, or at least, a secret kept from the judge advocate.

'Could I find out the answer to my question? Could I?' Johl began to laugh. 'Yes, yes. There are many ways. Ten minutes in Raeder's hands would loosen Meyer's tongue. And I could ask you. And if I did not get an answer I could have you killed.

'But do you know how I have chosen to find out the truth?'

Quickly his hand swooped down to make his move, steadying the piece, setting it precisely at the heart of its square, then lifting his hand free with a theatrical flourish. For the first time Stern saw the board for what it might be, a physical metaphor for the camp itself, with the Jews as expendable pawns, shuffled forward through the squares.

'I will ask Rolf Meyer when he returns to the stand. Tomorrow, or later, if we have to abandon the camp. The moment will be all the sweeter for its postponement.

'It is in Meyer's favour that so far he has not actually lied. So far. This will be the test. If he tells the truth I am sure the court will then know why he had to shoot Jonas Keuper. It will be murder, of course. He'll be shot. If he lies, he'll hang.'

Johl leant forward and tried to widen his eyes to encompass the tactical situation on the board.

The klaxon blared from the water tower.

They heard another shot, this one very close, the sound distorted by the bungalow. Johl stood quickly, his thigh knocking the board so that all the pieces jumped, and several toppled, but not his king.

The judge was halfway along the alley at the side of the house, trailed by Stern, when they heard another shot. The guard, who had been sitting on the front terrace of the bungalow, was fumbling bullets into his rifle.

Eigrupper, in his white shirt, simply stood still among his flowerbeds. Stern's eye was caught by some movement on top of the water tower. He could see three figures against the sky, one of them with a handgun.

Looking down the slight incline towards the railway station, through the internal wire fence, nothing moved in the heat except a miniature whirlwind that darted between the huts in the turbulent air, kicking up dust.

'Raise the alarm,' snapped Johl, pushing the guard in the direction of the mess.

A door in one of the barrack huts opposite opened and a Ukrainian guard tripped down the steps and walked, clumsily, out into the middle of the wide grassy avenue. His black uniform was dirty, he had no cap, but one of his hands was bright red.

'The Jews have guns,' he said once, but his throat was too tight to make the sound carry. He held his hand out as if it was evidence for Johl to see, then filled his lungs to shout out, but a shot rang from the top of the water tower and he went down in the dust, a deadweight in free-fall.

Chapter 55

Kopp pulled open the sickbay door, and they were blinded by the sunlight, which seemed to have solidified in the afternoon air, thick with drifting dust. The machine-gun delivered a constant soundtrack, which made the bones in Irena's ears vibrate. The bell rang madly, in a frenzy, as if a fish seller had come to Borek and wanted everyone to see the silver dead, laid out in rows, in the sparkling ice.

Shadows moved in circles on the bare earth and, looking up, Irena saw the vultures wheeling clockwise, on outstretched, patient wings. A hundred yards away the gate in the inner fence hung open, two German guards sprawled in the dust: grey uniforms, on red dust, with no signs of blood.

Beyond the inner wire, the glowing tracer of bullets cut a swathe in the air, like flashes of horizontal lightning. An avenue led down to Left Luggage Corner, where several more bodies lay, spread-eagled on the ground, their limbs set at ugly angles.

'Go to the water tower,' said Kopp, pushing Irena away. 'The women will meet there. They'll tell you what to do next. Go, please. If I find Stern I'll bring him with us.'

Then he ran, picking a route between the German barrack huts away from the fence: two left turns, then a right, pausing at each hut corner, to look left, right and ahead, but never backwards. Coming within sight of the commandant's bungalow and the drill square beyond, he knelt down, watching for movement on the veranda of the officers' mess. Three SS guards ran across the open space carrying rifles, heads down, tunics undone.

Irena, who had ignored the kapo's orders and shadowed his zigzag run, slipped under a hut into the space between the wooden struts. She was determined to see for herself if Leo was still alive in the German compound. The shadows reeked of soiled laundry and toilets. But she had a view out at ground level, across the grass, so that she could see, in the lee of a petrol store, an armoured car: a vintage model, with high mudguards, old-fashioned spoked wheels, and rust between its bullet-proof plates. Kopp ran over open ground to join another slave in the shadows beside the vehicle, kneeling beside the caterpillar tracks. While Kopp cut away the camouflage with a kitchen knife, the other prisoner, who had a vivid tattoo of the hammer and sickle on his arm, scrambled up on to the bonnet, and then to the top hatch, moving his hands quickly over the gunmetal shell of the vehicle, as if it were a hotplate.

The Russian clutched the circular lock on the hatch, turning it three times before it opened, and then dropped inside, in an expert, fluid movement, feet first. Kopp clambered up, awkwardly, then dropped head-first into the turret.

One second, two, three: then the engine burst into life, black exhaust, and gouts of oil, belching from the pipe. Gunfire raked the air from the direction of the mess. The vehicle jolted forward a few feet, only for the engine to cut out. Was it her key, stolen from the officer's coat pocket, that had turned the ignition? A starter motor coughed, then the engine caught again, a cloud of exhaust roaring out, concealing the whole vehicle in smoke. For a moment it was lost, as if hit by incoming artillery fire. Then, emerging from its own cloud of fumes, it lurched forward. Irena could smell the flying bullets. For a moment her courage failed her, and she buried her face in the dirt.

When she looked up, the armoured car stood in open ground, in plain sight, its rear armour facing the mess and the main gate. The small top turret swung round. There was a loud metallic sound, a wrenching, then a single beat before the canon on the turret punched out a series of shells, each marked by a tongue of yellow fire; one hit the mess veranda, the wood splintering in a plume of debris. The next exploded by the main gate. A third shattered the triple-arched window of the courtroom.

Chapter 56

After the opening shots Johl marched Stern at gunpoint across the German compound from the commandant's bungalow towards the water tower, passing through the inner wire. They left Eigrupper sitting in his garden, apparently unmoved by the prisoners' revolt. They found the tower surrounded by women, most of them armed with pieces of wood, or kitchen knives. The crowd was in constant motion, the women hugging, clasping, touching each other's heads.

They fell silent only when Johl fired three times over their heads.

'Go back to your huts,' he shouted. 'The guards are coming. You will be shot if they find you here.'

The women moved back, but in a single group.

One held her hands aloft and shouted: 'Stay sisters. When the wire comes down, they'll ring the bell again. Then we run!'

Stern's eyes raked the faces, looking for Irena, until Johl pressed the pistol into his back and told him to enter the tower.

After the incessant glare of the sunlight it was almost impossible to see once they crossed the threshold. The first image to emerge from the shadows was a body hanging in mid-air, a rope going up to the rafters. It was Brunner, the guard. One of his feet was bare, the other booted. He had not, it seemed, been dead long, because the body still swung perceptibly from one side to the other. Stern imagined Brunner looking up from his bunk, a book in one hand, as his killers appeared out of the simmering sunlight beyond the open door to sabotage the generator. His small kindnesses had perhaps concealed a calculating mind, but in death Stern felt he looked like an innocent.

Johl stood by the telephonist's chair, connecting and disconnecting wires, a headset held to his left ear. With the index finger of his right hand he played on a single key of the teletype machine: Stern noted that he picked the 'I', the percussion matching the rapid discharge of the distant machine-gun at the station. Johl's frustration with the dead line deepened, until he threw the headset down on the floor. Pulling out the seat he began manically trying various connections by plugging and unplugging leads into sockets.

He set the pistol aside on the desktop; a careless mistake, which betrayed his assessment of Stern as a civilian, unable to take independent action. Or worse: a civilian Jew, cowed and passive, of no consequence in the world of action. The doctor was simply an adjunct to Johl's life: witness, chess adversary, and now docile prisoner.

Stern took three quick steps forward, picked up the gun, adjusting it in his hand so that he could put pressure on the trigger, and pressed it into the downy hair at the back of Johl's neck. The last time he'd touched a gun had been before the war, when he'd hunted rabbits with Johann Keuper. That was a shotgun: this felt very different, like an extension of his own body. He went on applying the pressure, pushing the skull forward and down, until the judge advocate had to tilt his head to the right, so that he could lay his cheek flat on the desk. Stern then shifted the pistol barrel from the neck to the exposed temple.

A mine exploded out near the perimeter wire and the seismic shock made the water tower's iron beams groan. Dust fell in loose curtains from the pipes above. Brunner's body danced slightly on its taut rope. The air pressure in the room appeared to fluctuate as thousands of gallons of water shifted in the tank.

A nervous shudder made the doctor's arm jolt and Stern couldn't stop himself jabbing the gun into Johl's skin so that the judge cried out: 'My God!' and tried to raise his arms and hands in further surrender.

'Stand up,' said Stern. 'Or I will kill you.'

As a father, Stern knew that the voice betrays the heart. If he felt real anger with Judi or Hanna, they would instantly obey his commands. If he manufactured his emotions, they ignored him.

Johl stood up.

Stern fired the gun over the German's head, missing by a margin of less than three feet. If he had not pulled the trigger then, he would have never fired the gun. Now he knew he could do it if Johl pushed him too far. The bullet deflected off the wall and ricocheted into the metal piping. The noise in the enclosed space was deafening and Johl, one hand held up to ward off a second shot, fell to his knees. Stern first took this as a sign that the German's nervous system had shorted out, not a signal of submission, but when he saw the fear in the lawyer's eyes he thought he might be wrong.

Johl's hand shook as he brushed it across his lips. 'This is ludicrous, Stern. If you want to die in the woods, run. If you want to wait for Raeder's return from Weissenstein, put the pistol down. In a moment the guards will be back in control of the camp. They'll cut you down.'

Stern grabbed the judge by the braces that crossed on his back and hauled him to the door. It was satisfying to see him stumble, his carefully maintained patina of calm control destroyed in a few steps, so that he fell over the threshold and into the sunlit dust outside. Stern told him to make a star of his arms and legs. Kneeling on Johl's back, he used his own belt to tie the judge's hands.

The crowd of women watched in wonder. One walked forward with both her hands up, her tunic stretched over a pregnant belly. 'Leo,' she said. 'It's me, Esther. Don't shoot.' He was thankful that she'd identified herself so clearly, because fear and adrenalin were distorting Stern's eyesight so that even nearby faces were indistinct.

'Have you seen them, Esther?'

'I'm sorry, Leo,' she said, and gave him the wooden toy he'd given Hanna: the chess piece, carved by Brunner. 'This was on the path to the gas chamber.'

Stern took the toy and held it to his cheek. 'I know it now,' he said, unable to say the outright truth: that his wife and daughter lay on the field of the dead. 'They've gone from us. It's just that I felt they were alive, Esther. Close by.' It was the moment he could have given up, sinking to his knees, waiting for his own death.

They heard an explosion, muffled and low-octane. Black smoke billowed into the air from the railway station. The bell rang three times, calling the women. From the minefield they felt another blast, and a towering plume of earth rose up, in apparent slow motion. The women cheered and ran down the slight incline, towards the first square, sprinting, some holding hands, towards the sound of gunfire.

'Tomma is alive, Leo,' said Esther, holding his face. 'I'm sure of it. The woodcutter's squad know the forest paths, so they're to lead everyone through the minefield. I must go. Come with me, Leo.'

'No. I'll stay. Running away seems like a betrayal. Go – find Tomma.'

Esther kissed Stern roughly and ran after the rest as best she could.

Johl lay with his face in the dust, spread-eagled and immobile.

Stern placed a foot on the judge's back as a new, powerful idea took hold of him.

Chapter 57

The Himmelstrasse itself was deserted. In the shade by the gate Stern found a wooden chair and a child's painted stool, both of which he collected in one hand, leaving the other free for the pistol. Johl walked ahead, moving in and out of the slanting sunlight that pierced the canopy of leaves. The boles of the silver birch trees reminded Stern of bones, as if he were progressing through the skeleton of some beast that had died on its way to the gas chamber, a tunnel of ribcage and spine, fibula and ulna. He could see one of the orange-painted bull-dozers through the mesh fence, its sheet-metal skin shimmering in the heat. Tipped over into one of the pits from which the bodies had been lifted, it too looked like a stricken animal; its engine still running, although only in a spluttering way, the rhythm threatening to peter out entirely with each pause, like a faltering heart.

Johl shuffled stoically ahead, his hands tied behind him with the belt. On the back of his prisoner's skull Stern could see the welt where he'd struck the judge once with the pistol-butt to persuade him to step under the archway at the start of the path. That blow had been the first he'd ever delivered with violent intent to another human being, and the resulting wound was strangely fascinating, as if by causing it Stern had acquired part-ownership of the victim's body. Such an intimacy made Stern feel unclean; it gave him an insight into the strange alchemy of physical power, a hint of the fascination inherent in domination.

One hundred yards along the path they found Hackendorf. The German was drunk and had been badly beaten. A bottle wrapped in brown paper lay by his side, his flies gaped, his trousers were splashed and soiled. Through a hellish mask of dried blood, he struggled to open his eyes when Johl kicked his shin.

'Shoot him,' said the judge, looking away in disgust. 'He's a disgrace.' The judge concentrated on the field of fires, glimpsed through the wire mesh, as if he might find something uplifting or noble by comparison among the smouldering pits.

Hackendorf's left arm had been broken in at least two places so that it lay in a zigzag in the dust.

'Just walk,' said Stern, pushing Johl's shoulder roughly, and then bending down and stripping the leather belt out of Hackendorf's trousers.

The multiple doors of the gas chamber were open, but Hackendorf's tank was silent, the showerheads as clean and cold as ice. The building held no aura of death or suffering, as if those who had perished here had left their spirits behind them somewhere on the journey to the place of execution; perhaps in the Pariser Platz, or even in the boxcars, or back in the ghetto, or – possibly – when they'd first glimpsed the future: on *Kristallnacht*, or on seeing the first broken body in the street, or the casual, minor cruelty of a state official.

'Go inside,' said Stern, putting down the chair and the stool, and gripping the handle of the pistol.

Johl blinked behind the heavy glasses.

'Go inside the gas chamber,' repeated Stern. 'If you don't walk in, I'll shoot you in the legs and drag you in. Whatever else happens today you will enter this place with me. Nothing else is of any interest or importance.'

'I won't,' said Johl, so Stern shot, once, at his legs. The nerves in his arm and wrist jangled so badly that the bullet missed, hitting a tree, with a fleshy sound on impact. Johl's nerve broke, and he stepped quickly up to one of the open doors, not looking back, only resting his shoulder briefly on the wooden jamb before taking the final step.

'What does this achieve?' he asked, his voice echoing slightly within the empty building.

Stern pushed him further inside, so that he fell forward on the concrete floor, before positioning the chair at one end of the room, the stool to one side.

'Sit,' he said, lifting Johl up from the floor. Circling behind his prisoner Stern used Hackendorf's belt to tie one of the judge's ankles to the chair leg. Then he closed the doors, one by one, noting the incremental increase in pressure this exerted on his eardrums.

Johl's breathing had become laboured, and his shirt was wet with sweat so that the hairs on his chest showed through, like black worms.

Stern took Hanna's wooden toy out of his pocket and placed it on the concrete floor, then sat on the stool.

'Exhibit No. 1,' he said. 'My daughter died in this room. You are responsible. The charge is murder.'

Johl's jowls shook with indignation. 'I am a senior judge in the SS legal division. In what sense have I committed a crime? In what sense is it *my* crime?'

'Isn't it what the lawyers call a specimen charge? It represents other, similar crimes. Other murders for which you are responsible, other murders for which your fellow officers are responsible. Thousands of murders, perhaps millions. Today we'll just deal with Hanna. You could have saved her. She was an embarrassment in your court – but did she deserve death? You did nothing to save her. Why?'

Johl dismissed the question with his breath. 'You are a civilised man, a sophisticated man, but you pose these juvenile questions? You know the way the world works.'

'I speak for the child,' said Stern, and he felt his daughter's presence. 'What did she know of the world before you took her life?'

Johl's eyes ran round the interior of the chamber, slipping from the peepholes, to the doors, the hinges, the pipes.

Stern thought: *he thinks he can escape, and so now he will try and buy time by answering the question.*

'I am a guardian of the law,' said Johl. 'What has happened in this room is legal. It is tedious to keep repeating the obvious. Let's be concise at least. It is a despicable law, in this particular case. I do not *aspire* to uphold this law. I *must* uphold it. The continuation of the rule of law is more important than any of its separate parts. You think I should resist this law?'

Johl's oyster-like eyes met Stern's.

'Others resist,' said Stern. 'When Germans resist – non-Jews – the authorities give way. You know this. Remember the Rosenstrasse protest. German wives, with cardboard placards, against machine-guns.'

'Christ!' Johl looked up at the ceiling above him. The sight of the showerheads made him pause. 'You think Goebbels will not have his way in the end? Berlin will be *judenfrei*, and soon.'

Stern nodded. 'There are still crucifixes hanging in the classrooms of Bavaria. Berlin ordered that they be replaced with swastikas. The people rebelled. Not all these victories are short-lived.'

'Crucifixes.' Johl spat the word out.

In the distance they heard a landmine explode. The showerheads vibrated, and the doors shuddered in their frames.

'And T4?' asked Stern. 'T4 was closed down. Think what a precedent that could have been, Johl. Did some clever, moral, courageous man take up this precedent?'

Johl slumped in his chair. 'As you pointed out in my own courtroom, Stern, T4 did not stop. Misshapen adults, the sullen and the haunted, still die. State euthanasia has simply retired from public view.'

'Yes. But it is no longer legal – *is it*?'

Johl licked his lips.

'Well – is it?' demanded Stern. 'You cannot have it both ways. The state lives by the law or it does not. Which is it?'

Johl would not meet his eyes.

Stern persisted. 'If the state must act outside the law, in secret, how long will its strength last? It admits its weakness by subterfuge. How long will this state of yours last, Johl? Another five years? A year?'

Stern's vision was fogged, and for a moment he thought gas was leaking out of the showerheads. He wanted to go now, out through the far doors, and into the field beyond, to find his family.

'Where did Meyer take you at night?' asked Johl.

'My court, my questions.'

'Why don't you shoot me. End it now.'

Stern smiled, seeing for the first time that the judge had misunderstood. 'A bullet? You think that will be the verdict of this court of mine, that you should die by a bullet?'

He stood. 'No, you're going to die here, like my friends, my neighbours, my wife and daughter.'

A jolt of nervous energy went through Johl, so that both of his shoes scraped on the floor.

'All executions under the military code are by firing squad,' he said. A little rivulet of saliva had escaped his puffy lips.

'Forgive me, judge. In this case I am going to impose my own law. You'll die like your victims, except you'll die alone,' said Stern. 'Did you ever imagine it would end like that?'

'I do not waste time thinking about my own death.'

'Did you not think you might have to answer for the laws you enforce?'

'Yes. Of course. If Germany loses the war – and, I know, Germany *will* lose the war, we all know this. Since Stalingrad we have all known this, since the invasion of Russia we have all known this. So, when we lose, the Permanent Court of International Justice will sit, as it did after the last war. It will set out the crimes committed in this war by the vanquished. The crimes of the victors will not be judged for a lifetime, if ever. All of this will take years – a generation. Most of the guilty will be dead. The prime movers will not allow themselves to be taken alive.

'So a few will be tried – the left-behind. This is how stupid the *people* are – they must empathise, they must sympathise, they must understand, and to do this they seek out the individual, not the crowd. So a few men will stand trial, watched by the world, and this will please the people because they can only encompass something that mirrors their own lack of complexity. Murder takes our fancy – as the pebble takes the eye of the magpie. These few unhappy men will be found guilty, and then forgotten. And their victims will be forgotten too.'

Stern closed his eyes, feeling his heart beat slow. 'This court is more timely,' he said. 'This court finds you guilty today, of moral absence: guilty of the murder of Hanna Stern, aged six.'

'I do not accept the jurisdiction of the court,' said Johl, scraping his boot on the concrete, beginning to struggle, but without any signs of panic.

Stern walked to one of the spy-hole doors and opened it wide. Beyond lay the pits, piled with bodies, and beyond them the pyres. He felt immeasurably tired.

'There will be survivors,' he said. 'However diligent you have been, a few will walk away. The survivor is a victim, too. It is their burden to tell the story of the dead. And they will tell that story. It will be my burden to tell your story when you are dead, Johl. At least for as long as I live. I will remind the world of Georg Johl, and his failure to be what he was at heart: a good man.'

Chapter 58

As Stern closed the door of the gas chamber, he heard a foot-fall behind him. His body tensed for a blow to the head, or the impact of a bullet.

Instead, he heard a woman's voice in polite inquiry: 'What has he done?'

It was Hackendorf's slave, the thin woman with the long shining jet-black hair. She had a dash of blood across her cheek, but there appeared to be no wound.

Stern stood back. 'He's one of the German officers who let this happen; the gas chamber, and the pits. I want him to die here, as my daughter died here. And my wife.

'Can you help make the tank engine work one last time?'

Her face, through the hair that hung down, appeared impassive. The idea that this request might mark the end of her duties at the gas chamber finally registered; she stepped back, a hand to her mouth.

'They made me help, but I am guilty too,' she said. 'Will you kill me?'

Because her intonation was flat, he couldn't be sure if this was a question or a request.

'You've nothing to fear. I do not blame you; no one blames you. My name is Leo Stern,' he said, holding out both hands, palm upwards.

'I know who you are. They took you away when The Puppet was shot,' she said. 'I am Rachel.'

The musical quality to her voice was darkly hypnotic. 'I had a sister – a year older than I. She walked the Himmelstrasse too. You had daughters. I remember them.'

Despite Stern's promise that he would not hurt her, she took a step back. 'No one has told us what to do.'

Us? Looking beyond the woman Stern saw what he had not seen before. Standing beside the funeral fires were the slaves who worked here in the compound beyond the high fence, those whose job it was to drag the bodies from the gas chamber, throw the dead into the pits, or place them on the grids above the flames. Each one of these slaves stood alone. Stern counted twenty, both men and women, still and ash-grey, their hair long, their faces turned towards the gas chamber.

'There's a rebellion in the camp,' said Stern, astonished these prisoners had not tried to run away with the others. 'The rest of the slaves have broken out through the fence.'

Rachel brushed some hair aside. Stern wondered what working as Hackendorf's handmaiden had done to her mind, and what duties lay beyond the German's bed. She appeared disengaged from her surroundings, as if everything she saw, and heard, and touched, was perceived through a glass wall. Why did they not all run for the wire? Did they fear retribution from their own people?

'Have you seen Hackendorf?' she asked.

'He's dead, or dying; we passed him on the path.'

'He liked my hair long,' she said, catching at the strands that hung down in front of her eyes.

'I want the gas chamber to work one last time,' said Stern. 'Can you do this?'

'Of course,' she said, her hand rising to lightly touch the wall of the chamber. 'But there must be a name,' she added, as if she were the clerk of works.

So perhaps that had been her duty, thought Stern: to keep a record.

'His name is Johl, Georg Johl, a German officer. A judge. If you don't want to do it, then show me how.'

Rachel's eyes widened. 'No, no. Not the *victim's* name. Your name. We always record the name of the officiating officer. In this case, that must be you. I won't write it down, but I have to know, in case they ask.'

'It's Dr Leopold Stern,' he said. 'Can I help you start the engine?'

Rachel appeared jealous of her position, for without a word, she climbed up on the cowling of the tank and dropped from sight. It happened so quickly, and with such supple agility, that Stern was reminded again of Anton, rising like a spider into the attic at the sawmill.

The engine fired first time, although the cylinders were loose. Climbing back out, Rachel slid down the metalwork to the rear of the vehicle and turned the spigots, as Hackendorf had done. Stern put a hand on the metal pipe and felt the warmth immediately. Then she threw the two brass levers on the pipes that led to the wall of the gas chamber.

'What shall I do with the body?'

'Follow procedure,' said Stern.

She looked around the field of the dead. 'They never think of us, because we live beyond the gas chamber. It's as if we are dead with the rest.' Stern was unsure if the 'they' referred to the Germans, or the slaves, or the kapos.

'If we get sick, or tired, the Germans shoot us. There's no going back. When the shooting started, our three German guards ran down the Himmelstrasse. We think they will re-turn to finish burning the bodies. There must be nothing left.'

Stern thought about Irena and Hanna. Their bodies were here too, on the field of the dead. He could see some corpses laid out near the trees, while others were being carried to the fires, others dug up from open pits where they had been bur-ied. The drifting smoke, and the heat, made the whole scene shimmer and buckle.

Stern knew then he couldn't search for them, that walking between the dead, trying to see their faces, would be too much. In the chaos he could miss them or fail to recognise them in death. Becalmed, he remembered his duty; Irena, kindly, had made it clear. If he could save Judi, he must.

He should go to the sawmill, but he still found it impossible to leave. From his pocket he took out the chess piece. 'You said you remembered the girls? If you see the little one, here, among the dead, leave this with her. It's a gift from her father. She dropped it on the Himmelstrasse.'

He gave her the chess piece.

'Will you promise to do that?'

'Yes. I promise.'

Stern handed her the gun, pressing it into her hand.

'If you need to, use this. Don't stay. You're right, they will make you work – if there's time – and then they'll kill you too. Just run. Or come with me? You could come with me, into the forest, away from them …'

The rest of the slaves had edged closer and stood mute, in a half-circle.

She shook her head, but she was staring at the gun in her hand, delicately running her fingertips over the bevelled grip.

Stern squinted through the nearest spy-hole of the gas chamber. Johl sat quite still in the chair, his head forward, his shoulders back. The air in the gas chamber already carried a strong bluish hue. Johl coughed once, then looked up and blinked, catching sight of Stern. His eyes were flat and dull, as if focused within, rather than on the interior of the chamber. Stern had told the judge that he would die alone, so he broke eye contact, and stepped back.

'I found him guilty of his crimes,' said Stern. 'I find you in-nocent, Rachel. Live. With God's blessing we will meet again, if not in this life.'

Chapter 59

A shadowy doorway in East Berlin was not difficult to find.
They were opposite the *Prinzessa*, fifty yards up the street towards Stalin Allee, just beyond the bombsite. What was left of
the day was in the sky, a slash of cherry-red to the west, over
the rooftops. To the east, night was rising, a purple bruise revealing stars as it seeped, arcing, over Friedrichshain towards
the Brandenburg Gate.

They heard footsteps and a man went by at the top of the
street, dropped his newspaper and paused to pick it up, so
Peter leant back, taking Hanna with him. But it wasn't *Der
Shatten*; they'd lost him by taking a cab at Alexanderplatz, and
then getting out a hundred yards away in an alleyway. Clarke
had denied putting a tail on them, and he claimed to doubt
that Krikalev would bother either, but they'd come to distrust
the motives of both.

'Relax,' said Peter, lighting an f6. 'We've lost him this time.
The last thing we want tonight is a Stasi tail.'

The air was cold, the first hint of a coming autumn, and so
Peter unbuttoned his old great coat and wrapped it around
Hanna, pressing her close to him. Hanna wore the print dress
designed by Vanessa, and she felt better for her short hair;
light, even buoyant, despite the weight of the baby. Yesterday,
in the Zil on the long road back to Berlin, they'd held each
other on the back seat. What had happened at Borek had recast Hanna's world; past, present, future existed in their proper order. Sinking to her knees in the black earth of Borek she
had given herself up to who she was, and Peter had helped her
stand again, and go forward. Last night, back at the attic loft

in bed together, they hadn't talked at all, but made love amid a chaos of linen and then fallen asleep beneath the studio's skylights.

When dawn had broken, Peter must have sensed she was awake too. 'Hanna?'

He never called her Hanna.

She turned over, but it was still too gloomy to see his face.

'It's all right,' he said. 'Go back if you have to. Do what you have to do for the child. You're right, it's your life, your choice. I'll be waiting if you want to come back.'

It was a statement of fact, so she let it stand.

She'd lain on her back, focused on the square of light above them.

'I'm happy now, Pete. Right now – in this second,' she said. 'I feel like there has to be a future. Everything's changed now. They're alive too, my family. I know it. I can feel it.

'I'll find them one day. Or at least I have to try. If only I could remember what happened to us all beyond the shower block. But it's still a blank.'

She sat up on her knees. 'Vogel's the key. She lied about escaping from Borek. How did she really get out? Why won't she tell us?'

Peter turned on the reading light and got out of bed, retrieving a folder of documents hidden in the wardrobe, and spreading them out on the sheet.

'She'll never talk, not at the *Kino*,' he said. 'Clarke made it pretty clear they'd been thoroughly checked out by the Stasi – and that must include bugging the flat. They'll suspect as much. We need to catch her off the premises.'

Hanna pushed her hair back. 'My flight back's tomorrow, Pete. I can't …'

He held up a hand. 'Visas,' he said, brandishing the slips of paper, adorned with official stamps. 'Clarke got us these for the trip to Poland – *via the Soviet Sector*. They're valid for three more days.

'And *this* is the Stasi file on the Vogels,' he said, wielding a blue folder. 'Well, a summary of it. Another gift from the US Mission. The Vogels live an ordered life, Han. And a blameless one it seems. Every Thursday evening, they go out for an innocent night on the town. Well, it's Thursday morning, Han. Let's join them.'

Which is what had brought them to their shadowy doorstep on Kreutzigerstrasse.

As if on cue, the façade of the *Kino* became a symphony of receding light: first the bulbs over the advertising board went out, then the portholes in the projection room, and finally the ornate lamp over the foyer doors, while the shadows crept upwards from the street. The only light left shone from the Vogels' flat in the attic, where three grand dormer windows gave a glimpse of plasterwork ceilings adorned with imperial flourishes: cherubs and the masks of tragedy and comedy.

An old mirror, the mottled silver surface blushed with condensation from an unseen kitchen, reflected a flickering TV screen. An athlete ran, a crowd watched, the channel switched to a talking head. They could see cigar smoke rising, the fumes slightly green, knotted and visceral, substantial enough to produce shadows within, revealing an internal fluid geometry.

Peter lit another f6. Hanna reached out, took the cigarette, put it between her lips and took a single breath before handing it back, a habit from their first life together.

'You're sure they'll go out?' she asked.

'At one minute past ten precisely,' said Peter, smiling. 'The routine is sacred. They'll leave together. Elke, the child, has already been dropped off for a sleepover with friends – Vogel has a Trabant, parked on waste ground at the end of the street.

It's a Thursday – so there was a full matinee performance, but they're closed tonight. They're going to let their hair down – East Berlin-style.'

He looked up again at the flat. 'What more do you want to know? They use Spee washing powder, and Florena face cream, and lots of Bautzner Senf, the lurid yellow mustard for the inevitable sausages. Once a month they have a bottle of Rotkaeppchen.

'The Stasi start with your rubbish bins.

'But they don't stop there. On sleepovers the girl tells her friends her father snores heavily and her mother has night-mares. Most nights they listen to East German TV. They chat about the news, the cinema takings, Elke's homework. She sews. He smokes his cigars. This summer they plan to go back to a cabin near Leipzig that they rented last year. The child will swim. They'll eat. They often talk about the menu at the local *gasthaus*.'

'And tonight they go to the District Six social club. They leave at a minute after the hour – so, very soon. We can follow them. There's a dance floor, apparently. And a band – al-though, given it's the East, it may be rustic.'

Childlike, Peter watched the clock on the distant pepper-pot tower of the Frankfurter Tor, his lips parted, eyes bright.

'One minute,' he said.

At the top of the street they could see a group of workmen taking down one of the large street signs that stood in the cen-tral reservation of the boulevard.

'And here's another thing Clarke said: Stalin Allee is a thing of the past. They're renaming bits of the city now. Not that we don't do it in the West of course, rubbing out the names the Nazis put up to obliterate the Democrats, who rubbed out the Kaisers. Each generation makes its mark.

'Anyway, Stalin's for the history books. Enter Karl Marx Allee.'

Peter shrugged. 'If you don't remember the names, the past can slip away.'

'The cigar smoke's gone,' said Hanna, staring up into the Vogels' private world. It was almost dark in the street.

The well-oiled lock of the *Prinzessa*'s foyer door turned, and Hans Vogel stepped out into the shadows, looking up and down the street, his round spectacles catching the light. His wife followed, checking a handbag. A red glow revealed the end of the cigar, and a cloud of smoke hung in the air as they strolled away.

For twenty minutes they walked, arm in arm, not on the pavements, but on the cobbles. The city was largely flat, but there was a discernible incline, leading them towards the River Spree. They paused at a street corner. Beyond lay a vast space, one of the city's deserts of rubble.

The Vogels, poised on the kerb, appeared to gather themselves up, as if about to step from one world to another. Rachel looked quickly over her shoulder, before her husband propelled her forward at last. Half a mile distant, set in a line, stood the five narrow tower blocks of District Six. Four were lit within: thousands of kitchen windows, and living rooms, creating an illuminated vertical game board of identical squares, which reminded Hanna of a great chessboard. Steam rose from ducts, as if the interiors were boiling over. The fifth block was in darkness, a casualty of one of the East's intermittent power cuts, for as they watched it flickered back to life.

The Vogels set out over the wasteland. Paths, lit by occasional electric pylons, criss-crossed the void. Rachel's step was brisk and purposeful, but Hanna noted that Hans hobbled slightly, trailing a damaged leg. For the first time she realised the difference in their ages – twenty years perhaps, or more. They passed a boy pushing a bicycle, a couple clutching a bottle of vodka. The track vaulted the river on a metal bridge, the water below in a concrete culvert, giving off a gaseous cloud of ammonia, the sharp acid failing to obscure the gravid core of human excrement.

The burnt-out wreck of an armoured car marked a forking of the path. Hans Vogel, still trailing cigar smoke, led his wife left.

The block they chose was simply marked with the numeral 3. The ground floor had a main entrance, brightly lit, which promised a BAR and TANZ NACHT. A dance floor, a chipboard oval, separated tables from a bar. There must have been a hundred people sitting, drinking, watching the athletics on a TV mounted on a kind of ceremonial plinth emblazoned with the letters GDR. The sound of the commentator was drowned out by voices, and piped music.

Hans Vogel bought himself a glass of beer and his wife a small glass of white wine, although the liquid held that odd tinge of orange that seemed to characterise the vineyards of the so-called republic. Rachel Vogel chose them a booth, where she was greeted by several women, all of them displaying brittle hair, set in bouffant curves. Hans settled on the end of a banquette, the belt of his trousers forming a rim, so that the cinema owner's torso sat inside this circle like a pile of flour in a mixing bowl. He was a man undefined by muscle or bone. Everyone in the bar was smoking, so there was a peculiar interior *sfumato*, the far corners of the room tending to blue, like the horizon at sea.

It was easy to find an obscure corner. Peter bought two beers, declining the glasses.

'The band is on later – so we've that to look forward to,' he said, tilting his head back to drink from the bottle.

'I could just go over and sit down opposite her,' said Hanna.

Peter put an arm around her, holding her back.

'Wait. Why create a scene? We've got plenty of time; let's watch.'

But there wasn't time. Hanna felt that she'd wasted so much – twenty-two years – and now she had to make up for what she'd lost. Watching the world had always been enough, but now it felt as if she should step into the moving tide of the present.

She caught the eye of a woman at a nearby table who was watching them both, with a frank curiosity, her mouth open. Their clothes betrayed them, Peter's collar-length hair, her jeans, the way they drank beer from the bottle.

The Vogels' table was marked by a pall of greenish cigar smoke. Out of the gloom emerged Rachel Vogel, heading for the cloakroom.

'This is perfect,' said Hanna, standing. 'Wait here.' She headed straight across the dance floor towards the toilets.

Peter watched Hans Vogel out of the corner of his eye, examining a new cigar, turning it in his hand, looking at the circular label that carried the manufacturer's name.

But the cinema owner isn't really contemplating his cigar at all; he's considering what's happening, trying coolly to assess the present danger. His wife spotted the Stern girl and her American on the way to the club. Vogel whispered to her then, on the edge of the wasteland around District Six, that they had nothing to fear, but they both know this isn't true. They have nothing to fear *if* they keep their composure and remember to stick to their story. But Vogel knows his wife's nerves are poor, which is why she's fled to the powder room to gather herself. So he is alarmed to see the Stern girl follow, noting the energy in her arms and legs, the fluid movement despite the child she carries, as if she's a hunter in pursuit of her quarry. His wife will face more questions, no doubt, about the lost father. In all the years, she has never buckled or broken. Is this the day?

One of their friends asks him for a light for a cigarette and enquires if he would like another drink, but he declines. He keeps his voice steady and perfectly pitched because all they have to do is keep their silence and their secret is safe. The Stasi can pick through their dustbins as much as they like. They can waste their time listening through the microphone in the chandelier. There is no way that they can ever know what happened, because that moment is buried, not in the earth or the ash, but in geological time, when the city of today was born, at *Stunde Null.* Zero hour.

As he lights up the cigar, watching the surface leaves bubble, he is back in that moment, lying beside Rachel in a bombed-out cellar on the eastern edge of the city in the final days of the war. It is the moment that haunts their lives.

The snow is falling through a shattered roof, high above them. They look out like animals from a burrow, watching the stars wheel. The moonlight creeps over the basement floor, revealing a child's ball, the frame of a pram, a woodpile. (They must not light a fire, as the dispossessed roam the ruins, and snipers fire at the light.)

Too cold to sleep, he sees the icy light reveal the fingertips of a human hand.

Rachel finds the haft of a spade and they shift the snow, then the coal dust, then a roof beam, until the corpse is revealed. A German soldier, the face destroyed, the body crushed. The cold makes it impossible to tell how long he has been dead. He notes the thick army greatcoat and has already got it half off the stiff torso when he feels the wad in the inside pocket: a wallet, some letters, even a snapshot of a football team. They have searched many corpses, but it is the first time they have not found all the valuables taken. The moment of good fortune is incredibly intense. It is the moment that makes them who they are. The soldier's dog tag has been severed in the blast that killed him, but it still lies by his neck: Corporal Hans Vogel. An ID card in his wallet reveals his profession: cinema technician.

Peter watched Rachel Vogel coming back from the ladies' room and noted the brittle smile, the make-up thick and crude.

Hanna, in her wake, returned to her seat and put a bottle of beer to her lips.

'What did she say?'

'That she could not help,' said Hanna. 'I've never seen anyone so frightened, Pete.'

The powder room itself had been empty, although an old woman sat in the vestibule, beside a tin dish for tips. A yellow neon light gave out a constant buzzing note. A mirror ran above the washbasins, and there were others on the walls and the cubicle doors. Rachel Vogel, agitated, had stopped applying lipstick and asked to be left alone. There were many reflected images of her, and in each Hanna could see her shaking.

'I went to Borek,' said Hanna, and Rachel flinched as if she'd cursed her.

'When the Red Army arrived at the camp, no one was left alive. Why did you lie? How *did* you escape?'

Rachel's face, always so blank, had rippled slightly – the muscles under the skin reacting as if to a blow. One shoe, with a low stumpy heel, shifted back.

'I've told the truth. Leave us alone.'

It was intuition only, but Hanna knew that 'us' referred to mother and child. That this was what was at stake.

They heard live band music from the bar.

'I have to go,' she said.

'Why won't you help?' asked Hanna.

Rachel's cheeks reddened as if the question was a slap. She gripped the edge of the basin, making a little play out of rearranging her hair.

But she couldn't keep up the piece of theatre, so she fled.

'Nothing more?' asked Peter now.

There was raucous laughter from the Vogels' table, where Rachel had taken her husband's arm.

'How can that be, Pete? That's her private hell – the sight of her own reflection in a neon-lit mirror in a ladies' room, and my simple question: why are you lying? She's so frightened she'll never talk. I know it.'

Chapter 60

Irena still lay in the shadows under the barrack hut. All the main avenues were deserted because the Germans had set up machine-gun posts at several vantage points, and if they spotted movement, the hot air would sing with bullets. Several corpses lay in the dust, and the sound of flies was constant. The echo of single shots came from the woods, but the gunfire was intermittent, and distant. The dogs, baying, faded in the blazing afternoon. Finally, the only sound was the fires burning all around.

As the sun fell, she slipped out from under the hut and surveyed the ruined officers' mess in the distance. The tank shell had destroyed the roof, and she could see the panelled courtroom burning. Was Leo dead in the ruins? Or had he broken out with the rest? The thought that he'd gone without her made her panic, and she turned away to make her way towards the station.

The alleyways between the serried barrack huts were about ten feet wide. A guard ran past in the distance. Seeing her he shouted something, then fired his pistol, but ran on. It was clear that attempts to curtail the panic and chaos brought about by the revolt had only been partly successful. Out of the corner of her eye she saw someone emerging from under a hut: a boy, in ragged filthy clothes. Because he was looking away from her, he didn't see her, and it took him so long to stand up, unpacking stiff limbs, that she was upon him in a few seconds.

Once her hand closed around his arm, he dropped back to his knees and attempted to wriggle back under the hut. Irena, clinging on, followed him into the shadows, using her elbows to crawl forward over the dank soil. It smelt of old leaves underneath, but it also felt very safe. Their faces were close, the whites of their eyes like hard-boiled eggs. Both of them were breathing heavily, and the child's face was wet with tears.

'Be still,' she said in Yiddish. 'I won't hurt you.' She could see now that while she'd taken him to be a child, the boy might be twelve or thirteen. He had thin, bony limbs but a broad face, and a strong jaw.

Around them were lots of cans, beef and soup and vegetables. On a blanket were the remains of a meal of bread and cheese. There was also a book, broken open at the spine, to reveal verses in an old-fashioned German script, illustrated with etchings. A pile of winter coats, sawtoothed, tweeds, mohair – perhaps four or five in total – were bundled between the wooden struts, providing a kind of nest.

In the time Irena had spent in the German compound she had never seen someone so small or so young. The children who arrived on the train from Lodz were either taken away to the lazarette or left to walk the Himmelstrasse with their parents. The only child who lived among the slaves was the boy with the litter cart.

'What's your name?' she asked.

The boy strung together several profanities.

Irena felt a hot bolt of energy in her limbs. She set this string of ugly words the boy had uttered against the mute manners of her daughter, who had walked away towards the gas chamber without her mother. Despite the cramped space, she cuffed him around the side of the head with an open palm. Fresh tears spilt out of his eyes, perhaps from shame.

'My daughter died in the gas chamber; why have you survived, runt?'

He struggled again, kicking his feet out, trying to find a purchase in the dust.

'What is your name?' demanded Irena. 'Tell me that and you can go.'

'Baruck,' he said.

'Why are you here, Baruck? Tell me quickly. Where are your parents?'

'I was taken away,' said the boy. 'I kicked and fought but they did this …'

He tilted his head round and Irena saw that he'd been struck in the face and had lost all the teeth from the left side of his lower jaw.

'The Germans beat you?'

'No – the guards, the pigs in black.'

'Why did they beat you?'

Baruck struggled again. 'You said you'd let me go.'

Irena tightened her grip. 'Why did they beat you?'

'I was chosen, three of us were chosen, by the kapos,' said the boy. 'I didn't want to go. My mother was in the barbers' shop, but my father clapped, and shooed me away, and said they'd have a bath for me, and that we'd meet later when the train came to take us east. I dug my heels in, so one of the guards hit me. Then they dragged me off the square.'

He massaged his cheekbone. 'But now everyone's fighting, so there'll be no train. I don't think I'll see them again, do you?'

He tried to affect a lack of interest in the answer to this question, but his eyes shone in the dark.

'When did you arrive at the camp?' asked Irena, releasing her grip, leaving his heart-breaking question unanswered.

'Two days ago.'

They heard the thudding of feet and half a dozen German soldiers ran down the alleyway between the huts. They saw their boots and socks, and smelt the scent of leather bullet belts, and then they were gone.

'So what did they want you for?' she whispered. 'Why did they choose you? There are no jobs for you. The kapos choose only the skilled and the strong.'

'You're wrong there, old woman,' he said, hitching up his belt. 'There was a special job. An SS officer told us we were going to play pirates and look for treasure. He said they'd lost some gold and they needed us to find it. They showed us what to look for – coins, and watches, and rings.'

The child held up two hands as if to ward off Irena's laughter. 'No, it's true. Treasure – jewels as well. The officer said that an evil man had stolen the loot and it was up to us to find it, and that if we did, they'd give us lots to eat.

'I'm starving now, but I've eaten lots. There's something wrong with my guts.'

'Where did you look for the gold?' asked Irena.

'In lofts, and down the well, and here, places like this. And in pipes, and toilets, and drains. Anywhere the fat Germans couldn't get their fat arses. They said we were small enough and that they'd lost a soldier who'd got stuck under a hut and broke his arm and that another had fallen out of a loft and broken his leg.

'After a day and a night, they told us the treasure had been found and we'd have to go and have the bath we were promised. That was this morning. They said we'd be joining other prisoners, from a place called Hungary. That's a country to the south.'

'Why do you need the coats?' asked Irena, running the edge of an overcoat between her finger and thumb.

'I took these just now from the tailors' hut, and there was food in the kitchens. The cooks are hiding. If we get out into the woods we can sleep and not get cold, even if winter comes.'

'We?'

Baruck pulled back the nearest coat, a heavy wool jacket with frayed cuffs. Underneath was a child with her eyes open in terror. It was Hanna.

Chapter 61

Stern fled the gas chamber and headed towards the station and the hole in the wire beyond, determined now to circle the camp and, if he could, pick up the path to the sawmill. Dusk provided cover as he slipped down the alleyway between the squares. The slave camp was deserted. The dead lay where they had fallen. From the distant officers' compound the sound of a gramophone suddenly blared out a few bars of jazz, and then fell silent, then started again, playing a scratchy melody. The Germans, he guessed, would wait for dawn and the safety of sunlight to search the slave camp, leaving the overnight patrols to the Ukrainie, who must still be out in the woods.

A pile of suitcases still smouldered at Left Luggage Corner. The station house itself was burnt out, thin smoke rising from blackened beams. Looking back, Stern saw the silhouette of the water tower, and on the roof several soldiers working by lantern in the half-light. If they could restart the generator, power the lights, and reconnect the telegraph wires, they would be back in control of the camp.

Ahead lay the wire, and the wide gap punched through, no doubt by Kopp and the armoured car.

About to follow, taking his first step over the railway line, Stern paused to look back at the huts: many times, in the years to come, he would re-enact in his head exactly what happened next. In the synagogue, when the time of peace and prayer brought silence, it was of this moment he thought: the glance back into the dusk that saved him from the future that lay in the woods, where the dogs roamed, and the Ukrainie listened.

The darkness was creeping rapidly out of the forest, but the moon was rising, and the paths were silvery, and pale. At home, in Weissenstein, he'd always been wary of moonlight; it held within it an expectation that something – a figure, an animal, a spirit of the night – would appear in its ambit, as if it were limelight set at the edge of a stage. A more vivid imagination might have conjured up a vision, piecing together shards of black, and grey, and silver.

But there was no doubt: two figures had appeared, making their way down a grassy avenue, towards the station. Not two figures – he saw that now – three: a woman carrying a child and holding a young boy by the hand.

The recognition of any human being by their gait is precise; hair, posture, clothes, hand gestures, are all idiosyncratic, but from a hundred yards the manner in which a human being walks is as individual as a fingerprint. This woman put most of her weight on her right foot, while on her left hip she struggled to carry the child. Her free hand was held by the boy, who danced with his feet, like a girl. What was unusual about the woman's step was that she set her feet down quite widely – to the left and right – but just before footfall her hip brought the foot back in towards the centre of gravity in a graceful curve, as if she trod an imaginary line.

Stern didn't think the woman had seen him. There was no doubt she was heading for the station, and the gap in the wire. Her entire concentration was reserved for the child clinging to her hip, so that her face was held down, and turned to the left, lost in shadow. Stern was terrified that as he watched her get closer, she would dissolve in the night air; shimmer away, a product of his unbalanced mind. He stepped back around the corner, into the shadow of what was left of the ticket office, and simply waited for his fate to unfold. He emptied his mind, desperate that the image he'd seen would become flesh and blood.

Their footsteps approached, as did the boy's high, fluting voice. Not once did Stern let the woman's name form as a word in his head; instead, he kept the *idea* of her just beyond a conscious form. When he was a child he'd often wake at home without a clear notion of where he was, or even who he was, and he'd been able to suspend this exciting anonymity for several minutes by refusing to engage his consciousness. He was able to live in the world of the possible – undefined, but limitless, floating without the tiresome ballast provided by the real world; the sandbags of fact, such as a name, an address, a past, a routine.

They were almost upon him, so he stepped out into the path.

'Leo.' A woman's voice, one he recognised as well as his own.

'Is this him?' said the boy.

Stern walked forward until he could have touched her.

'Irena,' he said, uttering the word at last.

Then he looked at the child: the little girl who, in another version of his time on earth, had dropped her toy on the Himmelstrasse.

'I've been alive, and you've both been dead,' he said. It was too much for thought, and so his body began to shake, his eyes suddenly pooled with tears.

They embraced. Stern put his nose next to Hanna's and they shared a breath. Irena kissed his neck and felt something give inside herself, like a tendon snapping, so that she had to hold on to his waist. Between their three faces they shared the same soft air: damp, warm, and earthy.

'The Germans took the children to help search for the commandant's gold,' said Irena, her head inclined back so that she could see Stern's eyes. 'It's a miracle.'

Then she scanned the wreckage of the platform. 'Kopp, the red-haired kapo, told me that the plan was for the women to follow the men through the wire. We're late. Are we too late?'

They could hear dogs returning through the woods.

'The revolt is over,' said Stern. 'The guards are coming back because the woods are dangerous; too dangerous for us now. We can't stay here.'

'This is Baruck,' said Irena. 'He saved Hanna's life. He was taken away from his parents. He's been brave, and kept Hanna safe.'

Stern, sensing what was right, shook Baruck's hand.

'What shall we do, Leo? We must help Judi.'

She let Hanna return to her own two feet on the ground.

Stern thought how quickly it had come to this: the joy of reunion suddenly overtaken by the responsibility for others.

'She is in the woods, at the old sawmill. We must go there, too. Come …'

A voice came from behind them, in the shadows beyond the arch that led into the first square.

'*Not that way, doctor. And not now.*'

Stern's eyes had switched to night vision so that all he saw was in black and white: Meyer's death-mask of a face appearing, his uniform buttons catching the moonlight. Irena clutched at her husband's shirt, pulling Hanna close.

Meyer stepped closer. 'Freida is unwell and struggles to feed the child,' he said. His left arm hung limply by his side and Stern noted a black, glistening wound, and a gunshot hole in the left sleeve of his uniform.

'We had a contract, I think. The revolt changes nothing. Order has been restored.

'I have been to the bunkhouse. There is a party, a last night of pleasure. Your daughter is safe, but Freida and the child need their doctor. The Ukrainie are returning. We must hide in the camp until dawn and then slip away to the sawmill. If Freida can travel, we may all have to take to the wide woods.'

Chapter 62

Meyer hid them in the shower block and went out to find food. The camp was dark: the generator, expertly vandalised by the escaping prisoners, who had executed its nominated guard – young Brunner – could not be fixed without new parts, according to another guard set at the door. A small work group laboured to repair the perimeter wire. The Ukrainie, back from the woods, built a large fire at Left Luggage Corner. They'd brought vodka into the compound, and snatches of song weaved through the darkness. They pitched empty bottles into the flames, so that clouds of sparks, like fireflies, rose into the night sky. At the officers' mess, candles, set in china saucers, lit the half-wrecked veranda. Several officers stood drinking while watching the dull flashes of artillery fire in the east.

Meyer collected bread and cheese from the kitchen and slipped back to the shower block.

They all lay down on the cool tiles and tried to sleep. An hour before dawn, the German woke them and led them to the gate in the wire. There were no guards in the watchtowers, so they were soon safely in the woods. At the clearing they found the image of a hammer and sickle carved into three of the tree stumps. The styles of each sculptor were quite distinctive: one showed the hammer's grip, criss-crossed with leather straps; another the sickle blade with a serrated edge.

'Partisans,' said Meyer, working his fingers into the wood. 'They want us to know the Ivans are close. They want us to be afraid. They have succeeded. They must know of the sawmill, the girls. I wouldn't be surprised if we have long had a spy in our midst. It's an old tactic – sleeping with the enemy. They rested here – last night, perhaps. A few hours past.'

Irena hugged Hanna. 'Have they gone?'

No one answered.

They said goodbye now to Baruck. His uncle, who had travelled to Borek on the same transport with the boy's parents, had been taken away by the kapos on Pariser Platz. He was a fine carpenter – the best in Nordheim – and had therefore certainly worked for Kopp, who had helped organise the revolt. Baruck believed that his uncle would be alive in the woods to the east, and his plan was to track him down. With a winter coat and a knapsack of food, he walked away without looking back. It pained Stern to think of the boy alone, but he would not listen to their pleas for him to stay. Hanna articulated his name *BA – ROOK*, even though it contained such ugly, awkward vowels. She cried when the trees crowded round him and he was gone.

They walked on, fearful of what might be hiding in the woods. Whenever they stopped, the crackling of twigs seemed to run on, a second, perhaps three. For no apparent reason, crows, in smoky flocks, clattered unseen out of their high nests. Most of all Stern *smelt* them: damp clothes, a hint of nicotine, the earthy pungent reek of sweat and piss. Looking back down the woodland track, this certainty that they were being trailed was vivid enough to conjure up a vision: a partisan, with clay-clogged boots and gimlet eyes.

The sawmill, when it came in sight, looked deserted. They paused on the threshold of the trees hoping to hear a voice of welcome, but there was silence. Inside, through the unlocked front door, champagne bottles littered the floor, and a rat dashed the length of the corridor to the kitchen. A chicken carcass lay on the table, ants crawling over the bones. The house smelt of the girls, their perfume and powder, the reek of cheap soap and cigarettes, the salty tang of sex.

Meyer stood at the foot of the ladder and shouted: 'Olga? Natasza?'

'Where's Judi, Leo?' asked Irena, shouting out her daughter's name, running from room to room.

Meyer kicked open the back door. In one corner of the garden stood a walnut tree, and from a single branch hung the bodies of his comrades, Bertolt, Anton, and his old friend Julius Sandberger. He felt no sense of loss, as he'd not expected to see them again alive. In death they hardly resembled the men he'd known, their bodies stiff, the limbs at ugly angles, their faces distorted by gravity, and the ropes around their necks.

'The Poles have taken revenge,' he said, walking ahead.

The rest held back, wary of the makeshift gallows and its victims.

In the cottage Meyer found a note on Freida's bed, which he read and then brought back to Stern and Irena.

'They've gone. I've got one of the lumber company maps, so we can catch them up. They left in the night by cart, but they'll be slow because Freida is still weak, and the old peasant with the horse treats her like a child, so he won't push the pace.'

He lit a cigarette, and thought of Sandberger's two boys, who they'd taken to Charlottenburg to fly kites while on leave. He tried to recall names, and faces, but they'd slipped his mind.

He turned on the rest. 'Search for food. All of you. We have to catch them up.'

He gave the note to Stern, who held it in front of Irena's eyes.

> *Rolf, forgive this, but there is no time.*
> *The Armia came and killed your friends. We hid in the woods. It is three hours before dawn, and we are gathering food, but we must go. I feel better, stronger.*
> *Natasza has money – she'd hidden it in a metal box in the garden. We are all going to town in the cart, along the lumber path.*

We are to go to Natasza's estate. She knows a place where we will be welcome. I doubt this, but it is the only hope we have. If we survive, I will take the boy home, to Berlin.

Do not follow, Rolf.

If you want my blessing you can have it.

I told Judi that you might be able to get this to her father – she adds her own note.

Freida.

Stern gripped the single page of paper and read the message out loud.

Natasza says when the war is over, we can live in a world of books. Love to you, father. J

'She's alive,' said Irena, embracing her husband. 'We will be together soon.'

In the garden outside, Stern heard the distinct sound of a shovel being driven into the soil. He found Meyer digging a shallow grave. Beside it lay the body of Julius Sandberger, cut down from the trees.

Meyer stopped, wiping sweat from his face, and climbed out to drink from a water bottle he'd filled in the kitchen.

'I don't know why Julius is here,' he said. 'He never came with us into the woods. Bertolt and Anton lived for its pleasures. Perhaps he was looking for me.'

He shook his head.

'It's too cruel to think they'll find him here and that the story might travel back to Berlin; that they found him at the whore-house in the woods. He has a dutiful wife, a loving family.

'Better posted missing for ever. Better missing in action – or just lost in the chaos of war.'

He stepped back down into the shallow, narrow grave.

Chapter 63

Meyer's map had been drawn by cartographers employed by the provincial government of the Lublin Voivodeship in 1934, specifically for the use of lumber companies interested in developing the woods of Borek. Laying it out for Stern, the German traced a path through the cobweb-like network of tracks that covered the miles of pine forest; woodland featureless but for a few streams, a scattering of old mine shafts, erratic rock outcrops, and the sawmill that had been built, according to an italic legend, in 1903.

Two paths led away from the mill: an abandoned narrow-gauge rail track, and the original path that had preceded it, along which horses had once dragged lumber to market. One other feature stood out: a single electricity power line, running from the site to the main road twenty miles away, by which three villages clustered, although Meyer said they were hardly hamlets. The Ukrainie had terrorised the local peasants, building their own bunkhouses in each, and setting up vodka stills.

'We must keep clear of the villages,' said Meyer. 'And this …'

He held the map down and drew, with a heavy pencil, the line of the tarmac road the Germans had constructed to link the camp with the outside world in 1942.

'The girls have taken the old lumber path,' he said, indicating the winding track that followed the subtle contours of the sandy plain on which the trees grew, twisting to avoid the low hills and rocky tors hidden within the forest canopy. The old railway track was more direct, but, said Meyer, much rougher under foot.

'If we're going to catch them, we'll have to follow the railway. It's a short cut. With luck we'll come out here … ahead of them, where the two routes cross, but it will be tough work.'

Despite a search of the bunkhouse, they found little food. The larders had been ransacked and even the peasants' chickens, which usually foraged for crumbs and seeds in the mill, were gone, although there were feathers all over the yard.

Still hungry, they set out. The rotting sleepers of the railway line led into the shadows of the forest, the measured stride between them too short for Meyer, and too long for Irena, so that they stumbled and stuttered on their way, Stern was at the rear with a sack of blankets he'd collected from the attic in case they had to spend a night under the stars. Hanna's brown eyes scanned the trees in hope, as if she expected Baruck to stumble back out of the forest, still hauling his treasury of coats.

The forest, a jigsaw of greens and browns, closed over their heads and blocked out any view of the sky. Twice they heard gunfire, first as a distant crackle, and then as a single shot. Meyer held up a hand and they stood, stupidly silent for a minute, before trudging on. After two hours they reached a clearing and the remains of a woodpile. Resting, they all felt the unsaid reality: that they were encircled, tracked. Meyer stood on a fallen tree, smoking, his eyes on the track ahead. Stern, lying on his back, watched a single bomber cross the patch of blue above his head, trailing a line of smoke in its wake.

Another two miles and they fell out of the trees on to the lumber path as Meyer had predicted; a pale sinuous track of rotting leaf mould mixed with ash, lit now, as the sun was high. The railway ran beside the path. They took another break, squatting down at a shady spot. Meyer let them rest, convinced they had reached the junction first. Exhaustion overtook Stern, so he lay in the grass again and slept, to be awoken by the sound of a horse approaching, clopping on the ash, accompanied by the rumble of a cart's wheels.

Scrambling to his feet he found they were all standing, looking back along the path. The little caravan appeared around the distant bend. The old peasant brought the horses to a stop, peering ahead, allowing the dust to settle, afraid that the Germans had set a trap. Stern waved his arms and shouted Judi's name. Then Irena waved too, and Meyer clapped his hands above his head as if trying to call a ferryman across the river. The carthorse broke into a trot. The chickens, in wicker cages, fluttered so that their feathers rose in the sunbeams.

Judi was unable to contain her joy, jumping down from the cart to run to her mother and sister, so that they all clasped each other, Irena on her knees. And that is how Stern thought it would end, or at least, that is how he thought the rest of their lives would begin: on a hot Polish lumber track in the Borek forest, sixteen miles from the railhead at Kraśnik: the point on the surface of the earth where the Stern family was reunited at last.

Heat made the track shimmer, the trees buckle, while the forest canopy was still.

Meyer, climbing aboard the cart, took the child from Freida and held him in the sunlight.

What little food was stashed on the cart was shared around.

Stern kissed Judi and then left them all eating and drinking water, taking half a dozen steps into the shadows of the forest, telling himself that the strange immediate presence that he felt, which was as tangible as the iron-rimmed wheels of the cart, was an illusion. What lurked in the half-light? Not the aura of an individual partisan, or soldier, but that of a crowd – more, a multitude. This is what Leo Stern thought he felt on the lumber path that noonday moment when his family was so thrillingly alive: the company of the dead, who had shuffled in single file away from the gas chamber, and now watched him from the green shadows.

Chapter 64

Hanna slipped out of bed at dawn, leaving Peter sprawled on the sheets, naked, his face lit by the skylight above. She padded upstairs, made herself coffee, and sat in the studio. Since their return from Borek this had been the new routine. Three days, three new canvases, the series *Green, Silver, Red* unleashed, and with it the past. Her mind was crowded with a six-year-old's clutter of sudden, vivid, and often random images. These flashed before her, faded, then flashed again. Why had she remembered a great pile of ash, with licking yellow flames, and a boy sitting on a chair asleep? Or three arched windows through which sunlight poured on to the floor of a courtroom? The past helped decode the paintings, each one a stepping-stone to the next, as if she was rebuilding who she'd once been, becoming the living image of the lost child.

Peter told her that she'd changed on the outside too: her body seemed freer despite the weight of the baby, and she talked with her hands, as well as her lips.

'And your eyes,' he'd said that night, by the light of a candle. 'They look out, not in.'

One day she might remember what had happened to her family. But that was their only hope. Rachel Vogel had refused to give up her secret. There were other witnesses, unread files, but Clarke and Krikalev had stopped answering calls. A secretary at Spandau said that the Russian had been recalled to Moscow, but this might be a lie. The Cold War was deepening. Her time in Berlin was drawing to a close – at least for now. Her rescheduled flight left in three days.

What lay beyond that was still uncertain: Peter dared not ask, and she dared not speak.

It was still early, and the house slept, so when the phone rang, she dashed out into the stairwell to still the harsh sound of the bell.

'Miss Stern?' The Polish accent was thick but she recognised the fleshy sibilance of the voice immediately.

'Mr Ochab?'

She saw again the superintendent of the orphanage behind his desk in the cottage at Łabędzie.

'I am sorry for the hour. Lines are difficult to secure. I must be brief.'

'Go on.' She heard Peter turning over in the bedroom below.

'Moscow is sending workers back to Poland from the East, men and women they took after the war. They're broken, most of them; it's terribly cruel. But there's a man called Karel, who worked as the caretaker in the big house for the SS.

'He turned up here for a job as a night-watchman. It's true he knows the place well. And he's diligent enough. We talked, and I mentioned your story. A broken man as I say, but he remembers the Mazurek girl, and you – the 'silent child'.

'Yes, I see,' she said, because Mr Ochab seemed to be waiting for her to say something.

'The woman Natasza put on the train, with her baby boy, never knew of course that her saviour died on the way back to the estate. She wrote to her, the next year, to say she'd got to Berlin with the boy and that she was grateful. The letter came to the house. The Russians had moved in, the Germans were long gone. Karel was what passed for authority, so he read the letter.'

'He has the letter?' asked Hanna.

'No, no. I am sorry – not that. *He remembers the name.* And that she had found work at the Krupkat State Laundry.'

Peter's bleary face appeared below and Hanna mimed a pencil.

'What was her name, Mr Ochab?'

'Klumbacher. Freida Klumbacher. The boy was Eden, as we know. The laundry is in East Berlin, but she may have moved on. I thought it was fate, so I had to let you know as soon as I could. I'm sorry to wake you.'

'Can you spell the name, Mr Ochab?'

She repeated each letter and Peter wrote it down along with the name of the laundry.

She thanked the superintendent and promised to write properly to tell him what they found.

Then she sat on the step beside Peter, crushed together by the narrow stairwell, and told him what Ochab had said. She always felt hot in the mornings, although she hadn't felt sick for months, but the racing of her heart was nothing to do with the baby.

'There's one day left on the visas Clarke got us,' she said. 'Let's go, Pete. Now, today. We must find Freida Klumbacher. It's the end of the path. I know it is.'

Chapter 65

The state laundry was two miles east of the Brandenburg Gate, a district of unrelieved poverty, where ruined houses still stood on the edge of bombsites. The vast brick tenement blocks, built around communal yards, cut the light from the narrow streets. They'd almost stumbled at the first fence: the checkpoint, bristling with barbed wire, had let them through only after a lengthy examination of their visas, and at least one telephone call, possibly to Clarke's office. They'd stated the reason for their journey as research for the United Jewish Appeal, and a visit to a GDR archive in the old law courts. This seemed, at last, to satisfy the guards.

Their real goal seemed daunting; to find Freida Klumbacher, laundress, in this maze of brick and rubble and squalor. Berlin, beyond its blackened imperial heart, was a city that appeared to swallow people. Now that they were looking for an individual, the city had taken on the cloak of the crowd.

Hanna's excitement began to waver. What if Klumbacher had married, or moved away? But then the chaotic joy returned; the possibility of finding someone who knew what had happened to her family was intoxicating. This woman had travelled with Hanna and Natasza – she would know their story. Hanna's own family might even be here, living in a dusty backstreet in East Berlin. Hanna might meet them today, reach out and touch them, kiss them.

Peter kept reminding her that it was *sixteen years* since Klumbacher had written to thank Natasza for saving their lives. But at least there was no sign of *Der Shatten*, which made them think he'd been Clarke's man all along, and that the US

Mission had lost interest in Borek; that he'd finally been allowed to stop following them and go back to a dull office and a filing cabinet, and endless paperwork.

By the time they reached the laundry, Hanna had begun to shake. There was something childlike and hysterical about her energy, as if she was back in the playground at Upware, this time running with the rest of the children in a Fen wind, hand in hand.

The Krupkat State Laundry was a vast, three-storey warehouse, the windows of which belched steam in theatrical billows. There was a front office, where a woman sat with a telephone to her ear. Nonetheless, she waved them forward.

'We're looking for Freida Klumbacher,' said Hanna, wondering if everyone could detect the tremor in her voice.

Time stood still, as she knew it would.

'Klumbacher?' said the woman, deftly turning a directory on the desktop, the phone still to her ear.

'She's on the third shift. Six to midnight – laundry No. 5.'

Relief swept through Hanna like a drug. But now the thought of waiting to catch Klumbacher at the start of her shift that evening was intolerable. She'd already waited a lifetime.

'She was recommended by a friend,' she said, pretending to search through her bag for papers. 'I have some work for her, you see – it's urgent. It would be better if I could see her at home. An address perhaps?'

The woman abruptly ended her call.

'Private work is forbidden,' she said.

'We'll be discreet,' said Peter, in his textbook German, and the woman looked at him for a moment longer than is polite.

She began to write out a note.

'We all need two jobs just to put food on the table,' she said, with a note of genuine anger. She handed over the slip of paper.

1671 Lumbert Gotfried Strasse
Apartment 35H

'Twenty minutes on foot – towards the railway yards. There's a map on the wall.'

For Hanna, the urge to run, rather than walk, was almost impossible to resist.

Children played football outside open doors. The tenement blocks exuded a particular aroma of sweat and peppery cabbage. Laundry hung from networks of wire, so that the cobblestones beneath reeked of soap. Hanna thought there was an odd echo here of pictures she'd seen in Marcin's books at Swan House. At the end of the war, when the city was lost, survivors had hung sheets from windows as tokens of surrender.

They reached the street, but Peter grabbed her hand and steered her into the doorway of a boarded-up bakery.

'Our friend's back again,' he said.

They both pretended to read Peter's newspaper as *Der Shatten* passed on the far side, the umbrella under his arm. In fifty yards he'd been swallowed up by the crowds on the pavement.

Peter checked the address. 'It's on that side. It must be a way still.'

He ran a hand back through his thick hair, eyes closed. 'If we just blunder on, he might see where we go. What if he is Stasi after all? Do we have the right, Han?

'If we just knock on the door there'll be consequences – a visit from the secret police, interrogation even. And then what?'

Here, on their own in the Soviet Sector, without the protection of Clarke and Pierce, Peter felt cautious, even afraid.

'I'm not going back, now,' said Hanna. 'This is our chance, Pete. We have to take it. I've got a right to the truth.'

So, they agreed a plan: the tenement blocks were vast. Each entrance led to a staircase, and dozens of flats – hundreds of people. As long as they could obscure the *precise* address Klumbacher would be safe.

They edged down the street until they were opposite a doorway marked 1650–1680 in large stencilled numbers on the concrete lintel.

They crossed quickly to a locked communal entrance with a glass door. Beyond it stood a desk, a battered armchair, and a small sink and stove. The concierge, an old woman, opened the door by two inches and asked them who they wished to see.

Peter acted as lookout, making sure *Der Shatten* wasn't in sight.

Hanna showed her a ten-dollar bill and watched her eyes widen.

She let them in, a broad grin on her face making Hanna feel really afraid, as if they'd been tempted into a trap. A wooden board showed that KLUMBACHER was on the fifth floor. They left the woman at her post and went down a corridor and round a corner to the bottom of a stairwell. Peter sat here, so he'd have a plain view of the lift doors and the steps. The small landing was crowded with a nest of mops and pails, and a cleaner's trolley. Peter lit a cigarette, preparing to stand guard.

Hanna summoned the lift, then let it fly empty up to the third floor, while climbing the steps as silently as she could, determined that the vigilant woman at the door, or the missing cleaning lady, would not be able to guess her ultimate destination.

Looking down from the top of the stairwell, breathless, she could just see the top of Peter's head, the distinct double-whorl of his twin crown, wreathed in smoke. She heard the clatter of a pail, and some scraps of conversation, and then laughter.

She pushed open a metal fire door on to an exterior balcony. Rooftops ran into the mid-distance, while below in the yard a crowd of women wandered between the stalls of a small market. Flat 35H was at the end of the balcony. The kitchen window stood open, steam churning out, while inside a radio played dance music.

Behind Hanna, at the end of the balcony, was the lift. The sound of the cables and a whirring electric motor made her stop and wait. There was a light indicator board showing the letters A–H, but it wasn't working. When the motor stopped there was a pause of three seconds and then the doors opened.

It was Peter, and as she looked at his face, she saw that his eyes were focused on some distant point. His features – nose, chin, hair, cheek-bones – seemed misaligned, as if she was looking at a distant cousin, or a sibling she'd never met. In that moment, she felt her blood drain away, and couldn't think, just watch, or she might have screamed. The detail that unlocked the moment was Peter's blue lips, which moved, and she heard the simple words: '*Der Shatten.*'

Stepping forward, bent at the waist, Peter held both hands to his stomach, but he had to take one away to cling to the guiderail on the wall, revealing a large bloodstain. He'd got the checked shirt open a few buttons from the bottom, clear of his belt, and she saw into the wound, to the dark rust-red within.

He knelt down.

She took a step towards him, but he held up his hand and said: 'Get help.'

The last thing she remembered clearly was hitting the door of flat 35H with her hands, then splaying one against the frosted pane of glass and screaming so that her lips touched its clinical ice-cold surface. A distorted figure approached.

Then the baby inside her seemed to tumble and Hanna passed out.

Chapter 66

At three in the afternoon, on the old path through the forest of Borek, they brought the cart to a halt and shared what water and food they had left. The woods were still silent, even the mosquitos stricken by the solid heat. Stern was still haunted by the palpable presence of the dead, the ghosts who watched from within the green shadows. The rest seemed oblivious, except for little Hanna, who ran ahead, and then stood looking into the trees, quite still, her hands held slightly out from her body as if spellbound. Stern went to stand by his daughter, and they shared what was left of the water in one of the wine bottles they'd filled back at the sawmill.

'The horse suffers for water and the weight,' said the carter to Meyer. 'We should use the shadow and let noon pass.' Stern noticed how the words had no echo, but were swallowed in the hot, buckling air. Everyone else looked exhausted. Irena and Judi sat together in the grass, back to back as they had once done on picnics in the woods at home. Freida fed the child, her bare shoulder dappled by the trees. Natasza had made a nest of sorts among their bundles in the back of the cart and was lying as if asleep.

'No, we cannot rest too long,' said Meyer, slapping the flank of the horse. 'More of us must walk and lighten the load. You lead the way with Freida, and the luggage. Take Natasza, she's a delicate flower, and clearly thinks she's baggage too.

'We must keep moving. They will have patrols out and reinforcements will arrive today at the camp, perhaps tomorrow. We have to get beyond the forest by nightfall and then travel by night. This is our only chance. Then we can rest.'

Judi, who had explained to them all that the horse was called Cesarz, led the way holding its halter. Hanna danced at her sister's feet.

In the end it was Judi who changed everything; the course of the future, the shape of their lives to come. The heat began to make her dizzy and her mother had the water bottle, so she let go of the horse and picked up her little sister, although Hanna's feet only just left the ground. They stepped to one side, and let the iron-rimmed wheels pass, crushing the clods of hard red soil. At the last moment Judi passed Hanna up to Natasza in the cart and joined her parents in the wake of the little procession.

The path ran beside an old ditch, with a trickle of water in its depths. The shadows were lengthening, and clouds of insects had appeared above their heads. They were all weary, and their pace slackened, so that the cart got ahead of them, still piled high with suitcases, and mattresses, and chickens. Stern could see Natasza, and Freida, slumped slightly to one side, cradling the child. Where was Hanna? There! In the back, sitting beside Natasza, playing with one of the chickens through the bars of a crate.

At this moment, which will haunt Leo Stern for the rest of his life, a soldier emerges from the trees to stand between them and the distant plodding cart. A grey soldier. There is a red insignia on his coat. He carries an old-fashioned rifle. He doesn't look like one of the desperate degenerates they'd been told to fear, thirsty for blood and food. He has a pair of binoculars around his neck, and on his back a radio pack. An aerial swings in the air over his bare head. His helmet hangs from his rifle butt, and he's smoking a cigarette.

He's more surprised than they are.

There's a gunshot. The Russian falls to one knee but appears unhurt. Meyer, who was behind Stern, now runs past him, towards the enemy soldier, a pistol in his hand. Stern smells the fresh cordite on the air. The grey soldier brings his rifle up to his shoulder and fires. Stern hears the breath forced out of Meyer's body as he falls. There is a stiffening of the limbs, a sudden abandon in the spread-eagled arms, which tells him Eden's father is dead before he hits the dusty path.

In the distance a cloud of dust rises up around the wheels of the cart as the horse bolts at the sound of the bullets. Stern can see Cesarz's white mane rippling. At a twist in the road the whole caravan lurches as if it might topple into the ditch, but then it holds the bend, and is gone. Even the sound of it disappears, soaked up by the forest.

The grey soldier stands and begins to walk slowly towards them.

Voices, speaking a savage tongue, call out to him from the forest.

Irena and Judi hold each other tight, and Leo Stern raises his hands in surrender.

Chapter 67

When Hanna came round she found herself in a white world: lying in an old armchair, among neat stacks of folded sheets, wicker baskets of soiled laundry, and – outside the window – a pulley wire pegged with drying shirts, stretching across the void to the opposite block. Everything smelt of a newly made bed, as if she'd woken up at Swan House the morning after washing day.

A woman knelt on a threadbare rug beside her, holding a glass of water. Her skin was white too, bloodless, against which jet-black ringlets of hair fell over her forehead. She reached out and touched Hanna's cheek with the back of her hand, as if to check for fever.

'Mother says your man will be fine. It's a flesh wound, with a knife, so he has been lucky in this. But he'll need stitches.' For a moment Hanna felt the dizzy spin of disorientation: the voice was light, clear, but most definitely not that of a woman. And the washerwoman's face had not moved. Who had spoken?

She heard footsteps and then he was in front of her: a young man, with his mother's hair and skin, but blue eyes.

'*Mein Kind*,' said the woman slowly, standing up to hug him. 'My child.'

Then she smiled, radiating pride in the boy, but also something else, which Hanna recognised with a thrill as an intimate introduction, as if they were all of one family, which had been kept apart.

'I'm Eden,' said the young man. 'This is my mother.'

'The American is sleeping now because the old woman in H4 gave him a concoction. We're still in the land of witchcraft here, but we trust her. And she doesn't gossip.

'However, he did keep talking until the drug worked. So we know who you are, and why you came. It seems strange, but we have met before, you and I it seems, in a Polish sawmill near a place called Borek. The dreadful place where I was born.

'We haven't told the police because we don't want any trouble,' he added. 'But someone *will* whisper, and once the story is told everyone will know in an hour.

'So we'll have to move you both, and get a doctor. But that's no trouble. The problem's getting back to the West.

'Your man said your papers run out tonight, and they're searching everyone at the checkpoints after dark anyway, so they'll ask questions and they might find his wound. It could be bad for us.'

'I'm sorry,' said Hanna.

'Kirtchen, the door-keeper? She says it definitely wasn't Stasi. He pushed his way in, and that's not their style at all. They have ID. They move slowly. And they never use knives.

'Apparently your man came down the steps and asked him why he was following you: *that he had no right …*'

Eden laughed. 'Sadly, that's not how it works here. There's no right and wrong. Kirtchen said he pulled the knife and cut him; she said it was a practised move, but lacked conviction. Then he said: 'Give it up' – and fled. So it's a warning.'

Hanna nodded, a sudden pain in her head making her see coloured lights, so that she closed her eyes.

When she opened them again, Freida pressed a glass of water to her lips for her to drink, and then said something peremptory to her son, of which Hanna caught only the words 'documents' and 'stitches'.

Then she turned to Hanna. 'I must go,' she said, consulting her watch. 'You look like your father,' she continued, holding a hand to Hanna's forehead. They looked at each other for a few seconds, and Hanna sensed she was reliving a lost moment of the past.

'Eden can answer your questions,' she said, taking her hand away. 'We won't meet again this time. But next time. And then perhaps there will be a child, God willing.'

Hanna felt desperate, as if a meeting for which she had waited a lifetime was already lost. 'I came to ask about my family. I thought they were still alive; I thought you'd know where. Do you, Freida?'

Eden put a hand on her arm. 'We know a little – don't worry, I'll tell you everything.'

Freida bent down awkwardly and held Hanna's head, kissing her hair. Then she kissed her son, and burst into tears, going out quickly and slamming the door, a wicker basket against her hip.

Eden made sweet tea. Hanna felt better, sitting quietly, and the baby rolled slowly as it often did when she drank something hot. She thought how strange it was to be in the company of someone who'd known her other life, her forgotten life. Despite their years of separation, she felt comfortable with the silence.

'Do you want to see your man?' he asked.

He took her out into the corridor to an open door. Peter lay on a single bed on top of the covers, his midriff fiercely bandaged.

'He'll be fine,' Eden told her. 'It's just the pill. We're good at our own medicine, using the old ways. So, we have a few hours. I can answer your questions, but I must make a call first. I will be back.'

Alone, Hanna wanted to close her eyes and sleep, but she didn't want to take her eyes off Peter, whose breath came in whistles. She felt dizzy with anxiety and wondered if they'd put something in her glass of water. Peter had edged towards the window, turning his back, so she was able to lie down behind him and slip an arm across his chest.

Her lips were very close to his ear.

'Can you hear me, Pete?'

The image of the lift doors opening, and his altered face, kept flashing in her head. At first she'd had an overwhelming urge to stop the blood, to *remake* him, as if by some alchemy she could push the severed flesh back together and smooth over his skin.

'I didn't want to go, Pete,' she said now, in a whisper. 'If I left you – lost sight of you – I thought you'd die and when I got back, you'd be gone. *This* would be there …' She hugged him gently, until she picked up a faint echo of his heartbeat. 'But your life would be gone, and I'd see that in your eyes, despite the fact everyone would be telling me it would be all right. But I'd know it was over.

'But now I know it isn't.'

She put her forehead against the back of his neck.

Eden woke her up. He'd brought a tray of sausage and curry sauce from a stall and a cup of the dreadful chicory coffee. She sat up on the bed. Peter stirred but didn't wake.

Eden sat on the floor with his back to the door. 'I'll tell you everything I know. But it's best if I start in the woods around Borek. The last time Mother saw your family – Leo and Irena and Judi – was on a forest path …'

Chapter 68

Travelling south by taxi after dark, in the back with Peter, Hanna welcomed a rain shower by winding down the window, and letting the drops chill her skin. The streetscape told two stories: at first there were very few lights, and they slipped past Soviet suburbs, the curved white-painted apartment blocks of what Eden announced to be The First Five Year Programme. But then they entered Prenzlauer Berg, on the edge of the old city; this too was shadowy, but the pavements were crowded, and neon signs advertised subterranean bars, and even music.

Peter, waking again from his drug-induced sleep, looked at the street outside and asked if they'd crossed into the West.

Eden, in the passenger seat next to the cab driver, shook his head. 'It's the student quarter. It's 1961. We're catching up.'

He'd set out their timetable. They'd tackle crossing back to the West in the small hours. Eden said there was a place, but it was best if they knew nothing of the details until the moment came. Right now, they needed food, somewhere out of the way, and a doctor for Peter. They were headed to a café run by friends – an artists' haunt, so they'd like it, Eden told them, and the food was good: not just German potatoes and pickles and meat. He'd stay with them until the last moment – at the border out on the edge of the city. If they kept their nerve all would be well. He'd taken a note of addresses and telephone numbers and his mother would write, and he'd call. One day – perhaps soon, the city would be open again and they could meet and talk. Freida had promised, he said, that they'd never be strangers again.

They crossed a square, each side comprising tenements, but these were hardly typical: flags hung from windows, as did banners, proclaiming the titles of books, the names of jazz bands. On the first floor of one, a girl sat on the window ledge smoking; at a window above, red and blue lights strobed. A portrait of Che Guevara hung in the high portal that led into one of the central yards.

'A squat,' said Eden, turning to smile.

'This is allowed?' asked Peter.

'Until it's not,' said the cab driver. 'Then it is a good idea to be somewhere else.'

The cab stopped at a traffic light.

'And there,' said Eden, pointing across the street to a building on the far corner, 'there is our synagogue. Mother goes every week but says there are still very few of us and they can't afford a decent roof.'

Hanna saw the Star of David then, picked out in brick, the grim façade's only motif. It looked like a fortress, with a high arch over the entrance, and no lights showing at the slim, arrow-slit windows. One side of a pair of copper doors opened and a figure shuffled out, fumbling with the handle, so that for a moment she saw a lit interior of polished wood and a hanging chandelier with only one bulb glowing.

'Please – I want to see inside. Is there time?' It was her own voice, but she was surprised by the question.

The taxi driver pulled up at the kerb.

'Not too long,' said Eden, looking at her in the rear-view mirror.

Peter had fallen asleep on the back seat.

The heavy door swung in on oiled hinges. There were several rows of old benches, which looked as if they'd started life in another place. The wooden interior itself, the shape of a ship's hull, was older, and scarred by the war. There were two men on the right, sitting in the shadowy light of a menorah, its candles lit. She took a place on the left, near a pair of short pillars, which rose up to nothing, but were both blackened by fire. A woman, watching shyly, smiled at the signs of the baby Hanna was carrying. There was a light in a metal dish over what she took to be the Ark – its decorative marble exterior chipped and cracked.

There were boards on the wall inscribed with names in Hebrew, and a few small votive candles flickered. She saw now that several windows had been boarded up and to the side of a speaker's platform at the front a series of buckets had been set out to catch raindrops.

It was peaceful, and she was glad to be alone among others.

She wanted to sit quietly and re-live that final scene, described so vividly by Eden: her father and mother and sister left in the distance, as she was swept away around the bend on the cart. The parting tore at her despite the intervening years. The painful memory of it was gone, perhaps for ever, and she was thankful for that loss. But the prospect of the search ahead made her feel pitifully weak. Her lost family could be anywhere within the Soviet empire: her father possibly playing chess here, in a café in Berlin – or Poland, or East Germany, but most probably in some backwater of the USSR.

And then, inevitably, there was a new memory. This happened to her now, and always without warning. It was dark and she was in a cell in the camp. Her mother sat on a mattress braiding Judi's hair. Her father wasn't there but every now and then they heard his voice. Hanna had just eaten – this was particularly vivid – a piece of sausage and bread and clear water in a tin. The day that had passed had been full of fear and everyone had been scared except her father. But now there was a sense of brittle calm. Her mother had told them a story, and they'd played a family game in which they tried to guess what their neighbours were doing in Lodz.

Then a voice she knew – not her father this time – said they should look out the window. Her mother held her up to the square stone frame – the window was open, but there were bars in the shape of a cross. Down below they could see huts in lines, and at the windows of one the seven lights of a menorah seemed to hover, then move on, then cross to the next hut. Shadows of people moved. Then her mother told her of celebrations at the synagogue: the lights, the food, the dancing, and somewhere unseen, in the crowd, her own father clapping his hands in time to the music.

Hanna sat still, feeling herself suspended within the building, floating perhaps like the child within her. The subtle, Ark-like shape of the synagogue suggested another thought: that beyond this place of worship, but perhaps in another, sat Leo, Irena and Judith. At this very moment they might be thinking of her. Perhaps she would have to accept one day that this might be the end of the path after all.

Chapter 69

The cab reached a bombsite, slewing round in an arc to reveal a line of buildings, several held up with wooden struts, all perched on a sharp hillside. The café they were headed for was called Zone 5, but the name was hand-painted over an original – Der Prinz Berg. There were tables inside but no customers. The walls were crowded with paintings, mostly unframed. There was a jukebox playing jazz. It did feel safe, as Eden had promised, and the owner calmly led Peter to an upstairs bedroom. Hanna followed, and when she threw up the window to let some air in, she saw something she had not realised she had missed: a view. Berlin was flat: that was its *leitmotif*, a two-dimensional maze, but here, they were on a ledge, looking over the old city.

Peter slept on the bed until a doctor arrived, sweating, overweight, and possibly drunk. He ushered Hanna out of the room, so she sat with Eden outside on the café's stoop. The drinks were mysterious; the owner – a hyperactive young man with a tattoo on his wrist of an eye – produced a tray of small glasses full of a dense spirit made of ginger and chilli. Then Eden ordered beer and water, as a few people began to arrive to eat inside. The rest of the scene – the wide bombsite, and the rickety buildings – was deserted.

Eden said the whole street was built on a mountain of rubble left after the war. 'It's a cemetery but nobody talks about it,' he added. 'Sometimes the gases bubble up and catch fire.' It was clear he found this detail thrilling. He talked about his studies in chemistry at the Free University in the West. He had a calm grasp of facts and seemed much older than his years. Hanna wondered if Freida had ever married. While they'd waited for the cab in the flat, she'd checked the pictures on the walls, the books, the kitchen. There was no trace of a man, other than the teenage boy.

The old bombsite was still. Hanna had the distinct impression they were on a stage, and that the curtain was about to rise. Water dripped from the awning, so that they looked out west towards the Funkturm radio tower's winking light through a curtain of rain.

Eden pointed out the four zones: the French was within reach, three blocks away, then the British, then the Americans to the south. In the mid-distance an aeroplane's lights banked in towards the airport at Tempelhof.

'And finally …' said Eden, indicating the city below. It looked as if a velvet black cloth had been laid over the Soviet Sector, through which lights peeped as if through moth holes.

'The *Neue West* – yes?' said Eden, pointing at the shard of garish colour that rose from the direction of the Ku-Damm. The lights looked like the crumbling, jewelled surface of a lava flow, as if the real life, the heat, lay below, and was creeping, inch by inch, towards them.

The doctor appeared and Hanna paid him $30 in ten-dollar bills.

'Try to make him rest,' he said, in excellent English, then drove away in a battered car. They ordered food – kebabs with a fiery chilli sauce, and a salad – then Peter appeared. He was still pale, but his eyes were in focus, and he'd bought a bottle of vodka at the bar, and cigarettes.

The owner, who'd been in a shadowy corner holding a young man's hand, appeared now with peanuts, energised perhaps by the sight of the dollar bills.

Hanna told Peter to go back to bed or eat, but he sat, arranged the small glasses, and poured vodka.

'What doesn't kill you makes you stronger,' he said.

'You should eat,' said Hanna.

'Not hungry,' he answered. 'I looked in the mirror and the doctor's done a decent job.'

'*Prost*,' said Eden, and the glasses were refilled.

'How will we get across the border?' asked Hanna.

'A midnight stroll. It's best not to know more,' said Eden.

Hanna was wary of the party mood. Peter's elation she put down to alcohol and the pills. But there was something about Eden's enthusiasm, a note of recklessness that made her feel afraid. She wondered if the border crossing was more dangerous than he liked to admit.

Peter wanted to know about the art scene in the East, if there were underground galleries, student art collectives. He said the canvases hung inside the café bar were fine, but that the West led the way in the abstract, and it didn't look like the East wanted to follow.

'The best art is on the streets,' said Eden, slightly flushed with the drink. 'We are catching up. Public art – yes?'

He grinned then, a broad evolving smile.

'It's why we're here. The Zone 5 is good – but there are many cafés. I want to show you something new, provocative. It's not far. We can walk, if you can?'

Peter stood unsteadily, taking the bottle by the neck. 'How far?' he said.

'A few hundred yards – no more. Most of all I wanted to show *you*,' he added, turning to Hanna. 'It's about us.'

'Do we have time?' she asked.

'The cab will pick us up here in an hour.'

They walked two blocks to the entrance of a U-Bahn station, where the sign read Dimitroff Strasse. It was a back entrance, and the street was empty, the steps dusty and strewn with rubbish. They descended two flights and turned into a long subway, perhaps sixty yards in length, which was neon lit. Peter, wincing at the pain of the steps, drank from the vodka bottle, then set it down on the old tiles of the floor.

Both sides of the tunnel had been used for a monumental artwork. Newspaper cuttings, photographs and documents had been pasted to the curved concrete, then overlaid with painted figures, the *motif* dominated by the limp pale limbs of the dead, lying in mounds beside open pits.

The title ran along both walls, repeated and repeated, in blood red.

WHY SHOULD THEIR FACES BE FORGOTTEN?

At points along the wall, the names of the death camps were spelt out:

AUSCHWITZ, TREBLINKA, BELZEC …

Under each camp's name were photographic portraits. Each face in the work had been assigned a name in cut-out newspaper type, like a ransom note. Almost all were SS officers, and each was afforded the dignity of his rank.

The neon tubes that lit the subway had acquired small reservoirs of water where the damp had pooled. A train rumbled through the station below, and so the water vibrated, and rippled, and the curved walls appeared to flex.

The fizzing of the electrics was the only sound left after the train had pulled away.

Hanna saw the tunnel as if she was under water, the thick viscous air able to support fish, perhaps, and drifting weed. The shimmering aquatic light seemed to emit a hard, metallic note, an echo of the train that had just departed.

Peter, unsteady, put a hand against the wall, placing one foot on top of the other.

'Nothing too abstract here,' he said.

'It's the past,' said Eden. 'It has to be dealt with first.'

Eden took Hanna halfway down the tunnel until she stood opposite the giant letters that spelt: BOREK.

'Faces from our past,' said Eden.

She knelt down and started with the first picture, which – according to the caption – showed the commandant Eigrupper, pictured in a uniform in 1919, looking every inch the Prussian military hero. The fifth, almost at eye level, showed a man called Bertolt Soose; affable features offset by the strange affectation of an aristocratic monocle. This picture looked like a professional portrait, taken across a smart desk. Anton Oertel, next, had a symmetrical face, bland, if conventionally handsome, the tunic of his SS Hitler Youth uniform buttoned up tight under his chin. Lastly, at the top, she found Georg Johl, listed as an SS judge, a favourite uncle perhaps; jowly, with a slight smile, staring shyly out of the pages of a legal journal of 1936. The moist oyster-like eyes looked huge behind the thick plastic-framed spectacles.

Hanna reached out a hand, and touched the face, remembering what Colonel Krikalev had said in his office at Spandau when he'd shown them pictures of the missing SS officers from the camp. It was important, he said, to memorise the image in black and white, and then turn it in the mind, and add the years, and thin the hair. Then, one day, you might catch sight of the living man, the flesh and the blood, a face emerging from the crowd, or among the shadows of a machine, where he sits adjusting the focus on the fleeting images of moving light.

Chapter 70

The cab sped north from the café on a wide road bordered with ramshackle post-war tenements. Street lighting in the East was intermittent, and as they reached Pankow, and a level-crossing, the lamps failed and they watched a goods train pass in the shadows. Hanna felt uneasy, for the parallel with the junction at Borek was too raw, with the track leading off towards the water tower and the gas chamber, and the field of the dead. Which made her think of the face she'd recognised in the subway. She'd told Peter to take a picture, with the flashlight, and promised she'd explain when they were safe, and back in the West. There were others she had to tell: Clarke, and Pierce, even Krikalev if they could reach him.

And then the train was gone, and the barrier rose, and the headlamps revealed nothing more sinister than a country road leading to Rosenthal – according to the signpost – and they stopped here by a boarded-up roadside garage.

The cab driver was keen to go, and so he jumped out and went to the boot, and handed Eden a small knapsack. It was then that Hanna understood that he was coming with them, which explained his mother's parting tears back at their flat, and his own air of suppressed exhilaration. The university was in the West, the checkpoints might be closed for months, even years. If he had a future, it lay on the other side of the border.

After handshakes the cab was gone, tail-lights flickering out at a bend in the road.

They stood together, uncertain which way to turn. Hanna thought there was nothing quite as silent as a German village after dark. The night was cool, and Peter gave her his jacket.

'Follow me,' said Eden, and set off along what must have been the main street. The façades of the buildings were crumbling, and so they'd built wooden eaves over the pavements as they'd done in the old city, creating a boardwalk. There was a Rathaus, but it was a ruin, and only two Doric columns stood, covered in graffiti.

They heard a dog bark and then the sound of a window being edged down. Eden let them catch him up. 'Don't worry, everyone's used to this now. They turn a blind eye and no one ever raises the alarm. This is the easy bit.'

At the edge of the village there was a school – a concrete block like the rest in the city – and playing fields. A footpath took them round behind some goalposts and then they were in a copse of trees. Eden turned on a torch that lit his boots. They all crouched down when they got to the edge of the wood, a weak splash of moonlight illuminating a shadowy downhill slope.

Off to the left a mile distant, floodlights revealed a building site, and a line of dormant concrete mixers. Hannah could see the outline of a wire fence running south back to the city, and – in sections – a wall made of bricks.

The slope was a patchwork of allotments, and small sheds. '*Kleingarten*,' said Eden, pointing ahead. 'We need to wait.'

Hanna was worried about the baby now, because her body felt cold, and her back ached, and she knew that a nervous sentry with a rifle might fire a stray bullet and that the only protection she had was flesh. Peter was strangely quiet, clutching at his bandaged waist whenever they moved.

Eden's blue eyes caught a reflection of the distant lights.

'Where will you go – on the other side?' she asked, forcing herself to concentrate on someone else.

'I'll fade away, at least for a while. I have friends.'

They heard a burst of radio static carried on the still night air.

'A patrol – but don't worry, it's a long way away,' said Eden. 'The sound travels at night.'

A church clock close by marked the hour with a single stroke.

'This isn't difficult,' said Eden. 'Just keep quiet, keep moving, and do what I do.'

In single file they emerged from the trees and made their way down the hillside, following a path between the smallholdings, which smelt of leeks and greens and – hypnotically – jasmine.

The gentle valley was shielded from the lights of the construction site. To their right Hanna saw the silhouette of a squat ugly building that looked like a pumping station. There was only one light here, a single bulb.

As they descended the wide field the sound of a river grew stronger, and Hanna caught the smell of fresh water. She was dizzy now, and worried that the baby felt different, moving within her to a new place. The stream ran between reeds, and was alive with bubbles, as if it had just emerged from a mill race or a weir.

'It's two feet deep in the middle,' said Eden. 'Hold hands.'

Hanna sat down and took off her shoes, then put her foot in the black water, feeling its shocking chill. She thought of Marcin's waders, and the flood on Long Fen, and the night she'd edged out along the path in the storm. That version of herself seemed like a stranger, caught naked in the cold reflection of a mirror.

Peter put an arm around her and lifted her on to her feet. The bed of the river was pebbles, and these shifted slightly under her weight. Eden realised quickly he was wrong, the stream was deeper than he'd thought, and the current had begun to tug at them. He took Hanna's arm on the other side, so that the three of them were locked together. If they were to slip, and be swept away, it occurred to Hanna now that the secret would go with them, the identity of the face she'd recognised on the U-Bahn wall.

Mid-stream, Eden held up a hand.

She heard it too, the disorderly tramping of boots on a gravel track, and then, breaking the horizon, they saw them, a platoon, perhaps half a dozen soldiers. The guards stopped, and Hanna heard the crackle of a radio, and several cigarette ends bloomed in the dark.

For a minute, two, nothing moved but the river.

Then the radio again, muffled, and a brisk order, and they were gone, marching away back down the line.

Peter led the way to the far bank and lifted Hanna up. They all stood dripping, until he broke the spell. 'Are we safe?'

'No,' said Eden. 'The border's ahead. There's more *Kleingarten*, and a wire. I've never got this far before, but I've talked to others who have. We must stay silent.'

The next line of smallholdings was over the hill, each one with its shed and stove. The wire when they reached it was ten foot high, raking forwards, and zigzagging past a ruined farmhouse. Eden led them to a spot in the shadows and, after a brief search by torchlight, lifted back a section as though it were a door, and they crawled through, which for Hanna was the worst moment because the nerves in her back went into spasm, and she cried out.

A few chickens clucked in response, and a pig snuffled.

They walked away from the wire towards a large shed that showed light around a door. They'd seen many stove-pipes, but this was the first one from which smoke drifted. Somewhere a radio was playing; not the crackle of the military wavelengths, but a big dance band.

Behind them they heard a footfall, so they turned on their heels, and were blinded by torchlight.

'*Vy ne dolzhny lomat' zabor*,' said a weary voice.

The wire was between them: Hanna recognised the words; they were Russian, but it meant nothing. The blinding light was coming through the wire mesh. The patrol had returned, and she saw one soldier raise a rifle, while another pulled at the wire, as if searching for the gap.

They stood, transfixed. Then the door of the shed opened: she never forgot what she saw, a cameo that was to become part of her family history. A soldier stood in silhouette, behind him a desk covered in paperwork, his gun leaning against the wooden wall, on which a rabbit hung from a nail. There was a telephone too, and the stove, and a coffee pot on the top.

She couldn't see the brand of the cigarette the soldier was smoking, but she recognised the fragrant drift of its smoke: *Gitanes*.

The soldier stepped into the light and they saw him smile.

'*Tu l'as fait*,' he said, in a strangely clipped accent.

'*Bienvenue dans la zone Française*.'

The black-and-white film flickered like an exhausted eyelid. Behind the soundtrack they could hear the mechanics of the projector, a celluloid spool looping, a fluttering like a bird's wings. Then the title music filled the *Prinzessa*: that peculiar Hollywood confection of a thunderous orchestra and tubular bells that signals to any audience the mysterious Orient: China, the Forbidden City, and beyond.

Hanna, still blinded by the sun on the Berlin pavements, stood in the dark. She'd let her eyes narrow, accommodating the light, as the film began not with a distant view of pagodas or peasants stooped in the rice fields, but with a fog-choked London backstreet, a gas lamp revealing a figure gliding from doorway to doorway. A ship sounded a mournful note from the docks, although the soundtrack persisted with the Chinese motif.

The matinee was not popular. The Wall had interrupted the release of new features, and re-runs of *Charlie Chan* had dated badly. Cigarette smoke rose from an audience of three men, in the middle of the *Kino*, not too close for the screen to overwhelm them, not too far away to strain the eyes.

Rachel Vogel sat in the middle of the back row, her hair up, wreathed like most of the men in smoke, a cigarette held in the fingers of the right hand, her elbow on an armrest. On her knee was a folded linen napkin, upon which she'd balanced a cup of coffee.

Hanna sat beside the manageress.

'The last time we met,' said Vogel, smiling, not taking her eyes from the screen, 'in the powder room at District Six – at the club – I was so scared I could only look at you in the mirror. We were never safe, however much Hans said we were. He'd asked a friend of a friend to watch your American. He is good with a knife, if paid. It was meant to be a warning, but he went too far.'

'My friend could have died.'

'Men are stupid, but they hold power in this world, so what are we to do?'

She seemed a different person, as if the tension obscuring her real self had suddenly dissolved.

'Hans told me it would end like this, but I sent you the letter anyway, and the wooden chess piece.' She nodded to herself, as if this had been a job well done.

'*You?* There was evidence it might have come from the Stasi …'

Vogel smiled. 'No doubt. They tampered with our post over the years. They tamper with everyone's – especially international mail. But this was innocent enough to a dull bureaucrat's eyes – a family feud, a gift for a child. They must have let it go.'

Hanna twisted in her seat to see the projectionist's window. 'Are the police still with Hans?' she asked.

Krikalev had brought them all in a convoy of Zils to the cinema, with two Stasi officers in plain clothes and a military driver. Clarke had appeared at Peter's flat at the appointed hour. They'd been picked up on the Ku'Damm in the flag car and whisked through the checkpoint at Bernauer Strasse. The world might be paralysed by the Cold War, with missiles massed in German fields, but the name of Georg Johl had cleared a miraculous path.

Krikalev and Clarke had climbed the spiral staircase together, ignoring the manageress's demands to abide by the notices. One of the Stasi men searched the office, while Rachel Vogel was banished to the cinema, another officer guarding the only exit.

'If you sent the letter, you know where my father is,' Hanna said.

'No. Only Hans knows that. When the police have finished with him, I'm sure he will tell you everything. But he would not tell me. He said it would lead them to us – the police, the Russians, even the Americans. He was right.'

She ground her cigarette stub into the little steel ashtray provided on the arm of the chair.

The urge to leave this woman now, and climb the steps to the projection room, was almost too much to bear. But she was right: Krikalev and Clarke had been adamant. It was their prerogative to question the judge first. Hanna suspected that a deal had been struck. The Soviets would get custody of Johl, but Clarke would get to ask his questions.

'How did he survive the camp?' asked Hanna, lighting a cigarette.

Vogel twisted her spine so that she could look directly at Hanna. Peter had said, one Sunday afternoon on the towpath above Swan House, that we look into people's eyes because it's the one part of us that doesn't age, so that in some ways it's like looking into the past. But the sad reality is that eyes age too. Vogel's looked ancient, as if she peered out of a marble statue.

'At the end, when the rebels broke down the outer wire by the station, your father – the white-haired doctor – came to the gas chamber with Hans … he is always Hans to me.

'He thought he had lost his beloved daughter. Hans was to blame. It had been the judge's court, he had sent her to walk the Himmelstrasse, and so now he must face his own trial, and then execution. Your father was both judge and jury.

'We operated the gas chamber together to enact the sentence. I was left to complete the process.'

She went to touch Hanna's hand, but withdrew at the last inch. 'Your father was a kind man. He'd found Hans guilty, but he took the time to find me innocent. I had operated the chamber, but he said I should run, run free, into the woods. I was forgiven. This is something I have never forgotten.'

Her eyes flooded, but she went on in a calm voice: 'He said I could go with him, but I stayed. Most importantly, he gave me a gun. I watched Hans die in the gas chamber and then turned off the machine.

'I went to Hackendorf's hut and took up the floorboard where he kept his money. He had bandages too, and salve for wounds. But I could not stay there. The Germans said they would be back.

'So I hid in the trees on the Himmelstrasse. The Ukrainie were on the luggage square – I could hear their drunken voices – but they dared not leave their fire.

'Before dawn I heard the German lorries leaving. I knew the Russians were close behind. I had to escape, and the forest was the only place left to hide. I went back to the field of the dead. There was silence. Then I heard a voice from the gas chamber.

'I had failed your father. Hans was not dead, but he'd suffered a stroke. He was helpless: one arm was useless, and he limped badly. The Germans had gone. He said we had to go west before the Red Army arrived.'

She smiled. 'I failed your father. I let Hans live. He promised escape, and life. He was a fugitive, as was I. He said something deft: that we could be a *disguise* for each other. Hans had money too, in a leather satchel.

'I got him as far as the edge of the woods and we rested until nightfall. By the next morning he could walk, although badly. Then the journey began. We joined the long march at Kraśnik with the other Jews, one step ahead of the Ivans …

'All for this …'

She waved her hand to indicate the smoky *Kino*.

'And for the child who would be Elke. She's at school. What will she find when she comes home?' She looked away then, and Hanna felt that for the first time the reality of the situation had overcome her: the child was lost to her mother, the mother to the child.

Vogel's hand was still on the back of the seat between them, so Hanna reached out and took it. To have survived, but to endure such a nightmare now, was cruel. Hanna realised that simply walking away from Borek was not in itself an escape. Rachel Vogel had spent her whole life a prisoner. But for *der Springer*, and this woman's courage, Hanna would have followed the same path.

On screen the scene had shifted to a luxurious ocean liner below decks, where passengers watched a stage-show, a man throwing daggers at a woman tied to a large, circular board representing the zodiac.

'We have lived together for fifteen years,' said Vogel, finally, recovering her composure. 'Of that dreadful place, and that dreadful time, we have never talked. Can you believe this?'

'Time is short,' said Hanna, ignoring the question.

'Hans told me your father was alive – no more. He had never forgotten *Herr Doktor*. And I had kept the chess piece. Your father wanted me to put it with your body on the field of the dead, but you were not there. Hans said it was the lost child's precious toy. I wanted to remember your father, so I kept it safe. I had promised.

'So it was right to send you back the gift. It was yours, not mine. I could say no more than what I said. I wish I could say more even now, but *I* know no more. Hans would not tell me how the news came to us here, in Berlin. He feared discovery. But now, I think, he will tell you what you need to know.

'Go quickly. As I said, our friend's friend went too far. We did not ask him to use a knife on the American – this was never what we wanted. He came here for payment but Hans withheld his fee. And now Hans has paid for that …'

She turned over the white linen on her lap and Hanna saw it was soaked on one side with blood.

Chapter 72

'You are as clear-eyed as I expected,' said Georg Johl. 'Your father exuded a certain moral tone, a kind of clarity in itself. Sit – sit. You've come far, and I see a new Stern will be with us soon.'

As he spoke, he held a blood-soaked bandage to his shirt, just above the belt. 'Rachel has done her best, but the bleeding will not stop,' he added. 'The Colonel has sent for medical help, and it is most needed …'

Hanna had her back to the door, with its porthole window, through which she'd glimpsed the judge on that first visit, sitting in his metallic niche, embedded within the projector: a human cog. So it had not been difficult to recognise him in the U-Bahn tunnel beneath Zone 5, as his face in old age was a predictable version of the middle-aged, jowly lawyer.

'How do you know my father is alive?' she asked. 'Rachel says you know this. How? You must tell me. I have a right to know.'

Johl's face had succumbed to the gravity of the years, indeed his whole body seemed weighted, as if being here – on the mezzanine – in some way accentuated the Newtonian forces at work.

'I will answer your questions,' he said, smiling in a crooked way. 'But I will have to be brief. My hireling has done more harm than we feared. Perhaps it is best. A Stasi prison promises no comforts – certainly no cigars.

'Why don't you sit?' he asked, indicating a single seat that had been fitted to the wall beneath the observer's window.

He wore a heavy striped dressing gown that he now tied at the waist to cover the wound, which was not in the stomach, but higher, close to the heart.

Hanna went back to the door and opened it, calling down to Peter: 'Tell them to hurry. It is worse than he told them.'

She closed the door so that they were alone. They could see Rachel Vogel, still sitting below, the Stasi officer now at the end of the row.

'Sometimes she will sit for hours,' said Johl. 'Her eyes are open, but when I touch her arm she seems to wake from a dream. What goes on beneath the surface goes on beneath the surface, but each year that passed the tension grew. She knew this and feared the inevitable day. Perhaps it is a release after all.'

His eyes swam out of focus, and he quickly moved his feet to stop himself falling, but Hanna felt no pity. She didn't hate this man – she had no personal memory of cruelty or violence – but his arrogance, his oily confidence, made her see him for what he was: manipulative and scheming.

'You need a doctor,' said Hanna.

'I need a coffin. No – I *want* a coffin. I should have died that day in Borek when your father dragged me to the gas chamber. It was his courtroom, you see. I was the accused. Do you know the charge?' His eyebrows leapt above quick, liquid eyes.

'The murder of Hanna Stern! Yes. So, a legal flaw there I think, don't you?' He began to laugh, and this sparked a fit of coughing.

'We don't have time for your story,' said Hanna, her voice betraying a bitter impatience. 'The Stasi will not give us long.'

Johl nodded, letting his hand edge its way along the canopy of the projector to a small shelf from which he retrieved a glass of what looked like sticky water.

'I was found guilty by your father's court,' he said, knocking back the liquid in one gulp, ignoring Hanna. 'The sentence was death. But justice was not done, Hanna Stern. Only now it comes, delivered by a young girl once too frightened to speak in my courtroom.

'The case against me, the case brought in the gas chamber, was hardly watertight. But your father made some salient points with reference to my character; he highlighted certain defects that in another time would have made no difference to the greater world. A tendency – no, a *failure* to engage with strategy. This he saw in the way I played chess.

'Did you know we played? Yes – twice. Tactics – that is my downfall. Tactics are here, yes …' He circled his thumb over his fingertips. 'In the everyday. I live, I enjoy, I observe. I do not see ahead. Or any distance from my own concerns. Your father pinpointed this lack … of what? I could call it nobility of spirit. Or, if I was hard on myself, humanity.'

Johl rearranged his bones as if each joint were sore.

'These defects in character are very small, even your father acknowledged that. But there is a cumulative effect. It reminds me of the scientific parable of the frog left in the pan of water on the stove. An experiment first carried out here by the way, in Germany, by a fine physiologist called Goltz. If I remember my student notes, he heated the pan very, very slowly. The frog, which has evolved to react only to sudden rises in temperature, does not move. The water becomes warm, the frog waits. The water becomes hot, the frog waits. The water boils, the frog dies. So – I also fail to react to subtle changes in the moral temperature, until it is too late. I became a judge who did not know right from wrong. I delivered injustice.'

Johl shrugged.

'You admit that a doctor is needed,' said Hanna, standing. 'The time has come. If you die without telling me where my father is, then will we add that to the list of your crimes?' She paused, calculating, 'Will we add it to the list of *Rachel's* crimes?

'I repeat: how do you know my father is alive?'

'Very well,' he said, holding up his hands. 'One thing: it may help Rachel's case if you offer them this information. I have not told the Russian or the American. On the long road back to Berlin we passed a crossroads. The Red Army was ahead of us – to the west. A German SS officer had been lynched. It was a man called Raeder – from Borek. He left with the lorry carrying the gold. This means that either Moscow has the gold, or some Red Army officers took it. I suspect the first. This intelligence may help my family. I doubt this truth has been widely shared.

'Keep it to yourself today. Tell the Americans when the time is right.'

He struggled to his feet. 'How do I know Leo Stern is alive? I still play chess. I still play chess, badly. One day I found this …'

He crossed the room, trailing a leg, a last vestige perhaps of the disabilities that had come in the wake of the stroke. On the floor, in a rough pile, stood a column of bound volumes. He took one by the corner and expertly cartwheeled it into his open hand. It was the *Soviet Cultural Review 1957*, Volume IV.

'It's marked,' he said, offering her the tint-edged reverse of the spine, from which a bookmark protruded.

The page contained a series of announcements about a literary festival. The print was set across eight columns, but the story only filled seven. In the spare space the results of the 18th Gorky Inter-Zonal Chess Tournament in Arzamas were listed.

She skimmed down the page, letting her eye focus for a second on each name.

I.G.L. AGREEST
Y. DOLMATOV
L.E.L. STERN (GM)
A.V. KHOUDGARIAN

Her eye, flying onwards, taking snapshots, missed it the first time, but tracked back.

She reached behind her, flipped down the seat, and sat, transfixed by the print.

There it was:

L.E.L. STERN

She sat back and said it out loud: 'L.E.L. Stern.'

'Leopold Emmanuel Lasker,' said Johl. 'He was named after the great man himself – so your grandfather played too, I think. A noble tradition.'

'He is alive,' she said.

'Four years ago, certainly.'

For the first time she thought of the child inside her as a *grand*child, a great-grandchild.

Johl examined Hanna's face.

'Tears at last,' he said. 'I hope you meet him soon.'

He went back to his seat. 'As I say, we have a strange marriage, Rachel and I. Very little is said. One morning, when she brought the coffee, I told her that Dr Stern was alive. I realised my mistake too late and told her no more. Dr Stern's story leads to mine, and that is the secret we had to keep.

'But she is a resourceful woman. She enlisted help from Jewish organisations to try and track down your family. It was immediately clear that there was no record of the Sterns except for one daughter: yourself. A Polish family living in England had made a request for documents in 1946, on behalf of this daughter. There was an address, near Cambridge. She's a brave woman, Rachel.

'She told me to my face she'd sent the parcel. I said it would end badly. I was wrong. It has ended well. This is how it should end.'

Hanna was still staring at the report on the chess tournament. 'I don't understand. Where can I find my father?'

On the wall Johl had a framed colour map of the Soviet Union indicating postal zones. Taking short, shuffling steps, he went to it and put his finger on a stretch of Russia, hundreds of miles east of Moscow.

'This is Arzamas. It is on the road to Siberia, to the gulags. A way-station. Perhaps the family settled there. Your father was a doctor, so he was of value to them. The chess tournament was in a school hall – so a local competition. Perhaps he lives nearby.

'He was a very fine player. And now a Grand Master I see. The Soviets love their chess players. They are privileged, they travel, they fight the Cold War by proxy. But he is an old man now, so perhaps his powers have waned.

'What does it mean? It means he is alive – or was – and living in retirement in this small town on the road to nowhere. If he still has privileges, he may even have a telephone. Perhaps your new friends can secure a line.'

He tore the page out of the book and gave it to Hanna.

'You could have told Rachel the truth,' she said.

'I could not trust Rachel to keep our secret. We have survived by never being of interest to anyone. She wanted to tell you of your father's gifts: forgiveness of course, and the gun. The gun was very useful.

'We never talk of the past. The subject was closed until you appeared on our doorstep.

'Forgive me. I wished only to preserve the version of my life I have presented to the world. The story I have given my daughter. She does not know who her father is, let alone who he was. Can you imagine? My daughter is an innocent. And this is how ludicrous my life has become. The only thing that matters is the illusion I have created in a pretty girl's head: that her father is a cinema technician who likes cigars.

'This is all that mattered, and now I have lost her.'

He struggled to his feet. 'She will soon know the truth about her father. I wish you the same fate, Hanna Stern.'

Chapter 73

They carried Georg Johl out of the *Kino* on a stretcher and loaded him into the back of a military ambulance, while his wife was taken away in an unmarked car by the Stasi. Krikalev told the driver to take her to Ruschestrasse, the street of no footsteps, and then to pick up the daughter from the District Six school.

Hanna took Peter's hand as they watched the cars turn out into the newly christened Karl Marx Allee, a motorcycle escort appearing in their wake as they headed east, away from the city centre. Kreutzigerstrasse returned immediately to its former guise; a half-ruined backstreet in which drama was limited to the silver screen of the *Prinzessa*.

Krikalev examined Major Clarke's fresh signature on their new visas and agreed they had a day of freedom in the East. If they wished they could return to the West on foot.

While they'd waited for the doctor, Krikalev had asked Hanna to repeat her conversations with Rachel and Hans.

'And they said nothing more?' he asked now, flicking closed a notebook before slipping it neatly into a breast pocket on his uniform.

'Nothing,' said Hanna, lying easily.

Krikalev patted the pocket. 'I would use the time you have left wisely,' he said. 'We are a divided city. The wall only gets higher.'

'What will happen to them?' asked Hanna. She felt responsible for the fate of the Vogels, perhaps that of the child most acutely. 'The little girl is innocent. And her mother is a victim, surely – of the camps, the Nazis, the past.'

Krikalev held out helpless hands. 'Even I will not know what becomes of them,' he said, smiling. 'It is a matter for a higher power.'

He touched the peak of his cap and waved his hand, calling forth a Zil that had been parked on the bombsite. A single soldier was left on guard in the street as a carpenter nailed boards across the door of the *Kino*.

Up on the main boulevard they found a kiosk beside a concrete bench. Peter's wound had been cleaned and bandaged, but he needed a rest and a fresh packet of f6. They bought two bottles of lukewarm beer. Hanna felt light-headed. Everything she could see she saw with an unnatural clarity of light: the way back towards the Alexanderplatz, the trundling Trabants in mustard yellow and mould green, the Red Army trucks, a convoy passing with tarpaulins flapping, the policeman on point-duty, directing traffic with his white gloves.

She got up with her bottle of beer, stood on the kerb of the road and faced east, one hand on the child, her back arched.

'How far, Pete?' she asked, pointing.

'To Moscow? A thousand miles – more.'

'So this is all it would take …' She took one step.

'Or a telephone call? Clarke can get us a line if we can find a number,' said Peter.

'But I could walk,' said Hanna, thrilled by the idea.

'If I kept going, I'd get to Moscow, and then if I walked on – another few hundred miles – I would get to Arzamas. The Sterns will have a flat, possibly a nice one, reserved for a man of privilege, a doctor and a chess player. A Grand Master. And if God is on my side, his wife, Irena, will be with him. Perhaps, on the mantelpiece, there will be a picture of their daughter Judith – married now? So even grandchildren.

'It's the old family game,' she said, remembering how they would try and guess what the neighbours were doing in Lodz. 'He'll be by the window in front of a chess board. She'll be in the kitchen planning a meal for Shabbat – that's the weekly feast: the cleaner in your block's a Jew and I've been catching up. Or perhaps they go across town to Judith's house – to see the children.

'And then one day – after how many steps? – I knock on the door.' She looked at Peter and knew the true shape of the future. '*We'll* knock on the door. And then Leo and Irena will be my parents again. Judith will be my sister. What was lost will be remade.'

The image was captivating, and within reach. She hadn't expected to get this far along the path, but now she felt she would get to the end. Even one day soon.

She stole a hand over the baby. For the first time, she knew it was a girl.

A pain ran across her stomach, tightening into a circle around her spine. A dull ache seemed to deepen, wane, and then deepen again. It was six weeks until the baby was due, and so she'd ignored the signs that were becoming increasingly clear: the baby had moved down, giving her more room to breathe, while her own arms and legs seemed looser, oiled at their joints.

'Pete,' she said, thinking that the joy she'd felt looking east had tipped the balance within her, 'it's too early, but I think the baby's coming.'

She lurched towards the seat and sat beside him.

'*Now?*' said Peter. '*Here?*'

A new wave of pain began to build.

Chapter 74

The driver of the cab had a framed picture hanging from the rear-view mirror of a village church with a cupola. He talked non-stop about *his* three children, all born at home by candle-light, and each one perfect. At the checkpoint the guard's face was framed in the side window – a young man with a harelip, and light grey eyes, which widened with wonder when he saw Hanna clutching herself. They must have walked across the border, because she was at the white line between East and West when her waters finally broke, and she remembered later Peter saying, 'Clarke's sent a car'. And then they were driving through the pillars of Andrews Barracks, and she saw the long windows of the Olympic pool.

Then the pain, rhythmic, obliterated all her other senses.

The first time she came round in the hospital ward it was deserted. The crisp linen reminded her of Freida Klumbacher. A long line of empty beds, neatly made, led into the distance, where a nurse sat at a desk, reading under a light. A bowl of water was on a stand, and she could see it was tinged with blood. She was appallingly thirsty, so she called to the nurse, who brought her a glass with ice, but when she tipped it back the liquid never reached her lips, which made her open her eyes and realise it was all an illusion, which immediately began to repeat itself.

She wanted desperately to see Peter, because she had to ask him if the baby had been born, and if it was alive. If *she* was alive.

The second time she regained consciousness she saw the nurse in the distance again, this time bathed in sunshine, talking to Vanessa. Which made no sense. She couldn't hear what was being said because a woman with a mop was working her way down the middle of the ward pushing the pail along the floorboards. And there was another patient, a woman, three beds away, lying still. Hanna wanted to cry out, but her tongue was sluggish and swollen. The effort, the extra breath, sparked a sharp pain across her belly, and she felt as if she might come apart. Tormented, she straightened her back and heard the bedsprings creak, and saw above her the two suspended bottles, the blood and plasma, and the plastic tubes that led to her arm.

The third time she came round, it was late evening. The window was open and she could see a bright light outside, a floodlight, and hear feet scraping on asphalt, a ball bouncing, the cries of players, and a whistle. The linen on the bed felt crisp and cool, not damp and hot, and she could smell something familiar: aftershave, and the bitter edge of cheap tobacco.

A hand touched her forehead and she turned to see Peter's face, very close, and then the child was given to her, and she felt time begin again in its proper place, as if zero hour had struck for them all.

Stunde Null.

Chapter 75

The apartment on rue Delambre was a constant reminder to Hanna of the extent to which she was no longer a prisoner of the past. The moment when Mr Hasard-with-one-S had held her hand and knocked on the door in the bitter winter of 1945 seemed to her a scene from another life. Inside the apartment, the tall windows, separated by the full-length gilt mirrors, still gave the same illusion, making it impossible to tell if she was looking at the reality of Paris outside, or its reflection inside. But when she captured her own image, it was no longer ghost-like and insubstantial.

This morning she looked slim, in white overalls over a blue shirt, and a red-and-orange headscarf. She'd had her hair cut again at an exorbitant price, an exquisite bob, so that she looked as elegant as the furniture, which was still all pre-war, but which had been re-upholstered in spring colours. The flat had been the Wotyas', and Lydia's sister had been happy for them to have it for a fortnight. Normally an agency rented it out, although the cachet of Montparnasse had faded since the war, and now only office workers strolled in the cemetery.

She heard footsteps, so light they hardly made the floorboards creak.

Lydia paused at the door. 'Good morning, Hanna. Coffee?'

Hanna shook her head. 'It's going to be hot again today. I'll walk to the gallery while I can. The pictures may have arrived. Peter's night train is in at eight from Berlin. He said he'd go straight there. There's so much to do.'

She'd met her aunt at the Gare du Nord the day before. She'd looked sprightly, her sharp blackbird eyes catching the light, even in the clouds of smoke and steam trapped beneath the great roof.

Lydia set off reluctantly for the kitchen. It was the only room in the apartment she didn't seem to find familiar. She'd had servants then, before the war: a cook and a maid, even a driver. Hanna sensed her aunt was not at peace in Paris. She'd left her cases in the hall. After the private view she would take the train to Venice to stay with her sister for several months, possibly for good. She had planned to sell Swan House, but Hanna wanted to go back in the spring and open up the attic with skylights to the Fen sky.

Lydia was back, a cup balanced on a fragile saucer, *Le Monde* folded under her arm.

'Perhaps Peter will bring news,' she said, coming in and sitting down on one of the fussy chairs. Hanna felt her aunt always sat down as if she was in public or posing for a society photograph.

'I doubt it. It may take years, Aunt. Or longer.'

The search for her family was a frustrating one. There had been no lightning bolt of communication, no voice cutting through the static of a long-distance phone call. The Cold War had begun to sour relations at all levels. The Russians had shot down a US spy plane. Hanna's letters to Moscow went unanswered. The British Embassy had been polite, but Peter said you could hear the wheels of bureaucracy trundling in the dust. And, after all, what did they really know? Only that a man called L.E.L. Stern had played a game of chess in a school hall in 1957 in a town called Arzamas in central Russia. Only one letter had been answered, by an assistant postmaster in Gorky, politely informing them that there were no Sterns in the Arzamas telephone directory, or indeed anywhere in the *oblast* – a district of nearly sixty thousand residents.

Their search had widened. Letters had been sent to chess clubs and federations. Despite everything, the post always brought hope. She no longer felt her father was receding, fading away. He was as substantial as his lost daughter had become. She felt confident he was there, less so that she would ever touch him.

'You will find him,' said Lydia.

Opening a window, Hanna caught the unmistakable buttery aroma of fresh bread on the warm air. Unbidden, the memory of Spandau returned, the French newly departed to make way for the Russians, leaving behind them a hint of the *boulangerie* on the air.

'I must go while there are still shadows,' she said, collecting her portfolio case from beside the door.

Der Springer stood on the small table in the hall set aside for the telephone – a baroque creation in gold and marble in keeping with the rest of the decor. In Berlin she kept it on the bookcase by their bed, so that even at night the light from the clock revealed its hand-carved surfaces. She opened her bag, undid a zip within, and slipped it inside a safe pocket. She felt excited about the day ahead, joyful even, so that she couldn't stop smiling, but something made her feel the need of a talisman.

The street was already a canyon of heat. A moped accelerated away from the kerb, expelling a cloud of blue fumes, which caught at the back of her throat. She sought the shady side of the street and headed for the Left Bank. Her usual café was in a dank alleyway that reeked of dogs, but inside it was cool and often empty. It was full of brown wood, and smoky, with chessboards inlaid in the tabletops.

She lit a *Gitane*, and ordered breakfast, letting her eyes settle on the TV, although her mind raced over other images – her canvases, and how they would look on the gallery wall. She'd made a careful plan, with the help of a curator, and she replayed in her mind the issues of balance and drama, isolation and connection. It struck her that it had come to this – that she could organise the past, channel it into colour, shape and texture.

The TV was showing the RTF news. A column of black smoke rose over suburban rooftops. The reporter said it was a car bomb, and three people had been killed, in the southern suburbs. In the studio a man in a dark suit with narrow lapels said the attack was the work of right-wing extremists – the OAS – trying to stop Algerian independence. He said they were without a conscience and had resorted to 'Nazi methods'.

A siren pulsed somewhere close by, but quickly faded.

She ordered a second coffee and retrieved a letter from her wallet that had come the day before. Rachel Vogel had written many times. In the end she had walked across the white line at the Glienicke Bridge into the West, holding Elke's hand. The information Hanna had been able to pass to Clarke concerning the Nazi gold had been of little value. The gold was in Moscow, and always had been. But Hanna did have news for Krikalev: a long letter from Freida Klumbacher revealed the name of Eden's father – Obersturmführer Rolf Meyer, and the fate of his loyal friend Julius Sandberger. So Krikalev could close those files – a favour that eased Rachel and Elke's walk to freedom. Mother and daughter were well, although there was no smile in the enclosed snapshot, which showed them on a park bench by what looked like the Rhine.

Hanna's croissant and jam arrived, so she ate and watched sport on the TV: a bleached-out image of tennis players chasing their shadows across a court.

She had a sun-hat, but it was already too hot, and the prospect of the walk was deadening, so when she left the café, she ducked into the Metro at Duroc. The long summer break was over, and the crowded carriage reeked of cigarette ash and raw garlic. She declined a seat because the scar across her stomach often made it uncomfortable to sit. She emerged at *Champs-Élysées*, and felt better in the fresh air, heading south to the river, which was grey under a sky that seemed to be darkening for rain.

The grand entrance to the Palais de Tokyo was along the bank. She could see the white modernist columns, the flags limp in the humid air. The sight of it made her smile, and she imagined the crowds queuing once the show was open. In Berlin, when a gallery off the Ku'Damm had first taken her work, she was known as Peter Portland Cassidy's girlfriend. Now she was an artist in her own right.

Even from a distance she could see the banner strung between the two wings, over the entrance:

OUT OF THE SHADOW:
The Shoah and the new abstract: 1945–62

A bone-white wall ran round the perimeter of the museum, and as she got closer, Hanna passed large individual posters of each of the artists. She was shocked to see that Mark Rothko's had been defaced with a red swastika, and further along, Lee Krasner's with the single word 'JEWESS!' Her own image was untouched, perhaps because she was the newcomer of whom nobody had heard.

She saw now that outside the entrance to the museum a small crowd was waiting, on each side of the steps. As Hanna got closer she noted the placards, their message synchronised:

L'HOLOCAUSTE
LE GRAND MENSONGE

Hannah's French was workaday, so she struggled to turn *mensonge* into *lie*.

Distracted, considering too late the goods entrance at the rear, she forgot that her portfolio case betrayed her as an artist.

A voice boomed from a loud hailer: '*Rassinier dit la vérité!*'

Hanna's hand went to the Star of David she wore on a chain around her neck. She recognised the name Rassinier; it was that of an historian who claimed that the death toll in the Nazi camps had been exaggerated. France, Peter had warned her, was a crucible for denial. In Berlin it had been unspoken, but here it had become the summer fashion.

This was the first time she had encountered such ideas on the street, rather than on the page of a newspaper, or a poster on the wall, She noted two armed gendarmes standing idly together by a newsstand, a radio crackling, a pair of Alsatians on limp leads.

Rassinier's name seemed to galvanise the protestors. Many had been sitting on the pavement, but they jumped up, and waved their placards, chanting. Hanna saw that a TV crew had set up at the top of the steps. A sudden blinding floodlight made her hesitate, so that the protestors had time to block her way forward.

She began to climb the steps, walking the path between angry faces. A woman spat on to the clean steps in front of her. A man with wrecked teeth got so close she could see the broken blood vessels in his eyes. She felt a familiar dread – of what lay at the end of the path – and at that moment the dogs barked.

The protestors shouted in her ears: '*La Juive!*' And, in English: 'It's all a lie!'

Hanna felt a hand under her arm that almost lifted her up, and she was suddenly aware of a gendarme, the harsh fabric of his uniform. For a second her arm touched the cool steel of a gun. And then she was free of them. One of the museum attendants ran out to meet her and took her in through the open copper doors to the atrium. A group of women with buckets and mops stood at a plate-glass window watching the police try to regain order outside. A van had arrived, siren flashing. The dogs bayed.

One of the curators asked in French if she needed a doctor. '*Je vais bien*,' said Hanna. But her heart was rocking, and she'd felt, fleetingly, the terrors of a six-year-old on a silver path. But the confrontation itself had felt oddly staged. She did not feel like a victim, while they felt like actors, mouthing words written by others. And the work – the canvases – existed and therefore could not be denied.

Several people made a fuss of her, and told her more police were on the way, and that she would be safe.

Then she heard someone say her name and she turned to find Vanessa coming through the copper doors.

'What a hideous crowd,' she said, kissing Hanna. 'What exactly are the French police *for*?'

Hanna linked her arm inside her friend's. 'I ran the gauntlet too, but everyone's been kind. It's just a bit of a fuss – why don't we go and see if the work's up?'

Liberty's was interested in a new range of French patterns and Vanessa had decided that she could charge them the cost of a few days in Paris spent in the Louvre looking for inspiration. They'd stretched to the cost of a hotel room as well, which had saved her the ordeal of Lydia's company.

They set off arm in arm. The museum was closed to the public ahead of the official opening at the weekend. Here and there packing cases stood, but most of the American work was yet to arrive by ship. Hanna had left Berlin early because her pictures – especially the series *Green, Silver, Red* – needed to be hung to their precise pattern, in sequence.

They passed an electrician on a set of ladders fixing a light, and another posse of women with mops. After that they were on their own, the sound of the demonstration fading quickly.

The silence was deep, and Vanessa said white walls always made her think of cotton wool.

The *palais* was on a heroic scale, with polished wooden floors, sweeping walls, open staircases, and – facing south – windows that seemed to hang from the sky. They stood for a moment before the plate glass: rain was falling and the Eiffel Tower was a grey silhouette on the far bank of the river, but the sun was shining too, and caught the buoyant gold dome of Les Invalides.

'A rainbow soon,' said Hanna.

'You look well,' said Vanessa. 'Radiant. Domestic life obviously suits you.'

Hanna had taken a flat in Berlin with Peter. There was a balcony with a view of the sailing boats on the Havel. Vanessa had visited and promised a selection of prints for chairs and curtains.

'How is he?' she asked.

'Good. They've offered another year on the contract and he's taken it, but I suspect the results may cause a scandal. Colour – lots of it. The angry black three-dimensional nightmare is gone. I think we'll probably be back in New York by the summer – or at Swan House, if he can banish the idea of Lydia lurking at his shoulder.'

'Good luck,' said Vanessa.

She was about to add something acidic when she stopped in her tracks and gripped Hanna's wrist. Ahead, sixty yards away at the end of the whitewashed vista, hung *Green, Silver, Red III*.

'Well, that's a show-stopper,' she said.

'I had it shipped from the Fens,' said Hanna. 'I thought it might look weak – half-hearted – but you're right. It can hold its own.'

When they reached the gallery set aside for Hanna, they found seven pictures hung to the plan she'd set out, linked by a series of crayon lines in yellow and blue and orange on the walls, in imitation of her childhood scrawls at Swan House.

'Inspired,' said Vanessa. 'It's like being inside your head. Which, as we know, is a strange but beautiful place.'

Vanessa waved a cigarette packet at Hanna.

'No. I need to measure all this up and I want to get on. The rear exit is just through that door – the goods-in. You can smoke there.'

'Grand. You get to work. There's lunch to consider. I've found a place on the rue Tholozé – we deserve it.'

Alone, Hanna followed each of the coloured lines, which provided various routes that all led eventually to a tall, door-less opening, beyond which she knew the final picture hung in isolation. It was set to the left, not visible from the main gallery, so that the viewer had to enter a void, arrive, and then turn to follow the crayon lines to their final destination.

Hanna stepped through the arch and turned.

A man was standing in front of the picture. He was tall, or had been, as age had bent his long spine. His hair was thin and white. He had no walking stick, although his right hand pivoted rhythmically at the wrist, as if one was usually there.

His hearing must have been poor because Hanna could see him register footsteps, but not with any certainty, so that he turned slowly, the head leading over the right shoulder.

'Hanna?'

A gasp slipped from his mouth after the word, just the smallest of whispers.

Hanna didn't move, struggling with sensible questions: who was this man who knew her? A protestor about to deface the work? Yet at the same time she saw in the old man's eyes – once brown, now dimmed behind the tracing paper of age – a reflection of her own.

He took a step towards her, but rearranged his feet, coming to an unsteady stop.

'It's your father, Hanna. Do you not know me?'

She struggled to translate his strange, archaic German.

He held out his hands, which extended from the cuffs of an old, shapeless suit.

'You can't be,' she said, but softly. 'He's in Russia – we don't know where. We're searching. He plays chess.'

The old man seemed to struggle with *her* German, then smiled.

'Yes. He does. Quite poorly now. But for a while the Soviet state needed its Grand Masters to fight the Cold War on a chessboard. They let us travel – they *make* us travel, even when we are old and confused.'

He took another step. 'It is me, child.'

Hanna's blood knew the truth, because it flooded into her heart, and her feet seemed to lose touch with the polished floor. But she still couldn't move. The distance between them, the air itself, seemed a barrier. The old man was both a stranger and intensely familiar, a contradiction she couldn't resolve.

'The tournament is at the Luxembourg Palace ...' He began to nod, as if agreeing with himself. 'In the gardens the people play under the trees, while we sweat in a ballroom. These days I do not shine.'

Hanna had begun to search inside her bag. She needed a key to open the door to the past.

The old man watched but went on talking. 'Mikhail reads *Le Figaro* – he's a Jew too of course. We're all Jews but we're asked to forget that. He showed me an article about the gallery, the exhibition ... And its rising star, Hanna Stern. The name just a coincidence of course – but just a mile away, so no harm in checking. And then I saw your pictures...'

He raised his hands to indicate the canvases in the outer gallery.

Hanna, released at last, walked forward with *der Springer* in her hand.

As the old man took the chess piece, their hands touched, and Hanna thought: *This isn't the past, it's the present, and will be the future*.

'Brunner, the guard, made it,' he said, holding *der Springer* out to the light. 'But it was a gift from me. I thought I would never see it again. I thought I would never see *you* again. But I tried, Hanna. We tried. At Natasza's estate they said you were dead.'

The old man's face was wet, although she hadn't seen the tears fall.

'I know,' she said. She wanted to touch him again, to feel the heft of him, the weight of bones and flesh.

'I should have tried harder,' he said, and his face seemed to collapse.

They heard a distant voice in a faraway gallery, and the noise appeared to affect the old man, so that one leg gave way, and he stepped abruptly sideways, almost falling.

'Wait,' said Hanna.

She fetched a stool set aside for the attendant, and the old man's stick, which she found against the wall.

'Don't cry, Hanna,' he said, as she helped him sit.

She knelt on the floor. She placed her hand on his knee, while his hand settled on her head, but every touch was light and fragile, as if they were handling wrapping paper around delicate presents.

He made an effort to fill his lungs. 'For years I did not travel abroad,' he said. 'In Russia, yes. Local tournaments, small towns, draughty halls.'

He touched his chest. 'But my heart was weak so even that is too much. And your mother was not well. They sent us to a gulag – in the East, in '46. Then to a city called Magadan – a bleak place. But we had a life. An apartment.

'Your mother did not thrive, Hanna. I am sorry. She missed you so much.'

He covered his mouth with a hand. 'Last year was her last.'

He raised the hand to his forehead and then drew it vertically down his face in a gesture she knew must be a habit.

'I am sorry. She loved you very much. Missed you here …' He thudded a fist against his chest.

'We survived Borek – but they took our lives, Hanna, the lives we could have had, the lives we could have had together.'

She put an arm around his shoulders, thinking that she didn't recognise the smell of him: the tobacco, the old suit, the skin beneath the thinning hair.

He took a deep breath. 'I was lonely. Judi is in Moscow. She married a teacher; he's in the Party, a worthy man. She's not a happy person, Hanna. She wishes she'd gone West with Natasza, like her little sister. So I said, this year, now Irena's gone, I would travel again. But this is my last trip.'

Hanna gripped his hand. 'We can't visit you in Russia, Father. It's closed to us.'

He smiled. 'It's my last trip, Hanna, because I'm not going back.'

He took out a piece of paper. 'Here. We could take a taxi, yes? Place Louis Lepine – the Paris Prefecture, beside Notre-Dame. You have to start with the police. I am not the first, you see, so we know what to do; defection is the secret desire of us all, but the others have families, homes.

'I have my papers. I am ready.'

'So am I,' said Hanna, seeing a future for them both, however short it might be.

He held her head. 'I was not really sure it was you until I saw *this* painting.'

Struggling to his feet he took the stick and her arm, and they went up to the final canvas.

It was the end of the *Green, Silver, Red* series. The canvas comprised the three coloured panels, each one forming an arched window, set on a black base, riven with a horizontal red fissure, which seemed to burn with inner fire. Across all three panels smoke drifted. The charcoal lines were stronger here: stylised figures coalesced in a crowd, and dozens of numerals had been added, in various fonts, 9s and **4**s, 3s and 7s, all rising with the heat.

'I saw it, Hanna, and I remembered.

'I was on that path again, between the forest and the field of the dead: the path that led to that dreadful place. It is a miracle that I still carry this memory – but even more so that my little daughter has brought it to life. This is justice, Hanna. Justice for the dead.'

Below the picture was a small brass nameplate, which the old man could not read until, with Hanna's help, he knelt awkwardly:

DIE HIMMELSTRAßE

They heard footsteps coming from the corridor that led to the goods entrance – and Vanessa's voice, an octave higher than usual, enquiring about the colour of a dress.

Hanna turned stiffly, supporting the old man, in time to see a child coming through the archway, her steps uncertain, until she tumbled to the floor.

Peter appeared, an unlit cigarette between his lips, Vanessa in his wake. He saw Hanna holding an old man by the arm, their heads together.

The child raised itself and stumped forward, collapsing once again at Hanna's feet.

'This is my daughter, Irena,' said Hanna.

Acknowledgements

In 2010 I received an invitation to a wedding in Krakow, Poland. A friend, Michael Houten, was marrying Justyna Kita, in St Mary's Basilica, on the city's great square. A few days before the celebrations a group of us visited Auschwitz-Birkenau. In 1979, working as a journalist, I had visited Bergen-Belsen in Lower Saxony, with officials of the British Army of the Rhine (BAOR) At Belsen all vestiges of the camp had been swept away, the soil seeded with lime to counter disease, so that there was nothing for the birds to eat, so they did not sing. But Auschwitz did sing – all its terrible songs are alive today. The idea for this book was born that day. So I must thank Michael and Justyna for the invitation, and Justyna doubly, for helping transliterate the Polish in *The Silent Child*.

The greatest debt I owe is to the few survivors of the camps in the East who recorded their testimony. For several months I visited the University Library at Cambridge, and I must thank them for my treasured reader's ticket. On one of the upper floors, which are shadowy and often deserted, and where you have to twist switches to ensure a few minutes of ticking light, I found their stories, and soon I was walking with these men, women and children, the dust clearing as the trains arrived at Treblinka, Sobibor, Belzec, Chelmno or Majdanek. I have taken these memories and made a new story, which would otherwise have been impossible to tell. I hope every reader of *The Silent Child* will take time to remember them.

Several friends read early drafts of *The Silent Child*. Their support for the book, and their comments, kept the project alive. Veronica Forwood, Ian Glossop, Rowan Haysom, and

Rosy Thornton not only encouraged me to press on but provided vivid pointers for the way forward. My then agent, Faith Evans, brilliantly pin-pointed the project's early weaknesses. My wife, Midge Gillies, found time over the years in between writing her own books to provide advice on characters, and judgement on plot, although it has been her constant belief in the story which has carried me through. The book would not exist without her.

My agent, Teresa Chris, has become *The Silent Child*'s fearless advocate. The book's publication is a testament to her skills. Her enthusiasm for the story is a force of nature. Jo Dickenson, my publisher at Hodder & Stoughton, skilfully identified the heart of the book, and its final shape owes much to her editorial insight. Lily Cooper, commissioning editor, has been a joy to work with, and quietly brought to the manuscript her own painstaking talents, and those of proof-readers and copy editors.

Christopher Theel MA, of the University of Dresden, deserves a special mention. He is an expert in the internal legal system devised and administered by the SS. This provides a central pillar of the narrative. He provided expert answers to my many questions. I have gone far beyond ordinary legal practice in *The Silent Child* – allowing, for example, a Jew to take the stand in court – and I take responsibility for any errors or omissions.

Jim Kelly
July 2021